Just
in Time *for*
Christmas

CAROLYN
BROWN

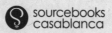
sourcebooks
casablanca

Published by Sourcebooks Casablanca, an imprint of Sourcebooks
P.O. Box 4410, Naperville, Illinois 60567-4410
(630) 961-3900
sourcebooks.com

Printed and bound in Canada.
MBP 10 9 8 7 6 5 4 3 2 1

Chapter 1

IT WAS JUST A WHITE FRAME HOUSE AT THE END of a long lane.

But it did not have wheels, and to Liz that meant it was a mansion.

She squinted against the sun sinking in the west and imagined the house with multicolored Christmas lights strung all around the porch, the windows, even in the cedar tree off to the left side. In her vision, it was a Griswold house from *Christmas Vacation* that lit up the whole state of Texas. She hoped that when she flipped the electricity on she didn't cause a major blackout because in a few weeks it was going to look like the house in that old movie that she loved.

Now where is the cowboy to complete the package? the voice in her head asked.

Christmas lights on a house without wheels and a cowboy in tight-fittin' jeans and boots—that's what she asked for every year when her mother asked for her Christmas list. She didn't remember the place being so big when she visited her uncle those two times. Once when she was ten and then again when she was fourteen, but back then she'd been quite taken with the young cowboy next door and didn't pay much attention to the house. The brisk Texas wind whipped around her skirt tail as if saying that it could send her right back to east Texas.

"I don't think so," she said with half a giggle. "I'm here to stay, and I know a thing or two about Texas wind. It would take more than a class five tornado to get rid of me. This is what I've wanted all my life, and I think it's the prettiest house in Montague County. It's sittin' on a foundation, and..." She clamped a hand over her mouth in disbelief when she saw her uncle's old dog, Hooter, slowly come down off the porch, head down and wagging his tail. Blister, the black-and-white cat, eyed her suspiciously from the ladder-back chair on the tiny porch.

"Uncle Haskell, I could kiss you!" she said as she slung open the truck door. The wind pushed its way inside, bringing a few fall leaves with it, but she didn't even stop to brush them away. Aunt Tressa would say that was an omen—that the place was welcoming her into its arms. Her mother would say that the wind was blowing her back to the carnival where she belonged.

Her high heels sank into the soft earth, leaving holes as she rushed across the yard toward the yellow dog. She squatted down, hugged the big yellow mutt, and scratched his ears. "You beautiful old boy. You are the icing on the cake. Now I've got animals and a house. Who cares about a cowboy? I can't have it all, now can I?"

The key was under the chair, tucked away in a faded ceramic frog, just where her Uncle Haskell said it would be when she talked to him earlier that afternoon. But he hadn't mentioned leaving the two animals. She'd thank him for that surprise later on when she called him.

She opened the wooden screen door and was about to put the key in the lock when the door swung open. There stood Raylen O'Donnell, all grown up and even sexier than she remembered. Her heart thumped so hard she could feel it pushing against her bra. Her hands shook and her knees went weak, but she took a deep breath, willed her hands to be still, and locked her knees in place.

"If it's religion you're sellin' or anything else, we're not interested," Raylen said in a deep Texas drawl. He held a glass of tea in one hand and the door handle in the other, and the expression on his face said he was as shocked as she was. "I wonder why Hooter didn't bark?"

"Maybe because he knows me," Liz answered.

She felt the heat of his gaze as he started at her spike heels and traveled all the way to the top of her head. She reached up and tucked several strands of her jet-black hair into a shiny silver clasp.

"You *are* Raylen, aren't you?" she asked.

"Yes, I am, and who are you?" he asked.

"I'm Liz, and I now own this place and land," she said with a flick of her hand to take in more than just the house.

"Liz?" Raylen's expression changed to one of disbelief.

"Surprise!" she said with a smile. "What are you doing here?"

Could Raylen really be the cowboy Santa was going to leave under her Christmas tree? He'd sure enough been the one she had in mind when she asked for a cowboy. She'd visualized him in tight-fittin' jeans and boots when she was younger. Lately, she'd changed her vision to nothing but a Santa hat and the boots.

His hair was still a rich, dark brown, almost black until the sunlight lit up the deep chestnut color. His eyes were exactly as she remembered: pale, icy blue rimmed with dark brown lashes. It all added up to a heady combination, enough to make her want to tangle her hands up in all that dark hair and kiss him. She looked up, but there was no mistletoe hanging in the doorway. She'd have to remedy that when she decorated the house for the holiday.

Cowboys have roots, not wings. Don't get involved with one or you'll smother to death in a remote back-woods farm or else die of boredom. Her mother's voice whispered so close to her ear that she turned to make sure Marva Jo Hanson hadn't followed her to Ringgold, Texas.

Raylen stood to one side and motioned her into the house. "I came to feed and water Hooter and Blister. Haskell asked me to do that until you got here. We met when we were kids, remember?"

"I do," she answered. How could she forget? She'd been in love with Raylen O'Donnell since she was fourteen years old.

"Haskell said that if you didn't like it here, he'd sell me your twenty acres," he blurted out.

"That won't happen, and you sure are blunt," she said as she scanned the living room that was exactly like she remembered it, down to the well-worn leather sofa and hassock where she'd snuggled in to read romance books about cowboys the last time she was there. "I'm going to live here. Uncle Haskell said if I like it, he'll deed the place over to me in the spring. The place isn't for sale and won't ever be."

"And do what? Ringgold isn't very big." Raylen's tone was filled with exasperation.

She shrugged. "I don't know. Pet the cat. Feed the dog."

"That won't make a living, lady," Raylen said.

She propped both hands on her hips. "I don't reckon what I do for a living is one bit of your business, cowboy." Never in all the scenarios that she'd imagined had he been cross with her like this. He'd kissed her. He'd swept her off her feet and carried her to a big white pickup truck and they'd driven off into the Texas sunset. He'd smiled and said that he remembered her well and she'd grown up into a beautiful woman. But he hadn't argued.

She brushed against his chest as she headed into the kitchen to make herself a glass of tea. She'd had Raylen on a pedestal for more than a decade and he didn't even recognize her. He was probably married and had three or four kids too. That was the way her luck ran, so why should today be any different?

When she fanned past him, she got a whiff of his cologne—the same kind he'd worn all those years ago.

"I'll take over feeding the cat and dog," she said. "Thanks for what you've done until I could get here."

He dug into his pocket and handed her an old key ring with two keys on it. "Welcome to Ringgold, Liz. I still live on the ranch that surrounds this land. Haskell sold me most of his ranch six months ago, all but the part the house sits on."

"He told me," she said as she opened the nearly empty refrigerator and took out half a pitcher of sweet tea.

Raylen headed for the door. "The O'Donnells are your closest neighbors. Come around to see us sometime. Be seein' you."

She wanted to say something, but not one word would come out of her mouth. Raylen in her living room, looking even sexier than he had when he was seventeen and exercising the horses. Raylen all grown up, a man instead of a lanky teenager, was such a shock and a surprise that she was speechless. And that was strange territory for Lizelle Hanson.

"Dammit!" She stomped her foot and popped the heel off one of her shoes.

The noise of the truck engine filled the house for a moment then faded. She'd been so stunned to see him that she couldn't think straight. She hadn't known what to expect, but it sure wasn't what she got. She fished a cell phone from her jacket pocket and punched a speed dial number.

"I'm here," she said when her mother answered.

"And?"

Liz giggled nervously. "It's bigger than I remembered, and there's a sexy cowboy who lives next door, but he's probably married and has six kids because no guy that pretty isn't taken. I'd forgotten how big the house is after living in the carnie trailer."

"Have you unpacked? You can turn around and come back right now. You could be here in time to take your shift tomorrow night, and my brother can sell it to those horse ranchers next door to him," Marva Jo said.

"Not yet. I was on my way in the house when Raylen opened the door and startled me so badly I was almost speechless. Hooter and Blister are still alive and well. I'm not ready to throw in the towel yet."

"Raylen?" Marva Jo asked.

"The sexy cowboy. I met him both times I came to visit Uncle Haskell. Remember when I told you about the boy who tried to beat me at walkin' the fence when I was ten? That was Raylen." Liz sank down on the sofa and wasn't surprised to find it just as soft as she remembered.

"You're right. He's probably married and has a couple of kids. I was hoping the house would be butt-ugly to you," Marva Jo said with a giggle.

"No, ma'am. I squinted and even imagined it with Christmas lights. Looked great to me. Right now, wild horses couldn't drag me away," Liz said.

"We'll be in Bowie in a few weeks. By then you'll be sick to death of boredom. You were born for the carnie and travel," Marva Jo said.

"I will have the Christmas lights on the house when you get here," Liz said.

"A house not on wheels with Christmas lights and a cowboy." Marva Jo laughed. "Be careful that the cowboy doesn't cut off your beautiful wings."

"Good night, Mama. I love you," Liz said.

"Love you too, kid. Go prove me right about getting bored. It's only half an hour until time to tell fortunes and I still have to get my makeup on. Does that make you miss me?" Marva Jo asked.

"Not yet. I only saw you this morning. Hug Aunt Tressa for me and I'll see you in a few weeks."

———

Raylen drove down the lane and stopped. The left blinker was on, but he couldn't make himself pull out onto the highway. The whole incident at Haskell's place had been surreal. Haskell said his niece, Liz, was going to take over the property. He remembered Liz very well. She was the ten-year-old who'd walked the rail fence better than him even though he was older at thirteen. She was the fourteen-year-old who rested her elbows on the same rail fence and watched him exercise the horses. Now she was so pretty that just looking at her sucked every sane thought out of his brain.

He finally pulled out on Highway 81 and headed north a mile, then turned left into the O'Donnell horse ranch. She'd find out that a person couldn't make a living by petting the cat and feeding the dog, and when she did he intended to be the first in line to buy her twenty acres. It was the only property for a three-mile stretch down the highway that didn't belong to the O'Donnells.

He parked in the backyard, crawled out of the truck, and sat down on the porch step to his folks' house. His older brother Dewar drove up, parked next to him, hopped out of his truck, and swaggered to the porch. Just a year older than Raylen, Dewar was taller by several inches. His hair was so black that it had a faint blue cast as the sunrays bounced off it. His eyes were a strange mossy shade of green and his face square. His Wranglers were tight and dusty, and his boots were worn down at the heels and covered with mud.

"Y'all get those cattle worked at Rye's?" Raylen looked down at his own boots. They were just as worn down at the heels as his brother's were and covered with horse manure. His jeans had a hole in one knee and frayed hems on both pant legs. His shirt looked like it had been thrown out in the round horse corral for a solid week and then used for a dog bed after that. He let out a long, loud sigh. He'd planned on at least meeting Liz the first time in clean duds, not looking like a bum off the streets.

"Yes, we did, and we would've got them done sooner if our younger brother would've helped," Dewar said. "You look like you just saw a ghost and lost your best friend. What's going on?"

"If you worked harder and played with our niece Rachel less, you'd get more done, and nothing is wrong with me."

"You're just tryin' to find excuses," Dewar said with a grin.

Rachel was the first O'Donnell grandchild and only a few months old. Her father, Rye, was Raylen and Dewar's oldest brother. Her mother,

Austin, had been a Tulsa socialite until she inherited a watermelon farm across the river in Terral, Oklahoma, and fell in love with Rye. Rachel was getting to know her two uncles, and there was an ongoing battle about which one would be the favorite.

"Want a beer?" Dewar asked. "I swear I'm spittin' dust, and hot summer is long since past."

"I'd drink a beer with you," Raylen said. "And I believe what we've got going on now is just about the last warm weather we're going to see for a while, so don't get used to it."

Dewar disappeared into the house and in a few minutes he brought out two longneck bottles of Coors. He twisted the caps off both, and handed one to Raylen. "So, you got the chores done around here or am I going to have to do those too?"

"All finished. Everything with four legs has been fed and watered. Horses are all exercised, and even Haskell's dog and cat are fed. His niece is over there now. She can take care of Hooter and Blister from now on." He turned up the bottle and downed a fourth of it before coming up for air and a loud burp.

Dewar plopped down on the porch step beside Raylen. "Is she going to keep the place, or do you have a chance at buying it?"

"She says she's going to keep it. I asked her what she was going to do to make a living in Ringgold,

Texas, and she said she was going to feed the dog and pet the cat. If Haskell is giving her all of his money as well as those twenty acres, she won't *have* to do anything but feed a dog and pet a cat."

"What's she look like?"

"Damn fine. She's got jet-black hair and the darkest brown eyes you've ever seen."

"You took with her?"

"Not me. That could be a big problem if things don't go right, what with us being neighbors and all," Raylen answered.

Liz stood in the middle of the living room floor and turned around slowly. The room was bigger than the fifth-wheel travel trailer where she'd lived her entire life. A fireplace with a real chimney was centered on the north end with a stone apron in the front. Two brown leather recliners flanked the sofa. The coffee table sat on a real cowhide area rug. A wheeled cart on the east side of the fireplace held a small television set, and as if something had to be used to balance the arrangement, a ladder-back chair was on the other side with a pot of silk greenery on it. That whole arrangement scarcely took up half of the big room.

The south end was covered with empty bookcases, floor to ceiling. Uncle Haskell had said that she'd have to start her own collection because he was taking all his beloved Westerns with him. Another sofa faced the bookcase. That one was orange and yellow floral velvet, had deep cushions and big round arms that begged for someone to settle in with a good book. A wagon wheel chandelier hung in the middle of the room over a library table with a set of horse head bookends and a well-worn *Webster's Dictionary* in the middle. An antique oak business chair was set at an angle as if waiting for Uncle Haskell to come back and look up a word.

It wouldn't take a lot of rearranging to give the room a more open and less cut-up look. Take the table and put it in front of the bookcases. Move the floral sofa under the window to the east and angle the fireplace arrangement.

"Oh, oh! And a Christmas tree right there with lots of presents under it, and garland looped around the ceiling caught up with Christmas bulbs. And cedar boughs strewn on the mantel with a nativity scene in the middle." Liz talked to the dog and imagined just how things would look.

But that was another day's work. Right then she was hungry, and she hadn't even thought about bringing groceries with her. She wandered into a country kitchen with cabinets making a U on three sides and a small maple table and four chairs set right in the middle. A picture of her, back when she was ten, was stuck to the front of the refrigerator.

It had to have been taken that summer when she showed Raylen up by staying on the top of the fence longer than he did. There was only one more photo, but this one was framed and sitting on the window ledge above the sink. She was fourteen in that one. Those were the only two times her mother let her spend the day at Uncle Haskell's place.

She remembered her short, stocky uncle inviting her for the day and her mother shaking her head.

"What can it hurt, Marva Jo? She just wants to see my new puppy. His name is Hooter, and he loves little kids," Haskell had said. "Come on. I promise not to put fertilizer on her feet."

On the way to his house, she'd asked him why he'd want to put fertilizer on her feet. "It's a joke, Lizelle. Your mama is afraid if you see how I live that you'll like it."

Later, when she was older, her mother had admitted that she had seriously never wanted her to get acquainted with the way the other side of her family lived, for fear she'd want that instead of the carnie life.

"We were all born into the same family. All grew up in the carnival. But Haskell, the one who is supposed to be running this business, wanted roots. I don't want that for you, my child. I want freedom and wings for you. And I've been afraid you'd get more of his DNA than mine—that you'd want the other side's life. He is like Mama. She stayed with the carnival because she loved Daddy, but she always liked it best when we settled down for the winter months and were in one spot," Marva Jo had said.

Liz's stomach grumbled and she forgot about the pictures of her young self and looked inside the refrigerator again. It was empty except for a chunk of cheddar cheese and the half empty pitcher of sweet tea. She found half a loaf of bread still within its date on the cabinet. She opened a pantry door to find a walk-in room with loaded shelves on three sides. Supper would be soup and cheese, and soon, because she was starving. She'd left Jefferson, Texas, that morning with butterflies the size of dragons in her stomach, so she'd skipped lunch.

She heated a can of vegetable soup, leaned against the counter, and let the scene from two days ago replay in her mind. Her mother had come into the trailer late and opened a can of beer. She'd propped a hip against the cabinet in the tiny kitchen and took a long gulp as she watched Liz remove her fortune-teller's makeup.

"What do you want for Christmas, kid?" Marva Jo asked.

As if by rote, Liz grinned and said, "A house with no wheels and a sexy cowboy."

"Your Uncle Haskell called a couple of weeks ago. Poppa is ailing and needs full-time help these days. Tressa and I've been talkin' about one of us staying with him for the first half of the run next year, and then switching off and the second one staying with him the last half. But Haskell drove out to visit him last week and came up with another idea. He says that he's used to living in one place and is ready to retire. He's already sold off most of his ranch. We talked about it, and Poppa likes the idea of having his son nearby. Haskell bought one of those prefab houses and had it moved on the land. It's built to be wheelchair accessible so if Poppa gets to where he can't get around or take care of himself with Haskell's help, then he can live there too. Now here's the rest of the story. The part that I don't like but Haskell and Poppa both say is the right thing." Marva Jo had looked like she'd just come from a funeral, or worse yet was about to go to one.

Liz would never forget the pain on her mother's face. "Haskell is offering for you to move into his house on the last twenty acres of his ranch. If you like it, come spring he'll put the whole thing over in your name. We'll be in Bowie the last week in November just like always, so I will see you then. That's a month from now and by then I hope you have changed your mind about living in a real house. So, it's up to you, kid. You really want a house with no wheels, or has it been a big joke between us all these years?"

Liz had whispered, "Yes, Mama, I want it."

"Then pack your bags, girl. You're leavin' in the morning. If you decide you want to come back to the carnival, you're always welcome, and the people next door to Haskell's have already said they are interested in buying the acres and the house. Me, I hope that you hate the damn place in a week or even a day. I don't want you to go, but Haskell and Poppa are right. You are twenty-five. It's time for you to make your decision about being a carnie forever or quitting the business."

"And so here I am," Liz said to herself aloud as she poured the soup into a bowl. "I guess Raylen is the one Mama was talkin' about buying my property. Well, ain't that a mess! I've wanted to see his pretty blue eyes again for eleven years, and he just wants my house and land. I got what I wanted, but he doesn't get my house or my land, no matter what he offers me."

After she'd eaten two bowls of soup and a chunk of cheese, she washed up her dishes, a habit her mother had instilled in her from childhood. "In a trailer this size, there's no room for clutter," she'd said so many times that Liz couldn't count them.

She went back to the living room, found the light switch and flipped it on, then brought in the first load of her things. Four doors opened off the hallway. Haskell's bedroom was the first on the right, across the hall from the bathroom, and swept clean. Not even a lonesome old dust bunny scampered into the corner. The next two offered up two more bedrooms. One very small one was completely empty. She vaguely remembered a desk being in the room. She swung open the fourth door to find another bedroom with a four-poster bed, a dresser with a big round mirror above it, and one of those old-time vanities with a velvet bench that pulled up to a three-sided mirror. The bed looked like it covered an acre and made her feel small when she kicked off her shoes and stretched out on it.

The wind brushed a tree limb across the window screen and Hooter set up a long, low, lonesome howl right under the window. It sounded as if he were mourning the loss of his master, which sent chill bumps dancing up and down Liz's arms. She threw her legs over the side of the bed and hurried back down the hall, through the kitchen, and slung open the back door.

"What is it, old boy?" she asked.

If dogs could grin, Hooter did. He lowered his head and marched into the house, across the kitchen floor, and past the recliner in the living room. He smelled the cowhide rug, turned around three times before snuggling down for a nap. Liz had been so busy watching the process that she hadn't realized Blister had snuck in with Hooter until the cat brushed past her leg. She jumped straight up and let out a screech, her heart pounding so hard that she threw a hand on her chest to keep it from jumping out on the floor and shooting past her so fast that it would rival the cat.

Blister slowed down before she reached the recliner and touched noses with Hooter before settling down on the back of the chair like a fur collar on a fancy winter coat.

They both looked up at her mournfully as if asking why she didn't join them, but she shook her head. "I've got to haul suitcases and boxes into the house. I don't have time to sit around and watch television but thank you for the invitation. After I unpack, maybe I'll take you up on it later this evening."

Put them outside. Do not pet them or let them stay in the house. You'll get attached and it will make leaving even harder. You know what happened that time I was gone for two days, and you hid that kitten in the trailer, her mother's voice argued with her.

"I'm not leaving. I told Mama I wasn't teasing when I said I wanted a house and a cowboy for Christmas. Every time we go into a new town, I wonder what it would be like to live in one of the houses we pass on the streets. Now, I get to find out."

Hooter rolled his big, soulful eyes up at her as if asking what she was talking about. She reached down and scratched the dog's ears as she walked past him and out into the night. She had two more suitcases, a worn old fiddle case, and two boxes to unload. It wasn't much to show for twenty-five years, but when two people share a small travel trailer, there's not room to collect junk. Only the very precious items could be saved, and they were in the boxes. She carried in the suitcases and set them inside the door and went back for the boxes.

She looked north but couldn't see anything but the moon and one star hanging in the sky. Raylen lived over there. She'd never seen the house, but Uncle Haskell said that his nearest neighbor lived a mile to the north. Was he over there with his wife and a house full of kids? Were they loading up in his truck or van or whatever his wife drove to go to town for fast food and a movie? Would Liz get bored by the end of the winter season and be ready to go back on the road with the carnival?

She sighed and carried her fiddle case inside, then the two small boxes. She was now officially moved in, and it was exhilarating. The dog and cat looked up with soulful eyes and she told them, "Work first. Play later."

When she'd finished putting her crystal ball on the vanity, a snapshot of her mother and Tressa in full costume on the dresser, and her deck of worn Tarot cards on the bedside table, she felt more at home in the big room. She popped open the suitcases and hung jeans, flowing skirts, a few shirts, and a denim jacket in the closet, arranged underwear, pajamas, and three bright-colored costumes in dresser drawers, and set several pairs of high-heeled shoes, a pair of Nikes, and a pair of scuffed-up cowboy boots on the closet floor.

Work is done. Now I can play, she thought.

She headed up the hallway. Blister opened one eye but didn't budge from the recliner. Hooter raised his head and looked toward the door.

"Already wanting to go back outside, are you?" The words were barely out of her mouth when someone knocked hard on the door.

She hadn't heard a vehicle and the dog hadn't stirred. Some watchdog Hooter was. She opened the door to find Raylen leaning on the jamb.

"Evenin'," he said in a deep Texas drawl.

"Good evenin'," she said.

"You goin' to invite me in?" he asked.

In carnival life, few people came inside the trailer. When they knocked on the door, it usually came with an invitation to come outside, to eat supper at the community potluck, to take a walk around the grounds, or to pet the horses. It had to be serious between two people for them to spend time inside a trailer together. Her mother had never brought a man, carnival worker or any other, inside the trailer. Tressa was the only person Liz could remember ever sitting at the small kitchen table with them.

"Well?" Raylen asked.

She stepped aside. If she was going to embrace a normal life she'd have to get used to the rules.

"Come in. I'm sorry. I just got unpacked and my mind was off in la-la land."

Raylen grinned. "Been there."

He went straight for the recliner where Blister had taken up residence on the back and sank into it. Hooter raised his head and wagged his tail. Raylen scratched the dog's ears and then turned his attention to Blister.

"They miss Haskell. I'm glad you let them in the house."

"Hooter was howling like he was dyin'. I opened the door to see what was going on, and they both came in," she said. Should she sit in the other recliner or the sofa? She finally crossed in front of him and claimed the other chair.

"They're good animals. Blister has a litter box in the utility room off the kitchen. The litter is in the cabinet beside the washer and dryer. Hooter would explode before he'd make a mess, so there's nothing to worry about them bein' inside. Haskell said they were good company, and that Hooter knew all his secrets. He told me that he was glad the dog couldn't talk."

Liz smiled. "Too bad. He could tell me stories about my uncle, I'm sure."

"Yep, he could." Raylen grinned.

When he smiled, she remembered that crazy feeling in her chest when they were teenagers. He had smiled at her over the fence and her heart had done a couple of flip-flops.

Liz inhaled deeply to ease the antsy feeling in her gut, but it didn't help. All she got was a lung full of Raylen's shaving lotion. The man had cleaned up in the last couple of hours. His boots were spit-shined, his dark hair still glistened from a shower, and his Wranglers were starched and creased. He looked like sin on a stick when he was all sweaty and dirty—but cleaned up, he made her mouth go dry.

"So you are Uncle Haskell's nearest neighbor, now mine I guess, right?" she asked.

He pointed toward the fireplace. "Less than a mile as the crow flies, straight that way. Haskell's house and ours is probably set on a plumb line, but to drive there, you have to drive down your lane to the highway, hang a left, drive a mile, turn left down the lane, and then back to our ranch. But I jumped the fences and walked over tonight. Needed the exercise after Mama's supper."

I would shoot you between the eyes if you called me Mama. When I get a husband, even when I have kids, he's not calling me Mama, she thought.

"How many fences?" she asked.

"Well, you have the backyard fence, but it's got a gate. Then the corral fence, but it's got a gate too. After that there's the rail fence out into the horse pasture, but there's a stile over it, and then your fence. So, I suppose I only actually jumped one fence," he said with another grin and then asked, "Why are you looking at me like that?"

That grin was flirting. If he was her husband, he'd be in the doghouse with Hooter for looking at another woman the way he was staring at her. Liz couldn't remember when she didn't work at the carnival in some capacity or another. And she'd seen men walking down the midway with their arm around one woman and eyeing another just like Raylen was doing.

Raylen stood up so fast that Blister rolled down into the chair. "I came to invite you to Sunday dinner tomorrow. We are a neighborly bunch in this part of the world. We do the big family thing on Sunday, and Grandma wants to have music."

She pointed. "One mile straight across there?"

"That's right. At noon. My sisters, Gemma and Colleen, will be there and my brother Dewar. My other brother Rye and his wife and baby daughter Rachel live over in Terral, right across the river, and they'll be coming too. And of course Grandma and Grandpa and Mama and Daddy."

Liz's dark eyebrows knit together in a frown. Did he and his wife live with his mother and father?

Well, you lived with your mother until yesterday, so don't be casting stones! Aunt Tressa's gravelly voice seemed to whisper so close it sent an involuntary shiver up her spine.

"I'd love to come to dinner. At noon? Can I bring something? What's your wife's name?" she blurted out and wished she could cram the words right back in her mouth. God, that sounded so tacky.

"Wife?" he stammered.

"You didn't mention your wife's name. Your brother Rye is married to Austin. Are any of the rest of you married?" She had opened a can of worms. There was no putting them back now.

"I wouldn't be over here askin' you to dinner if I was married. That wouldn't be right." The words shot out of his mouth like a cannonball.

She cocked her head to one side. Were all the women in Ringgold, Texas, blind? Raylen filled out those Wranglers right well, and his biceps strained the seams on his Western-cut plaid shirt. How in the devil had he outrun all the women?

"Do you have a husband?" he asked bluntly.

It was her turn to blush and shake her head emphatically. "Carnies aren't the marryin' type."

"Carnies?" He wondered if that was a family name.

"That's right. You sure I can't bring something?" she asked.

"We plan on having a jam session in the afternoon," he said as he stood up and headed back toward the door. "If you play an instrument, bring it along. If not, just bring a healthy appetite."

Liz walked him to the door. He turned at the door and looked down into her eyes and she moistened her full lips with the tip of her tongue, but he just tipped his hat at her and walked out into the darkness. Liz wanted that kiss and felt cheated, then cheap. A woman didn't let a man kiss her just because he asked her to Sunday dinner. She might be a carnie, but she wasn't trashy. She took a step back and looked over her shoulder at the dog and cat.

"I'll see you tomorrow then," she said.

"Be lookin' for you. Want me to drive over and get you?" he asked.

"No, I'd either walk or bring my own truck," she answered.

"Okay, then. Good night, Liz."

"Night, Raylen." His name slipped off her tongue.

She plopped down in the recliner, and Hooter laid his head in her lap. Blister moved from the back of the chair to the arm and purred. The remnants of Raylen's shaving lotion surrounded her.

"I'd give you each a big T-bone if you could talk and tell me more about Raylen."

She dug her cell phone out of her purse and punched in the speed dial for her uncle. After five rings she was about to hang up when she heard his voice.

"Uncle Haskell, hi. I'm here and I'm unpacked, and I was so tickled to see Hooter and Blister. Do I really get to keep them? I've already made up my mind. I'm staying on the property, and I promise I'll spoil them even worse than you did."

"Whoa, girl. Slow down." Haskell chuckled. "Yes, you can keep Hooter and Blister. They wouldn't be happy anywhere but right there, and I know you'll do right by them. But you haven't been there long enough to make up your mind, so you have to stay until March when the carnival pulls out of this area before I sign it over to you legally. I told Raylen to water and feed Hooter and Blister. I guess he did?"

"Yes, he was in the house when I got here. He went home but he came back and invited me to the O'Donnells' for Sunday dinner. He said they're going to have music," Liz said.

"You'll enjoy that. That Raylen and Dewar both are good men, Lizelle. Take your fiddle and enjoy the day."

"Are you settling in out there?" Liz asked. It hadn't occurred to her in the flurry of excitement that her uncle might not be satisfied in Claude, out in the Texas panhandle, and would want to come back to Ringgold. What if she put down roots, and then her uncle wanted his place back?

"Yes, I am," Haskell answered. "Poppa and I are getting along pretty good. I'm still unpacking my books, but we're getting a few boxes done each day. Poppa borrowed some yesterday. I may make a reader of him yet. He's anxious for Marva Jo and Tressa to get here for the winter though. He loves helping revamp the carnie wagons every winter."

"I'm glad you are there, Uncle Haskell. He gets lonely. I promised Hooter and Blister some quality family time so I'm going to hang up and visit with them," Liz said.

"I'll be looking for reports at least once a week," Haskell said.

"You got 'em. Good night," Liz said.

Did that mean she could ask questions about Raylen once a week as well as give her uncle a report?

Chapter 2

LIZ BROUGHT UP A MARTINA MCBRIDE Christmas album on her phone and listened to the music as she drove down her lane toward the highway. The first song was an old tune that she and her mother and aunt listened to when they were in their winter quarters, "I'll Be Home for Christmas." The lyrics said that the holiday would find her where love light gleamed. Liz sang along with her and hoped that she would find love—maybe not this year, that would be too soon.

Maybe next Christmas Eve. It would take a miracle to have it this year, she thought.

She and her mother liked country music. Tressa hated it. Liz wondered where her Uncle Haskell stood on the issue. Somehow, she couldn't see her overall-clad uncle listening to the Irish melodies that Tressa loved. She'd bet her fiddle that he was a Willie Nelson and George Jones man.

Another three Christmas songs had played through when she made a left onto the O'Donnell property. She gasped when she saw the big two-story white house and all the vehicles parked out front. She'd expected to find something more like her house, a small ranch-style place with a dog on the porch.

Oh, stop it, she thought to herself. *You've been in real houses before. You're acting worse than you did on your first date nine years ago. And this isn't even a date. Raylen said he didn't have a wife. He didn't say anything about a girlfriend. He's probably just being a good neighbor.*

Folding chairs under a shade tree in the backyard had a guitar, banjo, and several other stringed instruments sitting on them. She wondered if she should add her fiddle to the mix but decided to leave it in the truck. By the time dinner was over, she might have had enough normalcy and be ready to get the hell out of Dodge.

The wind had died down from the night before, but a breeze whipped her long, flowing skirt around her ankles when she got out of the truck. She pulled her bright orange crocheted shawl around her shoulders and made her way to the door. Her finger headed for the doorbell, but it didn't reach its mark. The big wooden door swung open and Raylen stood a foot from her. How in the devil did he do that? Did he have a sixth sense that knew when she was about to ring a doorbell or unlock a door?

The slight breeze that fluttered the fall leaves on the trees wafted the scent of his cologne to her while she took in his black Wranglers, a black pearl-snap shirt, and shiny black boots.

Raylen stood to one side and motioned for her to come inside. "I heard a car door slam and hoped it was you. We're just about ready for Grandpa to say grace and then we can eat. I was afraid you wouldn't take me serious about the invitation, but I'm glad you are here."

"Hey, talk later. I'm starving," a dark-haired woman yelled as she made her way down the staircase.

"That's Gemma, my youngest sister," Raylen explained. "Let's have grace and then I'll introduce you to the family." He put his hand on her shoulder and steered her through the living room and into the kitchen.

The living room was a huge square with lots of tall windows letting in natural light. A brown leather sofa with deep cushions and wide arms was on either end of the big square room, with rocking chairs and recliners thrown in here and there with tables and lamps beside them. It was a room that invited family and friends to come right in and make themselves at home.

"We're all here, so Grandpa, would you say grace?" a man who looked a lot like Raylen asked.

Everyone bowed their heads.

Liz did the same and tried to listen to the words of thanks his grandfather delivered in a deep Texas drawl.

"Amen," Grandpa said.

Gemma extended her hand. "You must be our new neighbor. We'll miss Haskell. He's been a wonderful friend to our family."

Liz reached out and Gemma's shake was firm. She had black hair cut in short layers that framed an oval face, deep green eyes beneath arched dark eyebrows, heavy lashes, and a wide mouth. Her red three-inch high heels on a one-inch platform made her seem taller than she was.

With a slight pressure on her back, Raylen turned her around to face more family. "This is my father, Cash O'Donnell, and my mother, Maddie. And right beside them is my grandma Frannie and grandpa Tilman O'Donnell."

Frannie stepped forward first. "You can call me Grandma like all the other friends of this wild bunch does. I wanted to be called Granny, but Tilman told me that the grandbabies would call me Granny Frannie, and I didn't like that so well. Welcome to our area of the world. We're glad to have you for a neighbor."

"Thank you, Grandma." Liz smiled.

She shook hands with both grandparents and then Cash who was taller than Raylen. They shared the same hair color, but Raylen's eyes were clearer blue and his face squarer cut with a stronger chin.

Maddie bypassed her hand and hugged her. "Welcome to Ringgold, honey. We're here if you need anything. Come over if you get bored. Holler if you want company."

"Thank you," Liz said softly. Would the invitation still stand when they found out that she came from a long line of carnies? Or had Uncle Haskell told them about his two sisters' lifestyles?

Maddie had a few crow's-feet around her bright blue eyes, but there wasn't a single gray strand in her chestnut-colored hair. She was taller than her daughters and slim as a model. Any twenty-year-old woman would have been delighted to look that good in snug jeans.

"I've got to get the last pan of hot rolls out of the oven, so excuse me, but remember what I said," Maddie said.

"Thank you, I will."

"My sister Colleen," Raylen said.

Her hair was a strange burgundy color, and her face was slightly rounder than Gemma's angular planes, and her lips a wee bit wider. She was a little taller than Gemma but built on the same delicate frame.

"You have gorgeous hair," Liz said. She imagined Colleen in a costume with a long scarf tied around her forehead and all that hair flowing down her back.

Colleen nodded but didn't offer to hug her or shake her hand. "What kind of job are you lookin' for, or are you going to farm those twenty acres?"

"I haven't thought that far. Are you offering me a

job?" Liz asked. She'd been in catfights before, and Colleen's eyes said that she did not approve of her brother bringing a stray into the house for Sunday dinner.

"I work at the casino as a blackjack dealer up in Randlett, Oklahoma. I imagine I could put in a word for you if you're shopping around for a job," Colleen said.

"I'd rather have something closer," Liz said.

"Then go talk to Jasmine at Chicken Fried. She's going to need a waitress in a couple of days. I'm Austin, the sister-in-law, Rye's wife," a tall woman, with jet-black hair and beautiful blue eyes said from behind Maddie. "And that baby that Maddie is takin' from my husband is Rachel, our daughter."

It was plain that Rye and Raylen were brothers, only Rye was well over six feet tall. The baby that he was passing to his mother was a dark-haired little girl with her mother's eyes. Liz wondered if Rachel would be as tall as her mother too.

"I'm pleased to meet you," Liz said. "Who's Jasmine?"

A brunette in pink cowboy boots, jeans, and a cute flowing top raised her hand. "That'll be me. And anytime you want to work come see me. I'm lookin' for a waitress at the Chicken Fried, my café just up the highway. And I'm not sister or kin. I got into the family on Austin's shirttails. Welcome to the area. I love it here."

Before Liz could answer Jasmine, Grandma

slipped her arm around Liz's shoulders and knocked Raylen's off. "We sure miss Haskell around here. He and his wife were a big part of our community. You tell him hello for us next time you talk to him."

"I sure will." Liz wondered if these people accepted everyone like this, or if she was being given the royal treatment because she was with Raylen.

"I'm Dewar, his other brother," another cowboy said.

Dewar wasn't quite as tall as Rye but taller than Raylen and his face was fuller. He also sported a deeper dimple in his chin and a scar on his cheek. "So, are you getting unpacked over there? Got a truck coming in with your things? Need us to gather up a bunch of men and help you get it unloaded?"

"No, thank you, I'm handling it just fine," Liz answered.

"Well, you call us if you change your mind," Dewar said.

"You better stop yapping and get over here or I'm going to clean out the mashed potato bowl and you're goin' to be left out in the cold," Jasmine said.

"Got to go protect my dinner." Dewar headed to the table where all the food was laid out buffet style.

Thank you, Jasmine, Raylen thought.

His brother's eyes had lit up entirely too bright

when he saw Liz. And he was the next in line. Rye found Austin the year before, and it was Dewar's turn if Cash's prophecy about his children all getting married in the order of their birth was to come true. Raylen didn't care if his brother got married or to whom, as long as it wasn't the new neighbor. He might not even like her once he got to know her, but that tingle in his hand every time he laid it on her shoulder sure made him want a chance.

Raylen draped his arm around Liz's shoulders again. "We'd better elbow our way up to the buffet bar or else we'll go hungry."

Colleen shot Raylen a dirty look, but he ignored it. His sister had always been a force to deal with, and she'd been overprotective of him since they were toddlers. He winked at her, but it didn't help one bit. She set her mouth in a firm line and glared at him.

"I'm starving," Liz said. "A home cooked meal is so much better than burgers and fries on the road."

Rye handed her a plate. "I agree with you. If you need help settling in, just call me or Austin. We'll make sure you have our numbers before we leave. How are you liking Ringgold so far?"

"I haven't seen any of the actual town except Uncle Haskell's place and this one. How big is Ringgold, anyway?"

Raylen chuckled. "If we round up everyone from the Red River to halfway between us and Bowie, we could probably rustle up about a hundred people."

"Uncle Haskell told me it was tiny and that the fire from a few years ago burned up a lot of it," she said.

Rye draped his arm around his wife. "That was a disaster, but we were lucky. The fire only got a few acres of our ranch."

"Are you Irish?" Grandma asked.

Liz figured she'd be asked a lot of questions, but all the eyes on her made her a little uncomfortable. Sure, she had performed at the carnival for a crowd, but this was different.

"No, ma'am," she answered with a smile. "Not that I know about, anyway. Are you?"

"Oh, yes, I am. I come from a long line of Irish. With your dark looks I thought I saw some Irish. Maddie was an O'Malley before she married Cash," Grandma explained.

"I done good when I lassoed Maddie." Cash leaned over and kissed Maddie on the cheek. "She is what made this ranch what it is today. A good Irish woman is hard to come by."

"You got that right about my daughter-in-law." Grandma was piling her plate high. "Maddie can take a colt that's all gangly legs and turn it into a million-dollar racer."

Grandpa yelled from the dining room, "I could say the same about you, sugar."

Grandma grinned at Liz. "Got 'im fooled."

"And we've all got the temper to prove that we're

Irish," Gemma piped up. "And Raylen is the worst of the lot. That's why he's not married."

Colleen poked her sister on the arm. "He'd be runnin' a close race to you and—"

Dewar pointed. "Don't say it. Y'all come on over here and sit with us. Ain't room at that table to cuss a cat without gettin' a hair in your mouth," Dewar said when Raylen and Liz had their plates filled.

"You really interested in a job?" Jasmine asked when Liz sat down beside her.

"I could be," Liz answered.

Dewar reached out to steal Jasmine's hot roll and she aimed a fork at his fingers.

"Touch it and you are dead," she said.

"Don't be her friend, Liz. She's mean and hateful." Dewar grinned.

Jasmine shot right back, "Don't be his friend. He's a thief."

Liz picked up a chicken leg with her fingers and bit into the best fried chicken she had ever eaten. She didn't moan with pleasure but she wanted to. After just one afternoon, she would never be able to keep all the names, attitudes, and information straight in her mind, but she was having a great time. There wasn't all that much difference between a carnie family and a real one after all.

Jasmine talked between bites. "Lucy usually supplies me with waitresses, but she's out of stock right now. You'd have to be there at six in the morning, but you're done about two so your afternoons and evenings would be free."

"Lucy?" Liz asked.

"It's a long story. Pearl, who's been my friend since we were toddlers, inherited a motel over in Henrietta, Texas. Short version is that she took in Lucy to help her out when Lucy's abusive husband whipped on her the last time. When Pearl and Wil married, she turned the motel over to Lucy to manage. She helps other abused women find work when they decide to get out of their bad relationships. But she doesn't have anyone to send to me right now, and Amber is leaving on Wednesday to live around her folks in northeast Arkansas."

Dewar eyed her bottle of beer, and Jasmine air-slapped his shoulder. "You do not even want to think about touching my beer. I might stab you with my fork for messin' with my bread, but darlin', they won't even find your bones if you steal my beer."

"See?" Dewar said. "I told you she was mean."

Liz shrugged. "I'd say she's protectin' her property. A woman can't be lettin' a man come along and steal her property, can she?"

"You got that right," Jasmine said. "Me and you are going to get along just fine. So will you work for me?"

"Sure, I'll fill in until Lucy finds someone who needs a job." Liz wished she could reach up and snatch the words back into her mouth the minute they were out in the air. She should have at least slept on the idea before she took the job. She didn't need the money. She had plenty in her bank account to live a year without lifting a finger. But on the other hand, she would meet the local people, get to know them, and carve out a place in Montague County, Texas. Or else by the time the carnival was ready for another season, she'd be ready to give up her roots, slap on her wings, and fly away.

"Could you come in Tuesday and work with Amber to get the feel of it?" Jasmine asked.

"Sure. Where is it?" Liz replied.

"Right up the road a couple of miles. Same side of the highway. Next to Gemma's beauty shop," Jasmine said.

"Just waitress work, I hope. I'm not much of a cook," Liz said.

"I do the cookin'. That's why I bought the café. Just need someone to serve it up and run a cash register. You ever done any waitressing?"

"Little bit," Liz answered. Running a concession wagon was the same thing, wasn't it? She took orders. She served them. She took money and made change. There couldn't be a whole lot of difference.

"Tell me about your family. Was Haskell the only one from Texas?" Dewar asked. "He mentioned his sisters and having a niece, but he didn't ever say where you lived."

"Texas born and mostly raised in this state.

Mama was born out near Amarillo, little town named Claude. I was born over in Jefferson, Texas. I guess I'm truly a third generation Texan. Just never thought about it like that until now," Liz answered and started to tell them about the carnival, but she remembered what her mother had said about people judging the ones who lived and worked in carnivals or circuses.

"You didn't visit Haskell much, did you?" Dewar asked. "Raylen said that he remembers you being over there only a couple of times when you were a kid."

"We didn't come this way very often," Liz answered. "Uncle Haskell usually came to our winter place between Amarillo and Claude for Thanksgiving and Christmas every year, and we saw him in the fall of the year when we came through these parts. Grandma died when I was a little girl, but my grandfather is still alive and he's out in west Texas. But y'all knew that because that's where Uncle Haskell has relocated to help with Poppa. How long have the O'Donnells been in Ringgold?"

Raylen yelled over the din of voices all talking at once. "Daddy, how long has the family been in Ringgold?"

"Grandpa used to say we squatted in this area, and they built the town around us. I expect we've been somewhere up and down the Red River border for a hundred years or more," Cash answered.

"And the O'Malleys have been here every bit that long," Grandma said. "And if y'all don't eat your dinner, we ain't never goin' to get out there and do some playin'. I been lookin' forward to music all week, and all y'all want to do is jaw around. I guarantee you it's goin' to come up cold here pretty soon, what with Thanksgiving in a little more than a month, and we won't be able to play outside. Remember that year back in about ninety-one or ninety-two when the whole area iced up on Thanksgiving? It could happen again. And spring is a long way off if we get an early winter."

"Yes, ma'am." Dewar grinned.

"Who are the musicians?" Liz asked.

With a wave of her hand, Jasmine took in the whole family. "They all play something or sing."

"Really? You?" She looked at Dewar.

"Dulcimer is my specialty, but I can fill in on an acoustic guitar if Rye gets tired, and I can play a little bit of fiddle." He finished off his sweet tea. "And Raylen plays any of the instruments, too."

Gemma raised a hand. "Dobro and guitar."

"Colleen?" Liz asked.

"I'd be the banjo picker," she answered, but her voice wasn't as warm as the other members of the family.

"Grandma plays the dulcimer and the Dobro, and sometimes she can talk Grandpa into singing for us," Raylen said.

"Sounds like fun," Liz said.

"It is, darlin'," Grandma said, "especially if you like country music and good old Irish toe-stompin' tunes." She picked up her plate and headed for the kitchen with it. When she returned, she walked right on past the dining room table and toward the door. "I'll just be warmin' up the dulcimer while y'all finish up."

"She's usually not in this big of a hurry," Raylen said.

"I'm finished. I'm going on out there with her," Liz said.

Dewar shifted his eyes over toward Jasmine. "Speakin' of Thanksgiving, where are you going for the holiday?"

"Mama would tack my scalp to the garage door if I didn't go home for the holidays. I'll close up the Chicken Fried for the day and go have dinner with the family," Jasmine answered.

"You're welcome here if the weather gets bad," Dewar said.

"Maddie already said I was part of the family and didn't need any invitations to anything going on here, but thank you anyway. Where is Ace today?" Jasmine looked around the room.

Dewar chuckled. "He's over at Wil and Pearl's. Is that old ugly cowboy going to beat my time with you?"

Liz was already standing, plate in hand, but she stopped.

"You, darlin', ain't got no time to beat, and neither does Ace. He's just my friend, like you." Jasmine accentuated her words by stabbing her fork at him.

Dewar threw a hand over his chest. "You break my heart, Jasmine."

"Yeah, right! With all the women lining up for your attention, I'm not so sure you are interested in me. Finish your dinner so y'all can make Grandma happy," Jasmine said.

Raylen looked at Liz and explained, "Ace, Wil, and Rye were best friends. Rye and Austin got married last summer, and Wil and Pearl were married in February."

"And Ace?" she asked.

"Oh, that cowboy is too pretty to settle down with one woman the rest of his life." Jasmine shook her head. "And besides, the woman that got him would have to train him. He's not even housebroke."

Liz smiled. That reminded her of what Aunt Tressa had said about Blaze.

He's too handsome to ever settle down. And your temper is too volatile to put up with women hanging on him and his flirting, so don't be thinking that because you two aren't blood related there could ever be a relationship there.

Raylen pushed back his chair, picked up his plate, and led the way to the kitchen. "I'm finished too. I'll go with you, Liz."

When they reached the back yard, Grandma

was warming up with "Bill Bailey." Liz sat down on one of the two quilts that had been tossed out on the ground, her skirt fluffed out around her, and Raylen joined her.

"You're supposed to be playing, not sitting," Grandma called out.

Raylen started to get up, but his boot got tangled in the edge of the quilt. When he fell, he took Liz down with him. They landed with her snuggled up beside him as if they'd been napping on the quilt.

"That was on purpose," Dewar yelled from the back porch.

Raylen moved to a sitting position. "I'm so sorry. I'm usually not clumsy."

Liz moved away from him and sat up. "Forgiven. Accidents happen. What are you playing today?"

Raylen raised his broad shoulders in a shrug. "Whatever they want me to play, I guess. I was just going to sit down here and visit with you until they all get here."

Grandma stopped playing the dulcimer and guffawed. "Don't be judgin' him too quick. He might be a little clumsy today, but he can make a fiddle do everything but tell you a bedtime story, and honey, he's mighty smooth on his feet when it comes to dancin.'"

Liz raised a dark eyebrow. "Oh, really. Care for a contest?"

Raylen cocked his head to one side—just like he did that summer when she was fourteen and she'd thought it was so cute. "Are we talking about fiddlin' or dancin'? Want to show me what you've got? You can play my fiddle and I'll go in the house and get an old one."

She stood up. "Mine's in the truck. You told me if I play an instrument to bring it. You were serious, weren't you?"

"Yes, I was, and yes, I'll take you up on that contest. Want to bet on it?" he asked.

"Not until I see what you've got," she teased.

"Then you show me yours and I'll show you mine." Raylen grinned.

Jasmine piped up from the edge of the quilt where she was settling down to listen. "Raylen is the one that can play all of our instruments. I swear he could string up a stick with balin' wire and make it spit out a beautiful song. You might want to rethink challenging him to a contest!"

"I'll try to hold my own." Liz stood up and went to her truck for her fiddle. When she returned, Rye had handed Rachel off to Austin and picked up the guitar. Raylen had tuned a fine-looking fiddle. Colleen had a banjo strapped around her neck. Gemma picked at the Dobro. Dewar had a mandolin in his arms, and Maddie had a harmonica up to her mouth.

Liz tightened the strings on her fiddle, positioned it on her shoulder, and ran the bow down across them. She shook her head, made a few adjustments, and tried again. That time she was ready to play. Grandma raised an eyebrow at her, and Liz nodded that she was ready.

Rye struck up a chord, and they all fell in to begin the backyard concert with "Red River Valley," and followed that with "Bill Bailey."

Grandma stood up when they finished "Bill Bailey" and kissed Grandpa on the forehead. "Okay, honey. I'm goin' to sit this one out and we're goin' to have a fiddlin' contest. Liz, you know 'The Devil Went Down to Georgia'?"

Raylen dragged the bow across his fiddle, and the first chords of the song raised the hair on Liz's arms. She might have just met her match.

Raylen moved closer to Liz and their eyes met as the contest began. Gemma picked up the microphone and sang the words to the song as Liz and Raylen fought it out without blinking. Time seemed to stand still until the song was finished and then the applause began.

Liz had forgotten that there was anyone on the face of the earth but her and Raylen. She'd gotten lost in his blue eyes as they played facing each other. For a minute, she wondered where the audience came from and why they were clapping, then she remembered and bowed gracefully as if she'd just finished a set on the Grand Ole Opry stage.

"You goin' to lay that fiddle on the ground because I'm better than you?" Raylen asked.

"I beat the devil out of you, cowboy," Liz said.

Raylen's blue eyes twinkled. "Oh, no, you didn't. Ain't no one ever beat me on the fiddle."

She poked her bow at him. "Suck it up, cowboy. I beat you fair and square."

"I want a rematch," he said.

Grandma pointed at Raylen and then at Liz. "I'd say it's a draw and we'll have a rematch next time. For now, we're going to play some more. Don't be puttin' your fiddle down, girl. You're goin' to give him a run for his money the whole rest of the afternoon. Raylen, you don't get to play anything else today neither."

Grandpa nodded seriously. "The queen of Montague County has spoken. If you kids don't listen to her I'll hear about it all week."

Raylen shot a look at Liz.

She popped the fiddle on her shoulder and dragged the bow across the strings in an old Irish song that put even a bigger smile on Grandma's face.

"You sure you ain't Irish, darlin'?" Grandma clapped in time with the music.

Liz winked at Grandma and kept playing.

Raylen raised an eyebrow at her and matched her note for note.

Rye picked up the tune on the guitar and Colleen did the same with the banjo. Grandma placed the dulcimer in her lap and began to strum. When that song ended Grandma went right into "Rye

Whiskey," and Liz didn't miss a beat. She glanced over at Raylen and flashed her brightest smile.

You are flirting, Lizelle. She heard Aunt Tressa's voice and almost dropped her bow. *Less than twenty-four hours and you're letting a cowboy and a silly Christmas wish run your life, possibly even ruin it. You have the gift. I've told you that a million times, so why don't you stop fighting it and come back where you belong.*

She argued as she played. *I'm going to work on Tuesday morning. That should keep me away from him. And I'm not flirting, and I don't have any gift. I just watched you from the time I was born and learned to read people's expressions and emotions. It only takes a couple of well-placed questions and a pack of cards to tell a fortune. There's nothing to it.*

Liz's shoulder ached by the time Grandma finished the last fast tune and held up her hand. "I'm tired and ready for my Sunday nap now. You younguns can keep on playin' if you want to, but this old lady is going home."

Grandpa slowly made his way over to her side and held out a hand.

She passed the dulcimer off to Colleen, brushed back her gray hair, and looked up into his eyes. "Thank you, darlin'."

He looped her arm into his. "Anything for my sweetheart."

Aunt Tressa, where are you? Did you see that? That's what I want for Christmas: a love like theirs.

Before Aunt Tressa's voice could argue with her, Jasmine hollered from the quilt, "Hey, Liz. You want to follow me to the Chicken Fried? I'll show you around a little while it's empty, and you'll know where it is."

"Love to." Liz opened her fiddle case, loosened the strings, and put her instrument away. Raylen was playing a haunting rendition of "Danny Boy" when she got into her truck and followed Jasmine's SUV down the lane.

Chapter 3

THE BUFFET AT THE CAFÉ IN BOWIE WAS FILLED from one end to the other with comfort food. It was a very different café than the Chicken Fried. Jasmine's place was an old-fashioned plate lunch type of café where people sat down, ordered from a menu, and waited for their food to be served.

Liz was hungry enough that the pinto beans cooked with ham, fried okra and crispy brown squash, hash brown casserole, corn bread, and roast beef all looked good. Marva Jo called it comfort food. Aunt Tressa called it sin on a plate. Uncle Haskell called it down home cooking.

When she placed her tray on a corner table for two people, she couldn't believe that she'd put so much food on it. There was enough there for her, Tressa, Marva, and even Blaze. And Blaze could eat a small cow when he was hungry. Thank goodness she'd paid at the door and it was all-you-can-eat, but still she blushed slightly when she unloaded the bowls and plates from the tray.

"Mind if I join you?" Raylen asked.

He was close enough that she could feel the

warmth of his breath against the soft part of her neck right below her earlobe. She jerked her head around and looked right into his blue eyes.

"Raylen?"

"I'm not stalking you," he stammered.

She eased into her chair and motioned for him to sit across from her. "I didn't think you were."

He set his plate and bowls off the tray and picked up her tray to hand it to a waiter with his. Their hands brushed in the transfer, and she got that same feeling she'd had on Saturday night when he was close enough to kiss her, and on Sunday when he guided her through the O'Donnell house with his arm draped loosely around her shoulders.

"I was down here loading up on seed and fertilizer. What are you doing in Bowie?" he asked as he sat down.

"I've got to stock up at Walmart," she answered as she slathered butter on her cornbread. "Basics like cleansers, and I'm going to buy five books today because I can put them on my bookcase and not have to donate them to the next library."

"Why couldn't you keep them before now?" he asked.

"I've lived with my mother in a fifth-wheel trailer my whole life. We don't have room except for the necessities. I was twenty-five this past August and was thinking about getting my own trailer. I already have a truck big enough to pull it, and I can have a

riggin' put in the bed to hook up to with no problem. But Uncle Haskell left me his land, and I'm
talking too much." She blushed.

"I love to hear your voice, so talk away, but I do
want you to know that I would still buy that land
anytime you want to sell," Raylen said.

"It's not for sale," she said.

"I understand, but remember to call me if you
change your mind and decide to buy that trailer. So,
what did you think of the café? Are you going to
really take a waitress job?" he asked.

She nodded.

"It's tough work," he said.

"I'm a tough woman," she said.

Raylen chuckled.

"What's so funny?" Liz had a fork full of okra
headed toward her mouth, but it stopped mid-air.

"You don't look so tough," Raylen said.

"Oh? What can you tell about me just by
lookin'?" she asked.

He started at her forehead and scanned all the
way to where the top of the table stopped his eyes,
then leaned back, looked under the table, and let
his eyes travel down the length of her legs to her
black high-heeled shoes. She started to tell him
that he was being rude and crude, but she had chal-
lenged him.

He reached across the table, picked up her hands
and turned them over to look at the palms. He took

his time studying them, and then said, "You don't work with your hands. They don't have calluses like someone who works hard for a living. They're also not dry and wrinkled like someone who's done a job that involved lots of water like dishwashing. You are fit, so that means you either work out at an expensive gym or exercise on a regular basis. I'd say you come from a wealthy background and don't know jack squat about keeping house or taking care of twenty acres of land. How'd I do?"

He still had her hands in his when someone stopped at their table and laid her hand possessively on Raylen's shoulder. "Well, hello…" A stranger to Liz drew both words out in a long Southern drawl. "…Raylen O'Donnell. Where have you been keeping yourself, darlin'? I haven't seen you in weeks."

Raylen dropped Liz's hands. "Been busy, Becca."

Liz liked the way her small hands had fit into Raylen's big old rough cowboy hands, and she'd sure liked the sparks that shot every which way when he touched her. Liz wished that Becca, who-ever she was, would drop dead right there in the café. The woman pushed back her blond hair but didn't take her hand off Raylen's shoulder. Liz had asked if he was married, and he'd stuttered like a ten-year-old who'd got caught with a *Playboy* maga-zine. But she hadn't asked if he was engaged or had a girlfriend.

Becca looked down at Liz as if she was nothing

more than something she had tracked in after walking through a cow pasture.

"Who's this?" Becca asked.

"I'm sorry," Raylen said. "This is my neighbor, Haskell's niece, Liz. She's moved into his place."

"Well, well, well," Becca said. "Has Raylen offered you market price on the place?"

"It's nice to meet you, and my place isn't for sale at any price," Liz answered and went back to eating her dinner.

Becca leaned down and put her other hand, the one that wasn't on Raylen's shoulder, on the table in front of Liz. "I'll give you three times what the going price is for that land."

"Why? Is there gold or oil under the topsoil?" Liz asked.

Becca stood up straight and laughed aloud. "It's not what's under the dirt or even on top of the dirt that I'm interested in. It's what lives next door. See you around, Raylen." She blew a kiss toward Raylen as she left with her hips swaying.

Liz looked across the table at Raylen.

"What?" Raylen asked.

Liz shrugged. "Guess I'm sitting on a gold mine since *you* live next door. If I sold, would I owe you a commission?"

Raylen's face registered shock. "Me?"

"Who else lives next door?" Liz could hear the chill in her own voice.

"Dewar," Raylen said.

"So, is Becca interested in Dewar? Does Jasmine know?" Liz asked.

Raylen threw both hands up. "Jasmine isn't Dewar's girlfriend. Becca has been my friend since grade school. She's a handful and speaks her mind, but she's just my friend."

"So then it's not a love triangle?"

Raylen stuttered and stammered. "A what?"

"Never mind. So why does she want my land?"

"She lives down close to Stoneburg on a cattle ranch. And since we're friends, I guess she wants to live close to my family. I didn't even know she was interested in buying land in Ringgold. Her daddy owns three-fourths of Stoneburg," he said.

"A friend who wants more from you—maybe benefits," Liz said. "It's none of my business who you like, date, or love, but honey, you've got rocks for brains if you think that woman isn't interested in you."

"Becca is my friend and she never likes any of my…" He swallowed. "…other girl-type friends. Tell me about you." He took a deep breath and let it out slowly. "So, you grew up in a travel trailer. Why?"

Liz figured she might as well 'fess up. She was actually surprised that he didn't already know about Haskell and his carnival background, but then her uncle hadn't ever been proud of that part of his life—not like his sisters were. "I was born a carnie. My grandparents were carnies. My mother and her sister are carnies even yet. Didn't Uncle Haskell tell you?"

"Carnie? That a family name?"

Liz laughed. "Carnie as in carnival. Did you ever go to the carnival when it was in Bowie?"

Raylen cocked his head to one side. "Are you serious?"

"I am very serious. My grandparents owned the carnival. When Nanna died, Poppa, that's my grandfather, gave the business to his daughters since Uncle Haskell didn't want any part of that kind of life. Poppa still has his trailer, but it's parked out on the land where we winter. That would be out in west Texas, not far from Amarillo, but he refuses to take the wheels off or skirt the thing. We live there from the end of November until the first of March. We do maintenance, paint, grease, and whatever else is needed to put the show back on the road in the spring. Each year there's evidence that Grandpa is growing roots, but he'll never admit it. The carnival was doing a gig in Jefferson, Texas, when Mother had me, so I've truly been a carnie all my life. If you came to the carnival in Bowie when you were a little boy, our paths have probably crossed in the past."

Raylen had thought his brother Rye was crazy when he fell hard and fast for Austin, a big-city girl with a big-city job. There was no way Austin would ever leave everything she'd worked toward her entire life and move to tiny little Terral, Oklahoma, to run a watermelon farm, but Austin at least had had a conventional life with a house and a job. Liz had never had any at all, so chances of her falling for a deeply rooted rancher were slim and none.

"Did Haskell ever show interest in the carnival?" Raylen asked.

Liz shook her head and said between bites, "It was a sore spot between him and his sisters. One is my mother and the other is my aunt."

"Why?" Raylen asked.

"Uncle Haskell wanted to settle down when he met Aunt Sara. He left the carnival and bought that piece of property next to your ranch. He worked for a company in Nocona until they could make the ranch pay its way. They wanted a house full of kids, but Aunt Sara couldn't have any. I barely remember her. She died when I was about five, but she always came to the carnival in Bowie and brought me homemade cookies."

Raylen finished his dinner and sipped sweet tea. "I was eight when Miss Sara died. It was one of the first funerals I went to. I don't remember seeing you there."

"Aunt Tressa and Poppa came. Mother kept the carnival going," Liz told him.

"How did you go to school?" Raylen asked.

"I didn't. Aunt Tressa and Mama homeschooled me just like their mama did them. I got my associate's degree in business online before my sixteenth birthday. Mama said I could stay off the carnival rounds a couple of years and get my bachelor's degree, but I didn't want to."

"So you ran the business end of the carnival?"

Liz shook her head. "I'm not strong enough to wrestle that from Aunt Tressa. She's the financial head. I'm Madam Lizelle, The Great Drabami."

"The great what?"

"Drabami. It's a carnie word for fortune-teller. I tell fortunes, read your palm, lay out the cards, or look into the big crystal ball, and..." She took a deep breath and figured that she might as well spit it all out and hold nothing back.

"And what?" Raylen asked.

"I belly dance," she answered. "Aunt Tressa taught me, and I took over for her when she hurt her back."

Raylen took a sip of his tea and didn't answer.

Liz wondered if he hadn't heard her before he finally said something.

"You are waiting for me to bite. I'm not going to. You're not going to catch me with that story," he said with a wide grin. "You're just paying me back for not conceding to you over the fiddle contest."

"It's the truth. Throw your palm out here." She reached across the table.

Raylen wiped his hand on a paper napkin and flipped it out on the table. She picked it up with her left hand and cradled it in her right. She'd held men's hands in hers since she was sixteen when she did her first reading, but nothing prepared her for the way her heart pitched in an extra beat when she traced the curve of his lifeline from the middle of his wrist around his thumb.

"You will have a long and productive life, Raylen O'Donnell. You will have one successful marriage and fate will play a big part in your choice of a partner." She almost stopped there because her mother had read her palm with the same words not a week before, but she gently traced another line and said, "You let your head rule and not your heart, but that will change. Don't be afraid. It's in your future and you will fear giving up control, but in the end, you will see the wisdom in allowing love to come into your heart."

He pulled his hand back with a jerk. "That sounds like a bunch of hocus-pocus to me. I still don't believe you, but I have to tell you, if you are putting in a fortune tellin' shop in Ringgold, you won't get any business."

"I'm going to work for Jasmine starting tomorrow morning, and I have hung up my belly dancing outfits, and probably won't be reading cards for anyone, either," she told him. "But I'm not ashamed of who I am or where I come from. I own my past, and if that embarrasses you, then I'll stay on my side of the barbed wire fences separating my land from yours."

"Hey." He held up both palms in a defensive gesture. "I still think you are pulling my leg about that fortune tellin' business, but I believe you about going to work for Jasmine. I'm glad you are. She needs help and she's my friend. You'll like working with her." He laid his napkin on the table and stood up. "I've got to get back to work. See you around."

"Come over sometime and I'll get out the cards and do a real reading just for you. I might even put on my costume and dance for you," she teased.

"Still not biting!" He waved over his shoulder.

She finished her tea and tossed a couple of bills on the table for a tip. She'd planned to grab a hamburger at the Dairy Queen and hit Walmart for supplies when she left Ringgold that morning. But she'd seen the café on the west side of the highway as she came into town, and there were two police cars as well as dozens of trucks in the parking lot. Any place where ranchers and police both ate had to be good, and she had not been disappointed. As she walked out the door, she fished her phone from her purse and punched in the first number on speed dial. Blaze picked up on the first ring.

"Was I right? Are you on your way home?" he asked.

"You were *not* right and you had no right to yell

at me. Are you finished sulking? I want to tell you about Raylen."

"I wasn't sulking, and who is Raylen?" her best friend, Blaze, asked.

She told him all about everything that had happened since she arrived in Ringgold. "And I've got a job starting in the morning."

"You won't last," Blaze said. "Some people are born to be still. Others to travel. Me and you are travelers, sweetheart."

"Want to bet?" she asked.

"No, I don't want to take your money. You're goin' to need it to buy a trailer when you come back, but you can always crash on my couch," he said.

"I'm hanging up on that note. Good-bye, Blaze," she said.

"Bye, sweetheart," he said.

A warm wind blew up from the south, swirling leaves around her truck tires. Black birds hopped around in search of free food but found very little. Liz wished she'd tucked the leftover corn bread into her purse to give them. Next time she'd remember that they were there. She opened the door to her truck and slid into the driver's seat. She put in a Christmas CD called *Now That's What I Call a Country Christmas* that she'd gotten the year before. Kellie Pickler made Liz smile when she sang "Santa Baby" and talked about her Christmas list. Liz's list wasn't long. Maybe, just maybe, Santa would have time to throw that last item in the sleigh and she'd get her cowboy by Christmas.

She thought about what Blaze and her mother and aunt would be doing that day as she drove from the café to the Walmart store across town, and made a mental note to put laundry detergent on her shopping list. Doing laundry at home instead of in a commercial laundromat would be so different than Monday morning in the carnival business. That was the day the crew tore everything down, got the animals into the trucks, and got everything ready to roll to the next location. Those who weren't busy with that job used the time to visit the local coin-operated laundry. Tuesday and Wednesday were travel days, with the hopes of arriving at their next gig sometime before dark on Wednesday. From the time they pulled into the parking lot, pasture, or wherever they were paid to set up, a flurry of activity took place to get things ready for the opening night, which was usually Thursday. Then it was nonstop work until Sunday evening when they turned off the lights and started tearing down again.

Laundry day was the day that Liz had time to look through magazines. Even if they were years old, she loved poring over the pictures of the insides of houses, especially the before and after ones. Now she had a house of her own and she could redo it any way she wanted. But other than moving around the furniture, she wasn't sure she wanted to change anything at all.

Nothing other than decorate it for Christmas with twinkling lights and lots of stuff. Plain old Christmas stuff that I can keep from one year to the next. I don't care if I have a whole room full of it. Right now, there are two empty bedrooms and I can store it all there, she thought as she drove.

Walmart was all the way across town, but she wasn't in a big hurry, so she drove slowly, taking a long look at the storefronts. She'd been in Bowie once a year ever since she was born. She knew where the grocery store was located, right along with Walmart, the old location and the new one, the laundry, and the Dairy Queen. Aside from that, until that day, nothing else mattered. But now she noticed a couple of furniture stores, a western wear store, banks, and several other places that looked interesting.

She snagged a parking place close to the door and checked the price of gas. It was two cents cheaper at the place next to Walmart than the service station north of Bowie, so she made a mental note to fill up before she left town. She took her time in the store, looking at the new fall shirts and jackets before she started filling her cart with items from her list. She didn't even see Becca until their carts came within an inch of crashing together as she rounded the end of an aisle and came face-to-face with her.

"Well, hello again, Libby," Becca said with a fake smile.

"It's Liz, not Libby. And hello to you," Liz said.

Becca leaned on her overloaded cart filled with large bags of dog food. "So, are you all moved into Haskell's place?"

Liz pushed her cart to one side. "Yes, I am. It was nice seeing you again, Becca."

Becca reached out and grabbed the side of the cart. "Are you sure you don't want to sell and go back to whatever rock you crawled out from under?"

Liz controlled the burst of anger that boiled up from her toes to her chest. "I'm very sure. It's not even mine until spring. Uncle Haskell is letting me live there for a few months to be sure that I want to settle down in this area."

"And if you stay?" Becca asked.

"Then it's my property," Liz said.

Blaze would like Becca for sure. He tended to go for women with blond hair and green eyes, and he really liked tall, tough women who dressed like Becca. Blaze and Becca... It even sounded good together. She fit all the criteria, but Blaze didn't stick with anyone more than a week or two, so the bubble in her imagination about Becca running off to help in a carnival burst with a loud bang.

"So, what kind of work do you do?" Becca asked.

Becca was being downright nosy, and it didn't sit well with Liz, who was tempted to blurt out her whole life story just to watch Becca's jaw hit the floor.

"Right now, I'm going to work as a waitress at the Chicken Fried café for Jasmine. I start in the morning," Liz answered.

"How long have you known Raylen?" Becca asked.

Now we get to the real reason she's created this cart wreck in the middle of the store. I would do the same thing for Blaze.

"If you count from the first time we met, about fifteen years. But I'd only seen him twice before I moved into Uncle Haskell's house," Liz answered. "Now if you don't have any more questions, I need to get done with my shopping."

Aunt Tressa's advice was loud and clear in her mind. *Keep a poker face and don't give away jack squat. Watch their expressions and you'll learn enough to give you a good reading.*

Becca cocked her head to one side and frowned. *Confusion. Disbelief.* That's what showed on Becca's face, and that gave Liz the power that Becca only thought she had. "I understand that you went to school with Raylen. Have you always lived in this area?"

"That's right. Raylen and I have been friends since we were just kids," Becca said.

At the mention of Raylen's name Becca's eyes should have lit up like a Tilt-A-Whirl, but they didn't. Her mouth said words; her eyes didn't back them up.

"Nice to see you again." Liz pushed her cart forward a foot. "I've got a ton of things to do before work time tomorrow morning."

"Waitress, huh?" Becca said with a half-hearted giggle.

Pure happiness. That's what showed in Becca's expression now.

Evidently, she figured Raylen would never be interested in a waitress.

"That's right. You ever eat at Chicken Fried?" Liz asked.

"Oh, yeah. Love Jasmine's food. She has chocolate cream pie on Friday, so that's my regular day. Raylen and Dewar usually drop by on that day. Raylen is a chicken fried steak guy and Dewar likes Jasmine's double cheeseburgers," Becca said.

Happiness brings about confidence, Aunt Tressa said. *Confidence loosens the tongue, and that's when you keep your mouth shut and listen.*

Liz nodded. "Maybe I'll see you there at the end of the week, then."

An upward tilt of the chin said Becca had regained her superiority. "Oh, I'm sure you will. Raylen and I eat there pretty often."

Liz pushed her cart to the right and disappeared around the end of the next aisle as quickly as possible.

"Well, hello," Colleen said.

Liz groaned, but managed to paste on a smile. All she did was eat lunch with Raylen. It wasn't even a date. She'd paid for her own meal and simply sat with him. Why did she feel like she was being punished?

Colleen studied her like she was a bug under a microscope. "I hear you had lunch with my brother."

Liz tried to keep a blank expression like she'd been taught. "News must travel fast in this area."

Colleen shrugged. "He called to tell me to pick up a few things since I'm already here."

"Well, rats! If I'd known you were shopping for the neighborhood, I'd have called you with my list," Liz teased.

Colleen shook her head. "It's only because he's my brother that he can weasel me into getting him dish soap and a bag of potatoes. Anything more and he'd be in here himself."

"Well, I've got to get back to the pet aisle. See you around," Liz said, wondering the whole time why Raylen would need those two items if he still lived with his parents. Didn't Maddie buy the groceries and cleansers?

"Did you take that job at Jasmine's place?" Colleen asked.

Liz nodded.

"Have you ever done waitress work before?" Colleen asked.

"I guess you could call it that," Liz answered.

"Where?" Colleen asked.

"All over the state of Texas, some in Oklahoma, and over in Arkansas. We traveled a lot." Liz pushed her cart past Colleen's and hurried to the back of the store.

Her phone rang when she was safely hidden in the aisle with the pet food. She dug it out of her purse, saw that it was her mother, and pushed the button to answer it.

"Hello, Mama," she said with a long sigh.

"We're on the move. Next stop is Bells, Texas. You always liked that little town. Why don't you meet us there and give up this notion of living like the rest of the world?"

"After only two days? No, thank you. Besides, I've got a job. I'm going to work at the Chicken Fried café in the morning." Liz picked up a dozen cans of fancy cat food and put them in her cart.

"Doing what?" Marva Jo asked.

"Waitress for minimum wage," Liz told her.

Marva Jo laughed so loud that Liz held the phone out from her ear.

"What's so funny?" Liz asked when her mother calmed down.

Marva hiccupped. "Now I know you'll come home to the carnival where you belong. You doing waitress work... Girl, you haven't worked for that kind of money since you were fourteen. I couldn't have asked for a better job to teach you a lesson."

"I don't need the money, so it doesn't matter," Liz argued.

"Okay, let's talk about the cowboy next door," Marva Jo said. "Did you tell him that you don't have to work, that you have an inheritance big enough to buy his piece of Texas dirt?"

"I had lunch with him. And yesterday I went to his parents' house for Sunday dinner and music afterwards. And no, I didn't tell him anything about money. Why would I? I don't think it would be right to say, 'Hey, Raylen, I'm rich.' But he did almost beat me in a fiddlin' contest," Liz said.

"Dammit!" Marva Jo exclaimed.

"Is that not as funny as the minimum wage?" Liz asked.

"No, it is not! You slow that wagon down, girl. You know very well that you don't belong with a man who's earthbound," Marva Jo warned.

Liz sucked in a lungful of air and got ready for the age-old argument. "You fell in love with and married a man who wasn't a carnie. So, what's to say if I fall in love with one that—"

Aunt Tressa butted into the conversation. "Marva Jo has this phone on speaker, and I'm right here with her. Don't argue with your mama, and learn from her mistakes. She married an earth-bound man and it did not work. I don't care if you grow potatoes and marry a dirt farmer, but you will be nice to your mama. She misses you and wants you to come back where you belong. And Haskell might have mentioned that his niece has a nice big bank account, so be sure that *guy* isn't angling for more than twenty acres of tumbleweeds and chiggers before you start choosing him over family."

"And Raylen isn't that kind of man. If he loved a woman he wouldn't care if she had a dime or a million dollars," Liz protested. "I'm hanging up now and getting my shopping finished. Love you both. I can't wait to see everyone next month. I'm putting up the Christmas tree early so you can see it."

Chapter 4

LIZ UNLOADED SEVERAL SACKS, INCLUDING three bags of Christmas ornaments for her tree when she got one back to her place. She laid them on the kitchen table and admired each one of the bright shiny bells and balls. She'd looked at a six-foot tree but couldn't make up her mind whether to get a tall skinny one or one of those huge, fat ones. Once everything was put away, she stood in the middle of the living room and eyed the room. If she scooted the sofa back, there would be plenty of room for a big, round tree with lots and lots of ornaments and a star on top.

She envisioned a real cedar tree in the spot.

No, as long as I plan to leave my tree up, a real one would get all dried out. She sat down on the sofa and was thinking about how many lights it would take to go all around the top of the roof when the phone rang. Thinking it was her mother and Tressa again, she ignored it, but when it started again after less than a minute, she fished it out of her purse.

"Hello," she said without looking at the caller ID.

"Hey, kid. Thought I'd check on Hooter and Blister," Haskell said. "I forgot to tell you that their vet papers are in the drawer beside the refrigerator. Hooter will need his shots in February and Blister gets hers in March."

"I'll put those dates on my calendar so I don't forget. I bought ornaments for a Christmas tree today and there's plenty of room for me to store them, so do you have a fake tree hiding somewhere or did you cut a real one every year and—"

"Whoa!" Haskell said. "Slow down, Lizelle! You know how Sara liked Christmas, or maybe you didn't, since you were so little. When she was still with me, I always cut a real tree. But the last few years, I just put up a little bought one because the real ones shed so bad. Can't keep enough water in the pan to keep them happy."

"That's what I figured. I'm going to buy a big one and I'm going to have a house that puts the stars in the sky to shame," she said.

"Then, darlin'," Haskell said, "go out to the barn and look up in the loft. There are boxes and boxes of decorations out there."

"What barn?" Liz asked. "The one behind the house? I thought that was O'Donnell property."

Haskell chuckled. "It's a little tough to picture twenty acres when you've lived in a trailer your whole life, isn't it?"

"I figured it went from fence to fence after I left the highway and then to the back side of the yard," she said.

"From the yard fence, you go on back to the barn that you can see from the kitchen window, and then to the fence back behind that. Then you've got twenty acres. The Christmas stuff is in boxes, and they are all marked," Haskell told her.

Liz sucked in a lungful of air and let it out in a loud whoosh. "Do you mean I've got a whole barn to put stuff in? I may go back to Walmart this afternoon."

"So, you like it there?" Haskell asked.

"Been here two days and I'm not ready to run yet," she said. "And I go to work tomorrow morning."

"Lizelle, you don't have to work." Haskell's tone turned serious. "Take some time, girl. You've worked your whole life."

"I know, but I want to. It'll get me acquainted with more folks than the O'Donnells. Did I tell you that I had Sunday dinner with them yesterday and I played my fiddle and Raylen and I had a contest? I beat that cowboy, but his grandma called it a tie," she said.

Haskell chuckled again. "They are good people, the O'Donnells. Been fine neighbors all these years. Raise some of the best horses in the whole state. They would probably hire you to exercise their horses, instead of you working at a café."

"But I want to work at the café. I can't wait. It's going to be so much fun," Liz told him.

"You are as stubborn as..." Haskell started.

Liz butted in with: "...as you are?"

"Busted!" Haskell said, his voice now back to normal. "How's Blister and Hooter?"

"Spoiled and I'm making them even worse. How are you doing out there, Uncle Haskell? Tell me the truth."

"Dad and I are cleaning up the big barn so we can pull in one trailer at a time and do some serious repainting and repair. He's excited about all three of us being here together and he's even considering letting me underpin his trailer before serious winter sets in. He misses the carnival life so much, but he's wise enough to know he's not able for it anymore."

Liz breathed a quiet sigh of relief. Uncle Haskell sounded busy and happy, so he wouldn't want his land and house back in the spring, and that gave Liz a measure of hope that he really would sign it all over to her. If not, she might just look around the area for another twenty acres with a house that did not have wheels.

"Got to go now. I see Poppa headed out to the repair barn. If I don't get out there soon, he'll do too much."

She barely had time to utter "love you" before Haskell cut the connection. She hurried to the kitchen window and looked out at the barn—her barn. She rushed back to her bedroom, kicked off her shoes, stomped her feet down into cowboy boots, and grabbed her denim jacket.

"Merry Christmas to me," she sang as she headed out the back door toward the big metal building.

Not only did she have a house without wheels, but she also had a barn, which meant that she had tons of storage room. She could park the carnie trailer that she'd lived in her entire life inside that big building and have room left over to store whatever she wanted to buy.

She slid the door back and the smell of hay, feed, and leather all hit her nose at the same time. She'd grown up accustomed to that odor, only it came from a pen where the riding ponies were kept. The carnival had had Shetland ponies when she was a little girl, but as they got too old for the carnival, Tressa had replaced them with Rocky Mountain horses, and Liz had fallen in love with them. The extra tuft of hair on their feet made them look like they were flying when they pranced.

"I could have some right here. I could breed Rocky Mountain and have baby colts. There's plenty of room for a pair," she told the dog as they wandered through the big building, discovering a riding lawn mower and a small tractor. And a mama cat with a litter of kittens hiding in the back corner, but they were all so wild that she couldn't get near them. Located in the northeast corner of the barn, the tack room was about the size of her living room. Shelves lined the walls, and when she opened the door the leather smell overpowered the hay and feed smell. Boxes of every size and shape were shoved on the shelves and were labeled in Haskell's spidery handwriting.

She pulled an old ladder-back chair over from the worktable. She hopped up on it and grabbed the first box she could reach. It wasn't heavy, but when she moved it, the dust flew into her hair, her nose, and eyes. Once the box was on the table, she opened it with a knife that was lying on the table.

Inside the box she found old-fashioned Christmas lights, the kind with big, multicolored bulbs, and they had been wrapped carefully around a cardboard tube. She wouldn't even have to waste hours and hours untangling them when she got ready to put her tree up.

Bless your heart, Uncle Haskell, for keeping all this for me, Liz thought as she looked up to see dozens of other boxes marked CHRISTMAS.

The next one she removed very gently so the dust didn't gag or blind her. It held more lights, as did the third, fourth, and fifth ones. The sixth one was filled with ornaments wrapped individually in newspaper. She undid each one, lining them up on the table as she did. The last one had a nativity scene that would look lovely on the mantel.

It's Christmas before Christmas, she thought as she stood back and looked at all the treasures.

———

Glorious Danny Boy, a solid black quarter horse, pulled at the reins, but Raylen kept him to a steady trot the first time around the pasture. Danny Boy had put the O'Donnell Horse Ranch on the map a few years back, and when Maddie and Cash won the Texas Heritage Stakes again the next year with Major Jack, the ranch became famous. Nowadays, Maddie and Cash raised horses but didn't race them. Glorious Danny Boy and Major Jack had such sought-after bloodlines that Maddie was particular about what mares she'd even allowed to carry one of their colts. And each year, she sold half a dozen of her own prize colts sired by Danny Boy or Jack.

Raylen finally gave the big black stud enough rein to let him gallop around the pasture. "Do you feel like you are back in the race?" he asked the horse.

Danny Boy slowed down and went straight for the pasture fence. He neighed and several mares raised their heads.

"Are you checking on your harem? I can barely keep up with one woman at a time, old man." Raylen leaned forward and patted the horse on the neck. He hooked a leg over the saddle horn and let Danny Boy flirt with his women for a spell while he thought of Liz. He remembered Wil telling him about the night his wife, Pearl, convinced him that her full name was Minnie Pearl Richland.

Nice try, Liz Hanson, he thought. *Wake up, lady, I didn't just fall off the hay wagon, and you are not going to snooker me like Pearl did Wil.*

Was Liz's last name Hanson? Haskell's last name was Hanson, so it stood to reason that her mother and aunt were Hansons. But if her mother was married, then Liz's name wouldn't be Hanson. She hadn't mentioned a father, not even when she was trying to make him believe that farfetched story about belly dancing.

"I bet if I'd said I'd be over at six-thirty for a belly dancin' demonstration she would have back-tracked," he said.

Danny Boy took a step backwards. Raylen had just made the second round in the pasture when he noticed the barn door over at Haskell's place was wide open. He reined in and dismounted.

I wonder what she's doing in the barn, he thought as he looped the reins to the rail fence.

He jumped the fence and was almost to the barn when he heard a squeal. He picked up the pace and followed the next scream to the tack room. Most likely Liz had had her first encounter with a snake or a mouse. He slung open the door to find her with half a dozen open boxes surrounding her on the floor as well as on the table, and Christmas decorations everywhere.

"Liz, are you okay?" he asked.

She jumped and squealed again. "Dammit! Raylen, you scared me."

"Well, you scared me. I heard you yelp and thought you were hurt," he said.

"It was excitement, not hurt," she said. "I found all these gorgeous old decorations so I can make my house pretty for Christmas. Want to help me?"

He raised an eyebrow. "Tonight?"

"No, but before Thanksgiving. Mama and Aunt Tressa are coming the week before Thanksgiving, and I want it decorated by then." The light from the window made the ornaments glitter and glow.

"Sure," he said.

"What are you doing over here?" she asked and sniffed the air. "Have you been riding? I smell horses."

"You've got a good nose as well as a loud squeal," he said with a grin. "I was exercising Danny Boy, one of our prize stallions. That's my afternoon job several days a week."

"Tell you what, I'll trade off help," Liz said. "If you will help get my house decorated by the time my family gets here, I'll help you exercise the horses when I'm not at the cafe. I love horses," she said.

"You ride?" That was as believable as belly dancing.

She picked up an ornament, wrapped it and put it back in one of the boxes.

"Our carnival has pony rides for the kids. We used to have Shetlands, but now we have Rocky Mountains. Ever heard of them? I ride in the winter months every single day. And Poppa has bigger horses out on the property, the ones that we can't use for the carnival but he can't bring himself to sell. So, yes, I ride."

Raylen's face registered shock, but he threw up his palms. "Sorry I doubted you. And yes, I've heard of Rocky Mountains. Dewar could talk for hours about Vanner horses. He's been buggin' Mama to invest in a pair, but she told him if he wanted to play with the fancy horses then to go ahead, but to keep them on his property. And I'll take you up on that offer. I'll help decorate the house if you'll help me exercise the horses."

"Thank you," Liz said. "Dewar will have to come to the carnival when it comes to Bowie and see Aunt Tressa's four Rocky Mountains. They're spoiled rotten, and she treats them like babies."

"When he hears about the horses, I'm sure he'll be there." Raylen leaned on the edge of the table and pretended interest in the boxes. Liz had been dressed like she was that afternoon, back when they were both teenagers. He'd wanted to be a jockey, but even though he was the shortest O'Donnell brother, he was still too big to qualify as a jockey.

"And you? Will you go have a look at the horses?" Liz asked.

"Of course, but only if you show me around and introduce me to everyone," Raylen said.

"You got it," Liz said with a smile.

Her smile affected him just like it did that day back when they were teenagers and she had hung on the rail fence and watched him exercise Major Jack. He'd been mesmerized by it and her dark eyes that he felt could see right down into the depths of his soul.

He cleared his throat and said, "I'd better be going. I left my horse out back, tied up to the fence. Saw the barn door open and thought I'd better check on things."

Liz moved around the table. "I'll walk with you. Is it the same horse you rode back when we were kids?"

"No, this one is Danny Boy. I was riding Major Jack that day," Raylen answered.

She fell into step beside him. "Uncle Haskell said y'all have two over there that folks stand in line to get a chance at their bloodlines. Is one of those Danny Boy?"

"That'd be him right there." Raylen pointed. "And Major Jack. They both won the Texas Heritage Stakes and made the ranch what it is today. O'Donnell Ranch has a dozen blue-blooded mares that Mama and Daddy use to raise colts from those two. She's got a long list of folks interested in buying a colt from either one of them."

Liz reached up and ran her hand down the length of his nose and he nuzzled her hair. "He's a beauty."

"You really do like horses, don't you?" Raylen was amazed that Danny Boy let her touch him. He was usually skittish around strangers.

She nodded. "And cats and dogs and cows."

"Tell me the truth," Raylen insisted. "You've been teasing me, haven't you? You were really raised on a ranch out in west Texas, weren't you?"

She looked up and locked eyes with him. "I was raised in a carnival. I tell fortunes and do some belly dancin' to bring in the crowd when Aunt Tressa or Mama is telling fortunes. We winter out near Claude, Texas, from the last of November until the first week of March, and Poppa likes animals. I told you this before, and it's the gospel truth."

He leaned forward and she moistened her upper lip with the tip of her tongue. His pulse raced, but it was a slow-motion experience. When his lips claimed hers in a sweet but oh so passionate kiss, she kissed back with enough heat to almost melt the soles off his boots.

"I been wantin' to do that for eleven years," he said, and then hopped the fence, mounted up, and rode away.

Chapter 5

LIZ SAT STRAIGHT UP IN BED AND SLAPPED THE alarm clock so hard that it bounced off the far bedroom wall and kept buzzing. What was she thinking, telling Jasmine that she'd be at the café at six o'clock in the morning? Somewhere in the Good Book there had to be a verse that said "Thou shalt never see the pearly gates if thou riseth out of thy bed whilst it is still dark outside." She threw herself back on the pillows, but the alarm clock sounded even louder, pitching a buzzing hissy fit as it lay upside down on the hardwood floor. Finally, she threw off the covers and crossed the room, picked up the indestructible varmint, and pushed the off button. She trudged to the bathroom, flipped on the light, and covered her eyes with the back of her hand.

It was a cardinal sin to be awake at five o'clock, and a glance toward the mirror proved it. Liz's black hair looked like a whole nest of rats had had a party in it while she slept. She grabbed a brush and went to work, sweeping it up into a ponytail and twisting it into a sloppy bun. She slapped on barely enough makeup to be presentable in public and went back to the bedroom. Jasmine said jeans and a T-shirt were fine and that she provided aprons.

Her eyes were still half shut when she picked up her purse and keys from the kitchen table and stumbled out into the darkness. Hooter looked up from the corner of the porch with mournful eyes, and Blister ran to her empty food dish.

"I can't leave until I feed the livestock," Liz grumbled as she went back inside the house.

She filled the food dishes and made sure there was fresh water and headed toward her pickup truck again.

"Good mornin'," Raylen said cheerfully as he hopped over the fence in a swift movement.

Liz glared at him. "It's five thirty in the morning. What is good about that?"

"Going to be a beautiful day. Sun will be rising in another hour. Thought I'd stop by and tell you good luck on your first day at work. I'm getting ready to plow that field right there." He pointed toward the tractor sitting on the other side of the fence.

"Thank you for the good luck," she said.

He hurried to the truck and opened the door for her. "Have a good day."

"How can you be so happy at this time of day?" she asked.

"I'm an early riser. Love the morning when things are just waking up," he answered.

She brushed against him and the electricity between them woke her up so fast it made her head swim. So, the fire in his kiss wasn't a one-time episode.

"See you later. I may drop in today if I get this job done," he said as he slammed her truck door shut.

———————

Liz drove out to the end of the lane and turned north. It was a good thing he hadn't kissed her, or she'd have been tempted to just stay home and make out with him all day. By the carnie bible she was already sinning by getting up before the sun; she might as well go to hell for a big sin as a little one. She had a smile on her face when she opened the door to the café and saw Jasmine through the serving window in the kitchen.

"Hey, come on back here and get a cup of coffee. It'll be about ten or fifteen minutes before the crowd starts wandering in," Jasmine yelled.

Liz headed that way and stopped at the kitchen door.

Jasmine pointed at the coffee machine and the cups stacked up beside it. "Your breakfast and dinner are included with the job. If you want a sausage biscuit, help yourself." Jasmine nodded toward a plate with several already made up. "Want cream or sugar with your coffee?"

Liz filled a mug with coffee and picked up a

biscuit. "I hate to cook. I may be your waitress until my dying day."

A young woman, not as old as Liz, rushed through the door and into the dining room. She poured a cup of coffee, then added two heaping scoops of sugar and enough cream to turn it pale tan. Then she picked up a sausage biscuit and wolfed it down before grabbing another one.

While she nibbled at the second one, she dug in her jeans pocket and handed Liz a piece of paper. "I'm sorry. I was hungry and thought I was late. I'm Amber. I made a list of the way I do things to help you out. Before I leave in the evenings, I put out the breakfast menus and make sure the tables are ready for the next day. That'd be full salt and pepper shakers, ketchup bottle, and pepper sauce. I get the coffee pots ready so all we have to do is turn them on. Breakfast rush is from about six to eight thirty, and then there's a few drifters up to eleven when lunch starts. Then it's a madhouse until two."

"Pleased to meet you, and thank you for the notes," Liz said.

"I hate to leave. I've loved working here, but Mama is ailin' and I need to go home," Amber said.

"Whatever brought you to Texas anyway?" Liz asked.

"Worthless sumbitch I met in a café up in Rogers, Arkansas. He was a truck driver, and I was doin' waitress work. I'd just got out of a bad marriage and got right back into one even worse than the first one. Mama told me, but I wouldn't listen," Amber said.

"I'm sorry," Liz said.

"Me too. Could've saved myself a lot of pain and misery," Amber said. "But that's all behind me now and I got a grip on life. I won't make the same mistake a third time, thanks to Lucy over at the Longhorn Inn. That woman is a saint, let me tell you. She gives talks at the shelters around here and finds jobs for those of us who need them. I've been livin' in the motel and helpin' her out some in the evenin's to pay for my room for the last six months. A saint, I tell you, and Jasmine here ain't far behind her."

"You worked hard for every dime you made here," Jasmine said.

When Amber smiled her whole face lit up. "Yep, I did, and I learned more than how to fill up saltshakers. What's your story, Liz?"

"My Uncle Haskell gave me his house and twenty acres if I want it," she said.

"Haskell Hanson? Love that old feller. Wondered why we hadn't seen him in the café the last week. Is he sickly?" Amber asked.

"No, but my grandpa is, so Uncle Haskell moved out to west Texas to take care of Grandpa," Liz answered.

"That where you are from—out there in west Texas?" Amber asked.

Liz sipped her coffee. "No, I'm from all over the state, the lower half of Oklahoma, and even some of Arkansas. My mother and aunt own a carnival, so I grew up traveling."

"Well, that sure sounds like fun." She nodded toward the porch. "Looks like Slade Luckadeau and his grandma and aunt are our first customers today."

Liz looked up to see two elderly women and a handsome cowboy coming through the doors.

"I'll get it," she said.

"Okay, go get your feet wet, Miss Carnival." Amber giggled.

"Good morning, folks. What can I get you this morning?" Liz asked as she whipped the strings of a white apron around her waist and tied them in the front.

"These two old grouchy women didn't want to cook this morning, so we're eating before we go to a farm auction down in Chico." Slade, a tall, blond, blue-eyed cowboy, winked at her.

"Don't you be callin' us grouchy," one of the women said. "You're the one who was bitchin' about gettin' up too damn early. I'm Ellen and this is my sister, Nellie, and that's her grandson, Slade. We have to keep an eye on him, or he'll be buyin' nothing but culls. He's married to a woman who helps him buy good horse stock, but me and Nellie have to help him out with the cows."

"Don't listen to them two. They're just grumblin' around," Nellie said. "They're both so happy to be goin' somewhere today they could just dance a jig in a pig trough. I want the big breakfast, the one that comes on a platter with scrambled eggs, pancakes, sausage, and biscuits and gravy." She was tall and slim, wore jeans and boots, and had short gray hair.

"Me too," Ellen said. "Only I don't give a tiny rat's rump about cholesterol so bring me two pieces of sausage." She was shorter than her sister, had dyed hair swept up in a ratted hairdo popular in the seventies, and wore a sweeping, multicolored skirt with a bright orange ruffled top that reminded Liz of her Aunt Tressa.

"Make mine with bacon instead of sausage," Slade said.

Liz wrote everything down and carried the order to the kitchen. "That's one sexy cowboy out there."

"Yep, if he wasn't married, I'd be on the other side of this business flirtin' with him," Jasmine said.

Liz leaned against the doorjamb and kept an eye out for more customers.

Jasmine went on. "I'm just teasing. I'm not getting involved with anyone for a while. I don't have good sense when it comes to the opposite sex."

Amber nodded, her expression stone cold serious.

Liz cocked her head to one side and frowned.

Jasmine cracked eggs into a bowl. "But if I ever

trust another man it's goin' to be someone like Slade. He's so in love with his wife, Jane, that he's blind to other women. I swear, Angelina Jolie could walk right up to him and whisper in his ear and it wouldn't affect him. Jane is his whole life. Well, Jane and those two little girls they have."

"Are there any more Luckadeaus?" Liz asked.

"What would you be askin' that for? Raylen acted like he was almighty interested in you at Sunday dinner," Jasmine said.

"You think so?" Liz asked.

"The blush on your face says that you are interested in him, too," Jasmine said.

"More customers are coming in," Amber said. "Today, you take the orders and I'll deliver them, and we'll split the tips."

Liz picked up a pen and headed out into the dining room. "I'm in the learnin' stage. You keep the tips for your trip."

"You are a good woman. Jasmine, you keep her as long as you can," Amber said.

Liz took orders from the first table and turned around to see another group who'd pulled up chairs around the table next to the door. She made a quick trip to the kitchen and hurried back out.

"Just coffee for all of us," a man said.

"Except I'll take a slice of whatever pie Jasmine has back there," Becca said.

"Well, hello again." Liz pasted on a fake smile.

"Hello to you. Don't matter what kind of pie it is. I had breakfast in the bunkhouse with the guys, but I'm wantin' something sweet." Becca dismissed her with a wave of her hand.

Liz took the two orders to the back, filled four coffee cups and set them on a dark brown tray, picked up a slice of chocolate cream pie, and carried it out. Becca didn't say a word, not even "thank you" when Liz set the pie in front of her. As she carried the tray back to the kitchen, she met Amber coming out with an armload of orders.

"Watch that woman over there with all those men. Her name is Becca, and she is downright mean. She treats me like dirt," Amber said out the side of her mouth and kept walking.

"Why doesn't Becca like Amber, and why would she be ugly to her?" Liz asked Jasmine as she waited for orders to get ready.

Jasmine cracked four eggs into a bowl and whipped them until they were frothy. "Becca comes from money. Her dad owns the biggest spread in the county over around Stoneburg. She's got an ego bigger than Dallas and pretty much gets what she wants."

"I get the feeling she doesn't know what she wants," Liz said.

"You've met her?" Jasmine asked.

"She showed up at the café where I was having lunch yesterday. Raylen introduced her, and she looked down on me, too," Liz answered.

"I'll expect to hear more of that story when we aren't busy. She and Raylen are a strange pair, but they've been friends since they were babies. To my way of thinkin', she's got roundheelitis, but someday she expects to walk down the aisle with Raylen or Dewar. Her daddy doesn't really care which one." Jasmine lowered her voice. "A union with either one would unite two of the biggest ranches in this part of the state."

"Roundheel-whatis?" Liz asked.

"If a man winks at her, her round heels get off balance and she falls back on the bed and takes the man with her. It's a disease that antibiotics won't cure." Jasmine laughed.

Liz laughed with her. "Sounds serious. Is it contagious?"

"I don't know. Don't plan on getting close enough to her to find out, but she'd better think again if she's going to hoodwink one of my friends into marriage. I'd run interference for Dewar or Raylen either one," Jasmine said.

"Does she have a deadline as to when she's going to propose to one of them?" Liz asked.

"Her daddy is putting the pressure on her, but she likes the chase too well to be tied down, and rumor has it she has the hots for the new foreman out on her daddy's ranch," Jasmine said.

Liz took a long, steady look at the cowboy sitting beside Becca. Dark hair that hung down on his shirt collar. Even though it had an unkempt look about it, Liz knew a high-dollar haircut and the result of hair product when she saw it. Blaze had the same look about him, and his hair was his crowning glory.

The cowboy said something, and Becca handed him her fork. He ate a few bites of her pie and pushed it back. She made a show out of licking the fork clean before she started eating with it. Her eyes were sparkling and her body language spelled lust in all capital letters.

"Girl, what are you thinking about so hard?" Amber asked.

"Out in la-la land. More customers?" Liz asked as she looked around the dining area.

"Not yet, but I heard someone coming up on the porch," Jasmine said.

"Hey, Slade, what are you doin' out this early with such good-lookin' chicks? Does Jane know you're out cheatin' on her?" a cowboy yelled as he closed the door behind him.

"Don't you go tellin' on me, Ace. Remember that I know some stories on you," Slade said with a chuckle.

Ellen, the shorter one, crooked a finger at Ace. "Come on over here and sit with us, darlin'. For that sweet lie about me being young, I'll buy you breakfast. If you'll let me drive that truck of yours, I'll buy you dinner, too."

Liz started that way to take his order, and

stopped at the edge of the table where he'd pulled up a chair and sat down.

"Now Miz Ellen, I done heard how you drive too fast and drink too much. You are way too much of a party girl for me. Hey, Amber, bring me… You're not Amber," Ace said. His eyes did a slow scan from Liz's toes to her hair.

He was a pretty cowboy with his blond curls and blue eyes, but his flirting eyes did nothing to throw an extra beat into her heart like a glance from Raylen did.

"I'm Liz. Amber is leaving tomorrow and I'm taking her place. What can I get you?" she asked.

"Well, honey, how about dinner tomorrow night since Miz Ellen is too much woman for me to handle?" Ace said in a slow Texas drawl.

Liz leaned in close and whispered, "Darlin', you couldn't handle me either. You want the big breakfast or just coffee?"

"Now, there's a girl after my heart." Ellen giggled. "Reminds me of myself when I was young."

Nellie slapped her on the arm. "You never had black hair unless it come out of a bottle."

"Now don't go givin' away the family secrets, Nellie." Ellen gave her sister the old stink eye.

Jasmine yelled through the serving window between the dining area and the kitchen, "All Ace wants is coffee and some flirting. Those fellows in his bunkhouse cook a mean breakfast for him every morning, but he can't stay away from Chicken Fried because he likes to flirt."

"Mornin', Miz Jasmine," Ace said. "Would you go to dinner with me tomorrow night so my pride won't be wounded? Miz Ellen here is too fast for me, and your new waitress is just downright mean," Ace teased.

"Woman has to be mean around you. I saved you a slice of lemon pie. You want it now or later?" Jasmine asked.

"Right now. If I don't eat it in a hurry, Slade will talk you out of it," Ace answered.

Liz went to the kitchen, poured a cup of coffee, and put the last piece of lemon pie on a saucer. The place was full of good-natured cowboys, both bad boys and good guys, but not a one of them appealed to her.

She carried the coffee and pie out to Ace and set it before him, deliberately brushing his shoulder. Her heart didn't even skip half a beat. Nothing. Nada!

"I heard that Haskell gave his place to you. You want to sell it?" Ace asked.

"I do not. Why would you want it, anyway?" Liz asked.

"So I can get into a bidding war with Raylen and Becca and make a fortune. Those twenty acres might turn out to bring in more money than there is in Fort Knox. Raylen would pay me triple what I gave you for it. He wants that land so bad he'd drop down on one knee and propose to you to get it." Ace laughed.

"Well, it's not for sale. I'm going to live there forever," Liz said.

Liz's bubble popped with a loud cracking sound inside her head. While she'd been floating around in the land of passionate kisses, Raylen had just been sweet-talking his way into buying her twenty acres. Well, it would take more than one steamy hot kiss and a five o'clock good morning to get her land. Even if she had been in love with the man since she was a kid, he was not about to work that angle on her.

All men have an angle. They either want your money, they want to get in your underpants, or they want both. Aunt Tressa's words echoed in her head as she fell to earth with a hard thump.

"Dammit!" she whispered as she went back to the kitchen.

"What'd you think of Ace?" Jasmine asked.

"He's a bad boy lookin' for a woman with those round heels. I see that Becca isn't flirting with him, but she's batting her lashes at every other man in the place," Liz answered.

Jasmine laughed. "They dated some in high school. He went away to college, and the breakup was not a nice one."

"Do you know everything about everybody?" Liz asked.

"Almost. I've been here since last February, and

a small café is almost as good a gossip place as a beauty shop. What I don't hear, Gemma does, and we trade off." Jasmine set a plate on the window and Amber grabbed it. "What did you do in the carnival?" Jasmine asked Liz.

"I told fortunes and did some belly dancin'," Liz said.

"I'd have figured you for the one who tamed the lions," Jasmine said.

"It's a carnival, Jasmine, not a circus, but we do have pony rides," Liz told her.

Amber came back to the kitchen for the next order. "This place is a circus right now. Slade's aunt and granny are arguing as usual. Becca is flirting with the cowboy right next to her, and Raylen and Gemma are on their way in the door. It's fixin' to heat up out there."

Liz waited until they were seated before she went back out to the dining room. "Good mornin'. What can I get you two?" she asked.

"Pancakes for me. Raylen didn't cook this mornin', and then I had to drag him off the tractor to get him to bring me into town to feed me. It was his morning to cook," Gemma said. "And coffee, don't put any cream or sugar in it. This morning I need it to be black as sin."

"Same for me," Raylen said. "Gemma is a big girl, and she didn't want to get up early, so if I had cooked, it would have been cold anyway."

"You two live together?" Liz asked.

Gemma nodded. "Last year when I put in the shop the folks said I could live with them, and I did for a couple of weeks. But then Raylen said I could use one of his spare bedrooms, so I moved in with him. Mama is a better cook."

"But Mama is a lot nosier, ain't she?" Raylen countered. "She still don't like you letting a boyfriend sleep over, does she?"

"Maddie does like to know where her kids are at all times," Ace said from the table behind them. "But you gotta love her 'cause she's your mama."

"See?" Ellen said from her place at the table with Ace. "It's the law. You got to love your mama, your granny, and your aunt who is a lot younger than your granny."

Slade rolled his eyes. "How are things at the O'Donnell place? Y'all ready to sell Glorious Danny Boy yet? Jane would give you a blank check for that horse."

Raylen shook his head. "Mama wouldn't sell Danny Boy for half the dirt in Texas. She raised him up from a colt. She'd sell Gemma before she would Danny Boy."

Gemma slapped him on the shoulder. "No, she wouldn't. I'm the baby daughter. She'd probably sell you though. You're just a worthless old third son."

Liz had started back to the kitchen when Raylen

reached out and touched her arm. "What are you doin' when you get off work?"

"I'm looking into more Christmas boxes, and making a list of what I've got and what I need to buy."

Gemma clapped her hands. "Can I come to your house and play? I love Christmas. Do you have those old lights that are as big as jalapeno peppers?"

Liz nodded. "Yes, I do. Uncle Haskell told me that some of the ornaments belonged to my Aunt Sara's grandma. She must've liked Christmas because there's boxes and boxes that I haven't even opened."

"My last appointment is at three. I'll be over soon as I get her out the door, if that's all right with you," Gemma said.

"Come right on," Liz told her. "Soon as I take stock of what's out there, I intend to start putting up the lights. I want it all done before Thanksgiving. Mama and Aunt Tressa are coming the week before because they've got a gig in Bowie. I'll take all the help I can get. Raylen is coming too. We made a deal. He's going to help me do the Christmas stuff and then I'm going to exercise horses as payback." Liz fought the urge to rub the spot where Raylen's hand had touched her arm just to see if it was as hot as it felt.

"What's that?" Becca crossed the floor in long strides.

"I'm putting up Christmas before Thanksgiving.

Want to come help?" Liz asked, even though she knew what the answer would be.

Becca ignored Liz and touched Raylen on the shoulder. "I've got better things to do and so do you, Raylen."

Raylen shrugged off her hand. "Maybe so, but I'm going to help out my new neighbor and then the whole month of December she's going to be exercising horses."

Becca pulled out a chair to sit at their table. "You are an idiot, my friend."

"Be careful. You might not want to be friends with an idiot," Raylen teased.

Liz left them to their bantering and took their order to Jasmine.

"That hussy better not steal my help this afternoon," Liz mumbled.

"Help with what?" Jasmine asked.

"Raylen said he'd help get my Christmas decorations put up, and Becca is calling him an idiot for being friends with me," Liz answered.

Jasmine shook her head. "Don't pay any attention to her, Liz. The show is all for Ellen and Nellie's benefit. They'll play cards on Friday night with her great-aunt from down in Chico, and tell that they saw her flirting with Raylen. Great-aunt will call Becca's daddy and tell him. He'll be happy that she's not seriously interested in his new foreman, who is that guy out there with the dark hair and the come-hither-to-bed look in his eyes. And all will be good on Becca's ranch. Meanwhile, back at the soap opera, she'll be spending her nights in the bunkhouse with the hired help while Daddy entertains visions of merging two big ranches."

"A female Blaze, only Aunt Tressa don't care who he marries or if he's a playboy the rest of his life," Liz said.

"Who is Blaze?" Amber asked.

"He's a cracker-jack mechanic who takes care of the carnival equipment. He's so sexy that he ought to be a carnival attraction. Women flock to him like flies on a fresh cow patty. And that's exactly what he is: a pile of cow manure! But he's a nice piece of eye candy and he can charm the hair off a frog's hind end, so women don't have much chance when he smiles at them. He's my best friend, and when Blaze gets here, Miss Becca's liable to get an acute case of roundheelitis and fall into his bed."

"How about your bed? Raylen going to warm it up?" Amber asked as she loaded a tray of dishes into the dishwasher.

"What made you ask that?" Liz asked.

"A blind person could see the vibes between you two." Amber giggled. "And not every man in Montague County would offer to help put up decorations. You might be the fortune-teller, but you can't see what's right in front of your face."

"You want a job with a traveling carnival? With that kind of imagination, Aunt Tressa could turn you into a fortune-teller in no time," Liz teased.

Amber shook her head. "No, thank you. I'm goin' home."

Chapter 6

LIZ TURNED SLOWLY AND SURE ENOUGH, RAYLEN was leaning against the doorjamb leading into the tack room. Her sixth sense hadn't failed her, or maybe she should call it her lust sense because every time he was anywhere near, her pulse raced. Dirt was smeared across his forehead. He had hat hair and there was a band on his forehead where his straw cowboy hat had rested all day. His jeans were dusty and his chambray shirt sweaty. And her heart pitched in that extra beat she was getting all too familiar with.

"Gemma said to tell you she's sorry," Raylen drawled. "Ellen and Nellie walked in just as she was finishin' up with her last appointment for the day and asked if she had time to cut Nellie's hair and style Ellen's, so she won't be here for another couple of hours." He wiped sweat from his forehead and settled his straw hat back on his head. "I'm also supposed to tell you we're havin' a party next Monday night in my barn. We do it every year for Halloween. Gemma loves the holidays, and we always have Halloween at my place. Then Thanksgiving and Christmas is at the folks.'"

She raised a dark eyebrow and flirted a little. "Is that an invitation?"

"Yes, it is, and Gemma seems to believe you about that fortune telling stuff, so she's going to ask you to tell fortunes for everyone, so bring your crystal ball or your cards or whatever other hocus-pocus you need," he said.

"You want me to belly dance, too?" she asked.

"Sure, I do." He grinned. "How about a demonstration right here and now just for me? You got a skimpy little outfit to put on? Can I tell Gemma you said yes?"

"Yes, I'd love to tell fortunes, and yes, I'd love to go to a Halloween party. Never been to one. Is it dress-up? I'll wear my belly dancing costume and you can stop doubting me, Raylen O'Donnell."

"Yes, ma'am, it is dress-up. I'm going as a cowboy, and you sure can come as a belly dancer if you want to." He reached for a box on the third shelf that was marked OUTSIDE LIGHTS.

"I can do that," she said.

"I don't think so. I can barely reach it without a ladder," he argued.

"I'm not talking about getting to that box up there. I'm talking about wearing one of my costumes to the party," she said. "Should I wear orange, turquoise, or hot pink?"

"Whichever one you want to wear, and I'll believe you when I see you come into the barn wearing one. This isn't all of the decorations. The loft is full of stuff." He set the box on the table and pointed toward the ceiling. "I used to come over every year about this time and help Haskell get everything out. Your aunt Sara loved Christmas, and every year Haskell made her one thing new to go out in the yard. Even after she was gone, he kept on making a new piece every year. He kept them up there, all covered up with tarps. Want to go take a look? There's probably enough to reach from here to the road."

Liz forgot all about the costumes. "Are you serious? Uncle Haskell mentioned more stuff, but I figured it was just lights and decorations."

"Yes, I am serious," Raylen told her. "After Sara died, he didn't put the stuff out in the yard, but he kept making one thing a year. I found him up there once when I was a teenager, painting a funny lookin' wagon pulled by four horses. It was all painted in wild colors, but it had Santa sitting on the driver's seat and the top was covered with toys. I asked him what he was making, and he explained to me about how Sara had always liked for him to make her one wooden cutout a year and the wagon was his gift to her that year. Come on. I'll show you. There's got to be thirty or more of them up there."

The wooden ladder went straight up with only room for one person at a time. Raylen stood to one side and let her go before he did, waited until she was more than halfway up, and then put his boot on the bottom rung.

The loft was half as big as the barn and swept clean. Buckets of paint were arranged on shelves on the north side with brushes standing, handle down, in Mason jars. Everything was organized and very clean.

"This reminds me of our barn in west Texas. Poppa keeps his paint all lined up by color and his brushes cleaned and in jars ready to use. He works hard from the first of December to the first of March every year redoing our wagons. I love to watch him paint. His hands are so steady, and his combination of colors is breathtaking," she said.

"You miss it, don't you?" Raylen said. "Your voice has a haunting sound to it when you talk about your poppa and that place out in west Texas."

"Of course I miss it. Would you miss ranchin' if suddenly you lived in the middle of Dallas?" she asked.

His expression changed to dead serious. "I couldn't survive without ranchin' and horses and tractors. Missin' it wouldn't even cover the feelings. I'd probably wither up and die in the big city. Is that what you're going to do here, Liz? Wither up and die?" he asked.

Liz turned around and met his eyes. "No, I am not. I've wanted this forever and I'm going to grow roots right here. But I'll always miss a portion of carnie life. It's what my family is, not just what they do. Uncle Haskell was the only one who ever quit the business and even then, when he came home for the holidays at Christmas, he helped Poppa paint."

———————

Raylen heard an elusive thing in her voice that he couldn't put into words. Until that lonesome sound left when she talked about her family, he didn't figure there was enough good rich Red River dirt to grow roots on Liz's heart. Like she said, the carnival and constant movement was what her family was, not just what they did. And Hanson blood flowed in her veins. It was what she was and that involved wings that flew from one place to the other.

He removed the tarp from the first wooden cutout and revealed a dark-haired woman in a bright orange harem-looking outfit sitting in the fork of a Saguaro cactus. She was barefoot and had a Santa stocking on her head. The cactus had Christmas garland wrapped around it and holes drilled in it for lights.

"Guess this year's decoration is in celebration of you taking over the house. I hadn't seen it before but that is you, Liz. You look like a dark-haired *I Dream of Jeannie*. Evidently, I was wrong about the dancing costumes. Is that the one you are going to wear to the party?" Raylen asked.

His heart did a nose-dive into his boots. Every

cowboy in the whole county would be panting after her. He wouldn't have a snowball's chance in Hades of getting a date with her—and he was the one who had taunted her into wearing that skimpy thing.

"Yes, it is, Raylen. It's my orange belly dancing outfit, and I think I will wear it to the Halloween party. Orange goes with Halloween, doesn't it?" she asked as she folded her arms across her chest and studied the piece of art.

"There's holes in the cactus for Christmas lights." Raylen couldn't take his eyes off the cutout.

"Well, that does make it a little more Christmas-like. Let's look at the rest of them."

"You want to look at them from oldest to newest or in reverse?" Raylen asked.

"You mean they're organized?"

Raylen pointed to the bits of paper thumbtacked on the wall above the tarps around the room. Each one had five years penciled on it, beginning with 1975–1979.

"Oldest to newest," she said.

Raylen moved past her and dropped a dusty tarp from a group of flat wooden cutouts. The first one was Santa Claus in a cowboy hat and boots, and Mrs. Claus in an apron holding up her dress hem to reveal bright red cowboy boots.

Liz moved closer and held the other end as she peered behind it. "Look, there's a date on the back that says 1975, and what's this?"

She peeled off a thick envelope that had been stapled to the backside of the cutout. "It's got my name on the front," she said.

"Then it must be for you." Raylen would have rather been holding her than propping up Mr. and Mrs. Claus on the only wall of the loft that wasn't filled with tarp-covered ornaments.

She plopped down on the floor and opened the letter. "Uncle Haskell says that he doesn't have time to tell me all about each piece over the phone, but if he writes it all down I can go over them all later. This is like the best Christmas ever. This piece is the first Christmas he and Sara were together on the ranch, and he was working at Nocona for a boot company and he made her a pair of red boots and this cutout as a funny joke to put out in the yard. She loved it so much that she said he had to build one every year of something that happened in their lives."

"Okay, ready for 1976?" Raylen set Mr. and Mrs. Santa to one side to reveal the next one.

It was a four-by-eight-foot nativity scene so realistic that she reached up to touch the woolly lamb beside the shepherd. She got tears in her eyes when she ran her hand over baby Jesus in the manger.

"I didn't realize that my Uncle Haskell is more than just a good trailer painter. He is an artist," she said. "He has captured the love in Mary's and Joseph's eyes for their new baby."

"I've told him dozens of times that he should be selling things like this," Raylen said.

"He doesn't say what kind of reaction she had to his gifts. I would love to know if she got excited and clapped her hands or if she hugged him and danced around the living room because she was so happy," Liz said.

Raylen moved the nativity over and revealed the next piece. "I suppose that was private and he doesn't want to share those memories."

Liz laid the letter down and pointed. "That's a derrick. But I didn't see oil wells on the property. Look closely, Raylen. There are elves peeking out from the bottom."

"There aren't any oil wells on his land, but maybe he and Sara had an inside joke about them," Raylen said.

Liz read some more before she looked up to find Raylen staring at her.

"Aunt Sara inherited land that year from a great-aunt down near Beaumont. It had oil wells on it, and she had a share of the royalties. That was the year Uncle Haskell quit the factory and started ranchin' full time. Look, there's holes for lights in the derrick. No wonder there are boxes and boxes of lights in the tack room."

Two hours later the sun was going down and they weren't even halfway through uncovering the beautiful artwork or reading about it.

"So," Raylen held out a hand to help her up off the floor, "if you put all this stuff up it's going to look like a miniature Christmas light drive like the ones they put on in Dallas."

"Every year when we are in a town that has a light exhibit, Mama and I take a drive through it. Is there one around here?" Liz asked.

"The prettiest one is in Chickasha, Oklahoma. But if you put up all this, you can bet folks will come from miles around to drive down your lane," he said.

"I'll sit on the porch in the evening and hand out candy canes when they reach the house and turn around." She remembered the time that they'd gone through a light show in east Texas and there had been a donation booth at the end for a charity. The lady there had worn a Mrs. Claus suit and gave out candy canes. Did she have time to buy a costume like that? What would she look like in a white wig?

"You goin' to wear a belly dancin' outfit while you hand out candy canes?" Raylen teased as he pulled her up to her feet.

"Of course, and if anyone wants to put ten dollars in my jar, I'll do a dance out in the yard for them," she shot back.

His didn't let go of her hand once she was standing. "You can't do that. This is a small town, Liz, but that would draw idiots from everywhere and you might get hurt. Promise me you won't do that, or if you do, let me come over to protect you."

"I was teasing, but Raylen, I can take care of myself. I've been fending off people for years. I *was* thinking about a Mrs. Claus costume. You want to be Santa?" she said quickly.

"Thank God." Raylen breathed a sigh of relief, "And no, thank you."

He drew her closer, looking down into her dark eyes, trying to find the faint glimmer of something that would not fly away. But he didn't want to think about tomorrow or the future. He just wanted to think about the moment at hand—and kissing her.

His mouth lowered to hers, and she rolled up on her toes to meet him halfway. Lips devoured lips when they met in a clash of passion. She wrapped her arms around his back, her fingers digging into his tight muscles and broad shoulders.

"Hey, anyone here?" Gemma's voice came from the doorway.

Liz stepped out of Raylen's embrace and blushed.

"We're in the loft. Be down in a minute," Raylen called down.

"I've got food," Gemma singsonged back up.

Raylen pulled Liz back into his embrace and brushed a feathery soft kiss across her mouth. "You have the sweetest lips," he whispered.

"I bet you say that to all the girls, don't you?" she said.

He hugged her tightly and traced her jawline with his forefinger. "Only the belly dancers. You are so beautiful, Liz."

"You say that to all the girls, too?" she asked.

He sighed. "Only the ones who can walk the fence better than me."

Gemma yelled from the bottom of the ladder, "What are y'all doin' up there?"

"Looking at the yard ornaments. We're on our way down," Raylen hollered.

"Well, hurry up. Food is getting cold, and I don't like cold mashed potatoes," Gemma said.

"We're on our way." Liz started down the ladder. "What kind of food have you got?"

"I brought leftovers from Chicken Fried. Jasmine said she'd have to toss them so I figured we could eat while we look through boxes. Today's special was roast and potatoes, so she sent a container of that, some gravy, some green beans, and a few yeast rolls. It's still warm, so hurry up. I'm starving," Gemma said.

Liz didn't think she could swallow a bite what with the nervous jitters flitting around in her stomach. It was a good thing Gemma interrupted them or Liz would have tossed caution out the loft window and turned passion loose right there in the barn with baby Jesus looking on from the nativity scene.

"What all did you find up there? Did Haskell make a new lawn piece for this year?" Gemma asked.

"Yes, he did, and it's of me sitting in a cactus, and I'm wearing my belly dancing costume," Liz answered. "I wonder how many pieces are up there."

"About thirty-five, near as we can figure," Raylen answered, "and remember that there's lights for every one of them. We always say that Haskell is the Clark Griswold of Montague County."

And all the lights won't make as bright a light as went off in my head when Raylen touched my bare skin or kissed me. I'm still too giddy to swallow food and too wound up to sit still.

Gemma nodded. "He had thirty-four last year so one more would make thirty-five. You can count on me and Raylen and Dewar to help you get them up. It will be fun to help, won't it, Raylen? Daddy and Mama put up lights around the house and an enormous wreath on the door, and sometimes she makes Daddy drag those wire reindeer things out of the barn to go in the yard. Dewar has one of those pre-lit trees that sometimes he shoves in a corner of his house and sometimes he forgets all about."

Liz had entertained visions of just her and Raylen doing the decorating.

"We might need to ask Dewar," Liz said. "He might not want to help."

"Sure, he'll help. And I'll get Jasmine and Ace, too. The more hands, the quicker the work will get done. I think Dewar likes Liz, don't you?" Gemma said. "The way he was flirting around with her was kind of cute. And he is the next one in line."

"In line for what?" Liz asked. Was there a ritual that she didn't know about?

"Daddy says we have to get married in the order of our birth. Me and Colleen have been tryin' to find wives for these guys for years because we don't want to be eighty and pushin' a walker with our wedding bouquets roped to the front of it down the aisle. Now it's Dewar's turn and—"

"Things don't have to happen that way. Daddy was teasing," Raylen said quickly.

Gemma peeled back aluminum foil from the disposable trays and began to heap food onto her paper plate. "We'll see. Come on and fill up a plate. I brought paper ones from the beauty shop and even had enough plastic forks."

The tack room soon filled with the aroma of good food intermingled with the normal smells of leather, hay, and dust. Raylen and Gemma lit into the supper like two hungry coyote pups. Liz was still combating the effects of the make-out session. She drained the tall plastic takeout cup of sweet tea and could have drunk another one, but she barely nibbled around the edges of the small piece of roast she put on her plate.

Gemma talked between bites. "I hated to miss all the fun, but I can't ever turn down Nellie and Ellen.

They are a hoot. They get to arguing about some wild thing Ellen did in the past and bickering, and it's a lot better than Comedy Central. I tried to get them to come to the Halloween party next week, but they'd have none of it. Said they were babysitting the kids so Slade and Jane could come over to it," Gemma said.

"What kind of stories?" Liz asked. Outsiders sure discussed their lives with anyone who would listen more than carnies did.

"Real life," Gemma answered. "When Ellen was young, she liked to go too fast, flirt, date, and drive men wild. And she just loves to relive the stories. I like to listen, so we make a pair. She was tellin' today about the last time she got behind the wheel of a vehicle. I'd heard the story before, but she always puts in a few more details and it's a hoot to listen to her tell it."

Liz looked over at Raylen and wanted to lick that fleck of potato from the corner of his mouth. When his tongue flicked out and caught it, she gasped and hurriedly covered it with a fake cough in her napkin.

"I'd love to hear the story. Entertain me while we eat," Liz said to take her mind off Raylen.

"Nobody can tell that story like Ellen," Raylen said.

"But now my curiosity is aroused, so tell me what it's about anyway," Liz said.

"Okay," Gemma said. "We've all heard the story a hundred times, but every time they tell it, Ellen embellishes it even more. Ellen said she was fifty, but Nellie raised an eyebrow and mouthed behind her back that she was past sixty. Anyway, she was in a vintage Corvette with this guy. She couldn't remember if it was a '55 or '56 model, but it was one of those cute little red things according to her. He'd been smartin' off about how no woman was ever drivin' his Vette. When he got out at a service station to go to the men's room, Ellen noticed that he'd left the keys dangling in the ignition."

"Oh, I can see where this is going, and it reminds me of my Aunt Tressa." Liz giggled. "But go on, Gemma. Tell me the rest of it."

"Ellen said that he was a stupid sumbitch to trust her like that, and he deserved to be taught a lesson. She also admitted that she'd already had more than her share of a fifth of Jack Daniel's whiskey. She got about half a mile down the road when she lost control on a patch of gravel. She said she went ass over teakettle for a while, and when everything stopped moving, she was sitting in the edge of a farm pond where cows watered, and there was manure and dirty water up to her waist." Gemma was laughing so hard the last words came out one at a time during guffaws. Liz and Raylen got as tickled at her laughter as they did at the story, and soon they all three were wiping their eyes with paper napkins.

Liz hiccupped. "Was she hurt?"

Gemma shook her head. "That's the first thing I asked, but Nellie picked up the story there and said that she didn't even get a broken bone. But the front of that Corvette had kissed a pecan tree, and if Ellen hadn't been drunk as a skunk and limber as a wet rag, she would have been killed. Ellen said that Jack Daniel's saved her life and she'd keep a bottle in the house the rest of her life. She said that she came up sputtering and spitting filthy water and cussin' a bloody blue streak about getting mud and cow manure on her new boots. The owner of the car had called the police and reported his vehicle stolen and his girlfriend kidnapped. When they arrived a few minutes later, she was sitting beside the car with what was left of the bottle of Jack in her hands. Neither the bottle nor Ellen had a scratch. She offered the cops a drink for coming to her aid, but according to her, they didn't have much of a sense of humor, and they hauled her ass off to jail for stealing an automobile, driving while intoxicated, and a few more trumped-up charges. She said she was surprised they didn't throw in stealing cow patties along with all the other charges, since she took a fair share of them to jail with her in her boots."

Liz laughed but kept Raylen in her peripheral vision. Seemingly oblivious to anything around her, Gemma went on: "Nellie declared that it wasn't all that funny because she was the one who had to get up at two o'clock in the morning and go to Chico to get her. Ellen said that she wasn't about to use that public toilet in the corner of the jail cell, and all that whiskey hit her bladder at one time, so she was dancing in her boots by the time Nellie arrived. And all Nellie wanted to do was cuss and rant at her. Nellie paid the fines, for the car damage and the whole shebang. And you know what Ellen is still griping about after umpteen years?"

Liz shook her head.

"That she thought the judge was hot and she left her phone number on the table right in front of him, and he never did call her." Gemma laughed so hard she got the hiccups.

"I've got to get to know these women better. Do they come into the café often?" Liz asked.

"At least once a week. Ellen gets her hair fixed every week, and Nellie gets a cut about once a month. I tried to get them to come to the party and bring the kids, but Ellen said she would dress up like a flapper and bring a quart of moonshine with her. Nellie says she's not letting her out of the house," Gemma answered.

"What are you dressing up like?" Liz asked Gemma.

"Depends. If Creed says he's coming I might dress up like Daisy Duke. God, but that boy is pretty, and the less clothes I have on the less he has to take off," Gemma said with a grin.

"He's too damn young for you!" Raylen said.

"He's twenty-four, Brother. And I'm only twenty-five, and I didn't say I was going to marry him. I just thought I'd make his job easier if we did hook up," Gemma said.

"Jesus, Mary, and—"

"Forget Joseph. I'd rather have Creed." Gemma giggled.

"You…" Raylen's finger was a blur when it shot up to point at her.

Gemma slapped his finger away. "Right back at you. Just remember what's good for the goose is good for the gander. You O'Donnell guys can be wild, but us girls are supposed to be sweet little lilies? It don't work that way, Brother. If I want to take off my Daisy Duke cutoff jeans for Creed, then I will do so, and you can't stop me."

Liz had always wanted a sibling so she could argue just like Raylen and Gemma were doing right then. She switched her empty tea glass with Raylen's and sipped at his full one while they bickered.

So, the O'Donnell guys had a reputation for being a little on the wild side, did they? She'd bet dollars to funnel cakes that not a one of them could outdo Blaze. And if Gemma liked them wild and woolly, maybe she'd be the one to tame Blaze. Too bad he wouldn't be in Bowie over Halloween. Liz would have wrangled an invitation for him to the party and watched all the women flock around him.

Gemma poked her on the arm. "I asked what you were going to dress up like. What were you thinkin' about?"

"Blaze," Liz said honestly.

"You are dressing up like fire?" Raylen asked.

"No, I'm not. Blaze is...well, he works for the carnival. His mama was Aunt Tressa's winter friend in west Texas. It's a long story, but her friend died when Blaze was fourteen, so Tressa took him in and taught him the carnie business. He's kind of like a surrogate son to her. I was thirteen that year, so we were brought up together, kind of..."

"Kind of like a brother?" Raylen asked.

Liz busied herself with a box of ornaments. "Not at all. More like a best friend."

Gemma sat down on a stool close to Liz. "Tell me more."

"He's tall. Blond hair. Strange eyes that are almost gold like a wildcat's eyes. And he has this animal magnetism that draws women to him like he has supernatural powers or something. He's a lot of fun and I can't wait for you all to meet him," Liz said.

"Are you planning to marry him someday?" Gemma asked bluntly.

"Oh, no, ma'am! Not Blaze. I'm not so sure any one woman could rope him in on a full-time contract. He's my friend, not my boyfriend," Liz said without a moment's hesitation.

"Man, I'd like to try," Gemma said with a sigh. "I should be going. I promised Mama after I delivered supper and made sure things were going all right here that I'd come over to the house and cut her hair. She didn't have time to get to the shop today and she has that horse meeting in Wichita Falls tomorrow. I'll see you tomorrow at the café, Liz."

"Thanks for the food. Now that I know why there are so many boxes up there, I don't need to look in every one of them. I'll start putting things out right after Halloween. I want it all lit up so Mama can see it. I'll take pictures to send Uncle Haskell," Liz said.

Gemma headed toward the door. "Then we'll plan to work on it in the evenings after the big party. If you see me lookin' like Daisy Duke, then you'll know Creed is there. Dewar better hang a tag around your neck that says for everyone to back off or those Riley boys will gather round you like a bunch of struttin' bantam roosters."

"More like vultures," Raylen grumbled.

"What did you say?" Liz asked.

He wiped his hands on a paper towel and shook his head. "I was askin' if you want me to help put any boxes back before I go. I've still got some chores to do at home."

"No, they can all stay right here, and I'll clean up," Liz answered. "Thanks for showing me where the lawn things were hidden away, Raylen. I appreciate it."

Everything had felt so right in the hayloft when she was in his arms and kissing him, but now that Blaze had been set loose, along with a cowboy named Creed and his brothers, there was an awkwardness between them every bit as big as a full-grown Angus bull.

"Be seein' you around then." Raylen headed for the door and then turned abruptly. "Are you really dressing up like a belly dancer?"

"Guess I am. What other women are coming besides Gemma, Colleen, and Slade's wife?" Liz asked.

"The party is kind of an open invitation to everyone in this area. Becca will be there."

Liz's tone almost chilled her own heart. "And what does she usually wear?"

Raylen grinned. "As little as the law allows. Holler if you decide to get any of that stuff off the loft. It has to be lowered by rope out the door to get it out of there. Haskell cut them out and painted them right on the spot. I told him once that it reminded me of building a boat up there in the loft. He told me that he'd lower it down with ropes when he got ready to put it outside."

Liz nodded. She heard what he was saying, but "as little as the law allows" was playing through her mind like a marching band on a continuous loop. Becca was just playing with Raylen. She loved that hired hand with the pretty haircut.

Raylen waved and left her with a plate full of uneaten food and dusty boxes of decorations. She waved back, but wished Becca would suffer a strange virus brought on by roundheelitis that slapped her big, tall butt in bed for at least twenty-four hours on Halloween night.

She pushed all the leftovers into one aluminum tray, turned out the barn lights, and carried the food to the house where she set it on the porch for Hooter and Blister to fight over. She was still muttering about Becca when she went into the house. She turned on the lights and the house phone rang at the same time.

"Hello," she said.

"Hi, kiddo. How'd your first day at work go?" Uncle Haskell asked.

"It was great. I met Slade and his granny and her sister," she said.

"Nellie and Ellen. Two great old gals. They'll talk your ear off and entertain you with their stories. That Ellen was a rounder in her day. Did she tell you the Corvette story yet?" Haskell chuckled.

"No, but she told Gemma and Gemma told me. And there's this girl named Becca," Liz said cautiously.

"Don't worry about that filly. She's going to flit all around the roses and land on a pile of pure old cow manure one of these days. She's all flirt and no substance," Haskell told her. "So, how'd you like Jasmine?"

"She's great, and I liked Amber but she's leaving tomorrow morning, so we didn't have time to be real friends. But I really do like Gemma. I don't think Colleen is going to be friendly, though."

"Colleen is a strange one. Gemma is more outgoing. How about Raylen and Dewar?" Haskell laughed.

Liz paused. "Raylen helped me tonight and he's promised to help put up all the cutout pieces. Then after Thanksgiving, I'm going to help him exercise horses to pay him back. It's a pretty good business deal. We found all the things you made for Christmas. They are awesome, Uncle Haskell. I'm going to put them all up this year between here and the road. Is there enough power to turn on all the lights?"

"You bet there is," Haskell said. "I called tonight to tell you all about the yard ornaments. I'm glad you like them, and honey, you will have the gaudiest house in Montague County. So Raylen helped you, did he? I figured Dewar would have offered."

"Why?" Liz asked.

"Just that I know Dewar is ready to settle down, and his folks are really ready for him to stop playing around," Haskell said. "Poppa is here, and we're watching *NCIS* reruns on television tonight. He likes that show, and I made him banana pudding with whipped cream. Have fun, and I'm glad you are making friends. There are good people in Ringgold. You'll fit right in with them."

"Uncle Haskell, I'll take pictures of everything when the place is decorated. I love everything," she said.

"I knew you would. Sara always wished she could've had you, rather than God giving you to Marva Jo. But life does have a bunch of twists and turns. Call me and send pictures when you get all that situated," he said.

"Good night, Uncle Haskell," she said.

A warm feeling settled around her like a tightly crocheted shawl on a cold winter night. She wrapped her arms around her body to hold it closer and jumped when someone knocked on the door.

She opened it a crack and looked out to see Raylen standing with his hands shoved down in the pockets of his jeans, then she slung it open.

"Sorry, I just didn't want to scare you. I hopped over the fence and was in my yard before I remembered that I drove my truck over this morning and parked out by your barn. I was afraid you'd hear the engine and think someone was trying to steal your Christmas stuff," he explained.

"Come on in," she said.

"Can't. Still got some chores. Just wanted to let you know about the truck. Don't know what in the devil I was thinking," he said.

She opened the screen door and stepped out on the porch. "Thanks."

He cupped her face in his hands and looked

deeply into her brown eyes. "You really are very beautiful, Liz, and I *don't* say that to all the girls."

She didn't have time to answer before his lips found hers in a blaze that burned every thought of anyone or anything from her mind. All too soon, it was over, and he stepped back.

"Good night, Liz," he whispered and disappeared into the night.

Chapter 7

THE NIGHT WAS CLEAR WITH THE FAINTEST HINT of a crisp fall breeze. Wispy clouds strung out like spun strings of cotton candy over a waning moon that promised werewolves, witches, goblins, and maybe even shapeshifters later on in the evening. Across the river bridge in Terral, little children were at the community center eating hotdogs and nachos before their parents loaded them on the back of hay wagons and took them trick or treating. Some would even ride across the river bridge to Ringgold in their cute costumes to hold out their bags to aunts and uncles, grandmothers and friends. Excitement had danced in the air all day, and Liz was more excited than the trick-or-treaters as she thought about her very first Halloween party.

She wore her orange belly dancing outfit, pulled her dark hair up into a ponytail, and stretched a two-inch wide jeweled hair clip around the base. She artfully applied her stage makeup, which included extra eye shadow, liner, and a deep, dark burgundy lip liner and lipstick, then very carefully affixed the headpiece, a double row of dangling, sparkling crystals with a pear-cut topaz resting between her eyes.

A circlet of bangles that sounded like wind chimes when she walked were clipped around each ankle, with matching ones around her wrists. Shoes were nothing more than thin leather soles kept on her feet with the tiniest strap of leather across her toes. She removed them before she danced, because Aunt Tressa had taught her to feel the rhythm with her feet. However, it was only a costume that night. She was a fortune-teller, and no one had asked her to dance.

The orange costume was her very first grown-up dancer's outfit. Aunt Tressa gave it to her for her eighteenth birthday and she'd worn it when she danced that night on the small porch attached to the fortune-teller's wagon. After her dance, people had lined up for two blocks waiting to have their fortune told by the Egyptian Dharma. The bra top was covered in bright, shiny rhinestones and sequins, creating a pattern that glistened from every angle when she moved. A fringe cascade below her bustline hung at varying lengths, drawing the eye downward toward her belly button and the intricate belt topping off a sheer, handkerchief-hem skirt. The wide, V-shaped belt matched the bra with sequins and rhinestones.

She affixed a rhinestone the size of a lima bean to her belly button and picked up the most important piece of her costume—a two-by-six-foot length of chiffon, scattered with rhinestones and bugle beads, that served as both a veil and a shawl around her shoulders.

Raylen had offered to come for her, but she'd opted to take herself so that she could leave if she wanted. She slipped her leather jacket over her outfit and was careful not to close the truck door on her skirt or shawl when she left. A Texas Highway Patrol fell in behind her when she pulled out onto the highway.

Now that would take some explaining if he pulled me over for speeding. Yes, sir, Mr. Patrolman, I'm a real belly dancer and I'm on my way to tell fortunes. Flip your hand out here, and I'll be glad to tell you how long you will live. Oh, my, you are going to have a very short life unless you let me go without even a warning. She giggled nervously as she turned into the O'Donnells' lane.

The highway patrol turned with her.

She kept a check in her rearview mirror.

She drove past the two-story house and made a left turn, following the two ruts that made a path toward the big, lit-up barn which would have been no more than half a mile from her house if she'd walked straight west. She passed a log cabin and slowed down to a crawl. Light pouring through the windows cast a yellow glow on the shrubs. A hound dog was silhouetted on the porch, and while she eased past what had to be Raylen's house the lights suddenly went out, the front door opened, and the dog yipped. Gemma stepped out and waved at Liz.

Liz braked and parked in the front yard. Gemma trotted over to the truck and swung the door open.

"Wow, girl, when you dress up, you do it right!" Gemma said and then turned her attention to the police car that had come to a stop right behind Gemma. "Hey, Sammy, are you in costume or not?"

Liz stepped out and asked, "Is he for real?"

The patrolman waved. "Not. I just came by for a minute to see how things were going. Who's your friend?"

"New neighbor. She's tellin' fortunes tonight. You sure you can't stay?" Gemma asked.

"No, I'm on duty. Ten minutes tops and that's my break time," Sammy said.

Gemma turned her attention back to Liz. "Where did you get that getup?"

"Just one of my carnie costumes. I guess Creed isn't here tonight or you'd be Daisy Duke," Liz said with a grin.

Gemma was dressed as a witch in a short outfit with a neckline that scooped low enough to show a couple of inches of cleavage. Her pointed hat was covered in black sequins and glittered in the dark.

Gemma frowned, drawing her dark brows down until they were almost a solid line. "Oh, he's here, but I got word early that he was bringing along some girl he met in college. They are Mickey and Minnie Mouse. She's crazy, I'm tellin' you, just plumb crazy. Creed is so damn fine he should be Tarzan or Fabio, not Mickey Mouse. And he's crazy for letting her dress him tonight. I'd never dress something as sexy as Creed up like a Disney character. I might dress him up like a stud bull, but not a cartoon mouse!" Gemma fussed as the three of them walked toward the barn.

"He's too young for you anyway," Sammy told her.

"Probably so," Gemma agreed. "But Ace could pull off a Mickey costume better than Creed. Never did see what all the women saw in Ace anyway, but his brothers are a different matter with all that dark hair and those big old soulful blue eyes. Dalton and Ryder are too young for me, but Creed is just one year younger than me, and at my age what does a year matter?"

"Wow!" Liz gasped when she stepped inside the barn.

"We do get carried away. We buy new things every year and add them to what we have in storage, so each year gets better. Jasmine is running the bar for the next hour and then I have to relieve her. Pick a spot where you want to tell fortunes for us tonight."

"Palms or cards?" Liz asked.

At least Gemma hadn't asked her to dance in

front of the whole crowd. Dancing before strangers was easy; doing so before her newly found friends wouldn't be.

"I don't care if you read tea leaves, but when Becca gets here, you tell her that she's going to be dirt poor and wind up living in a trailer house with six kids and four hound dogs," Gemma whispered. "I do not want her for a sister-in-law."

"But what if she's destined to be an O'Donnell?" Liz asked.

"Then change her destiny." Gemma laughed. "I'm going to check on Jasmine. Grab a beer or a plate of food and mingle. You got about thirty minutes before fortunes begin."

———

Raylen had been watching the door for the past half hour. Becca had arrived and made a splash as Annie Oakley in jeans cut off so short that an inch of her butt cheeks showed when she was standing upright and hung lower on her hips than a bikini. When she bent over a table, even more of her cheeks peeked out, but there was not a single cellulite cell anywhere. She wore a sequined hat, had rhinestone-encrusted .38s strapped low around her hips and tied to her thigh with velvet ribbons, and a pearl-snap Western shirt that was knotted under her breasts, leaving her entire midriff bare. Her boots were as shiny as her hat and sparkled every time she took a step.

When Gemma and Liz came through the doors, and Liz removed her leather jacket, Raylen's breath caught in his chest. Someone yelled at Gemma from across the barn and she headed in that direction. Liz looked up and saw Raylen, waved, and made a bee-line toward him. He was glad for the few seconds to collect his thoughts before she reached him.

"Well, good evening, Indiana Jones," Liz said.

Raylen sported two days' worth of stubble, a hat like the one Harrison Ford wore in the movie, and he'd rolled the sleeves up on his gray work shirt, unbuttoned the first three buttons to show a little chest hair, and wore faded work pants rather than jeans. A leather whip circled around his left shoulder.

"And what do I call you?" Raylen touched her shawl gently.

"Madam Drabami. I'm here to tell fortunes to those who aren't faint of heart," she said.

"Did you figure out that he's Indiana Jones?" Dewar walked up behind her. "That's his costume every year. I keep tellin' him that he looks more like Crocodile Dundee."

"Oh, no, Crocodile Dundee wasn't near as hand-some," Liz said.

Raylen popped his brother, who was dressed like a pirate, on the shoulder.

"Did you leave your contacts out tonight, Miss Liz? Let me show you around." Dewar grinned.

Raylen looped Liz's arm through his and said, "Sorry, Brother. Indiana Jones knows more about Egyptian princesses than a pirate does."

"Are we going to find a lost treasure?" Liz asked. "Please tell me we won't have to go into a cave where there are snakes or rats."

"You afraid of snakes and rats? I figured something as beautiful as you could charm anything on the earth," Raylen said in a sexy, low drawl.

Liz laughed. "You are a silver-tongued rogue, not Indiana Jones. I bet there ain't even a treasure in here."

Raylen chuckled. "Oh, yeah, there is, and I've got it on my arm. A drink for Madam Damagamy?"

Liz giggled. "Drabami. It's the carnie word for fortune-teller, and she would love a cold beer."

He pushed a strand of fake cobwebs to the side and led her toward the bar, where six-foot black cat cutouts with green flashing eyes stood propped at each end. Cauldrons with billowing smoke sat on the bar and were scattered around the room on tables.

Ace reached up and grabbed Raylen's arm as they passed his table. "Hey, hey, you goin' to share, or do we have to have a duel? My pistol can outdo your whip for the harem lady."

Ace had been in and out of the café all week. He and Jasmine were best friends and he reminded Liz so much of Blaze it wasn't even funny. He had that confident swagger about his walk like Blaze, curly blond hair, and he flirted with every woman he met. The one thing that was different was the eyes. Ace had crystal clear blue eyes, not totally unlike Raylen's. But when he sized Liz up with those eyes, it didn't do a thing for her. Not one single bell or whistle went off like they did when Raylen graced her with a look and a smile.

Raylen grinned. "I'm pretty good with a bull-whip, pardner."

"Ace, get your sorry butt behind this bar and help me," Jasmine yelled and crooked her finger at him. "You are my backup and I'm swamped."

Ace strutted over to the bar. "You've been saved by the sexy bartender who is begging for my help."

"Who is he supposed to be?" Liz whispered to Raylen.

"John Wayne," Raylen answered.

"Yes?" Ace turned quickly. "Did someone call my name? Is there a cowgirl in distress?"

"Not right here. This is Madam Dammagrammy," Raylen said.

"Madam Drabami," Liz corrected him again, this time with a giggle. "I guess Indiana will have to save her. John Wayne doesn't save anyone but cowgirls."

Ace winked.

"Two bottles of Coors, please, Miz Bartender," Raylen said.

Jasmine popped the lids off two longnecks and set them on the bar. "Liz, can you really do the dance that goes with that getup?"

Liz nodded. "But not to the George Strait song that is playing right now."

"Guess we're slap out of luck then because all these cowboys listen to is country." Jasmine smiled.

"What can I get you, Becca?" Ace asked.

Liz bit back the groan before it escaped her lips.

"I'm not Becca. I'm Annie Oakley and I bet I can outshoot and outdance you." Becca's eyes were on the cowboy at the end of the bar that Jasmine had pointed out as Taylor, the foreman of her father's ranch.

Ace played along. "Well, Annie Oakley darlin', what can this slow cowboy get you to drink?"

"I'll have a whiskey and Coke," Becca said and turned around, propped her elbows on the bar, and leaned back, straining the snaps on her shirt. "So you're the fortune-teller tonight? Are you going to look into the crystal ball and tell me that I'll be walking down the aisle with Raylen in six months?"

"I don't use the ball. I use cards and your palm, and I'll tell you whatever it says," Liz said.

"You really believe all that bull crap?" Becca asked.

"Do you read your horoscope every day?" Liz asked right back.

Becca readjusted her position and claimed a bar

stool. "Yep, and it comes true about fifty percent of the time."

A man dressed like a pirate bellied up to the bar. "Hey, Raylen, are you going to introduce me to your lady?"

Raylen made introductions. "Liz, this is Dalton Riley. He's Ace's younger brother. And Dalton, this is my new neighbor, Liz."

Dalton got to his feet and bowed over Liz's hand. He brought it to his lips and gently kissed her fingertips. "May I have the next dance, Miz Liz?"

"Of course you can," Liz said. "But right now, Raylen and I are headed to the food table."

"I'll hold you to that dance," Dalton said.

Becca reached out and touched Raylen on the arm. "Be a sweetheart and get me a plate of nachos. Libby can sit here beside me, and we'll talk about the stars."

Raylen tilted his head and looked at Liz. "Her name is Liz, not Libby. You'll have to get your own nachos. Liz is supposed to start telling fortunes in fifteen minutes, so we're going to eat right now."

Becca pouted. "You ain't no fun and not even a good friend tonight, Raylen."

Raylen ignored her and steered Liz toward the long food table with a hand on the small of her back. Her body hummed with the excitement of his touch, and she wondered if she'd be able to read the cards or even see a lifeline on a palm.

All the strange people, the party atmosphere,

the decorations, and the night air reminded her of opening night at the carnival: new faces eager to win a stuffed animal, little children clamoring to ride the ponies or the Ferris wheel, the smell of funnel cakes and cotton candy, the hawkers drawing in the crowds, and Liz dancing to bring in people to the fortune telling wagon.

She missed it all.

Liz wasn't a spectator. She was a player. She liked to dance. She liked to be in the midst of the carnival. She liked to tell fortunes and watch the people and children. What in the hell ever made her think that she could settle down and never roam again?

Raylen pulled out a chair for her and sat close enough that he could drape his arm over her shoulders. Liz looked out across the people laughing, talking, milling about from one group to the other. The energy wasn't as electric as opening night at the carnival, but it was there, and it fed the atmosphere.

"Would you go steal a candle from one of those tables, Raylen? And ask Jasmine if I can have one of her smoky cauldrons, and then I want a handful of dirt in one of those orange paper plates," she said.

"Why?" Raylen asked.

"Props," she answered.

He raised an eyebrow in question.

"Earth, wind, and fire. I'll call on the spirits to steer me to the right future for the people," she said.

"Hocus-pocus." He chuckled.

"Spirits." She smiled.

"Honey, I would try to move earth, wind, and fire for you when you smile like that. I'd even talk the angels out of their wings and the devil out of his pitchfork for you tonight," Raylen whispered.

"That is one very good pick-up line," Liz told him.

"It's the gospel truth," Raylen said and headed straight to the table where Becca was holding court with half a dozen cowboys.

"Why are you stealing my candle?" Becca asked when Raylen picked up the candle in the middle of her table.

"Fire. Madam Drabami told me to bring her fire, and her wish is my command," he said.

"You're goin' to get burned," Becca said.

"Not if I don't stick my fingers in the jar," he told her. He carried the candle over to Liz and set it in front of her. "Smile at me again, and I'll go find you some wind and earth."

She flashed a bright smile and he picked up a plate and headed outside.

———

"What in the hell are you doing?" Colleen asked when she caught him carrying a plate full of dirt back into the barn.

"Taking earth to the fortune-teller," he said.

"You are crazy and you're goin' to get hurt," she said.

"Not if someone like you don't blow hot air across my dirt and get it in my eyes," he said.

He passed by the bar and picked up a cauldron.

"Hey!" Jasmine yelled.

"Got to have wind if the folks want their fortunes told," he said.

"Then take it and be off with you, knight-in-shining-Indiana-hat." She waved him away.

When he returned, Liz had a deck of cards in her hands, shuffling them. He'd never seen such quick hands or such speed. Colleen couldn't even put on a show like that, and she was a professional black-jack dealer.

Liz spread the cards on the table, quickly picked them back up, and did an air shuffle that reminded her of Blaze. She looked across the table and pictured him sitting there beside Raylen.

She blinked and it was gone, but she couldn't stop thinking about Blaze. They had shared everything, including one kiss along the way. She was eighteen and both had had one too many beers that evening. They'd been scraping and painting wagons all day with Poppa and they were tired and sweaty from the work inside the warm barn. She'd reached for a beer at the same time he did, and their hands and eyes met somewhere in the middle. Looking back, it was inevitable since they were thrown together so much, but it had been awkward instead of passionate.

When it was over, she wondered why the women acted like mama cats in heat every time they were around him. And he'd wiped the kiss away with the back of his hand.

"I don't kiss that bad," she'd said.

"No, but I feel like I just kissed my best friend, or worse yet, my sister." Blaze had shivered.

"Yep, that's what it felt like," Liz agreed.

"Guess we know now that we ain't meant to be together no matter what Tressa and Marva Jo think," he'd said.

"Guess so," Liz had told him.

And that was that. From then on, they talked every night about everything. She heard about his women. He heard about her crushes. She knew when he thought he was in real love with that woman from Amarillo. He knew when she lost her virginity to the son of an air conditioner repairman right there in Claude, Texas, during the winter months. Blaze had held her hair back while she threw up after drinking too much the night she broke up with the boy, and Blaze was the only person in the whole world who knew that she'd harbored a long-time crush on Raylen O'Donnell.

"I'd give a whole quarter for your thoughts right now instead of a penny," Raylen said.

"Sorry, I was thinking about fortunes," she said.

That was not a lie. She was thinking about her future and Blaze's, anyway.

Creed Riley drew up a chair across the table from Liz and right beside Raylen. "Is it time for the palm reading to begin? My girlfriend just went to the bathroom but she wants to be first, so she sent me to hold her place in line. You don't look like a witch. And why do you need old Indiana Jones to protect you?"

Liz looked up and giggled. "I'm not a witch. I'm a Drabami, that's carnie for fortune-teller. There's a big difference. And Indiana isn't protecting me, he's my wingman."

Creed couldn't have looked less like Ace's brother. He had brown hair, green eyes, and towered above his older brother. "So why do you need a wingman?"

"I don't tell people what they want to hear. I tell them what I see, and sometimes they'd just as soon no one else heard what I have to say, so my wingman keeps everyone back about ten feet and turns them loose one at a time. Kind of like one of those good-lookin' doormen at a fancy big-city club," she said.

Creed nodded. "Makes sense to me."

His girlfriend, Macy, sat down at the table and

plopped her hand out in front of Liz. "Tell me this cowboy is going to make a wonderful husband." She had a high squeaky voice and blond hair peeking out from behind the Minnie Mouse wig.

Liz fanned the air above the cauldron. "Wind, earth, and fire, descend on us and give us your power to see the future. Show us what lies in the morrow as well as in the distant future." She shuffled her cards one more time. "Macy, cut them and then lay out the top card on the table."

The woman laid out the top card and Liz said, "You will soon have a cheerful experience. Your birthday must be nearing."

"My birthday isn't until the end of March," Macy said.

"You will have a wonderful, exciting year beginning next spring. You'll have parties to attend, and I see long distance travel in your future with a new love interest that you will find while you are on one of your trips. There's a jackpot in your money sector if you take advantage of the financial opportunities. If not, you will find happiness, but it won't be ecstatic happiness."

"I'm not sure I like this fortune tellin'. It sounds like I'm going to find my true love away from Ringgold," Macy said.

Liz nodded. "You will be happy if you decide to stay in Montague County, but your real happiness and wealth awaits outside of Texas."

"Now I know this is all bull. I'm going to marry Creed and live on a cattle ranch," she said.

Liz smiled. "Just remember what I said when you travel."

At midnight Liz had read everyone's palm except Raylen's, and she didn't want to read his or lay out the cards for him either. She'd told Slade's wife that she would have a third pregnancy which would produce twin boys, and Rye's wife, Austin, that she would have a big family in the next ten years. Colleen's fortune said that she would marry someone who would take her to faraway places and make her an exotic princess.

"Now what do we do with earth, wind, and fire?" Raylen asked when the party finally broke up.

Liz shuffled her cards and returned them to her pocket. "We return earth to earth, blow out the fire, and turn off the wind with the button on the bottom of the cauldron."

Gemma sat down and propped her feet up on the table. "Well, darlin', you made the party tonight. It was the best we've ever had. Everyone was talking about what you said. Creed said he'd prove you wrong because his girlfriend was going to marry a cowboy, and Colleen says you are crazy because she's never leaving this area."

"We'll see." Liz smiled.

"Me, I want to believe you, darlin'. I want to think that by next Christmas I'll have found my own special cowboy. Matter-of-fact, I'm going to be damn good this whole year so Santa can bring him to me. I want him to show up on Christmas Day wearing nothing but one of those cute little Santa hats and cowboy boots. Whooo-wee, that makes my little hormones whine just thinkin' about it," Gemma said.

"God Almighty, Gemma!" Raylen said.

"Yep, God is Almighty, but Santa might be almighty too if he can bring me that by next Christmas. I'm goin' home. We'll pack up and clean up tomorrow night. Jasmine and Colleen are helping. You want to?" Gemma looked at Liz.

"Sure. What time do I need to be here?" Liz asked.

"Say about four o'clock? Supper is on the house for anyone who helps. It's leftover party food and whatever Jasmine brings," Gemma said. "See you tomorrow."

Raylen looked at Liz. "I'll drive you home."

"No need. I drove myself," she said.

"Then let me drive your truck home and I'll walk back through the pasture," he said.

Liz laughed. "I didn't see any devils or blackbirds in the cards."

Raylen frowned. "Blackbirds?"

"They signify dire misfortune," she said.

He laughed. "Well, there's crows between here and your place, so I better see you to the door."

"Okay," she agreed. "But that Dalton fellow really should be taking me home since I promised him a dance and got so busy that I never did dance with anyone."

Gemma took her feet off the table and stood up. "Hey, girl, let Raylen take you home. Dewar got hooked up with Angie Sutter and took her home. I really did think you and him would hit it off but guess I was wrong. Remember what you told him?"

Liz nodded. "That love was on its way to meet him, and he had a strange adventure in his future."

"What'd you tell Raylen? I didn't hear his fortune," Gemma asked as she switched off the lights.

"I didn't do his," Liz answered. "He was my wingman and we didn't have time to see what the earth, wind, and fire could conjure up for him. We'll have to read his cards next time around. Good night and thanks for inviting me."

"It's me who's thankin' you. I'll probably see you tomorrow at the café," Gemma said.

Liz and Raylen were both quiet on the way to her house until he parked in front of the porch. "You had a glow about you when you read the cards. It was downright exotic. You belong in a carnival, not on a horse ranch. I don't like to admit that, but it's the truth."

The evening had plumb worn Liz out. When she worked at the carnival, her hours were different. She worked until midnight, spent an hour locking everything up, another one talking to Blaze or Tressa and her mother, and then slept until midmorning. Tomorrow the alarm would go off at five. It didn't care if she'd told fortunes until midnight or if she'd gone to bed at ten o'clock. The café opened at six, and customers were usually sitting in their cars waiting for the doors to be unlocked.

Raylen got out of the truck, helped Liz out and walked her to the door, waited while she opened it, and stepped inside without being asked.

"Raylen, it's late," she said.

"I want three minutes of your time," he said.

She cocked her head to one side. "Why?"

"I want you to dance for me," he said.

"Why? Haven't you seen a belly dancer before, or do you think that because you just told me that I belong in a carnival that I'll pack up and leave tomorrow morning?" she asked.

He shook his head. "You are so beautiful, and I've imagined you dancing all evening. Please?"

"Okay," she agreed.

She picked out a song on her phone and started it. Raylen settled into one recliner while Blister claimed the other and Hooter slept on the floor in between. Liz went to the middle of the floor and turned her back. When the music started, her hands were up, with her shawl tangled up in them and one leg slightly cocked outward. Her body and the music became one entity.

She moved close to him and popped a hip out to brush against his hand.

He smiled.

Putting a hand on each side of the recliner, she did several torso rolls; the sequins and fringe became a sparkling blur in constant movement. She knew that she was putting more sexiness into the dance than she had ever done before. It was belly dance and pole dance combined, but she loved the hot desire in his eyes.

His eyes locked with hers and a fine bead of sweat popped out on his upper lip.

She stood up, locked her fingers above her head, and turned her back to him, hips rolling from one side to the other. So he was hot, was he? Well, her skin was on fire from the way he looked at her. If his eyes could do that to her, she could hardly imagine what sex would be like.

Raylen reached out, but she moved away like she'd done so many times when a man tried to touch her.

She swirled in front of his eyes, the scarf becoming fairy wings. One moment it flirted with his face and the next it was gone.

When the music ended, the shawl was dragging behind her and their eyes were locked together in a heated gaze that said only one thing would ever put the fire out.

"You are amazing," he whispered hoarsely.

She tangled her fingers in his thick dark hair and then stood back away from him. She extended her hand, and he let her lead him down the hallway to a bedroom.

Was it possible to have wings and have roots too? she wondered as she closed the door with her bare foot.

———————

The next morning, she awoke to the smell of fresh coffee brewing and crawled out of bed. She belted a robe around her waist and felt a blush as she walked out into the kitchen to find Raylen making pancakes.

"Raylen, you need to know that I'm not a slut. I don't fall into bed with any man that winks at me," she said.

He kissed her forehead. "I know that, Liz. I can see it in your eyes."

She searched his face and his eyes. "I believe you. Then, this is not a one-night stand?"

He poured a mug full of coffee and put it in her hands. "I hope not. I want to see you again. This could be the beginning of something wonderful. But please promise me you won't dance like that for another man."

"I've danced for years, Raylen, but that was a special dance and I promise I won't do it just like that for anyone else."

Chapter 8

LIZ PICKED A CLEAN APRON FROM A HOOK INSIDE the kitchen wall of the café and wrapped it around her waist, bringing the ties back around to tie in the front. She loaded the pocket with an order pad and two pens, poured a cup of black coffee, and sat down at the table.

Jasmine settled a pink baseball cap with the company logo on her head, pulled her brown ponytail out the back, and gave Liz a once-over. "You look like warmed-over sin, girl. Did they keep you telling fortunes all night?"

Liz covered a yawn with her hand. "Midnight."

"And then?" Jasmine asked.

"And then I did a stupid, stupid thing," Liz said.

"Dewar or Raylen?" Jasmine asked.

Liz swallowed fast to keep from spewing coffee across the kitchen. "What makes you ask that? It could have been one of Ace's brothers or even Ace."

"No, it was either Dewar or Raylen, and I think it was Raylen. He's the one that can't keep his eyes off you. Dewar notices because he's a man. Raylen's looks go deeper. Only a blind person would have trouble seeing that." Jasmine set about making a pan of biscuits.

Liz took a sip of her coffee and hoped the hands on the clock would miraculously spin around ten times and she'd be saved by customers coming into the cafe.

It didn't happen.

"Well? You better talk fast because doors open in ten minutes." Jasmine's green eyes twinkled. "Dewar or Raylen?"

"Raylen. It's always been Raylen. Since I was fourteen, it's been Raylen. I measured every boy and later every man by Raylen. He's so high up on a pedestal that even God looks up to him," Liz said.

Jasmine sat down in one of the three chairs surrounding the small table in the center of the kitchen. It was a workstation when she and Liz folded napkins, a resting station at the end of the day, and a place for her to set up shop for the business part of the café once a week. "Tell me about it. Raylen might be a sweetheart, but there ain't a man livin' who deserves to be on a pedestal that high."

Liz took another sip of coffee, and her phone rang.

Jasmine pointed. "If it ain't God, then get rid of them. I'm dying to hear what happened."

"Blaze, darlin'!" Liz said. "I can't wait to tell you everything that's happened, but the café opens in ten minutes, and that's not enough time."

"Okay, okay, you are forgiven for running away, but I still want you to come back to your real home.

I miss you." Blaze's deep laughter filled her ear and echoed out into the café. "I'm just crawling into my trailer. Last night's woman was beautiful but turned out to be a whiner, so that won't happen again. When I got home, I had to call and tell you that. The rest can wait until I get some sleep. Call me in the middle of the afternoon."

"Oh, I will, and I've got so much to tell you," Liz said.

"You know I love you," he said.

"And I love you. Good night, darlin'," Liz said.

Jasmine's expression was one of acute confusion. "You love Blaze but Raylen's on a pedestal?"

"That's right. I told you about Blaze," Liz answered. "He's my best friend, kind of like Pearl is to you. We were the only two kids on the carnival rounds since I was thirteen and he was fourteen. And he's my confidant like Gemma is yours, and then he's like my brother and my cousin. Blaze wears lots of different hats. But he's not Raylen."

Jasmine got up, poured a cup of coffee and sat back down. "Did Raylen spend the night?"

Liz blushed. "Not quite all of it."

"I watched you telling fortunes last night, girl. You miss that life. Your eyes were all glittery and you loved what you were doing. I can get a new waitress when you get bored in Montague County. Raylen's heart is a different matter," Jasmine said.

"I told you it was a stupid, stupid thing," Liz said, "but it was so worth it. My Aunt Tressa says that I have to own my victories, failures, and sex life, so this is me owning up to what happened, but I'm not sharing details."

"It could be stupid, or it could be a brilliant thing," Jasmine said. "Like Ellen says, it's all in how you look at it and what comes out of it in the end. It's time to unlock the door and let the customers come on in for coffee and breakfast. You ready?"

Liz nodded. "I reckon I'd better be."

There was a steady stream of regular morning coffee drinkers before Gemma showed up at eight o'clock. She snagged the last table in the corner and ordered biscuits and sausage gravy with a side order of hash browns.

"It ought to be a sin to look like you do after last night," Gemma told Liz when she brought her food.

"Oh?" Liz felt a blush creeping up her neck and filling her cheeks.

"I danced and flirted. You told fortunes. Both of which would tire a woman out, and what did we get for our efforts? Not a blessed thing. We both slept alone, and I don't know about you, but that made me cranky. And then of all things, you tell me I got to wait a whole year before my knight-in-shining-new-Chevrolet-truck is going to come carry me off. You could have shuffled the cards different, and he could be on his way right now to drop down on one knee and propose to me," Gemma said.

"Can't manipulate the cards," Liz said with a smile.

Gemma picked up her fork and started eating. "Can't manipulate my brother either. You could have told him that if he didn't cook my breakfast every day between now and next Christmas you were going to put an evil spell on him, but oh, no, you didn't even lay the cards out for him. That sorry sucker was still snoring when I left a while ago. He put a note on the kitchen table that said he was sleeping in and then going to start cleaning up the barn when he woke up."

"I'll be over after work to help you with cleanup." Liz pointed toward a group of deer hunters dressed in camouflage and made her escape toward them.

"I've got appointments until six. It'll be you and Raylen and maybe Dewar if you can rope him into helping until I get there," Gemma hollered across the room.

———

Raylen carefully removed the fake cobwebs from the walls and ceiling and packed them between layers of tissue in the cardboard boxes where they belonged. He'd almost finished that part of the job when Dewar showed up close to noon.

His voice echoed in the enormous barn where they held annual horse sales when he hollered, "Are you hungry?"

Raylen stopped what he was doing and wiped his hands on his jeans. "Starving. Want to go up to Chicken Fried?"

"No, Mama sent me to get you," Dewar answered. "She made dumplin's and pumpkin pies."

Raylen nodded and headed for the barn door. Part of him was glad that his mama had chosen that day to make his favorite dinner. The other part, the section that controlled his heart, longed to see Liz again, to make sure that an awkwardness had not sprung up between them that would send her scooting back to her carnival.

"Good party last night. Lots of people. That Liz was a hit with her fortunes," Dewar said as they walked a quarter of a mile back to the house.

"Yep," Raylen answered.

"She looked like that woman in that old show that Grandma still watches. I can't remember the name of it," Dewar said.

"Yep, it's *I Dream of Jeannie,*" Raylen reminded him.

"If she'd had blond hair instead of black, she'd have looked like her," Dewar said.

"Yep," Raylen said again.

"You stuck on that word, or do you know another one?" Dewar asked.

"Liz ain't as tall as that actress was and she's prettier," Raylen answered. "Is that enough words for you?"

"You got a thing for her?" Dewar asked.

"Why are you askin'?"

"Remember when we all went out to Wil's and took him huntin' with us?" Dewar asked.

Raylen remembered the night very well. True, they'd gone hunting that night, but it was more than that. They went to railroad Wil into admitting that he had feelings for Pearl, and it had worked.

"Yep."

"Well?" Dewar stopped at the back porch.

"Deep subject." Raylen grinned and hurried inside the house.

Dinner was on the table, with Maddie, Cash, Colleen, and the grandparents already seated and waiting. Grandpa said the blessing as soon as Dewar and Raylen sat down, and Cash began to pass the dishes.

"Got to go wash up," Raylen said. "Didn't want to hold up dinner since you were all already sittin' down. Colleen, you leave me some chicken."

Colleen grinned at her brother. "Yeah, right."

He washed his hands and face and took time to comb his dark hair straight back. The man looking at him in the mirror didn't look any different from the one who'd looked at him the morning before, but he sure felt different. How could having sex one time with a woman change a man so much, and yet no one else could even see it?

When he returned to the table everyone was talking, mostly about the party the night before. Grandpa looked up and winked as if he knew something, and Raylen felt a slow heat crawling up his neck. Then Grandpa pointed to Colleen's plate and Raylen saw all the extra chicken beside her dumplings.

Raylen sat down beside her and loaded his plate with dumplings and then deftly, while his sister was talking to Grandma, forked the chicken from her plate and raked part of his dumplings over it.

"Hey, where's my chicken?" she said when she looked down. "Raylen!"

"Don't look at me. I was in the bathroom. Dewar probably stole it," Raylen said.

Dewar threw up both palms defensively. "I'm innocent."

Colleen narrowed her dark green eyes and looked from one brother to the other. "Raylen, you did it. You can't hide nothing in your face. That's why you're a lousy poker player."

Raylen grinned and shoved food into his mouth.

"He's got the hots for our new neighbor and he's hidin' that pretty dang good," Dewar said.

The grin vanished and he shot his brother a dirty look. "She's a pretty woman, but you'd best be careful," Grandma said. "She's like a butterfly. They look so pretty flittin' around out there among the roses, but if you catch one and put it in a jar, it'll die."

"She'll get tired of plain livin'. She's a…" Colleen said.

"A carnie," Raylen finished for her. "Once a

rancher, always a rancher. Maybe that don't hold true for a carnie."

Dewar put in his two cents. "I'll bet you it does."

"I'll take that bet. Ten bucks says she stays," Raylen said.

"Ten says she goes before Christmas." Dewar stuck out his hand and they shook over the table.

"Twenty says she's gone by December fifteenth," Colleen said.

Raylen looked at Colleen. "You don't think anyone can change?"

"Person is raised one way, chances are they'll stay that way," Colleen told him. "I won't ever marry anyone but a rancher. It's in my blood."

"I'll put twenty on it." Raylen sipped his iced tea. "So you're sayin' if a man walked up on our porch, say, sellin' Bibles, and you looked at him and fell in love in an instant like Rye did when he looked at Austin, that you wouldn't be happy sellin' Bibles with him?"

Colleen giggled, then laughed aloud, then grabbed her napkin to wipe the tears. "Me sellin' Bibles? That ain't never goin' to happen, Brother. I'm marryin' a cowboy when I get around to fallin' in love. One who lives on a big ranch."

"Good girl," Maddie said.

"Never say never," Raylen said. "Gets a person in trouble every time."

Chapter 9

AFTER WORK, LIZ DROVE TO THE O'DONNELL ranch and straight back to the barn. She just sat there behind the steering wheel staring at the barn and letting every scene from the night before play through her head. One of the doors was open about three feet, and she was pretty sure that Raylen was cleaning up after last night's party. She had her hand on the truck's door handle when her cell phone rang, and she jerked back as if she'd been burned. She answered it without even checking ID, figuring that Raylen was calling to give her a hard time about dragging her feet.

"I'm on my way," she answered.

"Well, now, that's amazing news!" Blaze's deep voice almost made her drop the phone.

"I thought you were someone else," Liz said quickly.

"That's disappointing," Blaze said with a sigh. "I just woke up. I miss you. Come home."

"I *am* home," Liz told him. "I love it here and I can't wait for you to see my new home." She emphasized the last word. "It's as big as our winter place, and I've got a barn and a dog and a cat and enough Christmas decorations to light up half of Texas. And Raylen is next door and he's not married, Blaze. And I'm sitting here in my truck looking at the barn where we had a dress-up Halloween party last night, and I'm going to help Raylen with cleaning it all up this afternoon."

Blaze laughed. "That sounds like you are trying to convince yourself. What did you say you did last night?"

"I was next door at a Halloween party," she answered, "with a live band and open bar at the neighbors' ranch—Raylen's place—and I told fortunes."

"Did you wear the turquoise dancing outfit as a costume?" Blaze asked.

"No, orange," she answered and her face turned scarlet at the memories.

"And?" Blaze pressed.

"And Raylen took me home afterwards," she said.

"Damn, Lizelle. Tell me what happened. I feel like I'm pulling teeth," he groaned.

What had happened between her and Raylen was too personal and too intimate to even share with Blaze. "The setting was so easy because they had cauldrons with dry ice in them, so that gave me the wind, and fire came from a candle. Raylen brought dirt from outside to use. You showed up in one of the readings I was doing for a red-haired woman."

"What's her name, and how well do you know her?" His tone changed to the one she'd heard dozens of times when he was sweet talking a woman.

Liz bit back a giggle. "Her name is Colleen and she's Irish to the bone. She's got deep green eyes. You'll meet her when you come to visit when you are here for the Bowie gig. She's Raylen's sister and she works as a blackjack dealer at a casino over the border in Oklahoma."

"And what card did you see?" Blaze asked.

"Oh, no! I don't kiss and tell, not even to you, when it comes to cards. It was her personal future. If you want me to read the cards for you then you have to come see me at my house. I won't even do a reading for you when I visit y'all at the carnival," Liz told him.

"Tressa can do it anytime I want," he threatened.

"Yes, she can. I don't think you'd like Colleen anyway. She's independent as hell and doesn't stutter when she speaks her mind. The first time you looked at another woman she'd tie your carcass to an altar and cut off your family jewels. The cards must've been wrong to even suggest that you'd meet her in the future, or else they were right and you'd better go on down to the funeral home in Claude and get fitted for a casket."

"That's morbid, but you've got my curiosity roused. Besides, you know I like red hair. You are just tellin' me this crock of bull to keep from talkin' more about you and Raylen," Blaze said.

"I am not!" Liz protested loudly. "To prove it I will introduce you, but things would never, ever work between you two. If she caught you flirting she really would deep-fry the jewels and feed them to her cat."

"That made shivers up my back. Did you turn over the card that says I'm to run from her?" Blaze asked.

"I've overstepped the confidentiality boundaries between reader and client already," Liz said. "Now, I've got to go help clean up the mess. It's a neighbor thing. I'm helping them today and starting tomorrow they're going to help me put up my decorations so it will be all pretty when y'all get here."

"Lizelle, don't get too involved with Raylen." Blaze's voice went into his big brother tone. "He's just someone you met a couple of times when you were a kid and you've built him into a superhero. He's a real person, sweetheart, and real people aren't gods or heroes. Your heart will always be a wanderer. You know that old sayin' in the church about giving them a child until they are six and they'll never change. It works the same in lots of things—like carnivals."

Liz sighed. "You were fourteen."

"Yes, but my mother was a flower child, and

I loved the carnival my whole life, even if I didn't get to join it until I was fourteen. I'd stand by the fence and watch y'all leave in the spring, and my heart would hurt to go with you. We're carnies at heart, sweetheart. We'll never change. Promise me you will be careful," Blaze said.

"I promise," she said and meant it.

"Did you sleep with him already?" Blaze asked bluntly.

"I'm not going to kiss and tell on that either. Tell Mama hi," Liz said and ended the call.

She was halfway to the barn when Raylen stepped out and waved.

"Already done?" she called out.

He grinned. "You aren't that lucky. I've got the cobwebs down and part of the tables cleared off."

She was about to put her arms around him for a hug when Colleen called out, "Come right on in. You can strip down the tables, and I'll wash them. Then Raylen can take over and stack them on the rack. I bet Gemma took extra appointments today on purpose. She loves to get ready for a party but hates to do the work afterwards."

Liz quickly took a step back. "We'll make her work extra hard when we start putting up Christmas decorations tomorrow night, won't we? Are you going to help us too, Colleen?"

"Nope." Colleen grabbed Raylen by the arm and pulled him back toward the doors. "I've got plans in just a few minutes, and then I'm dealing blackjack for the next seven nights in a row. Six at night until six in the morning."

Liz followed them into the barn. "After last night, you'll be wiped completely out by end of shift."

"Didn't you work seven nights a week at the carnival?" Colleen asked.

"Guess I did in one capacity or the other," Liz answered. "We were set up and running four nights a week. I did fortunes two or three of those. We were usually tearing down and moving two days and setting up the next day. Those days it was all hands on deck from daylight to way past midnight. We slept and ate when we could."

"Do you miss it?" Colleen asked but she looked at Raylen.

"Of course. Would you miss blackjack?"

"I'd miss the excitement. There's something about people who gamble. They are…" Colleen stopped.

"Electric," Liz finished for her.

"That's it. There's static in the air and excitement," Colleen said with a nod.

"I imagine it's like a carnival inside a building." Liz smiled.

"How can you leave all that behind for a dog and a cat and a waitress job?" Colleen asked as she stripped a table of its orange plastic cloth, wadded it up and tossed it in an oversized trash can.

"What would it take for you to leave your job behind?" Liz cleared cups, plates, and napkins from the next table.

Colleen stripped off another tablecloth and shoved it into the trash can before she answered. "I'm not sure, but it would have to be huge."

"How huge?" Liz asked.

"Bigger than a waitress job at the Chicken Fried—and an old dog with arthritis and a temperamental mama cat," Colleen said.

"Hooter and Blister and my job are pretty big in my dream world," Liz said.

She didn't add Raylen or her house and land into the mix. Raylen had waved at her when she arrived, but that's all she got, which wasn't a lot after the hottest sex on the face of the earth. Maybe he wanted a friend with benefits. He could wish in one hand and spit in the other and see which one filled up fastest if that's what he had in mind. Liz wanted a whole lot more than that.

Colleen's cell phone rang, and she dug it out of her hip pocket. "Hello… Yes, I can… Be there as soon as I can… Good-bye."

She ended the call and put the phone back in her pocket. "My plans just got changed. That was my boss. One of the other dealers has the flu so I'm drawing down some serious overtime. Have fun. Gemma should be here soon," she said on her way out the door.

Liz heard the truck engine pull away from the barn before she crossed the floor of the arena and propped her hands on her hips. "I won't be a friend with benefits," she spat out.

"I didn't ask you to," he said.

"Then why did you act like last night didn't even happen?"

"It was the hardest thing I've ever done." He took her hands in his and drew her close to his chest. "I didn't know how you wanted to play it. If you want me to, I'll crawl up on the barn roof and shout that we slept together last night so loud folks over in Oklahoma can hear me."

"You. Wouldn't. Dare." She was so flustered that she could feel her face burning with a deep blush.

"Don't ever dare an O'Donnell. Besides, I'm not ashamed that I had sex with you, darlin'. Are you? If you want me to show you the steps to get to the roof, I'll be right glad to do so. We can both do some yellin'," he teased.

"I'm not quite ready for that," she whispered as she moistened her lips, closed her eyes and rolled up on her toes to meet his slightly parted lips as they sought hers.

"Hey, anybody here?" Gemma's voice sounded like it was coming from six miles away.

"We're at the back of the barn," he hollered.

"Is Liz with you?"

"She's right here. Where have you been?" Raylen asked.

Raylen took a step back and flipped a table over, folded the legs up under it, and asked, "Rooftop? Or keep this quiet for a while?"

"Let's take it slow." Liz blew him a kiss.

Chapter 10

FALL IN TEXAS CAN BE COLDER THAN A BRASS monkey on the North Pole or hot enough to go swimming in the lake, sometimes both within a three-day span. It's that time of year when folks turn on the heat in the morning but by midafternoon, the thermostat has to be switched to air-conditioning.

The afternoon that the O'Donnells came to put up Liz's yard decorations felt nothing like Christmas. She had made a pitcher of iced tea, a pot of coffee, and the makings for hot chocolate were on the countertop with a platter of chocolate chip cookies that she'd bought at a local bakery. She found her playlist of Christmas songs on her phone, plugged it into a set of small speakers and put them on the porch. Everyone arrived at the same time: Gemma, Raylen, Dewar, Jasmine, and Ace. The three guys grabbed a cold beer and went right to the barn while the ladies had a glass of tea, cookies, and half an hour of gossip while the guys set the cutouts up in the yard.

"Reckon they got it figured out yet?" Gemma asked.

"What?" Liz asked.

"Menfolks are different from us girls. They have to scratch their heads and measure and talk something to death before they get it done," Jasmine said.

"You got it. Then after they've done cussed and discussed, they do what we would have done to start with. We might as well go get the boxes of lights and have them ready," Gemma said.

Liz started for the door. "What you said about men isn't just cowboys and ranchers. It's the same thing in the carnival business. We can take my truck and load all the lights in it."

"Guess we didn't give them long enough," Gemma whispered when they found the guys still working on a plan to get everything lowered out of the loft.

Two hours later all the pieces were unloaded up against the fence on the south side of the property.

"You're the boss lady, Liz. You tell us where to put it," Ace said.

"How many are there in all?" Liz asked.

"Thirty-six," Raylen said.

"Then we'll divide them. Eighteen on each side."

"By theme, color, or what?" Dewar asked.

"Let's lay them all out on the ground and then decide where to put them," Ace suggested.

Liz swiped her hand across her forehead, smearing dirt and sweat from one side to the other. "How do they stand up when a strong wind hits?"

Raylen flipped a snowman around and pointed

to the bottom. "See that board with the holes in it? Stakes go through the holes and then two feet into the ground. Plus there's a prop, kind of like the back side of an easel, that keeps them steady. We've got hundreds of stakes in the back of my truck. Haskell had them all cut and boxed up."

Liz had lain awake the night before and planned out where each cutout would go, but now, looking out across the expanse of them, she was bewildered.

"Help!" she said.

Jasmine pushed her brown hair behind her ears. "You really want a Griswold effect?"

Liz nodded.

"Okay, then take every other one and put it on the other side of the lane. Don't pay a bit of attention to themes or content. Just arrange them haphazardly," Gemma suggested.

"Okay. That's the way we'll do it. But remember to arrange them so they are all as visible as possible from the road," Liz said.

Ace picked up Betty Boop standing in front of a Christmas tree and carried it to the other side of the lane. Raylen grabbed a four-by-eight piece of plywood with a painting of three snowmen and a yellow puppy playing at their base.

"That must've been the year he got Hooter," Liz said.

"And that one with the dancer and cactus was for this year, right?" Jasmine pointed to the latest one.

"I don't remember seeing that one, so it has to be," Gemma answered.

Dewar got a firm grip on Santa's sleigh. "I'll come back and get the reindeer that hooks up to this soon as I haul this little fat man to the other side of the lane."

"The boxes with lights should be marked as to where they go. I've helped Haskell do this job since I was a little boy," Raylen said.

"Mr. Braggy Butt," Gemma said.

"Miz Smart Mouth," Dewar taunted.

"Oh, hush! You'd agree with him just because it's guys against gals," she grumbled.

Jasmine touched Liz on the shoulder. "They argue like that all the time. It wasn't easy for me to get used to since I'm an only child. Pearl and I were friends and we seldom ever had a cross word. These O'Donnells fight like..."

"Irishmen." Gemma giggled. "It's fun. You ought to try it."

"I know exactly what you are talking about." Liz remembered the arguments she had had with Blaze through the years. He hated to be wrong almost as much as she did, and their arguments could get heated. Maybe the fact that he was Irish, too, was the explanation. Their worst argument ever had been when he couldn't talk her out of leaving the carnival and then he stayed in his trailer and refused to come out to wave good-bye to her.

"Okay, then, let's put Mr. and Mrs. Claus with their welcome sign way back at the house. That way, when the folks get to the end, the old couple will be saying, 'come right on in and have a cup of hot chocolate,'..." Gemma said.

Liz was shaking her head emphatically. "No! I want them right here at the very front of the property to welcome everyone to the whole light show. Not way back there where you can't even see them. Put them right here in the corner."

"I disagree," Jasmine said. "I think they should go in the other corner since most people are right-handed, and that's where they'll look first."

Liz moved to the corner beside the cattle guard and crossed her arms over her chest. "I want it right here."

Jasmine and Gemma both cracked up.

"What is so damn funny?" Liz asked.

"You argued with us. I'm proud of you, girl. You might make an O'Donnell yet!" Gemma said.

"You two are..."

"Pigs from hell?" Jasmine asked. "Ever see *Steel Magnolias*? I love that line."

"Yes, I did, and I love it, too. And FYI," Liz said, "I've argued with an expert and you two barely qualify as amateurs."

"You hear that, Raylen? She says she can out-argue us," Gemma said.

"When hell freezes over," he shot across the lane.

"Get ready for icicles on Lucifer's boogers!" Liz taunted.

"I don't think so, dar...lin.'" Raylen dragged out the last word. "I'm the third son and have two sisters. I'm a professional at arguing."

"I'm an only child, but I grew up with Blaze, who could argue the words off a stop sign," Liz shot back across the lane at him.

Gemma nodded and giggled at the same time. "She's pretty good, Raylen. You've met your match on the fiddle and in an argument, too."

"We'll see about that," he said as he carried a decorated Christmas tree to the other side. His arm brushed against Liz's as they passed each other. He caught her eye and winked. All the arguing left her in an instant and desire flooded her body. She wanted to send everyone home and drag Raylen into the house and into her bedroom.

Whoa, girl! Aunt Tressa's voice popped into her head. *Are you playing too loose and easy with this cowboy? Be a little hard to get so he doesn't get tired of you, and besides, you haven't figured out if he has an ulterior motive concerning this land. Slow this wagon down, Lizelle!*

"You are frowning." Jasmine nudged her on the shoulder. "This is supposed to be fun, not a chore."

"It is." Liz forced a smile. "Do you think we have enough to cover the whole lane as close as we're positioning them?"

"You were thinking about Raylen," Jasmine whispered. "I saw the way you looked at him and that wink he gave you. Did he make you mad?"

Liz put her fingers to her lips. "Shhhh, and no, he did not, but we need to go a lot slower than we started off."

Jasmine zipped her mouth shut.

"Are y'all telling secrets without me?" Gemma asked from a few feet away.

"This place is going to make Griswold's look puny," Jasmine said.

"I'm glad Uncle Haskell marked the boxes for me." Liz pulled a box with MR. AND MRS. CLAUS LIGHTS written in big bold letters on the top from the back of her truck.

"Are they all like that?" Jasmine asked.

"Yes, they are," Liz answered. "We'll just have to dig through the boxes. Hey, you know what we should do? Put each box by the cutout where it goes rather than digging through them all."

"You sound just like Raylen. Y'all might be kin to each other as organized as you are. Your Uncle Haskell is probably his great-great-seventeen-times-back-cousin or something," Gemma said.

"God, I hope not," Liz said.

"Why? Don't you want to be kin to the O'Donnells?" Gemma asked.

"No, ma'am. Y'all argue too much for me," Liz joked.

"It's Dewar, isn't it? I knew it from the first. You've got a crush on Dewar," Gemma whispered.

Liz threw up both palms. "No, ma'am, I do not!"

"Well, crap!" Gemma sighed. "I wanted you to fall for him. We've got to get him married, and then Raylen." Gemma crossed herself and went on, "God forbid, but then Colleen. I'm not sure there's a man on the earth I can bribe into takin' her off our hands."

"Why?" Liz asked.

Gemma picked up a box of lights and carried them over to Betty Boop. "Because she's so outspoken and pessimistic."

"Not why about Colleen. Why do you have to worry about your brothers and sisters falling in love?" Liz asked.

Jasmine stacked one box on the top of the other and carried them across the lane. "Because according to Cash, they have to get married in the order of their birth."

"I thought that was a joke," Liz said.

"I heard y'all," Dewar said, raising his voice. "And you might as well give it up, Gemma. I'm not being railroaded to the altar."

"We could drug him and pay the girl," Jasmine whispered.

"What was that?" Dewar asked.

"I heard her," Ace said. "She said she was going to help Gemma drug you and pay some old gal to marry you."

"Better bring your lunch because it'll be an all-day job," Dewar said.

Jasmine pointed a long, slim finger at him. "Darlin', I could put something in your chicken fried steak, and you'd wake up next to some woman wearing a wedding band. We would make her sign a prenup so she couldn't sue you for the farm in the divorce. You'd better think about that when Gemma starts lookin' at wedding books. Us girls got to stick together."

"I'd say you'd better be out girl huntin', or else hire you a taster like they did in the old days every time you go anywhere near these witchy women. They want you to think they are jokin', but they are all dead serious," Ace said.

Jasmine narrowed her eyes at him. "You'd better be careful. I can have you at the altar in a heartbeat. I know lots of women who'd take your sorry old hide any way they could get it. And if you aren't nice to me, I'll forget to have them sign the prenup."

"Look what you got me into, Dewar. I was mindin' my own business drivin' stakes and now I got to watch my back." He pointed at a barbed wire tat around his upper left arm. "You see this? Me and Rye got them to protect us against witchy women. Rye's wife Austin either got over or under Rye's barbed wire, but ain't no woman never goin' to get me to drop down on one knee. It ain't happenin', Jasmine darlin'. Not even you have got that much power."

"Power hasn't got nothing to do with good old-fashioned sleeping pills," Jasmine told him. "But it is time for me to get home. Y'all are about done here anyway. If you need help another night, just call me. I've got to make peach cobblers before I go to bed tonight, and it's startin' to get dark, and you've got chores to do. Your hired help was fussin' yesterday about you getting lazy."

"They were not! They know I work harder than any of them out there on that ranch," Ace protested.

Jasmine pointed her forefinger at him and pretended to shoot him. "Gotcha! But seriously I do need to get back to the café."

"Us too." Dewar nodded toward Gemma. "All that's left is putting a few lights into the last half dozen cutouts and taking the empty boxes back to the barn, and Raylen can help with that."

"I've got early appointments in the morning, but when you get ready to do the lights on the fences, I'll be here," Gemma said.

"Want to go with me, Liz?"

Ace unloaded two more boxes of stakes from the bed of his truck before he held the passenger's door open for Jasmine. They waved and drove off down the lane, honking when they reached the end. Dewar and Gemma got into his truck and fell in behind Ace's truck when they turned north toward Ringgold.

Raylen looked over at Liz and opened his arms. She walked into them, and they closed around her.

She looked up to find his eyes closed and his lips coming toward hers. She snapped her eyes shut and moistened her lips with the tip of her tongue. The kiss was hard and fiery and crackled the air around them.

"I can't stay. Mama and Daddy are expecting me to go over books with them tonight, but I had to kiss you. Are you ready to get up on that rooftop and tell everyone that we're dating?"

She shook her head. "But we aren't. We haven't been on a single date."

Raylen brushed soft kisses across her eyelids and forehead. "That can be fixed real quick. This is Wednesday. Tomorrow we'll finish this job. Friday, I've got to be in Wichita Falls for a horse meeting. So Miz Liz, would you have dinner with me on Saturday night? You don't have to work on Sunday, so we won't have to be home early."

She ignored her aunt's advice about playing hard to get and said, "Yes, I would."

"Then on Sunday afternoon, we'll go out for Sunday dinner, and if you want an artificial tree we can go to the mall and find one. Or if you want a real one then when we get home we can go to the woods and cut one down. On Monday we can put it up and spend however many nights we need to decorate it," he said.

She leaned back and looked at him. "You *are* organized."

"That's what they say, but I want you to have a perfect Christmas, even if it is the week before Thanksgiving."

He kissed her one more time, and she swore she heard bells and whistles off in the distance.

"Now I really have to go. Mama said seven and it's five minutes 'til. See you tomorrow after work."

Liz wished that Raylen wasn't so punctual or organized.

Chapter 11

JASMINE HAD TO MAKE A GROCERY STORE RUN to Bowie for the café after work on Thursday, so she couldn't go play Christmas with Liz. Gemma had three late appointments that would keep her tied up until dark. Dewar had promised Rye that he'd go with him to Breckenridge to look at a new longhorn bull he wanted to buy for rodeo stock, and they wouldn't be back until bedtime. Ace was up to his elbows in tractor repairs and didn't even have time to come to the Chicken Fried for a hamburger.

That left Raylen and Liz to finish stringing lights down the top of the fence around the front of the property. He crawled out of his truck in her front yard and shook the legs of his dusty jeans down over his scuffed-up cowboy boots. His chambray shirt was open down the front with a sweat-stained gauze muscle shirt underneath. He removed his straw cowboy hat and wiped sweat from his forehead with his shirtsleeve.

Liz had just parked her vehicle when Raylen got out of his truck. Her work T-shirt was stained where grease had splattered on her, and her makeup had long since gone.

"Where's the rest of the crew? I knew Dewar was going with Rye, but we were supposed to have some help," she asked.

If he'd known he was working alone with Liz, he damn sure would've taken time for a quick shower and a change of clothes.

"Jasmine had to go buy groceries. Gemma had late appointments. Ace called in and said he didn't even have time to run by the café for a burger," she explained.

"Well, I guess it's a two-man crew, then. You ready to get this job done? We've got a helluva lot of work to do, Mrs. Claus."

Liz looked down at her stained shirt. "I'm sure Mrs. Claus never looked like this."

"I'm pretty sure Santa probably had a shower before he crawled up in the seat of his sleigh." Raylen chuckled.

"Then I guess we'd better get busy. I've got so many plans to show my family, both natural and carnival, how much I love it here. There will be presents under the tree for everyone on the night of my party, so that means some shopping after we get this job done."

"For everyone? How do you do that when you don't even know how many will be there or what they'd like?"

"Boxes of candy and tins of popcorn. Everyone likes that, and it's fun to have a present," she answered.

He tucked her hand in his and paced his step to match hers. Hooter stretched and followed five feet behind them. Blister had a sudden burst of energy and bounded off the porch to run ahead of them.

The spark that was between them hadn't died, and that was saying a lot for Raylen, who had always been the love 'em and leave 'em type of cowboy. That old adage "out of sight, out of mind" did not apply when it came to Liz.

Which is not a good thing. Colleen whispered so clearly that he glanced over his shoulder to see if she was right behind him. *You could get hurt really bad, my brother.*

He squeezed Liz's hand and swung her around to face him. "I've been putting hay in the barn all day and…"

She took two steps forward and wrapped her arms around his neck. "I've been working around food all day, but I could use a long, passionate kiss."

Her lips were like water to a man who'd walked thirty miles in the desert without a canteen. He couldn't get enough of them. One long, steaming hot kiss led to another and then a dozen.

"If we don't stop, these lights aren't going to be working when your carnival family gets here, darlin'," he whispered.

"Right now, I'm all for instant gratification," she said.

"Me too, but when your family and friends arrive, I want everything to be perfect," Raylen said.

And I'm not backing away because of something you said, Colleen, he thought.

They'd barely begun putting the lights on a piece when Liz's phone rang. She checked Caller ID and answered it. "Hi, Blaze! You just wakin' up? I've already put in a day at the... Oh my God! Blister, my cat, just ran down a field mouse and she's eating it from the nose, yuck, to the tail and I can hear the bones crunching."

Raylen looked up with a quizzical expression, removed his hat, and hung it on a snowman as he wiped away sweat again.

"It's Blaze," she said as if that was all the explanation he needed. Liz sat down on the ground beside the eight-foot-tall wooden Christmas tree. "Yes, I live in the country and yes, I really have a cat. I've told you that a million times, and yes, she is really eating a mouse right now. So how did your day go?"

Raylen couldn't hear what Blaze said and didn't want to. She could have said that she was working, that her brand-new boyfriend had come over to help her and that she'd talk to him later, but oh, no, she just sat down like she was going to talk for a whole hour and ignored Raylen.

Raylen finished stringing the lights on a section

of the fence and fastening them down with clips so the wind wouldn't blow them halfway to the coast. She was still talking when he went on to the next section and opened the box of lights for that area.

"So you're on the way to Denton for the next-to-last gig of the year. Are you getting excited about sitting still for the winter?" she asked.

Raylen had so looked forward to spending as much time as he could with Liz that afternoon, and he certainly didn't like his few hours being interrupted by her old friend.

You are being a big baby. She misses him like a brother, and if you were in her shoes and Becca called, you wouldn't tell her to hang up and call back later, his conscience scolded him.

Yes, I would. If she cared as much about me as I do her, then she'd want to spend what precious time she could with me. And I wouldn't care if it made Becca mad at me, he argued.

"You are kidding me! Tell me what happened and don't leave out a single detail," Liz said.

She looked up to see Raylen frowning and then he turned around and started toward his truck in long strides.

"Gotta go. Call you later," she told Blaze and snapped the phone shut. "Okay, I'm ready to get back to work," she yelled.

He didn't even turn around, but just opened the truck door like he was leaving.

"What's the matter with you? Are you sick?" She jogged across the lawn.

"I'm sick of being used," he said.

She propped her hands on her hips. "What are you talking about?"

"You just spent time on the phone with your friend," he put air quotes around the last word, "while I kept working on *your* project. I'm going home. You can finish the job, or maybe your precious Blaze can drive over from Denton and help you."

She picked up his hat from the porch railing and threw it at him. "Then go! I don't like or want a jealous man in my life."

The hat sailed over his head and hit the ground in front of him. He picked it up, slapped the dirt and grass from it, and settled it on his head before he turned around and said with gritted teeth, "Do not ever treat my hat like that."

She grabbed his hat off the top of his head, slammed it down on the ground, and stomped on it. "There's what I think of your damned hat."

He was too mad to speak so he picked up the hat, punched it back into shape, crammed it on his head again, and slid in behind the steering wheel. She took a deep breath and watched him go.

"Dammit! I wasn't through with this fight!" she said. The phone rang, and hoping it was Raylen, she answered before she even looked at the ID.

"You pompous bastard. Don't you walk away from me when we are fighting."

"I've been called pompous," Blaze said, "and my parents weren't married so I guess I am legally a bastard. But I didn't walk away from you. I do believe you hung up on me, so I don't think this is about me. I called back to make sure you are all right."

"No, I'm not all right. I'm pissed and I'm going to fix it right now. I'm so mad my cussin' is liable to fry out my cell phone, but finish telling me what you were saying about Aunt Tressa before I go straighten out this mess."

"I'm glad I'm not on the other end of that hissy fit," Blaze said. "Tressa went to the urgent care place before we left our last gig. She got a shot, some antibiotics, and Marva Jo is going to take care of the fortune-telling wagon a few nights. It was the first time since I've been with the carnival that she was too sick to work. She says she's well enough to take over, but Marva Jo says she's done for this year. Your mama is going to be worn out, girl. We need you here to take some of the burden off her, at least for the Bowie job."

"Okay, okay," Liz agreed, but her mind was still on Raylen. "I'll be there every night, but right now I've got to go see what made Raylen so angry."

"Trouble in paradise?" Blaze asked.

"More than just a little, and it involves a lot more than me throwing his hat on the ground," she said.

"Whoa! You threw a cowboy's hat on the ground? Darlin', that's a sin worse than coveting your neighbor's ass as the Good Book says. Did you pick it up and hand it back to him nicely?" Blaze chuckled.

"I did not," Liz said. "I stomped it flat. So I guess I don't get to go to heaven tonight. Call me later." She ended the call.

———————

Raylen felt really stupid by the time he got home. He was glad that Gemma wasn't there so he could wallow in his self-proclaimed pity pool as long as he wanted. It was evident that Liz missed her carnie life. She missed her friend Blaze, a man of her own caliber she probably belonged with more than she did with an old cowboy like Raylen.

He hung his poor, abused hat on the rack beside the door along with his black felt dress hat and his good straw hat, shucked out of his jeans in the living room, threw his dirty shirt over a rocking chair, and kicked his boots off in the hallway. When he reached the bathroom, he was wearing nothing but his socks. He wadded those up in a ball and slung them at the far wall.

"Temperamental women anyway," he muttered as he turned on the shower and waited for the water to warm. *Nobody falls in love with their soul mate when they are kids. I don't care if she could have walked a barbed wire fence instead of a rail one in her bare feet. I've been a fool to think that she was the one for me. Any other woman wouldn't leave me standing cold while they talked to their best friend. How would she feel if I left her sitting there while I talked to Becca for half an hour? I wouldn't do that to her. I like her too much to have a phone conversation with anyone in the world when I could be spending time with her. And I would never, ever throw her favorite hat in the dirt and then step on it.* He fumed as he got into the shower and soaped up his body.

———

Liz didn't even knock on his door but plowed right inside without an invitation, then grabbed the hat she'd stomped on from the rack. She crammed it down on her head, and followed the string of clothes to the bathroom.

She could hear Raylen muttering about something over the noise of the shower before she slung the curtain back and glared at him.

"What the hell was that all about?" she demanded.

"What the hell are you doing in my house and why are you wearing my hat?"

"Having a fight with you, you mule-headed jackass! The door was open, and evidently this hat means more to you than I do, and since it started the fight, I figured it should be here for the next one. Now answer me!"

"Don't you treat me like dirt and then yell at me. I didn't cause this problem, lady. You did when you'd rather talk to your carnie boyfriend than me. Go on back and talk to him some more, and put my hat back on the rack. This steam will get it all out of shape."

"You are a jealous horse's ass. I wasn't talking to a boyfriend. That was Blaze. I told you that he is my friend, and Tressa's been sick. And this hat is so ugly it would take more than a stomping or steam to get it out of shape," she said.

"You are making excuses. And don't talk about my hat like that."

Liz narrowed her eyes. "Don't be hateful! This is your fault, Raylen O'Donnell. Your Irish temper put you in this pot of boiling water."

"You put me in this pot, not my temper," Raylen argued. "You'd rather talk to your carnie friend than me? Well, go on and talk to him. And don't let the door hit you in the ass on the way out."

She glared at him and tried to stay angry, but it didn't work. How could she be mad when he was standing there all wet and naked.

He reached out with both hands, slipped them under her armpits, and picked her up as easily as he would a feather pillow. He quickly removed his hat and pitched it out onto the vanity, set her down, clothes, shoes and all, under the shower spray, and kissed her hard.

One kiss and she forgot all about fighting, his hat, Blaze, or even the fact she'd said she would take over the fortune telling business while the carnival was in Bowie.

She stripped out of her clothes and pulled the shower curtain shut.

Later, when she was dressed in a pair of his pajama pants and a T-shirt that came to her knees, he drew her to the bed, stretched out beside her, and wrapped her up in his arms. "Are you sure you aren't Irish?"

"Maybe a little bit, but Aunt Tressa says that we're predominantly Italian. I might consider converting to Irish, though. Are there classes I have to take?" she teased.

"Not that I know of. We've got time to finish putting up the lights if you want to," he offered.

"I'd rather lie here with you, and," she kissed him on the cheek, "just so you know, I left my cell phone in the truck, but I'm still a little bit mad," she said.

"And my hat still has its feelings hurt," he countered. "Reckon we'd better have some more makin' up?"

Her eyes glittered. "I suppose it might help get rid of some more of our anger."

"I'd rather you danced for me first," he said.

"I will dance for you on Thursday," she said.

"Is that a promise?"

"It is. The carnival will be here, and I'll be dancing on the stage and you can watch," she said.

"You promised you wouldn't dance for another man," he said.

She raised up on one elbow. "I won't be. I'll just doing a plain old belly dance."

"Then I won't be there," he told her.

"I will dance on Thursday, after the carnival, living room for you. Is your hat feelin'

"ma'am," he drawled.

"m glad. It bothers me when your hat is mad at me," she teased.

The house phone beside his bed rang.

He kissed her on the end of the nose. "Sorry, darlin', but I didn't know you were coming over, and I didn't leave my phone in the truck."

He answered it, jumped out of bed, and grabbed a pair of pants from his closet, motioning to her the whole time. When he hung up, he said, "That was Dewar. Glorious Danny Boy has gotten out of the barn again. That horny horse takes off anytime he gets a chance. We've got to get him chased down, or Mama will have a heart attack."

"Call me later?" she said.

"Yes, I will, and you promised to dance for me on the Thursday of the carnival. You won't forget?" he said as he crammed his hat on his head and shoved his feet down in his boots. "Don't forget your wet clothes in the bathroom."

"I'll be thinking about it every minute. Don't you forget," she teased.

"Honey, I won't be able to keep my mind off it," he said as he ran out of the bedroom.

Chapter 12

IT WASN'T LIZ'S FIRST DATE.

But it was her first date after sex three times as a prelude and she was more jittery than she was the first time she danced before a crowd. Going to the Halloween party had been easy; she'd dressed up in one of her costumes. But going to dinner with Raylen and then shopping…with Raylen…for a Christmas tree and then coming home to after-date kisses with Raylen…that was a whole different matter.

She looked at all the clothes in her closet and threw herself back on the bed. She should have made time for a shopping trip to Bowie. She needed something new and exciting to wear that night on her first date with Raylen. Something that would make his eyes go all dreamy.

"I need something in red. No, that's not the exact lyrics of that old song that Mama plays all the time. She said that she was looking for something in red that was cut down to here." She remembered the Lorrie Morgan song from a few years back. The singer had talked about looking for a red dress that would knock her feller's eyes out in the first verse. Then she wanted something in white in the second, something in blue for a new baby boy in the third, and back to something in red in the fourth. Liz hummed the song as she pulled the filmy turquoise dancing outfit off the rack and held it up to her body. She imagined what it would look like without the top of her black lacy panties showing above the encrusted belt and without her black lace bra peeking out above the fancy sequined top.

I'm looking for something in turquoise. If I met him at the door in this and did three minutes of dance, I bet we'd forget about leaving the house and I wouldn't be worrying about our first date, she thought as she looked at her reflection in the mirror.

She hung it back up and picked up her robe. Maybe if she walked away from the closet and stopped fretting, everything would fall into place. She shoved her arms down into the black satin robe and headed toward the living room. Her phone rang and when she saw that it was her uncle, she answered on the second ring. "Hello, we've got those gorgeous ornaments out on the lawn and it's going to be beautiful and why did you put me in an old cactus?"

"Because it's your first year in the house, living in Ringgold, and making a lot of prickly decisions," he said.

"I want a new one every year," she said.

"I figured you'd say that," Haskell said.

"So what have you got in mind for next year?" she asked.

"Next year you get a manger scene with baby Jesus in it and a new puppy and a whole litter of multicolored kittens around the cradle," he said.

"Why?" she asked.

"By then you will know," he said.

"Come on, Uncle Haskell, why would you do that?" She went back to the closet and flipped through the hangers.

"Maybe because I want you to have a new baby by then, and old Hooter could use a new puppy if you are going to stay there, and there's always kittens in the spring," Haskell answered.

She pulled a bright red sweater from the closet. "It would take more than a miracle for all that to happen in one year." Her thoughts went to the O'Donnell decree that the children had to marry in the order in which they were born.

"Who said the days of miracles were over?" Haskell asked.

She closed her eyes tightly and made a wish that Haskell was right.

"I called to tell you to send me a picture when you get it all done. Now I've talked enough. Poppa is coming over for supper," he said.

"I love you, Uncle Haskell," she said.

"I've always loved you, Liz."

The screen went dark, and she put the sweater back in the closet, went to the living room, and flipped the switch to turn on her Christmas display. An adage that she'd heard for years came to mind. It said that when a person looks back on their life, it wouldn't be what they did that they would regret but what they didn't do. If she didn't get her butt into jeans and her feet into boots or shoes, she wouldn't be going on a real date with Raylen, and in twenty years she'd regret that decision.

She went back to the closet, pulled out a pair of skinny jeans, a black shirt with rhinestone buttons and long, fitted lace sleeves ending in a wide ruffle at the wrist, and a pair of black spike heels. When Raylen knocked on the door, she'd just finished running a brush through her hair one final time.

———————

Raylen didn't want to leave the dreams of Liz dancing in a field of clover the next morning when he awoke. In the dream, he was sprawled out on a quilt and she danced for him in that orange costume. The bells on her ankle bracelets jingled in his ears, and her body moved to music that they shared in their minds.

Time was going so slow that morning while he plowed a field that he started talking to himself.

"I think I'm falling in love, and it's miserable,"

he said as he drove in monotonous laps around the pasture.

He got through the noon meal at his grand-mother's house, but he was so distracted that Grandma asked him if he was coming down with the flu.

Sitting in a saddle usually made him happy, but that day he kept visualizing Liz riding a horse in her costume. Finally, he traded places with Dewar and offered to muck out stalls. By the time the day ended and he got to her front door, he was ready to jump right into bed. But that's not the way a real date started, so he knocked on the door and waited…impatiently.

Raylen didn't even look at what she was wearing until after he'd cupped her cheeks in his hands and planted a sexy kiss right on her lips. Then he laced his fingers in her hands and stepped back to scan her from toes to eyes.

"Beautiful doesn't begin to describe you, Liz. Your perfume makes me think of an exotic woman in a sexy orange outfit doing a belly dance. And you taste like something the angels brewed up," he said.

"You are a romantic, Raylen O'Donnell. And honey, looking at you makes my heart do double time," she said.

He motioned toward the door and said, "Darlin', we'd better get out of here soon or else we're going to wind up in bed and there'll be no Christmas tree when your mama arrives, but thank you, my Madam Dammybammy, for saying that I affect you like that," he said.

———————

She laughed. "Drabami."

"I'm just an old country cowboy who doesn't understand your carnival language," he said with a grin. "Are we ready to go? I'm starving. Haven't had anything since lunch and I've been looking forward to this date all day."

"I'm ready. Do I need a jacket?" she asked.

"Not now, but you will by the time we get home. Weather says there's a cold front on the way. Won't drop us down to freezing, but the wind is fixin' to be out of the north," he said.

She picked up her black leather jacket and purse. He kept her hand tucked into his all the way out to his truck.

"Do you like Italian food?" He opened the door for her.

"Love it." She buckled her seat belt.

"Good. It was a toss-up between the Texas Roadhouse for steaks or the Olive Garden for Italian," he said and then jogged around the truck.

"I've never eaten at the Olive Garden but I love Italian. Blaze makes amazing lasagna," she said when he was buckled in and driving down the lane.

"I can't wait for you to meet Blaze. You are going to like him. He's a lot like Ace."

She didn't miss his jaws clenching and unclenching or his grip on the steering wheel, or even the way his back went suddenly ramrod straight. It might not be the best time to bring up Blaze's name, but she hadn't done it intentionally. His name had just popped out when she thought about his cooking. And anyway, she wasn't going to walk on eggshells...not even for Raylen.

"Ace?" Raylen asked. "Why would he remind you of Ace?"

"Blaze is about Ace's size, and his passion is flirting. He's got a woman in every place we stop, and if he doesn't have one, there's a dozen waiting in line for a chance at him." She paused and glanced over at Raylen, who seemed to be relaxing. "I could never fall for a man like that. Every woman I ran into in Walmart or the Dairy Queen might be one of his conquests."

Raylen chuckled at first, then it turned into a full-fledged laugh that erased all the tension in the truck.

"One time Blaze and I both had one too many beers and wound up kissing. I don't know what the women see in him. I felt like I'd just kissed my brother and he actually wiped my kiss from his lips with the back of his hand. Said he felt like he'd kissed a sister," Liz told him. "Did you ever kiss anyone that felt like that?"

"Becca," he answered with a nod. "When we were in eighth grade, we were at a Valentine's party and got locked in a closet together after a game of spin the bottle. I don't know if I kissed her or if she kissed me, but it was like kissing a sister. I never did kiss her again."

A shot of jealousy flashed through Liz's heart. Why did he have to bring up Becca's name?

You just told him about kissing Blaze, so you have no right to be angry. Her aunt's voice was back in her head.

She clamped her mouth shut and counted to ten. It didn't work.

She tried it again, and had cooled down enough to point out the window and change the subject. "Look at those wire reindeer. I want some of those. Where can you buy them? Oh, look, there's a horse pulling a carriage made out of that stuff, too. They are open and airy, so they'd look good in among all the wood things."

"You can buy those things at Hobby Lobby or sometimes at Big Lots or in the Walmart garden center," he said. "I thought we'd start at Hobby Lobby looking for a tree since you decided on an artificial one, so you can check there first."

"I want a real one," she said, "but Uncle Haskell reminded me that they dry out even between Thanksgiving and Christmas, and they'd never stay fresh for as long as I intend to have it up and decorated. Do you think they'll have one that doesn't look perfect? I want it to look real even if it's not."

"They'll have dozens. We can always lop off a limb or two to make it look real," he teased.

She slapped him playfully on the shoulder. "Don't tease me. This is important."

"Why is it so important to you, Liz?" he asked. "I love Christmas, but you go beyond that."

She hesitated for a moment and then decided to be truthful. "Mama asked me every year what I wanted for Christmas, and I told her that I wanted a house without wheels. When I was a teenager, I added one more thing to my list and that was a sexy cowboy. So, this year I've got my house with no wheels and I want it to be special."

"And the cowboy?" Raylen turned to face her.

She met his gaze and didn't blink. "The jury is still out on that one, and besides, it's not Christmas until December 25th. I might have a cowboy by then."

"After Thanksgiving, Santa Claus will be at the mall. You might have to sit on his lap and ask for a cowboy," Raylen joked.

"Been doin' that every year since I was four. Uncle Haskell says it takes a long time to make a house with no wheels and a cowboy. They aren't like Barbie dolls or skateboards. Oh, look at those." She pointed while they were stopped at a red light in Henrietta. She motioned out the side window to a display of wooden picnic benches, chairs, and swings. "I want a swing in my yard like that so I can string lights around it at Christmas."

Raylen pulled into the driveway and braked.

"What are you doing?" Liz asked.

"Let's look at them," he said. "Can't get one tonight because we'll have your tree and your wire reindeer in the truck so we won't have room, but we can find out if he's here all the time or if he's ever over in Bowie." He was out of the truck and had her door open before she could blink.

"Evenin', kids. What can I talk you into buyin'? Missus interested in a picnic table? I'll make you a great deal. Picnickin' season is over and I'm tryin' to get rid of the rest of my stock." The man had two days' worth of white whiskers on his round face, a bald head, and bright blue eyes.

"How long you goin' to be set up in Henrietta?" Raylen asked.

"I live up the road a piece. I'll be here until Thanksgiving if there's anything left to sell. That's so I'll be out of Mama's hair while she fixes up the holiday dinner. Kids are all comin' home this year. Got six and it'll be a zoo at our house with them and all the grandkids," he said.

Raylen ran a hand over the swing. It was sturdy and well-built. "What are you askin' for it?"

"Summer price is three hundred, but it's the last one, so I've got it down to two hundred. I'd throw in one of them Adirondack chairs for that price too, just to get rid of the stock. You want one of them picnic tables for your backyard too? More you buy the better the price. I knock twenty-five off each big piece when you buy two or more," the man said. "I know you. You're one of Cash's boys, ain't you? He bought a set of them rockers over there for Maddie's Christmas. I'm haulin' them out to hide in his barn on Monday while she's over at the beauty shop. Want me to haul any of this stuff for you?"

"I'm his third son, Raylen. Guess I won't be needin' anything right now since Daddy already bought the rockers," he said.

"How 'bout you, missus?" the man asked.

"Not tonight. Maybe I'll be back in a couple of days. I really do like that swing," Liz said.

"Well, darlin', you and the husband, there, y'all have a seat in it for a few minutes. You'll really want it when you see how good it sits," he said.

Liz smiled. "I better not or Raylen will throw me out beside the road for griping all the way to Wichita Falls about how much I want it."

Raylen steered Liz toward the pickup. "Thank you so much for the generous offer, but we've got to be going tonight. We might stop back sometime."

"That is some sturdy furniture. I really, really like that swing," Liz said.

Raylen settled Liz into the truck and pretended to fish in his pocket. "I left my keys on the table over there. Laid them down to run my hand over the wood. Be right back."

The old fellow looked up and grinned. "Which pieces you want me to put in the barn, son?"

"The picnic table, the swing, and two of those chairs."

"I'll just charge you for the table and the swing. Throw them two chairs in like I said I would. Go on now and you can pay me when I deliver them on Tuesday. I knowed you'd come back. She can swing the new babies in that swing and your grandbabies will eat off that table. I don't do no shabby work," he said.

"Thank you." Raylen whistled all the way back to the truck.

When he was back in the truck, Liz glanced over at him and said, "That poor old fellow must get lonely. He sure likes to talk."

"Reminds me of my grandpa. What does your grandpa look like?" Raylen asked.

"He's six feet tall and thin as a rail. Totally unlike Uncle Haskell who took after Granny. She was short and round. Pictures tell a different story about her though. When she and my grandpa got married, she was built like a movie star of the forties. She had dark, wavy hair and this big, pretty smile. You could tell by the way he looked at her that Poppa always saw her as that gorgeous woman that he was lucky to get," Liz answered.

"Were they always carnival folks?" Raylen asked.

She nodded. "My great-grandparents bought the carnival in the thirties. It was cheap entertainment, and folks needed that. Then they retired and gave it to Poppa about the time he and Granny got married. You know the rest. Haskell decided he didn't want that kind of life but Mama and Aunt Tressa thrive on it."

She pointed out a western furniture store between Jolly and Wichita Falls. "I want to go there sometime. It's closed now, but when I get ready to redo the house, I'd like to look at their stock."

"What have you got in mind for the house?" Raylen asked.

"Comfortable western or maybe early attic," she said.

He raised an eyebrow.

"Mama and I lived in a trailer my whole life. We don't use travel trailers or RVs because we'd have to take it into town every time we had to make a grocery or laundry run. We use fifth wheelers that hook into our pickup. I've never had space like I've got in my new house, and I love it. Early attic is junk you'd find in estate sales. We never got to go to things like that or have anything that wasn't necessary. So, I might decorate with early attic just so I can buy junk," she said.

"Then next spring, you and Grandma can hit the estate sales. She loves to go, and Grandpa hates them," Raylen said.

"That would be great," she said. "Is that the Olive Garden we're going to? There's a mall and a Ross store and a Hobby Lobby. I'm in love."

The waitress seated them in a corner booth right away, took their drink order, and handed them menus. While they made their selections, she brought Raylen a beer and Liz a Diet Coke.

"I'll have the chicken fettuccine," Liz said.

"And I'll have spaghetti with meatballs," Raylen said.

"I'll be right back with your salad and bread. Hey, aren't you Raylen O'Donnell? I've seen you in here with Ace. Where is that cowboy? Haven't seen him in months. He used to come in once a week," the waitress said.

"Been busy. Lost his grandpa and inherited a ranch to run. Doesn't stray as far from home as he used to," Raylen said.

"Well, you tell him Katrina said hello." She hurried off to the kitchen with their order. Raylen and Liz burst out laughing.

So far, other than having to cool her jealousy by counting, the date had been wonderful. Conversation had been good. Stopping on a whim to look at outdoor furniture had been fun. The kiss that started off the evening had been awesome.

Raylen reached across the table and covered her hands with his. "Did I tell you that you look pretty tonight?"

"Yes, sir, you surely did. I think the words were beautiful, exotic, and something to do with heavenly," she answered.

"Did I tell you that your eyes fascinate me? That I thought of them all the time after that year when you were leaning on the fence watching me ride?" he asked.

She smiled and her dark eyes glittered. "No, but I sure like that talk so you can keep right on with it."

"Well, well, well, lookee who's out on the town tonight," a familiar voice said right behind Liz.

Liz turned slowly, hoping she'd been wrong about hearing Becca, but she wasn't.

"Hello, Becca," she said.

God hated her! Or maybe it was the devil messing with her life. Whichever one it was, she wished they'd go on back to passing down judgment or stokin' up Hell's furnace and forget all about Liz Hanson.

Becca slid into the booth with Raylen, plastering her side against his. "I bet I can tell you what Raylen ordered. He's a plain old spaghetti and meatballs man. Never does try anything new. That's his life. He'll never go out on a limb and put something new in his life."

Liz didn't need to stay up all night reading *Catfights for Dummies* to figure out Becca's underlying message. She was telling her that in the end Raylen would settle down with a woman from that area that he'd known his whole life, that he didn't have the nerve to fall for someone new.

Becca patted him on the arm. "Steady old reliable Raylen. Course, he'll be just the ticket for some woman. She can trust him and never fear that he'll cheat on her. Might bore her to death, but he wouldn't be unfaithful."

"I'd hate to have you for an enemy," Liz said.

Becca's smile faded. Her back straightened ramrod stiff and she toyed with her bracelet as she shot daggers across the table. "Why'd you say that?"

"Because all you've done is put Raylen down since you sat down. If you're his lifetime friend and you do that, God only knows what you'd do if you were his enemy," Liz said.

Raylen squeezed Liz's hands.

"You talk big for someone your size," Becca said.

"I just tell the truth. Size ain't got a lot to do with it." A tall, lanky cowboy stopped by their booth and held out his hand to Becca. "They've got a table for us now. Hello, Raylen. Hi, Liz. Nice to see you."

Raylen nodded. "Brennan."

"Y'all have a nice evenin'. We're off to the movies soon as we get something to eat," Brennan said.

"Have fun," Liz said.

When they were seated across the room, Raylen said, "That was interesting. Never had a woman take up for me before."

"Is she always that bitchy?" Liz asked.

"No, she's really not. She's usually a lot of fun," Raylen said.

"Then she just plain don't like me. How is that going to affect your relationship with her since y'all are besties?" Liz withdrew her hands and held them in her lap.

Raylen shrugged. "Don't take it personal. She doesn't like anyone I go out with. And she really hates Jasmine. She thinks Ace has a thing for Jasmine because he's always flirting with her, and Becca and Ace were an item back in high school."

"That was years ago, and besides, I'm there most of the time when Ace comes in. He and Jasmine are the best friends ever." She caught herself before she said, "Like me and Blaze."

Chapter 13

THE HOBBY LOBBY STORE BUZZED WITH EXCITEMENT. Anything that had to do with Halloween was seventy-five percent off, and Thanksgiving items were displayed on two long aisles. But Christmas was what took Liz's eye. Several aisles displayed thousands of bright, sparkly ornaments that hung from the floor to above Raylen's head. Pretty paper, shiny ribbons, glittery garland, and beautiful tree toppers were on another aisle, and Liz could have all she wanted of everything that year. In years past, Marva Jo had set up a two-foot tree on the kitchen table and scattered the presents around it. They'd always put lights on the trees outside Poppa's trailer, and sometimes he even had a small tree, but nothing that went from floor to ceiling. She'd always wanted to buy lots of pretty decorations and that night she had the basket full before she and Raylen even turned into the Christmas tree aisle.

"From the look in those pretty eyes, maybe we should've brought a horse trailer to get all your purchases back to Ringgold," Raylen said.

She pointed at the biggest tree on display. "Look at that big one. Will it fit in the truck?"

He hugged her tightly to his side. "They come dismantled and in a box, so the answer is yes, however you might want to reconsider. It says right here this tree is ten feet tall. It's eight feet from your floor to your ceiling. We'll have to cut at least two or three feet out of the top of that one," he said.

She cocked her head to one side. "You are saying I should buy a six-foot tree in order to get the topper on it?"

He brushed a sweet kiss across her lips. "That's right, but look at all the different six-footers. There's the skinny one that doesn't take up much room, and there's a fat one that'll cover a quarter of your living room." He pointed as he spoke.

Liz pushed her cart toward the six-footers, folded her arms, and studied each one. "I want the fat one. I don't care how much room it takes up. It looks like one we'd really cut down out in the woods. And I want some of that pine spray stuff to go on it so it will smell real. And..." She hesitated.

"And what?" Raylen asked.

"Can we cut a real tree down tomorrow and put it up in the barn? That's where we'll have our carnie dinner on Wednesday night. And I'd like to have a tree in the corner and presents for everyone who is there, and we could put up a cedar in the barn because it wouldn't have to last but a few days, and if anyone is allergic we could open the big doors and…"

Raylen drew her close to his side. "We'll go cut down a tree tomorrow and decorate one in the barn and one in the house."

She grabbed his cheeks with her hands and rolled up on her toes. The kiss was supposed to be quick, and no one was supposed to see it, but it lingered and grew more passionate by the second.

"Wow!" she said when she took a step back.

"Yep," he said.

"Did that really happen? Did anyone see us?" She blushed.

"I believe it did happen, and I don't think anyone was around, but if they did I bet they saw the smoke risin' off the fire we created. Do you picture that tree with a star or an angel on top?"

She smiled. "I know this cowboy with a cute butt that I might get to help me put a big star right on top of it. A star on the one in the house and an angel with fluffy wings on the one in the barn."

"Oh, really?" Raylen tilted his head to one side.

She looped her arm through his. "You reckon you are strong enough to chop down a cedar tree?"

"Just how cute is my butt?"

Liz hugged up close to him and whispered, "Mighty fine when it's soakin' wet in the shower and really fine the way it fills out a pair of tight-fittin' Wranglers."

Raylen planted a kiss on the top of her head. "If Madam Dallydinger will keep up that kind of talk, this cowboy just might even help her get the lights on her house tomorrow while she hangs half a gazillion ornaments on her two trees, and Sunday we can chop down a cedar tree, and Thursday you are going to dance for me again, remember?"

"Madam Drabami won't be hanging balls on the tree. She'd rather be outside watching her handsome cowboy's butt as he puts up lights. Now let's go find some wrapping paper. I've got dozens and dozens of boxes of candy and cans of popcorn to buy and wrap. And yes, I'm going to dance for you on Thursday night. I'm looking forward to it, darlin'."

"Candy? You were serious?" he asked.

"Darlin', if you can't eat it, wear it out, or use it up in a few weeks, you don't give it to a carnie. They have no place to put it," she explained as she led the way to the wrapping paper and bows. "Is my cowboy going to help me wrap presents too? And after the big carnie Christmas party, we'll go shopping again so I can buy presents for Jasmine and Gemma and your mama and even Ellen and Nellie. I'm so excited about Christmas that I could dance—"

"Oh, no, not here!" he said quickly.

She giggled and then said, "I was going to say dance a jig, not a belly dance."

"Okay, but don't expect me to help with wrapping. I'm all thumbs when it comes to wrapping, and tape comes to life and attacks me every time I get around the stuff."

"Then I guess I'd better buy you those soft little black velvet handcuffs instead of duct tape for Christmas," she teased.

"I'd rather use that fancy scarf thing you dance with," he whispered so close that the warmth of his breath kissed that soft spot right under her ear.

She shivered. "You are cheating."

"All's fair in love and war, Madam."

Chapter 14

Liz carried sacks filled with boxes of assorted chocolates and cookies along with tins of popcorn painted with Christmas scenes into the house. Raylen unloaded the Christmas tree into the living room and put all the new wire ornaments on the porch until he ran out of room and had to set up the rest on the lawn. Then he helped Liz tote in the rest of the sacks.

When they finished, the two empty bedrooms were filled with sacks, wrapping paper, tape, gift bags, ribbons, candy, and popcorn. She covered a yawn with her hand as she made her way back outside and noticed that it was two thirty in the morning. It had been a fantastic first date. She loved the food and atmosphere at Olive Garden and couldn't wait to tell Blaze about it. Raylen had been so patient in Walmart while she wiped the shelves free of boxes of chocolates and tins of butter cookies and popcorn that he deserved a big gold medal on a velvet Christmas ribbon.

"All done!" He made it to the recliner where he plopped down.

"Thank you," she said.

"You are very welcome. Shall we talk about those handcuffs now?"

She sat down in his lap and yawned again. "Rain check, please. I'm wiped plumb out."

He pulled her closer and kissed her forehead. "Thank God! I'm too tired to move."

She drew her knees up and snuggled down into his chest. "Pop up the footrest and push back so we can rest."

I wonder what sex in a recliner would be like. Oh, hush, I'm so tired a bout of hot sex would kill me dead. And besides, I think Raylen is already dozing.

She meant to close her eyes for only a minute. Just rest them long enough to garner enough energy to kiss Raylen good night. All good dates ended with a hot and heavy kiss that would hold a promise that he would call again. At least they did in the movies. When she opened her eyes, sunlight was streaming in the window and Gemma was standing beside the recliner with her hands on her hips and a grin as big as Dallas on her face.

"Good morning," Liz said weakly.

"Looks like it!" Gemma smiled.

Raylen opened his eyes slowly. "Guess we fell asleep. What are you doing here?"

"Lookin' for you," Gemma said.

"Why?" Raylen asked.

"Because you didn't come home last night

and there wasn't a note or a voicemail message. Remember what we agreed? We are adults and we don't have to answer to each other for our time, but if we aren't coming home then leave a message so the other one doesn't worry," she said. "So this is who you had a date with?"

"Yep," Raylen said.

"A date or dating?" Gemma asked.

"I promised to leave a message. For not doing that, I'm sorry. The rest is my business," Raylen said.

"I don't like it," Gemma said.

"Get over it," Raylen told her.

"Why?" Liz looked at Gemma.

"Because it complicates *our* friendship, Liz. You can't tell me details of your dates since you were out with my brother," Gemma answered.

Liz grinned but she didn't move from Raylen's lap. "You want details? We went to the Olive Garden, and I had fettuccine and Raylen had spaghetti, and Becca showed up and she doesn't like me, but that's okay, I understand, because Raylen doesn't like Blaze either and I'm not sure Blaze is going to like Raylen." Liz stopped and caught her breath. "And then we shopped at Hobby Lobby, where I bought that tree over there in the box. And then we went to Walmart, where I bought a truck load of presents. Are you any good at wrapping? If so would you help me get them done later today?

And then we came home and unloaded it all and fell asleep. Did I leave anything out, Raylen?"

"I kissed you in Hobby Lobby. I think if we kissed in Hobby Lobby, it's dating, not a date, isn't it?" he asked.

Liz's expression went dead serious. "There's a sign on the Hobby Lobby door right under the one with the hours the store is open. It's written in that little bitty print that no one hardly ever reads, but I did before we went in."

Gemma butted in, "What are you talking about?"

Liz held up a palm. "Let me finish. The print says anyone not dating will be charged with a misdemeanor and a hundred dollar fine if they are caught kissing in Hobby Lobby. But since Raylen didn't see the sign, maybe it isn't a law. I'm not sure if both parties have to see it or not."

"Okay, Gemma, would you please go out in the barn, get the ladder, crawl up on the roof of the house, and yell that I'm dating Liz. That way all the other cowboys in Montague County can crawl off behind a mesquite tree and lick their wounds," Raylen said.

"You two are nuts!" Gemma said. "I don't think you are dating at all. You heard me coming and you staged this just to tease me, didn't you? I'm going home to get ready for church. I'll be back to help you wrap presents after Sunday dinner, Liz. But just to pay you back, I intend to tell the whole family that you two are an item, and I may tell Becca too, since she never misses Sunday morning services."

"Becca would be there if she had to crawl on her knees through six feet of snow and all she had to wear was a little black lace teddy. She has to pray for a crop failure," Liz said.

Raylen leaned back and drew his eyebrows down. "Crop failure?"

"Standard practice for those who sow wild oats on Friday and Saturday nights. They go to church on Sunday and pray for a crop failure," Liz answered.

Gemma sat down on the sofa. "I didn't know I could do that."

"Now you know, so go do some serious praying. And if you would tell Becca, it will save me a phone call," Raylen said.

"If I give you Blaze's number, will you call him? But not until after church. He'll be breaking at least one heart this morning before he gets busy tearing down the equipment to move it to Bowie," Liz said.

Gemma shook her head. "You two can do your own announcing, but I am telling the family at dinner unless y'all beat me to it. So if this is a joke you'd better tell me now before I get to the door, or you're going to have some big explaining to do."

"Have fun. We're going to be out cutting down a tree for the barn," Raylen said.

Gemma stood up and headed for the door. "On

that note, I'm leaving. I don't even want to know why you are putting a tree in the barn."

When she was gone, Raylen hugged Liz even tighter. "Good morning, beautiful girlfriend."

Liz wiggled down into his embrace. "I like the way that sounds."

"So do I, but darlin', it's gettin' to the imperative stage that I get to the bathroom," he said.

"The honeymoon is over when the guy is comfortable enough to announce that he has a full bladder," she said.

She was surprised that she didn't feel like a pretzel after sleeping for hours in his arms with her knees all drawn up. Raylen pushed the footrest down and made his way down the hallway. When he returned, she was opening the Christmas tree box with a kitchen knife.

"Hey, I'll do that later. Right now, I'm going home, get a quick shower, and change into work clothes so we can go hunt down the best real tree in the county," he said.

"You could shower here," she said.

He wrapped his arms around her and kissed her hard, his lips lingering on hers for so long that she thought for sure they were headed for another bout of shower sex.

"If I shower here, there will be no tree because we'll spend the day in bed," he said softly. "And there'll be no lights on the house or wooden Santa

Claus on the roof, or tree in the barn. Your choice, new girlfriend."

"That's a tough decision. How about when it's all done?" she asked.

"Be back in half an hour with an ax."

"I'll be ready. The scarf will be tied to my bed-post for afterwards," she teased.

"Girl, you are evil," he said.

"Just don't let Becca change your mind when you call her," she told him.

He pulled her back into his arms and kissed her until her knees went weak again. "When you call Playboy Blaze, you tell him how you feel right now this minute."

———

Liz hadn't been prepared for so many cedar trees. She'd thought it would be like the Hobby Lobby store. A couple of dozen trees to choose from, and she'd stand back, eye them all at once, and pick out the one she wanted. But they'd traipsed through wooded areas with acres of mesquite and a cedar tree tossed in every few hundred yards, and then to an area that had dozens and dozens of trees.

Finally, she found one that appealed to her. She walked around the enormous tree and looked it up and down. With the decorations in the tack room and what she'd bought in her spare bedroom, she had plenty to decorate that very one plus the new one in the house.

"You'd have to get the ladder out to put the topper on it, but then I could see your sexy butt even better," she said.

"Is my butt cute enough for that job?" he asked.

"I'm not sure. Maybe you better bare it and let me make sure," she answered.

"Not in this cold wind, but later we'll talk about that idea. Is this the one?" he asked.

"Yes, it is. It's the one I want." She looked up and saw a tiny room on stilts. "What is that?"

"That is Rye's deer blind," he said.

"A what?" She frowned.

"It's what Rye sits in and waits for a deer to come by so he can shoot it. See the slits in the side there? That's where you slip the rifle out," he explained as he slung the tote bag from his back and removed a chain saw.

"I thought you were bringing an ax," she said.

"This will do the job faster." He revved it up and laid the blade next to the base of the tree.

"How do we get this thing back to the truck?" she yelled above the noise.

"Drag it, darlin'," he said and then removed a few lower limbs.

She meandered over to the deer blind. It didn't seem fair to her for hunters to hide up in a place like that, and then shoot the deer when it wasn't looking. A true hunter should have to chase it and give it a fighting chance. She climbed the ladder to the landing and slung open the door. It was empty except for a folding chair in one corner with what looked like a sleeping bag thrown over it.

Raylen watched the cedar tumble to its side and hoped he hadn't broken any branches. Even if he dreaded meeting Blaze and her carnie family, he wanted everything to be perfect for their visit to Liz's house.

"Okay, now it's time to take it home," he said as he put the chain saw back in the case and looked around. "Liz?" he yelled.

"Up here in the tree house," she said. "Come on up here. You can see all the way to the truck."

He made his way up the ladder and inside where she was staring out the small rectangular window.

"Why didn't you bring me up here to find the tree?" she asked. "I can see hundreds of them from here."

He wrapped his arms around her waist and snuggled up against her back. "Because your perspective is all off. How big does that one I just cut down look from this angle?"

"About three feet." She turned quickly and their lips met in a clash of passion. "I've wanted to do that the whole time we've been in the woods. Your lips are cold but they make my insides feel all bubbling hot."

"Same here. We should warm up our lips before we go home to work on Christmas stuff," he said.

A niggling thought about what Aunt Tressa had said about taking things slow played in the back of Liz's mind. Sure, he'd said they were dating, and he'd called her his girlfriend, but everything about their relationship was a whirlwind.

I don't want to slow down, she thought.

"This is our first make-out session since we are dating," he said.

She pulled his face over to hers for another series of kisses. "Can we come out here every day?"

"Why?" he asked.

"You can't get away from me, and nobody bothers us," she answered.

"Darlin', I see heaven in your eyes," Raylen said. "I see angels with fiddles and..."

"Angels have harps, not fiddles," she told him.

"Not in your eyes. They have fiddles. That's what makes the devil red. Because he's so mad that he can't have those fiddles," Raylen teased.

"You see that in my eyes?" She kissed him on the chin.

"Yes, I do," he answered.

"Whew! You should be a fortune-teller. Do you say that to all the girls?" She frowned.

"No, darlin'. Just the ones who entice me up to a deer blind," he said.

Liz leaned back and locked gazes with him. "And how many would that be?"

"One so far," he teased.

She giggled and buried her face in his shoulder. "We should go home, but it's so peaceful up here."

He covered his yawn with a hand. "We've got more than six hours' worth of work to do on these trees and the house. Aren't they coming to Bowie tomorrow?"

"Yes, but not to my house until next Monday. I wasn't thinkin' about a tree, but a nice long nap all wrapped up in this bag with you," she teased.

"Your choice, darlin'. Tree and house, or nap," Raylen said.

"Kiss me one more time and we'll start home," she whispered.

Chapter 15

THE TREE WAS TOO BIG FOR THE HOLDER THEY found in the tack room, so Raylen nailed a cross bar on the bottom, stuck the whole thing down in a galvanized wash tub, and filled it half full of water.

"That should keep it from drying out for a week," he said.

Liz clapped her hands and hugged him right in front of Ace, Jasmine, Gemma, and Dewar. "It's beautiful. I'll wrap the bottom with an old quilt to cover the wash tub and then use a couple more quilts for the tree skirt. You are a genius."

"Whoa! You'll swell up his ego until the rest of us plain old cowboys won't be able to endure his struttin' around like a bantam rooster," Ace said.

Jasmine slapped the air in front of his face. "Honey, there ain't an ego in Montague County as big as yours. And you strut in your sleep, so don't you be callin' the pot black. Now you guys go get a couple of ladders. You can put the lights on the top and us girls will take care of the bottom half. When we get this one decorated, we'll go in the house and do that one, then you fellers can take care of the outside lights while we wrap presents."

Ace poked her on the arm. "I'm going to work up an appetite."

Jasmine gave him a half smile. "I figured you'd say that, so I'm prepared. We'll all go to the café and grill some burgers and make some fries after everything is done. I've got half a chocolate cake and two pecan pies left over from yesterday."

"For pecan pie I will string lights from here to the North Pole," Ace said.

Liz led the way to the tack room. The women each picked up one box and the guys stacked up two each. Dewar and Ace crawled up on ladders and worked together, clipping the strands of lights to the tree as Raylen fed the wires up to them. Jasmine started at the bottom of the tree, Liz began her strands a foot up from Jasmine, and Gemma started in the middle.

When they'd finished that job, Dewar said, "While we are up here, we might as well put the garland on. Raylen, you can keep it coming just like you did the lights."

"And they accused me of being too organized," Raylen said.

"You got a girlfriend now. That erases all the sane thoughts from your head so me and Dewar get to be kings of organization," Ace said.

Jasmine started around the bottom of the tree

with wide gold garland. "I'm damn sure glad dating doesn't affect women like that."

"Hey, now," Raylen said.

"I still can't believe you two are an item," Gemma said. "Are you sure y'all ain't just putting on a show to tease us?"

"I told Becca," Raylen said.

"Well, it is set in stone now," Ace said.

"And?" Jasmine asked.

"She thinks I'm crazy," Raylen answered honestly.

"I can only imagine how mad she is," Gemma said. "She was saving you for the last hurrah, Raylen. When she got ready to buy that wedding dress, she was going to land in your arms."

"Now she'll have to land in Dewar's or Ace's," Raylen said.

"Hey, what'd we do to make you mad?" Ace asked.

"Not me. Brennan can have her," Dewar said.

Gemma blushed. "Brennan?"

"That's who Raylen said she was with last night," Ace said.

Gemma clamped her jaw tightly shut and kept looping gold tinsel over the cedar limbs. Liz could tell that she was about to explode.

"Okay, Gemma, what's this about Brennan?" Liz asked.

"Nothing!" Gemma snapped.

Jasmine shook her head at Liz.

"Nope, I'm not going to ignore it," Liz declared. "Gemma, what's wrong?"

"This is so Becca. She's known for years that I had a thing for Brennan and that we had started going out. She hates me and sabotages every hint of a relationship I might get into," Gemma answered.

Liz finished her garland and went back for another length. "You ever think that maybe he asked her out and she's showing you that he's not the one for you? Maybe she is your friend."

Raylen's ears were hearing things! Surely Liz hadn't just taken up for Becca. If Liz knew about the fit Becca threw when Raylen called her that morning before he told everyone that he and Liz were officially dating, she would be stringing the woman up by the thumbs. She wouldn't be taking up for her by any means.

"If it wasn't her going out with him, then it could be someone else. I didn't see a cowboy from this area in your cards when I read them, so Brennan isn't the one, honey," Liz said.

Gemma nodded but her eyes were still angry. "I hope she winds up with him. It would serve him right. I'm not high maintenance like her."

"You want to repeat that business about not being high maintenance?" Dewar asked.

She pointed up at him. "You hush or I'll shake you off that ladder. Liz, would you tell me again what you saw in my cards while I get some more garland out of the box?"

"I saw a blond cowboy. Tall, blond, and sexy. And he adored you." She didn't tell Gemma that the cowboy could very well be Ace because she couldn't see his face at all in her vision and the cards hadn't given her an exact description.

Gemma took out some garland and began to drape it around the tree limbs. "I think card reading is a bunch of hocus-pocus, but I need something to hang on to. By next Christmas, right?"

"In my vision, I definitely saw a Christmas tree," Liz said.

Gemma sing-songed. "Well, you are out of luck, Brennan. Noel, noel, noel!"

"Deck the halls with lots of cow patties," Jasmine chimed in.

"Rockin' around the Christmas tree, and it ain't with you." Liz added a line.

They all three cracked up in giggles and looped their arms together and went back to the tack room to bring in boxes of ornaments.

When they brought the boxes back, Gemma shook her finger at Raylen. "Don't be scratchin' your heads and measuring things. Shove a whole box up to Dewar and Ace. They can balance a box at a time on the ladder tops and get the top part done. You can help us work on the part we still can't reach."

In thirty minutes, the tree was covered with ornaments, and Liz brought out the angel for the top. It reminded her of what her mother had said about not letting anyone cut off her wings.

This is to prove that I can have wings and roots both. Gemma does, and Jasmine does, so I can too, she thought.

Liz carefully climbed the ladder to the top and then Raylen handed up the porcelain angel with real feather wings. She settled it on the branches, and then slowly descended to Raylen's waiting arms. He held her tightly and then handed her a box of silver icicles.

"And now for the finishing touch." Liz handed everyone a fistful of icicles. "Y'all help me get these all draped everywhere, and then we'll light it up."

When the tree was all aglitter with silver icicles, Raylen plugged in the lights and Liz gasped. It was more beautiful than any tree she'd ever seen in the windows of real houses or even in the malls she'd visited on her travels from one place to the other.

"Like it?" Raylen wrapped his arms around her waist and she leaned back into his chest.

"Love it. I hope the one in the house is half as pretty," she said.

"Okay, one down," Jasmine said. "One to go. Load up the rest of the boxes and let's go to the house."

"I'm glad we did this together," Liz told Raylen. "I will always remember this night."

"Me, too," he whispered.

Ace poked Jasmine on the arm. "You sure are bossy."

Jasmine laid a hand on his shoulder. "Think pecan pie when we are all done."

The tree in the house didn't take nearly as long because they followed the same routine. When Liz flipped the switch on the electrical cord, she was just as amazed as she had been with the one in the barn.

"Please don't tell me that you want one in the kitchen now," Raylen said with a laugh.

"I was thinking just a tiny one, and then one for the bathroom, and my bedroom," Liz teased.

"Think about all the work when you have to take all this down and pack it away," Gemma reminded her.

"Oh!" Liz gasped. "Y'all will come and help me, right?"

"Depends on if Jasmine is going to make pie for us to have afterwards," Ace answered.

Jasmine nudged Ace. "Of course I will. But we've still got gifts to help wrap while you three get Santa up on the rooftop, and then we'll have burgers and pie."

"Slave driver," Ace muttered, but he had a big smile on his face.

Gemma started singing the Christmas song about Santa being up on the rooftop. When she got to the part about him coming down through the chimney, they all joined in. "I can't believe that I've made such good friends in only a couple of months," Liz said when they finished singing.

"Friends?" Raylen raised a dark brow.

Liz raised up on her tiptoes and kissed him on the cheek. "And boyfriend."

———————

"It's beautiful." Liz couldn't see everything about her yard and house fast enough. Her eyes went from the side windows of Raylen's truck to the front, and then she twisted around as much as possible to look out the back. Jasmine and Ace were ahead of them in Ace's truck, and Gemma and Dewar led the parade going to the café in his vehicle.

"Just be glad that Haskell put in lots of high-powered wiring to provide the juice to run all that stuff. I bet the electricity meter is going so fast that it looks like a blur," Raylen said.

"I don't care how much it costs. It's worth every dime. I cannot believe we got it all done. Thank you. Thank you. Thank you," she repeated.

Raylen reached across the console and laid a hand on her shoulder. "Jasmine rounded up the posse and did a lot of the bossing. We just followed her orders."

She covered his hand and gave it a gentle

squeeze. "But they're your family and friends, and I wouldn't have known any of them if it weren't for you. And"—she paused, not really wanting to spoil the evening—"we need to talk about us before…"

"Before what?" Raylen asked. "Are you going to have Christmas and then go back to the carnival?"

"No, not that, but right now our relationship is new and hot, and we can't get enough of each other. I want to be with you all the time. Every time someone comes into the café my heart skips a beat because I think it might be you. But when the fire dies down and there's nothing but cold ashes left—what then?" she asked.

"Here's the way I see it," Raylen said. "Our hot kisses and love making is going to feed this fire for a long, long time, and then when we're old and gray we will sit in the ashes and remember the good times."

"So, you think we'll be old and gray together," she asked.

Raylen tapped the brakes, removed his hand from her shoulder and turned into the parking lot of the café. "Grandma says that it's a good thing we don't know what the future holds, so don't ever read cards for me. If there's a future without you, I don't want to know about it."

"That is the most romantic thing a guy has ever said to me." Liz's eyes filled with tears, but she didn't let them flow. Even if all the universe planned to give her was a house with no wheels and a cowboy for just one Christmas, she would have her miracle, but oh, how she wanted to grow old with Raylen O'Donnell.

Gemma knocked on the window and pointed toward the café.

"Maybe we should've kept our relationship a secret a lot longer," Liz said with a long sigh.

"Didn't have a choice. We got caught," Raylen said.

Liz unbuckled her seat belt. Raylen slid out of his truck to jog around the back and open the door for her.

He held her hand all the way to the door, then stopped abruptly and gave her a long, passionate kiss. When it ended, he said, "You landed in your new house during holiday season. I keep hoping and praying when the excitement of this is over that you don't get bored with life in our community. We party hard, but we also work hard, and that can get monotonous."

"After the holidays and after Jasmine's new waitress gets here, I will probably drive out to west Texas to spent a few days with my folks and see my Poppa," Liz said, "but I can already feel roots going down right here in Ringgold, and I love the feeling."

"You will come home, though, won't you?" Raylen asked.

"Yes, darlin'. I never knew how much I really

wanted permanent friends and roots until now," she assured him.

"And a boyfriend?" Raylen asked.

"That more than anything." She raised up on her toes and kissed him on the cheek.

Gemma slung the door open and said, "Y'all can't live on love forever, and the burgers are already on the grill."

"I'm not so sure about that," Raylen said.

"Me, either," Liz added, and realized that neither of them had said those three magic words—I love you—yet.

When Raylen and Liz reached the kitchen, Ace was complaining about starving and Dewar was busy pulling the last of six chairs down from a table in the dining area.

"You're like a little boy, Ace," Jasmine said.

"That's what makes me so lovable," he told her.

Liz filled six glasses with ice and set them beside the drink machine and thought about all her new friends. *Just one Sunday afternoon at the O'Donnell ranch and look at what I've got. How deep will the roots have gone by this time next year?*

Would Gemma really find love, and would Jasmine ever settle down with Ace? She glanced over at Raylen who was filling drink orders and carrying the glasses to the table. Would her Aunt Tressa's last reading for her come true? Would she spend her life sitting on a fence, wanting roots and wings both?

She thought about the way she'd felt back when she was ten years old and walked on the fence. With her outstretched arms, and the heady feeling of watching Raylen right ahead of her, she'd felt like she was flying. Then a few years later, when she hung onto that same rail fence with her feet on the ground, she'd wanted what he had.

You can't ride two horses with one hind end. Her Poppa's words came back to haunt her. *You got to choose which one to ride so choose carefully, darlin'.*

"Gather round and start building your burgers to suit you," Jasmine called out as she lifted a basket of fries from the hot grease, shook them a few times and then poured them out on a tray.

Ace was first in line and loaded a plate with two burgers and fries, then headed to the table. When everyone was seated, he held up his iced tea glass. "Here's to burgers, fries, good times like tonight, and most of all good friends."

"Hear, hear!" Raylen raised his glass and sent a sly wink toward Liz.

It's always been Raylen. Liz remembered what she'd said to Jasmine a few weeks before.

"Y'all are so cute," Jasmine said.

"And I'm jealous." Gemma dipped a french fry into ketchup and popped it into her mouth.

Dewar grinned. "Won't do you," he glanced at Raylen and then shifted his gaze back toward Gemma, "or you any good. You know Dad's rule. I'm next, and I'm going to be a cranky old bachelor."

"Who needs a marriage license?" Raylen asked.

"That's right!" Gemma chimed in.

"I'll marry you, Dewar," Jasmine offered. "We can get married one day and divorced the next. That way these two won't have to live in sin and upset Grandma."

Ace groaned dramatically. "Oh, no, you won't! I'm going to marry you someday, Jasmine. When I'm too old to chase women, I'm going to settle down with you."

"Why me?" Jasmine asked.

"Because you can cook," Ace said with a grin.

Liz loved getting her house decorated and presents wrapped for her carnival family party, but not even that had been as much fun as sitting around the table with friends.

Dewar raised his glass and said, "An Irish toast to us all: May the best day of our past be the worst day of our future."

Gemma's glass touched his and then Raylen's. "May luck be your friend wherever you go and may trouble never be your friend."

Ace raised his and chuckled. "May you live as long as you want, and never want as long as you live! May you live to be a hundred years, with one extra year to repent."

Raylen held his glass up, looked right into Liz's

eyes and said: "Wishing you a rainbow, for sunlight after showers, miles and miles of Irish smiles for golden happy hours, shamrocks at your doorway, for luck and laughter too, and a host of friends that never ends each day your whole life through."

Liz leaned over and kissed him. "I love every one of those toasts. I'll add the one that hangs in my mama's travel trailer: Even with fire in our blood, an unbridled spirit, and a wild heart, home will always be where the heart is, whether on the road or sitting still. So, here's to home."

Jasmine raised her glass. "Amen!"

Chapter 16

BY THE END OF THE DAY, THE DINING ROOM HAD thinned out to only one table of elderly men who were deep into a heated discussion concerning politics. From there, Liz heard them start worrying about the idea of imports and exports, and whether they'd have to bring in hay from another state that fall or if they had plenty of small bales in the barns and big round bales in the pasture to last.

Liz had long since removed their dinner plates, dessert plates, and kept their coffee cups filled as they solved the problems of the country.

"Hey, Liz," Gemma called out as she opened the door into the café. That stopped the old guys from their discussion of hay—for a minute—and then they went right back to it.

Liz forced a smile when she saw Colleen follow Gemma inside. "Hi, y'all. Are you hungry or just wanting a cup of coffee and a place to rest awhile?"

"Starving," Colleen said. "Got any of the special left?"

"Enough for y'all," Liz said. "You want the same, Gemma?"

"I'm not in the mood for turkey and dressin'. I'm saving that for Thanksgiving. Bring me a bacon cheeseburger basket." Gemma removed her jacket and hung it over the back of a chair before she sat down.

"You got it." Liz wrote down their orders and took them back to the kitchen.

"I'll holler when it's ready," Jasmine said.

"I'm procrastinating. Let's talk about what we're going to do to decorate this place for Christmas. I've got lots of decorations left at my house. Let's put a big old stuffed Santa in a rocking chair out on the porch and hang ornaments in different lengths from the ceiling on ribbon…no, on jute twine. I saw some horses, steer horns, and horseshoes ornaments on display that I want to buy. We can have a countrified Christmas theme. I saw one of those rough wood signs that we can hang above Santa on the porch that says, 'countrified and satisfied.' That goes with the Chicken Fried name really well."

"Whoa, girl." Jasmine threw a hamburger patty on the grill. "I like all those ideas, but I'd only planned to put up a little garland and a few lights the Sunday after Thanksgiving, but if you are offering your decorations, I'm game to dress the place up a little more than that. Who knows? We might get all kinds of traffic down this way for your light drive, and if they see everything lit up here, they'll drop by and give me some business. Now tell me why you are procrastinating? Usually when Gemma comes in, you sit with her for a while."

Liz shrugged. "Colleen hates me. I can see disapproval in her face."

Jasmine patted Liz on the back. "She was the same way with Austin. She loves her brothers, and I guess it's working with gamblers all the time that makes her not as trusting as Gemma. Besides, you've had it too good. You need some speed bumps."

"Speed bumps?" Liz asked.

"Life is like a highway. Got to have a few curves and speed bumps or else you start to take things for granted."

"I'll remind you of that when your road is too straight and perfect," Liz said.

Jasmine flipped a burger and added a slice of cheese to the top. "I bet you will!"

"Let's talk Christmas decorations some more," Liz said.

"Procrastination is over. Time to clean off a table." Jasmine pointed toward the dining room.

The elderly men had pushed back their chairs and were putting on their mustard-colored work coats. She could clean it, pocket the tip, and ignore the O'Donnell sisters until their food was ready, or she could wait a few minutes and use it as an excuse if the speed bumps got too dangerous. She bypassed the cluttered table and sat down beside

Gemma. "What brings you to town on a Tuesday, Colleen?"

"My hair. It was too long and needed some layers. Gemma just finished cutting it," Colleen answered.

"It looks great, but then it always does," Liz said. "Has anyone ever asked you to model for their hair products?" Liz asked.

"Not yet. Raylen told me that y'all are dating," Colleen blurted out.

Own your decisions, Aunt Tressa's voice said.

Liz stared right into Colleen's eyes without blinking. "Yes, we are."

Colleen stared back with the same determination. "Don't break his heart, or you will answer to me."

Liz nodded. "I won't, and if he breaks mine he will answer to more than one person."

Liz expected more threats, but Colleen smiled. "Raylen says your place looks like the Griswold house. I'm looking forward to seeing it."

Liz couldn't help but smile back at her. "It's the most beautiful thing you've ever seen. I've got presents under the tree, and it's huge," she gushed. "And speaking of my party, please join us for the fun. There's even a present under the tree for you, Colleen, and could I borrow your folding tables and chairs for my party next Wednesday night?" She stopped long enough to take a breath and went on, "I can't wait for y'all to meet all my carnie family, and for them to meet all y'all. Maybe then they'll stop bugging me about giving up my house and land to go back to the carnival life."

"Wow!" Colleen's eyes got big as saucers, and she gasped.

"Is that sarcasm?" Liz asked. "I know I talk too much and too fast when I'm excited but—"

Colleen tilted her head toward the door. "No sarcasm intended. That is one fine-looking—"

"Blaze!" Liz shouted, crossed the floor in a dead run, and jumped into his waiting arms.

"Hi, sweetheart! Who is that gorgeous red-head?" he whispered.

Liz's answer was somewhere between a laugh and a groan.

Colleen and Blaze?

The devil would be line dancing in heaven to Charlie Daniels's "Devil Went Down to Georgia" before Texas was big enough for that combination.

"There's two women back there. You sure you're lookin' at the redhead?"

He spun her around and set her down. "Yes, definitely. I'm looking at the gorgeous one with the red hair and the jean jacket. Introduce me if you know her."

She picked up his hand and led him to the table. "Gemma and Colleen, this is my best friend, my surrogate brother and cousin, and part of my carnie family, Blaze. Darlin', meet Gemma and Colleen, Raylen's two sisters."

Colleen held out her hand. "It's a pleasure to meet you."

Blaze's eyes never left her green ones as he shook her hand, holding it longer than necessary before letting go and turning to Gemma. "I understand you've been a big help in getting everything ready for Lizelle's Christmas party."

"We just call her Liz," Gemma said.

The man was dressed in black jeans and a black T-shirt that hugged a six-pack of hard abs and strained at the bulging biceps. His hair was blond, in need of a decent cut, and his eyes were as dark as Liz's. He had two days' worth of light brown scuff that matched his eyebrows, a slight dent in his chin, and dimples when he smiled.

"Order up!" Jasmine yelled.

Liz grabbed Blaze's arm. "Come on. You've got to meet Jasmine and…"

"Hey, y'all! Got any special left? I'm starving!" Raylen yelled as he came through the door.

"And Raylen." Liz could hear the excitement in her own voice.

Raylen extended a hand. "You have to be Blaze. Liz wasn't expecting to see you until this evening. It's nice of you to drive up here and surprise her."

"I couldn't wait to see my favorite girl," Blaze said.

"Order up!" Jasmine called again.

"Gotta go work. You want the special, Raylen?" Liz asked.

He brushed a quick kiss across her lips. "Yes, darlin', I want the special."

Then he turned back to Blaze. "Come on and sit with me and my sisters. I'll buy your lunch. Want some turkey and dressin' or one of the best burgers in the world?"

"I'd like one of those famous chicken fried steaks," Blaze answered.

Raylen led the way to the table. "Folks come from miles around to get Jasmine's chicken fried steaks. You won't be disappointed."

Raylen and Blaze were being polite, but the tension in the room reminded Liz of two tomcats that had just jumped on the yard fence at the same time. Time stood still. The sun was afraid to move. The clock stopped dead. Liz could imagine their fur fluffing out and their tails straighten up as they met in the middle of the café floor.

"Colleen was just barely a speed bump, but what's going on out there is a mountain," Liz whispered to Jasmine as she picked up the tray with Colleen and Gemma's orders.

"It's all relative. I'd say she was the speed bump that got you ready for the big hairpin curve instead of a mountain." Jasmine laughed. "He's pretty, but he doesn't make me have hot flashes. Go on out there and sit with them. I'll bring out the guys' orders when they are done and meet him."

Liz whispered, "Colleen is smitten and about to

get her heart broken. Blaze is one night stand material. He has commitment issues."

Jasmine leaned away from the grill and peeked out at the table. "She's flirting with him, and honey, Colleen might be the one who breaks his heart instead of the other way around."

"Blaze can charm a holy woman into bed. Colleen doesn't have a chance. And he'll be gone in a week. Raylen will break up with me if Blaze causes Colleen to cry." Liz groaned.

Jasmine shook her head slowly. "It'll take more than a tight shirt and dimples to get Colleen to commit. I'd say the two of them have each met their match."

Liz put on her best smile and carried out the tray. "Turkey and dressing for Colleen, and a bacon cheeseburger basket for Gemma. Jasmine said she'd bring y'all's on out when it's done."

Raylen pulled a chair from an empty table and wedged it in between him and Gemma. When Liz was seated, he brushed another kiss across her forehead and sat down beside her, taking her hand in his and resting their laced fingers on top of the table.

He's marking his territory, the niggling voice in her head said. *Are you going to put up with that?*

She pulled her hand free, and smiled across the table at Blaze. "Is everyone busy getting set up at the carnival?"

"They are working on it. We've got a nice big lot, so we aren't crowded. Marva Jo has been antsy for two days. She's missed you. Is that your place south of here that looks like a North Pole store?" Blaze asked.

"That's it. Uncle Haskell made most of it," she answered.

"So, you grew up next door to my Uncle Haskell?" Blaze focused on Colleen.

"Yes, I did. We all loved Haskell and Sara," Colleen answered.

If looks could kill, Blaze would be a pile of cold bones on the café floor right then from the looks that Raylen was shooting his way. Liz couldn't blame him. She had told him all about Blaze and his conquests and there he was, flirting blatantly with Colleen.

"What do you think of Liz's place?" Blaze's eyes never left Colleen's face.

"Haven't seen it since she moved in. I thought I'd drop by tonight and look at it. It's all Raylen and Gemma have talked about all week," Colleen said.

"I'm going to help with the setup and see Mama, but I should be back by nine," Liz told Colleen.

"Orders for the guys," Jasmine said at Liz's elbow. "I've heard a lot about you, Blaze. Are you looking forward to a long, slow winter?" She set their food on the table, dragged a chair from the nearest table, and sat down.

"Liz has talked about all of you. And yes, I'm looking forward to the winter this year, but I'll miss Liz. Thank goodness for cell phones so we can talk every night." He turned his attention back to Colleen. "Will you be takin' in the carnival?"

Colleen's eyes glittered. "I haven't been to a carnival since I was a kid."

"You should come see ours. It'll make you feel young again." Blaze flashed what Liz called his "come hither" smile.

Yep, that redhead is a sheep being led to the slaughter by a wolf, she thought.

"I'd think all those terrifying rides would scare a few years off a person," Colleen said.

Liz cut her eyes around to Colleen. There was heat when she looked at Blaze but something else. Rock-hard steel in her eyes said that she was attracted but she wasn't rolling back on her heels and falling into a motel bed with him. If he liked what he saw, he was going to work for it.

Gemma bounced a knee off Liz's and winked when Liz looked her way. Suddenly everything looked much better. Raylen wouldn't kill Blaze or break up with her. Blaze, bless his heart, didn't have any idea that the gorgeous redhead was a panther, and in the past he had only tamed little house kittens.

Blaze ate fast, complimented Jasmine on her cooking, flirted with Colleen, kissed Liz on the cheek, and told them all to come on out to the carnival and he'd see to it they had free wristbands, so they could ride anything all evening without paying. Then he was gone and the static electricity in the café settled down.

"Is he your aunt's son or what?" Colleen asked.

"It's a long story but I'll give y'all the short version. We winter about halfway between Amarillo and Claude, Texas. We're sixteen miles from Amarillo and fourteen from Claude. My mother's people had a lot of land in that area when the depression hit, and they sold it to buy a small carnival. They kept enough to park the carnival for the winter months, and that's where we've always gone the week before Thanksgiving. The nearest neighbor is half a mile up the road and they had a daughter, Mary Lou, who was friends with Aunt Tressa. She got mixed up with a hippie group that decided to go to Wyoming to live in a commune when she was about eighteen. That lasted until she got pregnant and decided communal living wasn't for her. She came home and had the baby. Her folks died the year after he was born in a small plane crash going to Brownsville. Then she got cancer and died when Blaze was fourteen. Aunt Tressa took him to raise. So he's not blood kin but just heart kin, as Aunt Tressa says."

"What about the ranch where he lived?" Gemma asked.

"By the time Mary Lou died, she'd sold it off to pay for medical bills until all that was left was a small trailer and two acres. Aunt Tressa sold that and put it in a trust for Blaze, gave him a job, and he's been a carnie ever since."

"How did he feel about being jerked out of one world and tossed into another?" Colleen asked.

"He loved it from day one. He told me that he used to hang on the fence out by their place as we drove away in the spring and wish he could go with us. He's got that hippie blood in him from his biological father, I guess," Liz answered.

"Why'd she name her baby something like Blaze?" Jasmine asked.

"I asked Aunt Tressa that back before he came to live with us. She said Mary Lou didn't want him to have a common name. She was going to name him Phoenix like the bird that rose from the ashes. But when she was in labor, she said the pain was like blazing fire, so that's what she named him. And there's no middle name. Just Blaze McIntire."

Gemma dropped the spoon she'd been fiddling with. "He's Irish?"

"To the bone. Mary Lou was an O'Riley and his father was a McIntire."

Colleen smiled. "Imagine that."

Chapter 17

LIZ FELT LIKE SHE'D COME HOME WHEN SHE walked into the place where the carnival was that evening. Everyone waved, yelled, or came out to hug her, tell her how much they'd missed her and/or ask when she was coming back. It was half an hour before she reached the middle of the concession row where Tressa was helping Joe and Linda set up the awning to the side of the funnel cake wagon. Joe, a tall, lanky man with a crop of gray hair that always needed cutting, had joined the family when Liz was only five years old, and brought his wife, Linda, with him.

Liz hugged all three and asked, "Where's Mama?"

"She just headed into the Porta Potty. She'll be out in a minute. Hold up this pole," Tressa said.

Liz's Aunt Tressa had flaming red hair and aqua-colored eyes. She was taller than Liz, but at fifty-six, she still had the same slim build.

When they finished, Linda tucked her brown hair back behind her ear and said, "We sure missed you, darlin' girl."

"I miss all of you every day, but I love my new life," Liz said.

"Hey, kid!" Marva Jo said so close to Liz's side that it startled her.

Liz turned and wrapped her arms around her mother. "You snuck up on me. I missed you so bad."

She kept Liz in an embrace for a moment, and then stepped back to give her daughter a thorough once-over. "You have put on five pounds. Much more and your belly dancing belt will be too tight."

Blaze appeared out of nowhere. "She doesn't miss us a bit. Don't let her lie to you. I saw her with her new friends, and she's settling down into that life pretty well."

Liz shot daggers at him. "You will always be in my life, even if you are not in my sight and if I'm mad at you which I am right now."

"Mad at me! I came all the way up to Podunk, Texas, to see you and you're mad at *me*?" Blaze laid a hand on his heart like he was hurt.

"I'm mad at you for saying that about not missin' my mama. I might even stomp on your hat," she said.

"You never did tell me what happened about that. See, she doesn't even confide in me anymore, Marva Jo. She doesn't love any of us," Blaze teased.

"Children, this is no time to fight. We've got work to do and lots of it," Tressa said. "Blaze, get back to the Ferris wheel. And you, young lady, come help your mama work on the fortune wagon so we can visit. We've got to have this show up and ready before we go to bed tomorrow night, because the people will start arriving at ten o'clock on Thursday morning."

Liz didn't realize how much she had missed the smell of oil and dust as they got everything ready for the opening. She loved the sounds of the drills and hammers, the horses complaining about being cooped up in a truck, and the people all talking at once as they worked. She looped her arm through Marva Jo's and they headed off toward the brightly colored fortune telling wagon together.

"All we have to do is check the electricity and snap down the wires," Marva Jo said. "Blaze couldn't wait to see you. He says your friends are okay, that one named Colleen is knock-down gorgeous, and that Raylen is not what he expected."

Liz waved at everyone they passed: vendors, hawkers, ride managers, and the maintenance crews. She knew them as well as their kids' and grandkids' names. Knew where they went home to winter after they had parked their wagons in Claude the week before Thanksgiving. And she had missed every one of them.

"Did you hear me, Lizelle?" Marva Jo asked.

"I was listenin'," Liz answered. "I just want to see everything and everyone and can't do that and talk, too. What did Blaze expect out of Raylen?"

Marva Jo was six inches taller than her daughter, had strawberry blond hair and blue eyes. She was heavier than her sister but still looked good in tight jeans and a fitted Levi's jacket.

Marva Jo threw an arm around Liz's shoulders. "The way you've talked about Raylen, Blaze thought he'd be six feet tall, bulletproof, and sitting on a big white horse."

"He's five feet ten inches tall, has dark hair with red highlights when he gets in the sun, the clearest blue eyes you've ever seen, even lighter than yours, and he fell off his pedestal the first time we had a big fight," Liz said.

"And what was that over?" Marva Jo asked.

"Blaze. I was talking to him on the phone and ignored Raylen who was putting up my Christmas lawn things so everything would be beautiful for y'all. And he stormed off to his truck in a fit of anger, forgetting his hat that he'd hung on the porch railing. I threw it at him. He got mad because of that precious hat, so I stomped it, too!"

Marva Jo laughed. "And I bet you dropped down on your knees and apologized and made nice, didn't you?"

"I plowed right into his house and told him he was a horse's ass," Liz told her. "His best friend is this awful woman named Becca and she hates me. At least Blaze treated Raylen like an equal. Becca looks down on me like she's so much better than I am."

Marva Jo laughed even harder. "How'd he react to a woman calling him names?"

Liz had backed herself into a corner. She took a deep breath and spit it out. "When I went into his house, I saw his hat on a rack, so I slapped it on my head and plowed right into the bathroom like a bulldozer. He was in the shower, so I threw back the curtain and we had our fight right there. When I got my piece said, he pulled me into the shower, clothes and all, and kissed me."

Marva Jo really guffawed. "Now that's a man I could like. He'll keep you on your toes. What happened to the hat?"

"He pitched it on the vanity before he jerked me in the shower."

Marva Jo couldn't stop laughing.

Liz didn't think the story was all that funny. "What did Blaze tell you about Colleen?"

Marva Jo swiped at her eyes with the cuff of her jacket. "He is smitten. Something I never thought I'd say about him, but after he told us about where you work, that girl was all he wanted to talk about. Here we are. I'll run the cord out to the main box and plug it in. You check the inside and out for burned bulbs. If it's all good, we'll snap it down."

Liz knew exactly what to do, and when she'd made sure everything worked, she yelled out across the lawn where Marva Jo was talking to Tressa, "It's all good. Where we goin' next?"

"To the midway. Fred needs someone to unpack and hang stuffed animals," Marva Jo said.

Liz hopped down from the porch where she'd danced at least twice a week for the past decade and walked with her mother toward the middle of the grounds. She'd always liked the Bowie gig. They had lots of room, and the grass was nice. She didn't like playing in Denton where they set up on concrete. Spilled drinks and food were messier to clean up on concrete than grass, so they had to hose it down every morning. When they set up on dirt and grass there was little cleanup except for picking up paper. The birds ate what food was dropped, and the ground soaked up the liquids.

Marva Jo hopped up into the back of a semi and handed Liz a cardboard box. "Are you as smitten with Raylen as Blaze is with Colleen?"

She held the box in her arms and said, "Maybe. Stack another one on top. They aren't heavy. I can carry two or three."

"What are you going to do about it?" Marva Jo asked. "You've got to be honest with him, Lizelle."

She peeked around the end of the two boxes. "Right now, I'm just happy where we are. We're having fun being together. I'm not in a hurry."

"That's good. Maybe you'll decide to come home. I'm thinkin' about shooting my brother for giving you that house and land." Marva Jo dragged three boxes to the edge of the truck and jumped down. She added another one to Liz's and then picked up the remaining two and led the way to the gallery.

"Stock is getting low," Liz said.

"It's right where I want it for the last gig of the year. We've got a couple of extra backup boxes, but I think we ordered supplies just about right last spring. We're going home with trucks that are almost empty. Are you going to dance and cover the wagon on Thursday and Friday to give Tressa a rest?" Marva Jo asked.

Liz nodded. "I'm lookin' forward to tellin' fortunes. Did I tell you that I told fortunes at Gemma's Halloween party? And I saw a blond-haired cowboy in Colleen's future."

"Well, glory be!" Marva Jo declared loudly. "You did say cowboy, didn't you?"

Liz gasped. "He had blond hair and…"

"He didn't have boots or a hat, did he?" Marva Jo whispered.

"It's just a reading." Liz felt the color leave her face. "And even though Aunt Tressa thinks they're the real thing, we know they're just for fun, right?"

"What?" Tressa ripped the tape from the top of a box and handed Liz small stuffed animals to hang on the wire at the back of the gallery.

"She saw a blond-haired man in Colleen's future," Marva Jo said.

"Well, that sucks!" Tressa said, "But there have to be dozens of men with blond hair floating around this part of Texas."

"It can't be Blaze. He won't ever settle down. You said it yourself," Liz said.

"I read his cards last night just for fun. I saw a red-headed girl in his future, and I turned over the wedding card," Tressa said.

"Dammit!" Liz doubled up her fist and slammed it into her other hand.

Raylen poked his head around the end of the gallery. "Hurt yourself?"

"Raylen! What are you doing here?" Liz squealed.

"I came to meet your carnie family and to help," he said.

Liz leaned out the booth window and kissed him on the cheek. "You got here at just the right time. You can meet Mama and Aunt Tressa at the same time." She made introductions.

Raylen shook Marva Jo's hand. "Where did Liz get black hair and dark eyes?"

"From her father who was Latino. His name was Eddie Garcia. I gave her our family name when she was born because he had already passed away, and it simplified matters," Marva Jo answered.

"And this is my Aunt Tressa," Liz said.

He dropped Marva Jo's hand and held it out to Tressa. "My sister, Colleen, has red hair. Not the same shade as yours but still red. It's a pleasure to meet you both."

Tressa started at his scuffed-up work boots,

slowly took in his clean but faded jeans and chambray shirt, up to his eyes and hair. "You said you'd come to help? Why?"

"Thought you could use it and I'm caught up on my plowing for today," he said.

"Good. I like a man who's willin' to work. Come with me and I'll show you what to do. I expect you can use a drill and hammer, right?" Tressa asked.

"Yes, ma'am," Raylen said.

"Good, you can help Blaze put up the Ferris wheel."

"But..." Liz stammered. Raylen hadn't come to the carnival to help Blaze. He'd come to spend time with her. Was Aunt Tressa just plain stupid?

Marva Jo laid a hand on Liz's shoulder and shook her head. "Let it be," she whispered.

"Why?"

"If he survives tonight, he'll pass the test," Marva Jo said.

———

Blaze had just busted a knuckle when a stubby screwdriver bounced off the platform leading up to the Ferris wheel. He was cussing a blue streak and holding one hand with the other when Raylen and Tressa walked up.

Tressa grabbed his hand and pulled a tissue from her jacket pocket. "Hold it tight and stop the caterwaulin'. That won't make it stop hurtin' or bleedin.'"

"It'll sure make me feel better." Blaze clamped the tissue down on his knuckle to stop the blood flow and glared at Raylen. "What's he doing here?"

"He came to see Liz, but I stole him. He's going to help you. Looks like you need it if you can't even get the ramp up," Tressa said.

"The screwdriver slipped," Blaze said through gritted teeth.

"Then be more careful. Raylen, do whatever he says. Two strappin' fellows like you ought to have this Ferris wheel up and runnin' by bedtime," Tressa said as she walked away.

"You any good with mechanics?" Blaze asked.

"I can tear down a tractor and put it back together," Raylen answered.

"Then I reckon you'll do. Right now, we just got to get this ramp put together and then bring the seats out of the truck and fasten them into place. Motor is runnin' good, especially for the end of the season." Blaze didn't want to work with Raylen, or even talk to him, but he *was* Colleen's brother.

"Got an extra screwdriver?" Raylen asked. "I didn't bring my toolbox. I thought I'd be hanging out with Liz, not helping you."

Blaze nodded toward a red metal box sitting about three feet from Raylen. "Too bad about that. Liz doesn't belong anywhere but in the carnival, so why don't you just get out of her life so she can make the right decisions."

"I reckon she's old enough to make up her own mind where she should live," Raylen said. "What do you need me to do?"

"I'll hold this end up if you'll get that one fastened down," Blaze said. "She's confused, but she won't ever be happy anywhere but with us. She'll regret it if you push her into a relationship, and then both of your lives will be miserable."

"What if we're miserable without each other?" Raylen asked.

"After this board, we can use the electric drill and it'll go faster. I'm determined to figure out a way to build a ramp that won't require teardown for next year. But right now, it's got to be dismantled, or else we'd have to buy a forklift to get it from here to the semi." Blaze stopped and checked the scratch on his hand. "You just think you know Liz. She's like a sister to me."

"I can see where that one would be a real problem, up underneath like that." Raylen leaned into the job and the three-inch screw went right into place. "If you love Liz, then let her make her own decisions."

"Liz is headstrong and—" He stopped in the middle of the sentence.

Raylen followed Blaze's eyes to find his two sisters and Liz coming toward them. "Maybe they came to get a key from Liz so Colleen can see the house all lit up."

When they were close enough, Liz gave Raylen a big hug and kissed him on the lips. "I'm going to show the girls the fortune wagon, and then we're going to set up toys in the dart gallery. When you guys get this done, come and find us. We want the trial ride on the wheel."

Blaze couldn't take his eyes off Colleen. Standing, she was even more stunning than she'd been sitting down at the café. She was taller than Gemma but not by much, putting her at just the right height for him to walk beside comfortably with his arm around her shoulders. Kind of like how Raylen and Liz fit together. He shook that picture out of his mind. He didn't want to like Raylen, and he didn't want Liz to really fall for the cowboy even if he did know how to use a screwdriver. He wanted her to come back to the carnival, not put down any more roots in Ringgold.

"Well, guess we'd best get to work," Raylen said hoarsely.

"Yep," Blaze agreed, glad that Raylen couldn't read his mind. If he'd known how Blaze was looking at his sister, he'd use that screwdriver in his hand for a lot more than putting a ramp together.

Chapter 18

LIZ COULD HARDLY SLEEP ON WEDNESDAY NIGHT and awoke long before the alarm clock went off the next morning. Like every opening day for the carnival, her first thought was weather. She raised the blinds in her bedroom to nothing but darkness and groaned. The sun hadn't even started to rise yet. She checked her laptop for the weather update to find that it hadn't changed since the night before. Eighty percent chance of rain, cold front moving in, and enough wind to bring the chill factor down. Thursday night of a carnival was usually the slowest one. Friday night business picked up and Saturday night it was booming. The Bowie gig was always touch-and-go with the weather. It either rained and was so cold that only the brave at heart brought their whining children out to the carnival, or else it was unseasonably warm and everyone wanted one last fling before winter set in—feast or famine was what Tressa called it.

She was so deep in her own thoughts that at first she thought she was hearing things, then she realized that the voice was real. She tiptoed down the hallway to the kitchen to find Hooter and Blister following Raylen's every move. "What are you doing here?"

"You talkin' to me or the livestock?" Raylen asked.

"I'm talking to you," she answered.

"You've been on the go so much this week that I haven't got to see you except when there was a hundred people around us. I'm making coffee. I was going to bring it to you in bed," he said.

"That's so sweet. I missed you too."

He turned around, dropped a kiss on the top of her head, and led her by the hand to the table where he sat down and pulled her into his lap. "So, what's the agenda for tonight?"

"Have you heard a weather forecast?" she asked.

"What's that got to do with anything?"

"In the carnival business, everything," she answered. "Nobody comes out in the rain to get on the rides or play the games."

"Guess it's more like ranchin' than I thought. I was plannin' on plowin' up the last forty acres surrounding you today, but there is already a fine mist out there, and the weatherman says rain all day, and the temperature is supposed to be around fifty with a wind chill factor of forty degrees," he said.

"It means business will be slow," she said.

He poured a mug full of coffee and set it in front of her. "According to the weatherman the sun will come out at noon tomorrow, but this cold front won't move out until Sunday."

She took a sip of her coffee and sighed.

Liz turned around, wrapped her arms around him, and snuggled close enough that she could listen to his heartbeat. Forget the carnival, forget the café.

"You promised me a dance tonight. Is the rain going to prevent that?" Raylen buried his face in her dark hair.

"I've been looking forward to dancing for you for days," she whispered into his ear, and then stood up. "As much as I'd like to go where this would lead us, darlin', I've got to get ready for work."

He nuzzled down into her hair. "Five more minutes."

A quick glance over his shoulder at the clock said it wasn't happening. "Can't or I'll be late."

She bent down to plant a steaming hot kiss on his lips. When she stood up again, Hooter was staring at them, head cocked to one side. Blister had jumped up on the counter, not six inches from Raylen's ear, and meowed loudly.

Liz giggled. "I think they're tellin' us that we'd best stop now or else I'll get fired."

"I am very fired up." Raylen looked down.

"Stay that way until tonight, and I'll dance for you after I tell fortunes at the carnival. Business might be slow, but there will be some that come out to see what the future holds," she said.

She made it to the café five minutes before opening, grabbed a cup of coffee, and wolfed down two bacon biscuits. "Does rain mean a slow day in the café business like it does in the carnie world?"

Jasmine poured a cup of coffee. "Not at all. If the ranchers can't work, they come to the café to talk ranchin', religion, and politics. So get ready for a very busy morning. I've got extra biscuits on the pans ready to put in the oven. They'll be orderin' sausage gravy and eggs to get the chill off. What happens to the carnival in rainy weather?"

"If it's rainy and cold, folks stay home. No amount of whining or begging from their kids can get them out in the nasty weather. We'll have a slow night and, according to the weatherman, the rest of the week is going to be chilly. If it's not raining, we might have a fairly decent weekend to finish up the year," she explained.

"You said 'we,' Liz. You're not completely cut away from it, are you?" Jasmine asked.

"No, but I'm workin' on it. I've been growing these wings for twenty-five years. I can't get rid of them in just a few weeks," she said.

"That's understandable and honest. Time to open the door. The parking lot is already half full. Get ready for a rush," Jasmine said.

Liz picked up her apron and tied it around her waist. She wondered if Raylen was still at her house.

If he'd left Hooter and Blister inside.

If he had ever told Becca about their sex life.

That put a frown on her face as she crossed the

dining room, flipped the sign around to say OPEN, and unlocked the door. Surely, he didn't tell personal things, even if Becca was his friend. She didn't share the intimate things about their relationship with Blaze.

"Mornin', Liz," a regular old timer said. "Bring us six cups of coffee. I'm buying breakfast for us this morning, so put our orders on one tab."

"Sure thing, Donny," she said and headed toward the coffee pot.

The hectic morning gave way to a busy lunch rush. Closing time snuck up on Liz and she realized that she hadn't seen Ace or any of the O'Donnell family all day.

She locked the door and grabbed a broom, but Jasmine took it out of her hands. "You need to get out of here and spend time with your family. I'll get my cakes done for tomorrow's dessert and then us girls are coming to the carnival."

"Thank you so much." Liz didn't even argue. "I can't wait for you to meet Mama and Aunt Tressa. Colleen and Gemma came by last night and helped me stock the midway. And Aunt Tressa made Raylen work with Blaze on the Ferris wheel."

Jasmine stopped and leaned on the broom handle. "I knew they were all coming, but we've been too busy to gossip."

Liz talked while she slipped her jacket on. "I was afraid they'd kill each other. I sure wouldn't want to have to work with Becca. Then when they got it finished, all five of us did the debut ride. Tressa ran the controls and let us go around about a dozen times before she declared it was ready for use."

"Keep going. Who rode in each bucket?" Jasmine asked.

"Blaze rigged it so that he and Colleen sat together," Liz said. "I'm worried about that."

"Who sat with you?"

"Raylen," Liz said.

"Would you want someone interfering with you and Raylen?" Jasmine asked.

Liz had already unlocked the door, but she turned around, "No, I would not!"

"Then leave Colleen and Blaze alone. They're both grown, and trust me, Colleen can take care of herself. Would you break up with Raylen if you had a brother who fell for Becca?" Jasmine asked.

"No, but I'd sure think about shooting Becca," Liz said.

"I rest my case," Jasmine told her.

———

Liz felt right at home in the travel trailer, sitting at the table with her makeup kit and mirrors around her. She wore a long, flowing multicolored skirt, a yellow blouse with billowing sleeves, with a turquoise scarf and beaded sandals. When she finished her makeup, she slipped six strands of different colored beads around her neck, a dozen silver bangle bracelets on one arm, and a tinkling charm bracelet on the other. Then she wrapped a long scarf around her head, tying it in a double knot right above her left ear and letting the ends fall over her shoulder.

She was checking her reflection when her mother stepped into the trailer. "You forgot something."

"I did?"

"Ah, my child. One month and you are already becoming a householder."

"I'm not an outsider, Mama. What did I forget?"

Marva Jo pointed at her feet. "Your ankle bracelets. The tinkling sound helps to feed the illusion."

"Thank you," Liz said.

Marva Jo went to the refrigerator and took out a Diet Coke. "I like your Raylen. He reminds me of your father except that your father had jet-black hair and eyes, like you have. And he was much shorter than Raylen."

"Then what is it about him that makes you think of my father?" Liz asked.

"The way he looks at you. Just remember our wanderlust is only appealing for a little while. It didn't last with your father. If he hadn't died, we would have divorced. Our marriage was on the rocks. It won't last with Raylen. Enjoy it while you have it and then let it go. Kind of like a butterfly on a pretty red flower. Stay until you tire of it and then fly away," Marva Jo said.

"What if I don't get tired of it?" Liz fastened charm bracelets with little brass bells around her ankles.

"It's not up to you. He'll get tired of it, and then you'll find out that the place for you is in the bosom of the carnie. He's the only reason you went there and the only thing that holds you. When it's over, you'll come home. History repeats itself." Marva Jo told her. "A mother knows these things."

"What if it's five years down the road and we're in a committed relationship?" Liz asked.

Marva Jo kissed her again on the forehead, being careful not to mess up her makeup. "What-ifs could go on all night. I wish you could dance tonight, but from what the weatherman says, it's going to be too cold. Such is life this late in the year. Sometimes it's nice and warm, and sometimes we don't even make enough to pay the electricity bill before we leave town."

"What did you think of Colleen and Gemma?" Liz asked.

"I liked them but I liked Colleen the best." Marva Jo finished her own makeup.

"You got to be kiddin' me!" Liz gasped.

"No, I'm not kiddin' you," Marva Jo assured her. "Now get out of here, and go do your job. You've got just enough time to get settled into the wagon and turn on the crystal ball light before your first customer."

She was on her way from the trailer to the carnival and had just waved at Blaze who was working the controls at the Ferris wheel when she heard someone yell her name. She was surprised to see Austin and Rye not five feet from her.

"I almost didn't recognize you," Austin said.

"It's me in living color." Liz twirled around a couple of times. "I'm telling fortunes tonight. The next two nights they've got me working the shooting gallery and Aunt Tressa will be back in the fortune telling wagon. Y'all are brave souls in this weather."

"This is the only night we get to come, and I love carnivals. Rye took me to a carnival on one of our first dates. I make him take me to one whenever it's close enough. Maddie is keeping Rachel for us," Austin said. "I don't care if I get wet. I've got dry clothes at home. And you didn't look like that at the Halloween party. You wore a genie outfit."

Liz smiled. "You're going to have to tell me the story of your romance when I have more time. Maybe we can all get together for a girls' night out sometime. And that outfit was my belly dancing outfit. This is my official fortune telling costume."

"Name the place and time. Maybe we can have it at my house, and you can teach us how to belly dance," Austin said.

Rye's face broke into a grin. "Can the guys have a guys' night out and watch?"

Austin kissed him soundly and giggled. "No, but you'll reap the benefits of our learning, I'm sure," she answered as she herded Rye off toward the Ferris wheel.

Liz noticed the paint was beginning to chip on the fortune-teller's wagon when she slipped inside and got it ready for business. She flipped a switch that turned on dim lights and another one that lit up the iridescent bulb at the base of the crystal ball. She struck a match and fired up two incense cones, and in a few seconds, the wagon smelled like sandalwood. Then she sat down and touched a button under the table that flipped a sign on the door to ENTER. While she was with a customer, she would touch the button again and the sign would flip over to say, DO NOT DISTURB.

She *had* missed the business. She'd missed the feeling of waiting for the first customer, the smell of the incense, the tinkling bells when she crossed and uncrossed her legs, and the pretty light in the crystal ball. And most of all the excitement in the faces of those who got their fortunes told.

That reminded her of Raylen that morning. Raylen was a complex, exciting man who kept her on her toes. She looked into the crystal ball and saw her own distorted face smiling back at her.

"Is this what I'll look like when I'm old?" she muttered. "Will Raylen love me with wrinkles in my cheeks and around my mouth?"

Chapter 19

The door swung open and Liz said, "Welcome to Madam Drabami's Fortunes," in a low voice.

Becca took two steps and sat down across the small table from Liz. "I came to see if you'd changed your mind about my fortune."

"Cards, ball, or palm?" Liz's tone came out blunt even though she had tried to keep it professional.

"What's the difference?" Becca asked.

"Palm is five dollars," Liz said, "and cards and crystal ball will cost you twenty."

Liz wanted to strip out of the costume, then go home to her dog and cat and Christmas decorations.

Becca threw a twenty on the table. "Give me the works. Tell me that I'm going to marry Raylen when you move on, and I pick up the pieces."

"I'll tell you exactly what I see, not necessarily what you want to hear," Liz said. "Do you want to change your mind before I start?"

Becca leaned across the table and said, "I don't like you. You are a fake and you're going to hurt Raylen."

"The works it is," Liz said. "Please lay your hands, palms up, on the table."

Becca laid them out with a thump. "Didn't you hear me?"

"I did, but you didn't put twenty dollars on the table to fight with me. You laid it out for a fortune. We can fight later. I don't charge for that." Liz picked up her hand. "I see a long, long life ahead of you. This line says you will be married for many years, and this short one here suggests that you'll marry again after that, but it won't last long. I would think the first time you marry it will be for love, and when that love has passed on in your old age, you will look for it again and not find it."

Becca jerked her hands back and held them in her lap. "That could be anyone's future."

Liz picked up the cards and shuffled them. "It could be, and it probably is for lots of people, but it is yours today," Liz said.

"I'll cut the cards and turn them. I don't want you to cheat," Becca said.

Liz handed the deck to her.

Becca reshuffled them, cut them, and then laid the deck on the table. She turned over the top card.

"You need to turn three cards and lay them out side-by-side. One card can mean one thing, but next to another one it takes on a very different meaning," Liz said.

Becca laid out two more cards and crossed her arms over her chest. "What does that mean?"

"You will have exceptionally good luck for a little while and then a reasonable measure of success, but you are walking on the edge of the cliff when it comes to your romantic side, and one misstep can put you over the edge. Be careful, or you will trade true love and happiness for contentment." Liz wanted to tell her that she was going to gain a hundred pounds and all her hair would fall out, but she stayed true to her craft.

Becca shivered. "Okay, now the ball."

Liz rubbed her hands over the glass ball and looked closely into it.

Becca leaned in, but she saw nothing but her own face.

"I see you at a birthday party. Is it yours?" Liz asked.

"Could be. My birthday is coming up soon," Becca said.

Liz kept her eyes on the ball. Becca was a Scorpio. No wonder she was so biting, with that zodiac sign. "You thrive under intensity. You like adversity, but your dreams are bearing down on you, and you have an ongoing thorn in your side right now. Balance is not easy for you. You are drawn like a moth to the flame when it comes to drama. You like to stir up trouble, and you are good at it. You need to let go of the control issue in your life and let your heart lead you. Those around you want one thing, but your heart wants something different, Becca.

The reason you are in conflict between heart and head is because you are walking close to the cliff when you give in to your head. Let your heart lead you away from the edge of that cliff, and success in romance, business, and life will be yours."

Becca stood up so fast the chair fell backwards with a loud crash.

"I don't love Raylen," she said bluntly. "I love him as a friend with all my heart. I'd kill for him as a friend, but I don't want to marry him. Daddy says it's either him or Dewar and has given me until June to make my decision or he's going to cut me off."

"Sit down." Liz got to her feet and set the chair back up.

"Tell me more. I don't care what it costs." Becca's face had turned ashen and tears welled up behind her eyelashes, but she sat down and held her hands out.

"You've paid enough, Becca," Liz said as she covered Becca's hands with hers. " I was raised in the carnival. I love it, but something in my heart keeps pointing me to another way of life. It's not easy. I want both but that's not an option. Mama says I have wings, not roots. Pulling the feathers out of my wings is not easy, but I do it every day because I'm determined to put down roots. Listen to your heart, Becca."

"I don't want to be poor," she whispered.

"It's the foreman, isn't it?" Liz asked.

Becca dabbed at her eyes with a tissue she pulled from her purse. "Taylor is his name. He's ten years older than I am, and he asked me to marry him. Daddy will fire him on the spot and cut me off."

"You sure about that? Talk to your dad. Can't do any more damage than what you've already worked up in your mind. Take Taylor with you and have an adult conversation with your father. Tell him you are ready to start working instead of playing. I bet you have a good head for organization and figures. It goes with the Scorpio sign," Liz said.

"Thank you," Becca said. "Don't tell Raylen."

"You'll tell him when the time is right," Liz said.

Becca left and Liz pinched her nose between her thumb and forefinger for a full minute before she flipped the switch under the table that turned the door sign to ENTER.

Liz applied cold cream to her face after she'd removed her costume. She had shut down the fortune telling business at ten and took a long look out across the midway: not much happening there. The Ferris wheel was still, and only the Tilt-A-Whirl was operating. There weren't twenty people milling around, and no one had looked like they were interested in palm readings or crystal balls. She stomped her bare feet down into cowboy boots and headed straight for the gyro wagon.

She ordered two sandwiches and a Diet Coke, found a seat under the awning, and sat down for a late supper. Before she could remove the paper wrapping and take a bite of the first one, Blaze had parked himself right beside her.

"Thought I'd find you here. Hope it picks up tomorrow night, or we might as well pack it up and go on to west Texas," he said.

"Oh, no!" she protested. "You are coming to my house on Monday and staying until Thursday. Tuesday is rest up day and Wednesday night we've got a Christmas party in the barn. It's all planned, and invitations have already been given."

"Who all has been invited?" he asked.

"All the O'Donnell family. They've been good to me. And Ace and his hired help which is four guys, and Wil and Pearl and their foreman. Austin and Rye are coming with their baby girl, and Slade and his wife and girls and his granny and aunt. You've got to meet Ellen. She's the grown-up, eighty-year-old version of the women you like," Liz said.

Blaze smiled brightly. "Darlin', I wouldn't miss your party for anything. Now talk to me about this O'Donnell family some more."

"The family or Colleen?" she asked.

Blaze's smile almost chased the dark clouds away. "You know me too well."

"Yes, I do," she agreed.

"And I know you just as well. You are in love, but is it real love or are you in love with the idea of being in love? That's the question you need to ponder in the crystal ball." He pushed his wet hair back. That night he'd shaved smooth, and Liz caught a whiff of his most expensive shaving lotion.

"So who's the lucky lady who'll be picking you up at midnight tonight?" She looked around.

"Could have a date. Don't have a date. Catching up on sleep tonight. Maybe tomorrow night someone will come along that takes my eye," he said.

Liz polished off her first gyro and unwrapped the second one. "I don't know if she's coming or not. Did you see Gemma tonight?"

"Yes, with your boss lady. They rode the wheel twice and ate Indian tacos and cotton candy. I heard her tell Jasmine that Colleen was going to love the tacos tomorrow night." Blaze grinned.

"She has roots. Deep ones," Liz said.

"You have wings. Big ones," he shot back.

"Be careful, Blaze."

"I can't. Not this time or I'll lose what my heart really wants, and you can't say a word because you're floating the same boat as I am," he said.

"Yes, I am," she admitted.

He held up a beer. "Here's to roots and wings. May they both have the ability to change."

"Last week you wouldn't have said that. You were begging me to give my house back to Uncle Haskell and come back to the carnival. And love at first sight is..."

He poked her playfully on the arm. "Love at first sight is a load of crap. But the heart can reach out and know its soul mate at first sight, and then the love can come later."

Liz finished her food, wadded up her papers and put them in the trash can at the end of the table. "Be careful, darlin'. Next thing you know, you'll be sprouting roots."

"No, I'm not," he declared, "but I can hope that someone else will sprout wings someday. Got to run. Tressa is motioning to me. I think she's about to call it a night and shut up an hour early. See you tomorrow night?"

"Oh, yeah. I'm running the dart gallery. Colleen ought to love it when she sees me hawking for customers," she groaned.

"We are what we are." Blaze waved good-bye to her.

Raylen opened the door when she walked up on the porch. Candles glimmered in the background and Christmas music floated out to meet her. He wore flannel pajama bottoms and no shirt.

He pulled her inside, kicked the door shut

with his bare foot. "I believe you owe me a dance, Madam Daragama."

She took him by the hand and led him to the recliner. "Wait right here and I'll be back in a few minutes."

"Wait is a four-letter word," he grumbled.

Suddenly something that sounded like snake charmer music began to play in the kitchen, and Liz appeared out of the darkness, taking tiny steps toward the center of the room as her arms moved to the flute music.

The drums started and she did a one-foot spin, landing on both feet so close to him that he gasped. Then she slowly turned around, her arms beckoning to him and her belly muscles rolling. The tempo picked up, and she leaned backwards until her black hair touched the floor, and she was looking at him upside down. When the flute took center stage again, she rolled back up, each graceful move as subtle as it was sexy.

Turquoise hip-slung pants hugged her legs to the knees where ruffles in silver and lighter blue flirted with him every time she moved.

The music changed slightly, bringing in a piano, and she did another one-foot spin and removed the skirt. She wrapped a long silver scarf around her hips and kept time to the music.

Liz liked this dance even better than the one she usually did when she wore the orange costume.

The piano added a salsa flavor that had Liz sweating bullets by the time she started winding down the dance.

"Promise me one more time that I'm the only man you'll ever dance for like that," he said.

"Only for you on your birthday and Christmas," she said as she sat down in his lap.

"And maybe July Fourth. We'll make our own fireworks," he teased.

———

Friday night was a little warmer and the stars were shining when the folks started coming out in droves to the carnival. Liz had made a hundred dollars from a man who'd been determined to win his girlfriend the biggest teddy bear on the rack. The poor fellow couldn't have hit the broad side of a barn with a river rock, but he kept trying. Liz wanted to cheer for him when he finally popped one balloon with a dart, and gave the lady her choice of the medium-sized animals as a consolation prize. The couple walked off with smiles on their faces, and Liz reset the game.

When she turned around to the next customer, she found Raylen sitting on a small stool at the end of the stuffed animal display. She blinked twice and then once more, but he didn't disappear. "Tressa said I could work with you tonight," he told her.

Tressa's voice was in her head. *The best way to truly get to know someone is to work with them.*

I already have worked with him, Liz mentally reminded her aunt.

"You look like you're having a mental argument with someone," Raylen said.

"I am, and her name is Aunt Tressa," she admitted.

He pulled her closer to his side. "I'm not stalking you, Liz, but the best way to get to know someone is to work alongside them. That's what Grandpa taught me when I was a boy."

"That's exactly, word-for-word, what Aunt Tressa just reminded me of. So I guess we were getting to know each other when we put up all those decorations, and when I helped clean up the barn after the party," she said.

"You've seen my world. Now I'm seeing yours, and I can see the appeal of living with so much excitement week after week," he said. "And here's a customer eyeing the big bear. You going to reel him in or want me to try?"

"Give it your best shot." She stood up.

"Hey, mister, your pretty girlfriend sure would like to take our big bear home with her. You can start to win it with only three darts. All you have to do is pop three of those five balloons and that gets you the first stuffed animal of your choice. Trade it back in and buy three more darts for the next size until you make it all the way to the big bear. What do you say?"

The man shook his head.

"Well, sweetheart, I guess you don't get that bear tonight. Or else you'll have to find another cowboy to win it for you," Raylen said.

The man laid out another dollar and popped three balloons. Liz blew up three more and Raylen tacked them to the corkboard.

"Keep it or try again?" Raylen said.

The cowboy shook his head.

The lady looked at the bear and stuck out her lower lip in a fake pout.

He laid out another bill and popped three balloons again. The woman traded her tiny piglet for a medium-sized zebra.

"That's it, Misty. You can either keep the zebra and go dancin' tomorrow night at the Twisted Spur, or else we'll try for the bear," he said.

Misty kissed the zebra and they walked off.

"If you'd been fishing, then that big old bass would have just flipped back into the water," Liz said.

Raylen squeezed her hand. "Your turn. If you put another hundred in your pocket before the next fish gets off the hook, I'll make you breakfast in bed."

"And if I don't?"

"Then you are breakfast in bed," he teased.

"Does that mean you are going to spend the night with me?" she asked.

He chuckled and tilted his head toward a soldier in uniform hugged up to his girlfriend. "Are you askin' me to sleep over at your house tonight?"

"I just might be," she whispered.

"What do I have to do to get that big bear?" the soldier asked.

Liz told him.

"Then let's play," he said and laid five dollars on the counter.

Twenty dollars later the soldier handed the big brown bear to his girlfriend.

"I bet that lucky guy is a sniper," Liz said.

Raylen pulled Liz to his side and gave her a hug. "He's not as lucky as I am."

Chapter 20

LIZ HAD ALREADY THROWN BACK THE COVERS when she remembered it was Sunday and she didn't have to go to work. She eased back down and snuggled up to Raylen's back.

Raylen turned over in his sleep, slipped one arm under her and another over the top, and snuggled up next to her, burying his face in her hair. Lying in his arms the past two nights, even without sex, felt so right, but doubts had begun to creep into her mind.

Leaving now would break her heart, but if they ever got married and it didn't last, she would die of a broken heart. Her mother knew men much better than Liz did.

Marva Jo's words played through her mind in a continuous loop. *Just remember our wanderlust is only appealing for a little while. It didn't last with your father. It won't last with Raylen. Enjoy it while you have it and then let it go. Kind of like a butterfly on a pretty red flower. Know when to fly away before it's too late.*

Give it until Christmas, Uncle Haskell's voice

argued. *You'll know by Christmas if you want to give up the land, and you can tell me when you come home to Claude for the holiday. Don't make a rash decision until then. You've only been there a few weeks, and you've just had four days of carnival. See how you feel when they're gone and you're back in your normal schedule.*

Maybe her uncle was giving her very different advice from her mother because Aunt Sara had often wished that she was Liz's mother. Or perhaps it could be because he knew how badly she wanted to settle down.

A broken heart is a broken heart whether it's the week before Thanksgiving or the day after Christmas, she thought as she eased out of Raylen's arms and padded barefoot to the kitchen. She started a pot of coffee, popped open a can of cinnamon rolls, put them in a pan, and slid them in the oven. While they cooked, she laid half a pound of bacon over a stand-up rack and stuck that into the microwave.

"I thought we were going to sleep in," Raylen said from the doorway.

"I woke up and couldn't go back to sleep, so I decided to cook breakfast for you," she said.

"When you wake up early, it means you are settling down into small town life," he said. Raylen crossed the room and hugged her tightly. "Liz, the past couple of nights have been wonderful, even if we were too tired for sex."

His phone rang and he grabbed it from the counter.

"That one is mine," she said.

Two phones side by side, she thought. Was it an omen that someday they might go through the rest of their lives together?

He laid her phone back down and picked his up in time to answer on the fourth ring.

"I'm on my way." He turned around and headed back to the bedroom in a hurry.

"What?" Liz asked.

"Glorious Danny Boy got out of the barn and jumped a fence or two. There's a mare out in the pasture that's about to bear his colt. I guess Danny Boy wants to check on her. She's going to drop a foal before long and we're just hoping all this excitement doesn't kill her. Dewar has already called the vet to be on standby. I'm sorry, darlin', but…" He left the sentence hanging.

She followed him back to the bedroom. "Do you need me to help?"

"Thanks, but no thanks. Dewar and I can take care of it. Are you going to help with the carnival tear-down?" Raylen asked as he got dressed.

"Call me as soon as you find him, please?" she asked. "Yes, I'll be at the carnival helping them tear things down and move up here for the night."

"I promise to keep you updated. See you later."

No quick kiss, just a rush out the door.

There's your omen, Marva Jo's voice whispered in her ear. *Ranch first for him. Carnival should be first for you.*

The microwave dinged as Raylen left, letting in Hooter and Blister at the same time. She pulled the bacon out and checked the cinnamon rolls. They were almost done, and the coffee had stopped dripping. She poured a cup and ate a piece of bacon while she waited on the rolls.

Blister jumped up on the counter and meowed.

Hooter looked up at her and yipped.

"Hungry, are you?" She shook dog food from the big bag into Hooter's dish and opened a can of cat food for Blister.

The cat bailed off the cabinet, smelled the food, and rubbed around Liz's legs. Hooter ate one bite before he sat down in front of the microwave and looked up. Liz reached down to rub Blister's ears, and the cat licked her fingers.

"What happens to you two if I go home to the carnival after Christmas? This is your home. I couldn't take you with me," she said.

The smell of baking bread and cinnamon filled the kitchen, reminding her of all the times when her mother heated up leftover sweet rolls in the microwave. When she and her mother had put away a pot of coffee and all the rolls were gone, then they'd go outside and begin tearing down the carnival.

That morning she took the rolls out of the oven

and found a fork in the drawer and ate two of them right out of the pan.

I miss you, Mama. She sighed.

━━━━━━

When Liz reached the carnival, Blaze was sitting on his trailer doorstep with a blanket wrapped around him. He had a cup of coffee in one hand and a toaster pastry in the other.

"Sit down and tell me your week has been better than mine. Want some breakfast?" he asked.

She scrunched in beside him. "I had hot cinnamon rolls and bacon. What are you whining about? My feller got called away to help find a runaway horse this morning while the bacon was still cookin.'"

"I'm whinin' because Colleen just breezed in and out of my life, and I want to know her better, and life is not fair," Blaze whined.

Liz laughed. "Aunt Tressa didn't sign a contract that life would be fair when she took you to raise. I believe the one she made you sign was pretty much like the one Mama made me sign that year. It talked about lots of work, good pay, and you didn't have to go to public school. And besides, you've still got a few days to woo her into going with you, or else staying here. You can always move into my spare bedroom."

"I found my soul mate and I didn't even get to sleep with her," Blaze said between bites of the left-over pastry.

"Colleen will be right next door until you leave. Did the warranty run out on the charm and you forgot to renew it? Come on, Blaze, if she's your soul mate, it will work. If she's not, there's lots of fish in the sea," Liz said.

Blaze finished the pastry and licked his fingers. "I don't want to fish anymore. I want a soul mate like you got in Raylen."

"How do you know that?" Liz asked.

"It's in the eyes and the way you look at each other," he answered.

"That's a load of romantic crap. I've seen women look at you the same way since you were fourteen," she told him.

Blaze threw an arm around her and hugged her up to his side. No bells or whistles sounded in her ears. Not a single spark sizzled in the air around her. No fireworks popped off in the distance.

"It's more than lust, Lizelle. It's something that can't be described. I knew when I looked at Colleen that she's my soul mate." Blaze's tone said that he was serious.

Liz had never seen him like this and wasn't quite sure what to say to him. "What about Janet?" she finally asked. "Seems like you had a fairly long-term thing going with her before we left last spring."

"Honey, she got married a few weeks ago, and she, along with all the other women who've been in my life, wasn't real. Colleen is," he said. "I haven't been to bed with anyone since I laid eyes on her."

"Holy smoke, Blaze. You are worse than…"

"You?" he asked.

"Far worse," she said.

He got up and opened the door into his trailer. "Don't leave. Maybe you can help me start taking the Ferris wheel down after I get dressed. We can talk more while we work. Everyone will be waking up soon, and they'll all want you to help them. We've missed you a lot, so I'm laying claim to you first."

Take down fever.

That's what the carnival family called today. The last gig of the season, and everyone was ready to go home for the winter. Come spring, the trailers would begin to come in, and *take off fever* would be in the air.

While Blaze was in his trailer, she wiped a tear from her cheek, and tried to say goodbye to the life she'd always known. Pickup trucks with tiny living quarters behind them were pulled up in a line. Semis and flatbed trucks carried the equipment, rides and vendors' wagons—five wagons to a flatbed. The ponies would soon be in the horse trailer and probably looking forward to being turned loose in a pasture for the next few months.

The next day they would depart, leaving nothing, not even a candy wrapper, in their wake. This year instead of heading due west, they'd go fifteen miles north to Liz's place. She had plenty of room for them to park and rest until Thursday morning when they'd be off to Claude. Poppa would be standing on the porch looking for them to parade onto the land by suppertime. Only this year, Uncle Haskell would be there too, for the first time, and Liz wouldn't be driving her truck and bringing up the rear of the parade. *How can I leave all this behind? It's my life.*

She smiled when her phone rang and she saw Raylen's name pop up on the screen. "Hello, Raylen. Did you find Danny Boy?"

"We've got him, but he's got a nasty cut on his foreleg that is going to need a few stitches and he'll need a round of antibiotics. He's in the barn and the vet is on the way. Mama is with him, and Daddy is trying to figure out how he got out. Near as we can tell something spooked him, and his gate stall wasn't fastened tightly. We're lucky he's not banged up even worse. Found him in a mesquite thicket, limping back toward the house. He'd jumped three fences."

"Is there anything I can do?" Liz asked.

"Not a thing. I just can't come help with the teardown business today. One of us will stay with him all day and night. I drew the shift from six to midnight. If you get home in time, you can come out to the barn and keep me company," he said.

"I'll be there, and I'll call before I leave so I can bring anything you need," she said.

"I just need you," he said.

"I'll be there soon as I can. Call me with updates," she said.

"I will. I see the vet pulling in now. See you later then?" he asked.

"I promise," she said.

Blaze cracked the door. "You promise what?"

She stood up and headed out across the grounds. "That I'll go by the barn and see about the horse that got out. Ever heard of Glorious Danny Boy?"

He grabbed a toolbox from the bed of his truck and followed her to the Ferris wheel. "Everyone that follows horse races like Tressa and I do knows that name. He's that famous quarter horse that won the Texas Heritage Stakes several years ago. When anyone talks about horse racing they say 'as good as old Glorious Danny Boy' or 'never as good as.' Why are you asking?"

"That's the horse that got loose this mornin'. Glorious Danny Boy. The O'Donnells own him and Major Jack," she explained.

Blaze gasped. "Those people are *the* O'Donnells?"

"Yes, they are," she answered. "Let's get things going here. Hand me the stubby. I'll get the first board off since my hands are smaller."

"And Colleen comes from *that family*," he groaned as he handed her the screwdriver.

Liz nodded.

"There's no way she'd ever be interested in any kind of relationship with me," Blaze said.

"Long-term or long-distance?"

"Either one," Blaze said. "What happened to the horse?"

"He got out of the horse barn, jumped a couple of fences, and they found him in a mesquite thicket with a torn foreleg. The vet had just gotten there. The family will stay with him all day and Raylen's drawn the straw for first shift tonight," Liz answered as she went to work on the troublesome screws.

Blaze got a battery powered drill from the toolbox and started helping. "If that horse belonged to me, the whole family would stay with him tonight. Colleen could read bedtime stories to him and keep him calm with her soft-as-silk voice."

Liz shook her head. "You are smitten."

"Yep, I am. Are you?"

"Oh, yeah! But I have been since I was a little girl," she admitted. "I fell in love with Raylen when I was ten years old."

Chapter 21

Liz had been on the phone with Raylen every minute of the way from Bowie to the O'Donnell ranch. She could see the lights shining out the open doors of the big barn, and then there was Colleen walking right toward them.

She put on the brakes and said, "Just a minute. Your sister is in front of me. Is she the one who will be relieving you?"

Raylen sighed. "I guess so if it's Colleen."

"Looks like her red hair."

Colleen stopped when Liz drove up beside her and opened the truck door. "I'll ride with you the rest of the way."

"Got a passenger and a guide. See you in a minute," Liz told Raylen and ended the call.

"The vet said we didn't have to sit up with Danny Boy, but Mama says different," Colleen said.

"Maddie loves that horse, doesn't she?" Liz asked.

"Yes, she does. She raised him from a newborn colt and always said he would be a winner, and she was right. We're more worried about her than the horse," Colleen said. "Mama is a strong woman, but…"

"But losing Danny Boy would crush her, right?" Liz asked.

Colleen nodded. "Mama and I will be in and out all night to check on him. Mostly she'll be keeping watch on the horse, and I'll be here for her. Gemma will take over at noon tomorrow since she doesn't have to work on Mondays. Dewar said he'll do a stint in the middle of the afternoon. By late tomorrow night, Mama says if he's doing well, we can stop baby-sitting. The vet will be here three times a day until we're sure his leg is healing right."

Liz nosed the truck in beside Raylen's vehicle. Before her hand reached the door handle, Raylen opened it.

"I'm so glad to see you." He leaned inside and kissed her right in front of Colleen.

"Hello to you too, Brother," Colleen said.

"Don't get snippy with me," Raylen said. "If Danny Boy gets an infection or—God forbid—that we have to put him down, I sure don't want to deal with Mama. Right now he is doing fine. Vet said he could eat whatever he wanted, so he's getting spoiled. I've already fed him three carrots and two apples, so don't believe him when he gives you that 'poor pitiful me' look."

He laced his fingers in Liz's hand and led her into the barn with Colleen right behind them. "The vet put in six stitches and gave him a healthy dose of antibiotics, which he gets three times a day for three days, along with dressing changes. He assures us Danny Boy will be good as new and doesn't think he was out more than a couple of hours. The blood wasn't dried on his wound and he didn't have any scratches anywhere else."

Liz let go of Raylen's hand and opened the gate to Danny Boy's stall. She went inside, rubbed his nose, and whispered, "Poor baby boy. Now you have to stay in the stall, and you won't get to see the Rocky Mountains and flirt with my girls. I've got a carrot in my pocket that was left over when we loaded the Vanner ladies into the horse wagon. Would you like to have it?" She offered it to him and he nuzzled her face before he accepted it.

"You're good with him," Colleen said.

"I love horses," Liz said as she stepped back out of the stall. "We've got several out in Claude that have been put out to pasture. They're too old for the carnival and I spend a lot of time with them in the winter."

"Vanners? You have Vanners?" Colleen asked.

"Six mares," Raylen answered for her. "Fancy stock, let me tell you. They use them for pony rides, believe it or not. Dewar is going to drool."

"I might drool with him," Colleen said. "I didn't see them when I was there."

"The pony rides are at the far end of the carnival.

Past the Ferris wheel. We keep them in a portable round pen. Blaze and Aunt Tressa take care of them. Blaze is really good with them. Knows his horses well. He and Aunt Tressa flew to Pennsylvania last February to buy a stud. Brought home Sweet Diamond Jessie. Poppa is of the opinion the Vanners are too fancy for carnival work. He wants us to leave them home next year."

"I agree. Shetlands can do carnival work. Rocky Mountains should be royalty," Colleen said.

Raylen threw open the stall door next to Danny Boy's. "Welcome to the babysitter's quarters."

Liz was amazed to see an army cot and two folding chairs. One chair held a laptop computer and one a baby monitor. She raised an eyebrow and Colleen laughed.

"There's one taped to Danny Boy's stall wall. We can hear him if he burps or whines," she explained.

Raylen tugged on her hand. "Sit by me."

Liz sat down on the cot, and he settled close to her. Colleen sat in the other metal chair and fidgeted with her fingers, lacing them together, then wringing them. She looked at the computer screen and then back at Raylen and Liz.

"I took a few days off work," Colleen said. "I figured I'd better come home and help with Danny Boy. When Mama called, she was frantic. Now I see y'all have it under control."

Raylen reached across the space and patted

Colleen's knee. "Thank you. You calm Mama's nerves more than any one of us kids. You need some time off anyway, and this is the week that Liz is having her big party. You'd hate to miss that."

Colleen shook her head. "I've got four weeks paid vacation coming. I took a week of that."

"How did you get that much vacation?" Liz asked.

"I've been there six years now. It builds up. So did y'all get the carnival torn down and ready to move things onto your place tomorrow?" Colleen asked.

"We did," Liz answered.

From the look in Colleen's eyes, Liz figured she wanted to know more about Blaze than she did about tearing down the carnival.

"I'd forgotten how much fun going to the carnival was," Colleen said, "and I really had a good time the other night. How about you, Raylen? I heard you'd been down there every night."

"Whole different view of carnivals now that I've helped get one ready to open. What time will they be here tomorrow? You going to light the place up for them?" Raylen asked Liz.

"Oh, yeah. I don't care if the sun is shining, it's going to be lit up. Mama is supposed to call me soon as they pull out, so I'll have time to turn everything on. Y'all were supposed to bring the tables over tomorrow evening for the barn. I know where they're stored. Is it all right if I bring Blaze and some of the guys over there and borrow them? You'll be busy with Danny Boy, I'm sure. Colleen, if you don't have to babysit, come on over and help us set up the party."

Colleen nodded. "Thanks for the invitation. If Danny Boy is better, I'd love to help. Do you have enough decorations? You are welcome to borrow the boxes of decorations we use for the ranch Christmas party. It's not until the second weekend in December."

"Got plenty but thanks for the offer," Liz told her.

"What time do you think your people will arrive?" Colleen asked.

"Sometime around three," Liz told her. "They'll have to do some last minute clean-up before they leave."

"I'll be there." Colleen stood up. "I should be getting back to the house. I'm sure Mama will be checking in with y'all at least every hour."

The minute Colleen cleared the end of the stall, Raylen picked Liz up and settled her onto his lap. and then his cell phone vibrated in his shirt pocket. He removed it and sighed. "Colleen says that Mama is on her way."

Liz quickly left her place in his lap and moved to the other end of the cot.

"Y'all back here? How's my Danny Boy?"

Maddie's voice echoed through the barn and Danny Boy's whinny came through the monitor.

Raylen yelled back as he pulled Liz down beside him and grabbed her hand. "He heard your voice and whimpered for you. Come on back here and check him out for yourself."

"I'll have to remember to give Colleen the same warning if she almost gets caught in a compromising situation with Blaze," Liz whispered.

"You do realize that's the real reason she took vacation time. She's dated a lot of cowboys in her day. Some guys I probably don't even know about, but she's never gone all tongue-tied over one like she has Blaze," Raylen said.

"And how do you feel about that?" Liz asked.

"I didn't like it at all. I hated it because of what you've told me about him. But then your Aunt Tressa sent me to work with him, and he's a good man. But..."

Maddie bypassed them and went straight to Danny Boy. She whispered in his ear and stroked his nose for a few minutes.

"But what?" Liz asked.

"But we'll talk about it later." Raylen lowered his voice. "Mama doesn't need to know about Blaze when Danny Boy is hurt."

Maddie settled into the metal chair in front of them. "He's lookin' good, and I appreciate all you kids chipping in to sit with him," Maddie said.

"When is your party, Liz? I'm hoping that Danny Boy is enough better that we can all come over to it."

"Wednesday night, and then they'll all roll out on Thursday and head home for the winter," Liz answered.

Maddie nodded and glanced back toward Danny Boy's stall.

"I'm sorry." Liz swallowed hard a couple of times before the lump in her throat went away enough that she could talk. "I can't imagine how worried you are. If we lost one of the Vanner horses, I would cry for a week, and I didn't raise them from babies. I shouldn't even be talking about a party when Danny Boy is hurt."

Maddie smiled and reached across the short space to pat Liz's hand. "Honey, we need a party worse now than we did two days ago. Danny Boy is going to be fine, and by Wednesday night, he'll be almost new. My mama is so excited to meet all your carnival family. She called four times this afternoon to see about Danny Boy and to talk about your party. She wants you and Raylen to play 'Fire on the Mountain' and 'The Devil Went Down to Georgia' together. She says that'll put the icing on any party."

"Well, if that's what she wants, it's what she'll get. Will she mind if some of the other folks bring their instruments and play?" Liz asked.

"Oh, no! The more the merrier. She loves music,

and she's convinced you are at least part Irish," Maddie said.

"When she sees Mama and Aunt Tressa, she'll believe it even more. They both have red hair and tempers. My dad was pure Latino. His name was Eddie Garcia," Liz said.

"Was?" Maddie asked.

"He died a few weeks before I was born. He and mother married on a whim. When the new wore off, he decided he didn't want a carnie wife. The divorce wasn't even final when he died. Mama gave me the Hanson name to avoid confusion, but if she'd given me his name, I would be a Garcia."

Maddie stood up. "Well, he and your mama sure made a pretty daughter. I'm going back to the house. Now that I've seen Danny Boy one more time, I can sleep better. If you need anything, holler and I'll send one of the girls or Dewar down here with it, or I'll bring it down myself."

"Thank you," Liz said.

When Maddie had been gone five minutes, Liz moved over to snuggle up to Raylen's side. "You reckon she could send one of the girls with a big king-size bed and some satin sheets?"

He buried his face in her hair. "I've gotten to see you every day for the past week, but I miss you every hour I'm not with you."

"I feel the same way," she said. "It seems like days since this morning."

He reached up above his head and flipped a switch. The stall went dark, with the dim lights out in the center aisle barely letting him see the hot desire in her dark eyes. He kicked the stall door shut and grinned.

"Ever made love in a horse stall?"

"No, but I'm plannin' on it right now," she said. "Before we do this, Raylen, we need to talk. I know we've only known each other as adults for a few weeks, but where are we going?"

The noise coming through the monitor told them that Danny Boy was restless.

"Guess we woke the baby," Raylen said as he flipped the light back on.

"Need to check on him?"

"Maybe for a few minutes. Stay right where you are, and we'll talk when I get back," he said as he opened the gate and headed over to the next stall.

She yawned. "I should go."

"Stay a little while. You said that we need to talk," he said.

She got to her feet and followed him out of the tiny stall. "We will, but not now. Danny Boy needs to have your full attention. Good night, darlin'. Please come to supper tomorrow evening. Aunt Tressa and Blaze are making Italian food in my big kitchen. Bring Colleen with you."

He checked on Danny Boy and then walked Liz out to her truck. "You sure that's wise?"

"Everyone at the carnival liked you," Liz told him. "Mama even wondered if you'd like to travel, and Aunt Tressa said there would always be a place for you in the carnival."

He grinned. "No, thank you. I could never leave this area. It's home. I wasn't talking about me, darlin'. Is it wise to invite Colleen and Blaze? Should we encourage or discourage whatever this is between them?"

Liz opened the door and turned to face Raylen. "Honey, Colleen might find out that Blaze is way too much for her to handle if they spend time together."

Raylen put an arm on either side of her and caged her against the door. "Or he might find out the same thing."

She raised up on her tiptoes, kissed him, and said, "Good night, Raylen. It's a quarter till twelve, and my truck might turn into a pumpkin if I'm not home by midnight."

Chapter 22

LIZ COULD HARDLY BELIEVE HER EARS WHEN her mother waved from her truck window and yelled, "It's just beautiful, Lizelle!"

That Marva Jo had agreed to set foot on Haskell's land was a miracle. She'd never quite forgiven her brother for leaving the carnival. Liz had envisioned all kinds of scenarios when her mother arrived, but pure old joy wasn't a part of any of them.

By the time the last flatbed had parked, Liz had jogged out to the barn and was making the rounds, showing them the barn, where the electrical outlets were, and where the portable bathrooms were placed out to the north of the barn. When Marva Jo and Tressa crawled out of their trucks, they didn't stop to get their trailers set up but headed straight to the barn. Liz ran ahead of them so she could see their faces when they saw the tree and all the presents.

"What do you think of it?" she asked.

Tressa looked all around as if she were measuring it in feet and inches. "It's big enough."

"For what?" Liz slipped an arm around each of them.

"Winter," Marva Jo said.

"You are thinkin' about changing the winter site to here? That would be awesome!" Liz swiped at a tear that escaped her eye and ran down her cheek.

"Not now. When you and Blaze take over the carnival. It would be ideal. Raylen could spend several months a year next to his folks and then y'all could travel the rest of it," Tressa said.

"Keep dreamin', ladies." She giggled. "It ain't happenin'. I wanted a cowboy for my Christmas present, not a carnie."

"And what's wrong with a carnie?" Blaze came up from behind and wrapped his big arms around all three of them.

"Not one thing," Liz said, and went all misty-eyed again. "I love you all, but I've made up my mind. I'd be over the moon for y'all to change your winter place when Poppa is gone, but I'm staying right here."

"That will be for the next generation to talk about. Blaze will oversee making decisions if you are serious, Lizelle," Marva Jo said.

"I am very serious," Liz said and yet there was a niggling little doubt still in the corner of her heart.

"That's not for years and years down the road," Blaze said. "Tressa and Marva Jo are still going to be running the big show when they are ninety. Now show me and Tressa to the kitchen. It's been years since I had a big kitchen to work inside."

Liz spun around, kissed him on the cheek, and whispered, "Thank you!"

"Is it this way?" Tressa pointed toward the tack room.

"No, it's in my house where you two are sleeping tonight."

Marva Jo shook her head. "We've decided that we'll eat in your house and cook in your house and maybe even enjoy a bubble bath in a real bathtub, but we aren't sleeping there. Neither of us would be able to get a wink of rest without wheels under us, and besides, look what sleeping in that house has done to you. Those roots might attack us in our sleep and never let us leave, and we've got a carnival to put on the road in four months."

Liz was only mildly disappointed. This year, she'd talked them into staying three nights and setting foot in her house. Next year, she might get them into a real bed. One baby step at a time and she could be a patient woman—when it came to some things.

"Then lead the way," Blaze said.

"I will, but you don't get to play in the kitchen until after you round up some guys to haul a bunch of tables and folding chairs from Raylen's barn to mine. I'm borrowing them for our dinner on Wednesday night," she said.

Blaze gave her an extra squeeze. "I can do that. You show these two women your house and then come back and take me to Raylen's barn. Can we make a side stop somewhere along the way and see Glorious Danny Boy and Major Jack?"

"No," she said without hesitation.

Blaze looked puzzled and hurt at the same time.

"Colleen is going to want to give you the tour of her folks' place, and I wouldn't deprive her of that for anything," Liz answered. "So you'll have to wait until after supper. I've invited her and Raylen to eat with us."

"I understand." Blaze's grin lit up the whole barn. "I'll get my trailer set up while you do what you got to do and see you back here in a few minutes."

Liz tucked one of her hands into her mother's and the other into Tressa's and led them back to the house. "You should have been here when I first discovered that barn was on my property. I thought it belonged to Raylen. And then we found the Christmas stuff up in the loft where Uncle Haskell had his wood shop, and Jasmine and Ace and Dewar and Gemma all pitched in to help me get it all up and lit before you got here. I wish you would have brought me here for Christmas so I could have seen everything all decorated."

"Haskell and Sara came out to our winter place for Christmas," Tressa reminded her.

"I know, but as a child I would have thought this place was magic," Liz said. "As an adult, it seems like that to me, and I can't wait for you to meet Jasmine.

She owns the café where I work. Don't look at me like that, Aunt Tressa. I know I'm rich and I don't have to work, but I want to. And I've invited everyone I know to the party so you can meet the whole community." She stopped at the back porch and took a long breath, then went on. "You'd never believe that Jasmine left a high paying corporate job to be a cook in her own little café, or that Pearl walked away from being a high-powered banker to run a motel over in Henrietta. And what do you think of this infatuation Blaze has with Colleen?" She finally let go of their hands and opened the door. "Welcome to my home."

"We've been here before," Marva Jo said.

"Not since it's belonged to me," Liz told her.

Tressa giggled. "You threw that last question about Blaze and Colleen in there pretty slick, girl."

"Yes, I did, but I'm worried about both of them. You'll remember Hooter and Blister." She pointed to the dog and cat meandering around the corner of the house. "He's a terrible watchdog, and I understand she has kittens two or three times a year. You've probably already met them, too, but if you've got a problem while you are here, just remember that they are wonderful listeners. Now please answer that question, Aunt Tressa. I've been dying to ask you, and Blaze is always around, and I'm dying to know what y'all think."

"You are missing our gossip sessions, aren't you?" Marva Jo said.

"Yes, I am," Liz admitted honestly.

The cat and dog followed all three of them into the house, through the kitchen and into the living room. Hooter jumped up on the sofa, and Blister found a place under the coffee table.

"What do you think?" Liz asked.

"Which question do you want answered first?" Tressa shot right back at her.

"The one about Blaze, and then tell me how you like all my decorations," Liz answered.

"Blaze is a big boy." Marva Jo walked around the tree and pointed to an ornament. "That one belonged to my mother. She gave it to Sara the first Christmas that she was in the family, and darlin' girl, I like Colleen. My instincts tell me she's a quick study and I can already see her in costume."

Liz's dark eyes almost popped right out of her head. "For what?"

"Telling fortunes." Tressa pointed to another ornament. "Mother handmade these little crocheted snowflakes for Sara the year Lizelle was born."

"You will be telling fortunes for years and years." Liz wasn't sure she was comfortable with turning over her job to Colleen.

"Yes, but I have to have help. I trained this one girl named Lizelle, but she's tired of the life. However," Tressa paused, "Colleen could be ready by spring to take over your job if you're really going to leave us."

"She would never leave her family and her job," Liz gasped.

"You did," Marva Jo answered. "Now show me the kitchen and the pantry. You remembered to get fresh garlic, didn't you? A good lasagna does not need to be made with dried flakes."

Liz nodded. "This way."

Marva Jo looped an arm around her daughter's waist. "I love the house. If I wasn't a carnie, it's exactly what I'd want. Big living room for the family. Big kitchen to cook in, and bedrooms on the other end. I can see why Haskell built it this way. Too bad he and Sara never had kids. I liked that woman. She would have made a good mother."

"You saying that means a lot to me. It can't be easy," Liz said.

"You'd better have more than one child. Have a house full, because at least one of my granddaughters is going to inherit my traveling blood, and I'm going to make you pay for your raisin' one of these days," Marva Jo said. "Until then, know that I love you enough not to send you on too big of a guilt trip."

Liz put both arms around her mother and hugged her. "You are the best mother in the whole world."

Marva Jo hugged her back and then took a step back. "Tell me that when I steal your favorite child and make her a carnie. It'll be in her bloodline, Lizelle. Don't forget where you came from."

"I can never forget that," Liz said. "Let's go cook before you make me cry."

Tressa laughed. "You cook? Darlin', have you told Raylen that the extent of your cooking ability lies with whatever you can pour out of a can or heat up in a microwave?"

Liz pointed toward the end of the living room. "His mama lives one mile that way and she is an amazing cook. I'm bettin' I can wrangle a meal or two a week over there. And don't forget I'm a waitress at a café. Jasmine is an artist in the kitchen, and her prices are reasonable. I can take him up to the Chicken Fried when Maddie or Grandma aren't cookin'. And on the nights we want to stay in I betcha he doesn't mind canned soup and microwave pizza at all."

Tressa threw back her head and roared. "We have raised a genius, Marva Jo." Then the laughter stopped abruptly, and she grew serious. "Too bad she's going to make this one bad decision, though."

"And that is?" Liz wished she hadn't even asked when the words were out there.

"I'm living proof that sometimes you just got to let a kid fall on her face, but when she comes to her senses and returns to the fold, we will take her back without saying 'I told you so'," Marva Jo said.

"Who's going to say I told you so?" Blaze asked as he opened the back door.

"I am," Tressa declared. "When Liz comes back

where she belongs in a few months, I'm going to say it even if Marva Jo doesn't."

"I am, too," Blaze said, "but this is a really sweet little place here."

"Wait until you see the O'Donnell ranch. It's downright huge, and if I come crawling back to the carnival, you can all gather round me and chant 'I told you so' for as long as you like," Liz said. "But don't hold your breath until it happens. None of you look good in that shade of blue."

Blaze stopped just inside the door and took stock of the kitchen. "This is even bigger than Poppa's kitchen out in the winter place."

"Yes, it is," Liz said. "Are you ready to get those tables?"

"Yes, I am, and the folks all love the idea of getting a little rest before we all split seven ways to Sunday. They said if we'll bring in the tables, they will set them up for their supper tonight. Frankie is making soup for all of them, and they'll be glad to have a place to sit around and enjoy the decorations out there," Blaze answered. "Let's get this show on the road. I can't wait to mess up this big old kitchen."

"What you can't wait for is a glimpse of Colleen, and remember, the rule applies in a big kitchen the same as a little one: what you mess up you clean up. Only thing I like less than cooking is washing dishes," Liz teased on the way out the back door.

Chapter 23

RAYLEN WAS FRESHLY SHAVEN, AND HANDED LIZ a bottle of his sister-in-law Austin's watermelon wine when she opened the door.

"You didn't have to knock," she whispered.

"Yes, I did," he said. "I want to make a good impression."

"You already did. They're talking about you joining the carnival." She continued to speak in a low tone. "Can I take your hat?"

"Depends on what you intend to do with it." He removed his black felt dress hat and finger-combed his dark hair.

"I'll turn it upside down right there on the coffee table, and I promise I won't stomp it or sit on it," she said.

He handed it to her. "I'm putting a lot of trust in you, darlin'. I've seen what you can do to a man's good hat."

"What have you seen?" Blaze asked from the doorway into the living room.

Raylen nodded to acknowledge Blaze. "I have seen with my own eyes that Liz has quite a temper. She threw my hat on the ground and then stomped it."

"Then you're doing good," Blaze said. "She will have her say or die, so if you are weak-hearted, you need to run right now."

"That's the Latina in her," Tressa called from the kitchen.

"Raylen brought watermelon wine," Liz said to divert the conversation away from herself.

"I had to beg for that bottle. Austin wanted to send a bottle of Granny Lanier's because she's sure it's a good vintage. But I made her give me a bottle of her first year's crop to celebrate tonight," Raylen said.

"That's so romantic." Tressa came into the living room and took the bottle from Liz. "I've only had this kind a couple of times, but I really liked the flavor. It will go well with tonight's supper."

Raylen slipped his arm around Liz. "Thank you. Colleen said she'll be along in a little bit. She wasn't through primping, and I have an idea she wants to bring her own vehicle tonight."

Liz turned away from Raylen and looked at Blaze. He had changed from his work clothes and was now dressed in Wranglers, boots, and a black shirt with two buttons open at the neck. His dark brown hair was feathered back, with a few drops of water still clinging to it.

"You two are certainly a couple of handsome fellers tonight," Liz said as she turned back to Raylen. "I suppose you've noticed that there's mistletoe over every doorway, and I don't know about Colleen, but I do not intend to waste any of it."

Blaze grinned, and his cat-like eyes glistened. "Thank you very much, Lizelle. And I forgot to tell you that the house is beautiful. It ought to be on one of those house tour things that they talk about in Amarillo."

"What I like most is that arrangement on the mantel," Tressa said. "Mother would have liked having a nativity in the house. She liked the spiritual side of the holiday and Poppa has always loved the silly side."

Raylen slipped an arm around Liz's shoulders. "What about you, darlin'? What do you like?"

"All of it. Nativity, Santa Claus, and every single bit of it. There's not a theme I don't like, and did I tell you that we're doing the cafe in a country Christmas theme? I can't wait to dive into that, too. Are you going to help me?"

"How cute is my butt?" From the slight redness in his face, he hadn't meant to say those words out loud.

"Cutest one in the house tonight." And then she whipped around to face her mother, Tressa, and Blaze. "I told him that his butt was cute when he was up on a ladder."

"Thank you, and darlin', you look amazing tonight," Raylen said.

"Yes, you do," Blaze said with a grin.

Raylen drew her even closer to his side. "She always

does. She wore this the first time she came to Sunday dinner at my folks'. I thought she was a princess."

"She is." Blaze smiled. "You two go on in the living room and sit with Marva Jo. Tressa and I will finish up in the kitchen. I still have a few adjustments to make to the table. I need to put out glasses for the wine."

"He cooks?" Raylen whispered on the way to the living room.

"Yes, he is a chef in the kitchen, and he's a neat freak and even does his own ironing because a laundry wouldn't do it to suit him."

"No wonder the women love him," Raylen said.

She shrugged. "Hadn't thought about it that way, but you are right."

Marva Jo caught the last of the conversation and pieced the rest together. "Liz does not cook. She knows how to do laundry and hates to iron. She had no choice but to keep things neat, but it's not by nature like it is with Blaze. It was by necessity because we lived in a small trailer."

Raylen sat down next to Liz. "Are you tryin' to scare me off?"

"Maybe," Marva Jo answered. "Is it working?"

"Not a bit," Raylen told her.

Liz patted Raylen on the knee. "He's not a neat freak, but he's not sloppy. His biggest problem is that he's organized and a perfectionist."

"Then he'd better reconsider a relationship with you," Marva Jo said.

"How does Colleen fit into the picture? She's your sister?" Marva Jo asked.

"We are peas in a pod, but she only cooks when she has to. Mama made all of us learn everything from kitchen work to cleaning to ranching. Boys had to learn just like girls, but she also made sure my sisters were able to run a ranch just like us boys. In the O'Donnell household, there is no division of men's and women's work." Raylen made lazy circles on the palm of Liz's hand with his thumb.

Liz vowed she'd get even later. It wasn't fair for him to heat her to the boiling point with nothing but his thumb, and right there in front of her mother.

The doorbell rang, and Liz started to hop up, but Raylen held her hand tightly and yelled, "Blaze, would you get that door?"

Liz shot him a look, but he just winked at her and said, "Us guys got to stick together."

"That's not fair. Why does she get to go to the kitchen?" Liz whispered.

Marva Jo shook her finger at Liz. "You've got all the pie you can eat right here in this living room, my child. Let Blaze have his in the kitchen. I guarantee you that Tressa won't let them do one thing more than I let you two get away with."

"Why do I feel like I'm sixteen and on my first date?" Liz asked.

Marva Jo smiled. "Because I said so."

Liz giggled. "I've heard that often enough."

Blaze yelled from the kitchen, "I heard that last remark. Colleen has invited me over to her place to meet her parents tonight and to see those two famous horses."

"Children, children! Forgive them, Colleen," Tressa said. "They've acted like siblings since the day I brought Blaze to the carnival. Marva Jo, bring your wayward daughter to the dinner table. We are ready to sit down."

———

Liz pulled the sheet up over her and Raylen. A fine sheen of sweat covered them both, and an afterglow that was almost visible surrounded them. She reached across the space between them and clasped his hand in hers.

"That was fantastic. Good night, darlin'," she said breathlessly.

"Always is," he panted. "But I'm not spending the night."

"Why?" she asked. "Mama and Aunt Tressa are in their trailers."

"I'm trying to show your mama and aunt that I'm one of the good guys, not a bad boy that only wants a romp in the hay, so I'm going home."

She held on tightly to his hand, but he shook free and in one swift movement he was off the bed and on his feet.

"You don't play fair," she said.

"That would be the pot calling the kettle black, darlin'." He dressed quickly and headed out of the bedroom.

She sat up and wrapped the sheet under her arms. "You think Colleen made Blaze's trailer rock?"

Raylen covered his ears. "I don't even want to think about that—Colleen is my sister!"

"You are *her* brother. You think she doesn't know we've been to bed?" Liz asked.

"Don't go there," Raylen said.

She whipped the sheet back and jumped out of bed, put her finger under his nose, and said, "Don't you talk to me in that tone. I was joking."

"If you had a brother, would you want me to tease about him sleeping with Becca?" Raylen's tone had a bit of a chill to it.

She took a step forward. "That's different, and Blaze is like a brother. I wouldn't get all hot under the collar if you wondered if he was out in the horse barn with Colleen. Go home. Evidently, you can't take teasing."

He whipped around and stormed out of the house. She threw herself back on the bed and pouted for five minutes before the tears started. Her short-lived relationship with Raylen was probably over. Most likely the whole reason fate had sent her to Ringgold was so that Colleen and Blaze could find each other.

"Life isn't fair," she sobbed into her pillow.

Her mother's voice popped into her head. *Oh, hush your whining! You think you are the only one who is unsure of herself in this relationship? What about Raylen? You are a carnie and your whole carnie family is surrounding you right now. Ever think that he might be scared you'll go with us when we leave?*

She wiped her eyes with the edge of the sheet and sniffled. *I'm not leaving. He's not running me off. I'm staying right here because it feels right*, she thought stoically. *But if Raylen isn't the one*—She broke down and wept again.

She couldn't call Blaze because he was busy with Colleen, and Liz wouldn't disturb that but she sure needed a friend. She finally slung her legs over the edge of the bed, grabbed the first nightgown in her drawer, and pulled it over her head. She pushed her feet down into her cowboy boots and picked up her truck keys from the kitchen counter and stormed out of the house.

She vowed she wouldn't shed another tear as she slid behind the wheel of her vehicle and drove down her lane to where it made a sharp left. By then sadness had turned to anger. She stomped the gas pedal, slung gravel halfway to Bowie, and headed toward the O'Donnell ranch. The truck fishtailed when she turned onto the gravel road back to Raylen's house. Lights were on in the house, but when she reached the porch and knocked on the door, no one answered.

"I'm not leaving until you open this door," she muttered and twisted the door knob, only to find it locked. "You are not going to lock me out until we talk."

Finally, he opened the door just a crack and stood before her in nothing but a towel. His hair stuck up every which way, and water dripped onto the floor.

"What do you want?" he asked.

She slung the door fully open, and he took two steps backward. "Don't you ever leave in the middle of a fight. You stay until we settle it and either break up with me or else have makeup sex, but don't just walk away."

"You told me to leave," he reminded her but still didn't invite her inside.

"Well, I didn't mean it. You are supposed to stand up and fight for us if we are important enough." She propped both hands on her hips. "Are we, Raylen, or are you tired of me already?"

"Don't you dare accuse me of being tired of you. I've wanted you since we were kids, dreamed about you, thought about you, and measured every other woman by the impossible yardstick you put in my mind. So don't you dare say I'm tired of you. I won't ever be tired of you. Maybe you just want to go back to the carnival, and this is your way of doing it. Fight with me so it'll make it all right," he said.

She stepped right up into his space, her nose not

six inches from his. "You are an idiot if you think that. I was crying my eyes out and made up my mind that Ringgold is where I belong. So, whether you are tired of me or not, I'm not leaving. You can just get used to having me for a neighbor, if that's all we are ever going to be to each other after tonight."

Gemma made her way into the living room and stared at them. "I don't even want to know. See you two in the morning." She went to her room, closed the door, and turned the music up.

"I'm sorry. It was stupid," Raylen said.

"I'm sorry too," Liz said. "It was ugly of me to talk like that about Colleen. You were right. If I had a brother, I'd be livid if I thought he was with Becca. And you've been so good about Colleen even after all that stuff you know about Blaze. Forgive me?"

"Of course I forgive you. I love you, Liz Hanson. I have since that day you were watching me ride. You were so beautiful leaning on the fence, but not as gorgeous as you are in that flannel nightshirt you are wearing right now," Raylen whispered.

"I love you too, and I have my whole life, it seems like. I'd like to rip that towel off you, but I'm going to turn around and go home," she said.

"Why?" Raylen asked. "Gemma knows you are here. The whole county probably knows you are here."

"Because when we have our makeup sex, it's not going to be with your sister across the hall."

He bookended her face with his big hands and kissed her hard. "I do love you."

"Me too!" She turned around and walked outside. All the way home she singsonged, "Raylen loves me. Raylen loves me."

Chapter 24

LIZ COULDN'T HAVE ASKED FOR A BETTER NIGHT for her party. The carnival folks had pulled the cinnamon bun wagon, the funnel cake wagon, and the gyro wagon off the flatbed and set them up inside the barn. Liz had made arrangements with Jasmine to cater in turkey and dressing and glazed ham. The rest was pure potluck. Bring whatever you like, put your name on the bottom of the dish, and go home with a full tummy and an empty dish.

"With all this food, why would you set up those wagons?" Gemma asked.

"Ovens. We needed more ovens," Liz explained.

Raylen slipped his arms around her waist and pulled her back to his chest. "Hello, darlin'."

"That sounded almost like Conway Twitty." Liz laughed.

Raylen buried his face in her hair and inhaled. "This is one big party."

She laughed again and turned around. "Yes, and I want to introduce you to each one of my carnival family."

He kissed her quickly and nodded toward the

corner of the barn where the musicians were tuning up their instruments. "I didn't know so many of your friends played. Does Blaze?"

"Blaze can dance the leather off a woman's boot soles. He can almost carry a tune, but he can't play anything. Not even a washboard because his rhythm is off," she said.

Grandpa O'Malley's big booming voice sounded even louder coming from a microphone that had been set up in the musicians' corner. "Liz tells me that it's time to announce the food is ready. We are thankful for the opportunity for everyone to get to mingle and know each other. And whoever made those cinnamon rolls, would you hide one pan of them under the table for me to take home? Don't tell my wife Franny. She and the doctor tell me I'm too fat, but those bathroom scales are the biggest liars in the world. Now load up your plates, and while you're doin' it Raylen and Liz are going to give us some fiddlin' to entertain us."

Raylen looked at Liz with a puzzled expression.

"I asked him to make the announcement," she explained. "It's kind of like mixing up our two families tonight. Is that a problem?"

"Not at all. I just didn't know we were supposed to play right now. I'd rather hold you as my fiddle," he answered.

"Later, darlin'," she whispered as she led the way to the stage area and picked up her fiddle.

Raylen followed right behind her.

Liz pulled the bow across the strings to make sure it was still in tune. "Ready?"

He smiled and locked his eyes with hers.

"Then let's give 'em something to talk about," she said.

She started the Bonnie Raitt tune, "Something to Talk About."

Liz didn't miss a beat when she stepped up to the microphone and sang as she played. The lyrics said that they were going to give them something to talk about and it was love, love, love.

When the last chords died, she turned to Raylen and said, "Is that yelling it from the rooftops?"

He nodded and mouthed, "My turn."

She recognized "Tennessee Whiskey" from the first note, and then he began to sing and play at the same time.

"Give us some 'Devil Went Down to Georgia,'" Grandpa yelled when they'd finished that one.

Liz and Raylen's bows hit the fiddles at the same time and the whole barn went silent as they watched the show. They faced each other and had a real contest and when the song ended, the applause was deafening.

"Ready to give me that fiddle?" he asked Liz.

"Are you ready to give me yours?"

"I beat you that time," Raylen argued. "I sang as well as played, and I didn't miss a beat."

"I didn't either." Liz didn't give up that easy. "Grandma, who won?"

Franny pushed back her chair and stood up. "I'm callin' it a second tie. You two belong together."

Raylen pulled the microphone to his mouth. "Yes, we do. Liz and I are together so all you other cowboys out there are out of luck."

"It's been announced to the whole county!" Gemma yelled from across the barn.

"We're hungry so we're takin' a break. Rest of you can play when you want and maybe we'll join you later," Raylen said.

"You ain't goin' to do 'Earl's Breakdown' before you go?" Blaze asked.

"Maybe later. I've got something better to hold right now." Raylen slung his arm around Liz's shoulders and looked up.

"What are you looking for?" she asked.

"Mistletoe," he answered.

"We've announced that we are together," she told him and tiptoed to kiss him. "We don't need mistletoe."

Raylen led Liz to the food table where they loaded up their plates and carried them to a table where a couple of chairs were left.

As soon as they sat down Blaze stood up.

"I've got a toast to give here in front of all these witnesses." Blaze held up his beer bottle. "I was wrong."

"The world is coming to an end!" Liz raised her voice. "Blaze just admitted he was wrong."

"There's a first time for everything," Blaze said. "Liz, I hate to admit it, but you belong right here. Roots look good on you."

"Hear, hear!" Colleen clinked her beer bottle with Blaze's.

"Raylen, be aware, she's got a temper," Blaze said.

"Oh, I've already seen that." Raylen laughed.

Colleen leaned over and whispered in Liz's ear, "When you get ready to sell those wings of yours for absolute sure, I'll give you top dollar for them."

One of Raylen's good friends, Wil, held up his beer. "My awesome wife Pearl and I have an announcement. It's twins and they're due in July. If they're girls, I'm hoping that they get their mama's red hair."

Liz wondered what it would be like to have twins—girls with Colleen's red hair, and maybe Gemma's carefree attitude. Would she and Raylen have blue-eyed children or would they have her dark hair and eyes?

"Congratulations!" Liz raised her tea glass. "I can't imagine having two kids at once."

"I can't imagine having one." Pearl smiled. "But then I couldn't imagine being married to Wil the first time he came into my motel. He was so cocky and full of himself—and still is—but that's what I love about him. There we were in the middle of a winter storm and the next morning the cops arrested him for murder."

"And?" Liz asked.

"It was a case of mistaken identity," Wil answered. "But she came to my rescue in her vintage Caddy, and I swear I was in love from that day."

"You were not! It took a shot contest to make you see you'd met your match," Pearl said.

Wil kissed her on the cheek. "Red, darlin', that's just when I admitted it to myself. My heart knew the first time your devil cat and Digger got into it."

"Red?" Liz leaned in closer and blocked out all the noise around her.

"She is Pearl to everyone else, believe me." Jasmine laughed. "But she lets Wil call her Red."

Liz smiled and shifted her gaze to Blaze. "Thanks for your toast. After the way you carried on, I know what that one cost you."

"My thanks, too," Raylen said. "I agree. Roots look good on her."

"You'll have to clip her wings every spring about the time we leave for the rounds," Blaze said. "She won't truly ever forget her previous life, but she does belong here with all y'all."

Tressa walked up behind Liz and laid a hand on her shoulder. "Great party, darlin' girl. But the truth is Raylen beat you on the fiddlin' contest."

"Aunt Tressa!" Liz could hardly believe that Tressa would say such a thing.

"But," Tressa held up a finger, "Raylen, you will never get her to admit defeat and give you that fiddle of hers. The only way you'll ever get it is to take the woman that goes with it. That's goin' to take some serious hard work. Good luck, son."

Liz's heart was full that evening. She had the best of both worlds, but tomorrow half of her heart would be leaving with her carnival family. Right then she wondered if Raylen would be content with just having the other half. She looked up at the angel on the top of the tree and a tear formed on her eyelashes. She was willing to give up her wings for love, but like Blaze said, it was coming at a cost.

The trip would be over before supper. The next day they'd winterize the travel trailers, unload the wagons and semi-trucks in a long row behind the barn. The horses would be put out to pasture.

Through the next few months, Poppa would use his little tractor to pull the vending wagons inside the barn for renovations. Then the last week in February, they'd come driving in, a few each day. Everyone would be excited, and the new year would begin the same way the previous one ended, with Poppa standing on the porch waving at everyone.

"It was a wonderful party," Raylen said.

She nodded. "But it's over."

He tipped up her chin with his fist and said, "Memories last forever. I remember this little girl who could stay on the fence longer than me. And one who watched me ride, and I wanted to show off for her even more than I did, but I was afraid Mama would kill me if I hurt my horse or myself either one. Those memories were etched into my mind for years before she came back."

"Don't be sweet to me," Liz groaned. "Fight with me. I want to kick something or pitch a fit. It's like when the winter ended, and it was time to go on the road. I was happy because everyone was so excited about a new year, but a little bit of me was angry because I didn't want to leave Poppa and our home there. It always made me cry to see him waving good-bye from the porch. I felt happy and sad at the same time, just like I do now," she said.

His cell phone rang in his shirt pocket so close to Liz's face that she jumped.

"It's Becca," he said.

Liz had found the perfect person to fight with even if she had to do it by phone.

"Hello. Why weren't you at Liz's party tonight? We missed you," he said.

Liz reached out and took the phone from Raylen and put it on speaker. "This was a big thing for me and Raylen both tonight. If you were really his friend, then you would have been here instead of staying home pouting. Are you mad because I told you what the cards said? You knew that I wouldn't lie when I laid those cards out, and besides—"

Becca raised her voice. "Shut up and listen to me."

Liz raised her voice two octaves. "What did you say to me?"

"I said shut up, Liz," Becca said with a giggle. "I wasn't there because Taylor and I got married today. I wanted you and Raylen to be the first to know. I did what you told me to do, and we told Daddy together. He wasn't happy, but he settled down and said I could have the down payment for a house to be built on the ranch or a big fancy wedding. Taylor and I decided to take the house and we flew to Las Vegas for three days. After that, I'm putting in ten-hour days at the ranch, learning what I should already know, so when the time comes I can keep it running. So shut up and wish me good luck."

"Are you serious?" Liz said barely above a stunned whisper.

Becca laughed. "I finally got the best of you."

"You did not!" Liz argued.

"Oh yes I did." Becca sounded happy. "Now let Raylen talk."

"He's going to be so disappointed, Becca. He wanted to be your maid of honor at your wedding, and now he's got this beautiful apricot-colored dress that he won't ever get to wear."

Becca's laughter echoed off the walls.

"Congratulations, and I do not have a dress of any color," Raylen said, "but why did you listen to Liz? I've been giving you the same advice for months."

Becca lowered her voice. "It took a woman's point of view, I suppose, and Raylen, she's a smart cookie. Hang on to her."

"Yes, ma'am."

"She'll make you toe the line like Taylor does me. Neither of us could ever be satisfied with a wimp."

"Yes, ma'am."

"Good night. I love him, Raylen. Have for a long time. This will change things between me and you, won't it?"

"Sometimes change ain't too bad," he answered.

Liz looked at him with questions on her face when he turned the phone off and laid it on the arm of the sofa.

He raised a dark eyebrow and grinned. "What?"

"Change is good? Do you really believe that?" Liz asked.

"With my whole heart," Raylen answered.

She rolled her eyes toward the ceiling. "I can't get a rousing good argument out of anyone."

"Why do you want to argue?" he asked.

"Because if I'm angry, then I won't be sad," she admitted.

"I'll be here when the exodus begins." He kissed

her. "And honey, until you aren't wishing, that you are ready to really give up your wings, you can't grow roots that will bind you to this place."

Liz walked him to the door, kissed him goodnight one more time, and was asleep two minutes after her head hit the pillow, but she was restless all night, tossing and turning, reaching out for Raylen only to find an empty pillow beside her.

Chapter 25

HUGS WERE GIVEN.

Promises made.

Then it was time for Liz to stand on the porch like her Poppa had done for years and wave as the parade went down her lane. Tears dripped off her cheeks and dropped onto her sweatshirt. She'd made up her mind and she was at peace with her decision. She liked her roots. She loved Raylen. But why did clipping her wings have to hurt so badly?

When the last taillight was out of sight, she tucked her head into Raylen's shoulder and sobbed. "Now I know how my Poppa felt when we all left him behind. I miss all of them, Raylen, and they're not even to the highway heading west yet."

"They're only hours from here, Liz. You can go see them any weekend that you want to. You can take off when you get off at two on Saturday and come home the next day. It's not like you won't see them for a year," he said.

"Oh, hush." Colleen rounded the end of the house and she was crying as hard as Liz.

Raylen held out his left arm to Colleen and she

walked into it, laid her head on his other shoulder, and sobbed. He didn't know what to do with one weeping woman and now he had two hugged up to him, soaking his shirt with their tears.

"You still want those wings?" Liz asked.

"More than ever. What's the price?" Colleen asked.

Liz wiped her cheeks with the back of her hands. "I'll sell them to you for your roots, but know this, if it hurts this bad to clip my wings, it's going to cause a lot of pain to rip up your roots."

"Right now, I would hand them to you on a silver platter. Watching him leave was the hardest thing I've ever done. How can I feel like this after only a week?" Colleen asked.

Liz smiled through the tears. "Craziest thing in the world, ain't it?"

"At least you don't have to have a long-distance relationship," Colleen said.

"Neither do you. Four hours out there. Take your vacation time and go spend it with him," Liz said.

Colleen swiped at her eyes with the sleeve of her denim jacket. "Mama will have a fit."

"Mine did, and it didn't kill me. Maddie will be angry, but you'll live. It's part of the price we have to pay to follow our hearts," Liz told her.

Colleen nodded and pulled out of Raylen's embrace. "I've got to go to Randlett. Got to be at work at four today. I'll call you, Liz."

Liz stepped away from Raylen and put a hand on Colleen's arm. "Think about going out there. He'll call you but…"

Colleen hugged Liz. "I know. He's cocky as hell, but there's a little insecurity there. I promise I'll think about it, but it takes at least a week after I put in a request for that kind of time. I'll let you know when I figure it all out."

"I'll be right here or at work or riding horses to pay for all the help with my party, but I'll have my phone," Liz said.

Colleen disappeared around to the backyard. Liz swallowed another lump in her throat just thinking about the decisions ahead of Colleen. If that had been Raylen driving away, her heart would have shattered.

"Well, that puts things in perspective," she mumbled.

"What's that?" Raylen asked.

"There could be a worse scenario than Mama and Aunt Tressa leaving," she said.

"And what would that be?" Raylen tucked her hand in his and started walking toward his truck.

"Watching you drive away," she answered.

"That ain't happenin', darlin'," he whispered as he sealed that vow with a long, lingering kiss.

"Where are you takin' me?" she asked.

"Mama says Danny Boy needs a slow walk around the pasture and she wants me to do that. But there's about a dozen mares that need some exercise. Want to ride off those tears?" Raylen asked.

Liz nodded. "Let's go."

———————

They rode to the horse barn in comfortable silence. Two very different emotions rattled around inside Raylen. Hearing Liz say that watching him leave would be painful made him happy, but it was short-lived. He could see the future as plain as Liz did when she read the cards. Colleen was pulling up her roots and growing carnival wings right before his eyes. He'd always figured all five of the O'Donnells would settle down right there close to Ringgold. They'd all come to Sunday dinner when Maddie called them in like a hen with her chickens. And raise their kids together. If Colleen and Blaze got serious and wound up together, Rachel would hardly know her carnie cousins.

And Gemma? What did the future have in store for her? Would both of his sisters wind up living far away?

Maddie waved at them from the barn door where she leaned on a scoop shovel. When Raylen got out of the truck and then opened the door for Liz, Maddie tossed her shovel to the side and met them halfway. She wrapped Liz up in her arms and said, "It can't be easy to watch your family leave like that. We've all lived in a close pile. I'm not so sure how much longer that'll be the way it is. I saw the way Blaze looked at my daughter and it scares me. Colleen has always been the one with the…" She stumbled.

"The most pessimism." Raylen smiled.

"No, the one who took care of everyone else," Liz said.

"That's right." Maddie nodded. "I always thought she'd probably wind up with a nearby rancher who'd adore her."

"Blaze is not a rancher, but he adores her," Liz said.

"And that is probably the most important part. But right now, this minute, I think you need some good old hard work. I understand you ride?"

"Yes, ma'am," Liz said.

"Well, start on the south side of the stables at the end. That'll be Missy. A couple of turns around the forty acres over there," Maddie pointed to her left, "should do it. You can ride as many as you have time for, and I appreciate the help."

"Thank you, Maddie."

"I'll clean out her stall while you ride," she said.

Raylen draped an arm around Liz's shoulder and directed her to Missy's stall. "She's partial to this." Raylen hefted a saddle from the stall and handed it to Liz. "Do you need me to put it on for you?"

Liz picked a bridle from a nail up above the

saddle and started talking softly to the horse. "I can do it myself."

Raylen backed up to the other side of the center aisle and crossed his arms over his chest. He'd make sure she had the hang of things before he went over to Danny Boy's stall. The saddle might be too heavy for her. She might have trouble getting Missy to stand still while she cinched it up. Or she might need a boost to get mounted up and ready.

Missy nudged Liz's shoulder. "Impatient, are you? Well, we'll have us a good ride right after we get you all ready, and then we'll have an apple or a carrot."

She hung the saddle back on the gate.

"What are you doing?" Raylen asked.

"I ride bareback," she told him.

He followed her as she led the horse out into the sunshine and rubbed Missy's ears for a minute before she grabbed a hunk of mane and swung up on the horse's bare back in one swift movement. She clamped her knees against Missy's flanks and the mare stepped high.

Maddie came out of the first stall and stared. "Is she one of them horse whisperers?"

Raylen shook his head. "She's pretty good, isn't she?"

Liz's dark hair fluffed out behind her as she led the horse into a soft trot. "Fast enough, little girl. That's all you're going to get today. Any more and you'll work up too much sweat."

Maddie and Raylen watched until she and Missy disappeared over a hill in the distance and then Maddie picked up the shovel. "She doesn't need me to advise her on horses. I'm going back to work."

Raylen brought Danny Boy out for his walk, and kept an eye out for Liz the whole time.

"I'm still in shock at that woman of mine. She's just full of surprises," Raylen said.

Danny Boy threw back his head and neighed as if he understood every word.

———

Liz finished the second round and brought Missy back to the front of the barn. She slid off her back, led her inside the barn, and grabbed up the equipment to rub her down before she put her back in the stall that Maddie had just finished mucking out.

"You're pretty good ridin' bareback," Maddie said.

"We got horses out in west Texas. I can saddle up if you want me to, but it's just extra time. Who's next?" Liz asked.

"Fire Red." She pointed to the name above the stall door.

"Her name mean she's got a temper?" Liz asked.

Maddie leaned on the shovel. "Gentlest mare I've got. She's birthed several of Danny Boy's colts for me. Got one that'll be in the sale this next fall. Beautiful boy that we haven't broken yet."

Liz itched to meet that horse. "Want me to start workin' with him?"

"Honey, Dewar would disown me if I let anyone near that horse but him. But there'll be more colts, and now that I've seen what you can do, you're goin' to have your hands full. You've got a full-time job here when you quit the café business. And I promise you will get to break one eventually," Maddie said.

Liz and Fire Red had made it halfway around the pasture when her phone rang. She fished it out of her hip pocket and shifted the reins to one hand. Fire Red kept up a steady trot around the perimeter of the pasture.

"We're out past Wichita Falls," Marva Jo said.

"Haskell called. Poppa is antsin' y'all to get there," Liz said, "and Mama, watching y'all leave was pretty tough."

"Change hurts sometimes, but you are where you should be. I should have married a carnie instead of your father! It was his genes that keeps you in one place. A third-generation carnie would have given you good genes."

Liz managed a weak giggle. "I'm riding bareback right now. I promised Raylen I'd help exercise horses if he'd help me take care of all my Christmas decorations and the party."

"You loved horses from the time you could walk. That's Daddy's genes coming out in you," Marva Jo said. "We're getting into Vernon and traffic is heavy. I'll call when we get there."

She'd barely ended that call when Blaze called. "I'm miserable." He sounded like he might cry, and Liz had only seen him shed tears one time in his life—that was the day they buried his mother.

"I'm glad." Liz sniffled. "When y'all left I sobbed like a baby, and now just hearing how sad you are makes me want to be there for you."

"I just now stopped snifflin' enough to call you. I'm in love, Liz," Blaze said. "I thought all that love at first sight stuff was a load of crap, but I believe now."

"It can happen. It did to me when I was just ten years old," Liz told him. "What are you going to do about it?"

"I don't know. It's brand-new territory for me. Got to go. Traffic is slowing us down. Call you later," he said, and the call ended.

The phone rang a third time. "Where'd you learn to ride like that?" Raylen asked when she answered.

"I started riding before Poppa or Mama knew it. I rescued an old wood stool from the barn and stood on it to mount up on the Shetland ponies. I was barely four, and Mama said I was too little to ride, but all I could think about was getting on that pony. I was too little to saddle up. I'd been riding a month or more when they figured out I wasn't playing with my Barbie dolls out there behind the barn."

"Stubborn little cuss, weren't you?" He chuckled.

"Always," she said. "I'm bringing Fire Red in now. Who's next?"

"Glory. She's one of Major Jack's first colts," Raylen told her. "She's got a lot of spirit like this belly dancer I know. She'll test you."

Liz scoffed. "As much as you do? Are you coming over tonight?"

"It's a date," he answered.

Maddie was still mucking out the stall when she rode Fire Red into the barn. Liz slid off the mare's back and rubbed her down.

The sun was a bright orange ball hanging right above the western horizon when they finished up. The inside of Raylen's truck smelled like hay, horses, and manure but neither Liz nor Raylen noticed. She wanted some time alone with Raylen.

"Just so you know, Mama invited us to have supper with them. I told her that I'd promised to help you eat up some Italian leftovers," Raylen said.

Liz patted him on the leg. "And you will. After we have a long, hot steamy bath—together."

"You don't stutter when it comes to speaking right up, do you?" Raylen's tone was serious, but his eyes twinkled.

"I told you about riding that pony when I was four. I get something in my head, I do it. I got something to say, I say it," Liz told him.

Raylen parked the truck, and asked, "Then why

didn't you tell me that summer when we were teen-agers how you felt about me?"

"I was just finding out that I could have feelings for a boy," she said.

She hopped out of the truck before he had time to open the door for her and hit the porch in a dead run. Hooter looked up, but she didn't invite him or Blister into the house.

"You sure are slow." She grinned as she kicked off her boots and headed for the bathroom, leaving a string of clothes to mark the path for him.

"Who's slow?" He shucked out of his clothing and beat her to the bathroom.

Her phone rang somewhere out in the hallway, but she wouldn't have answered it if it had been right beside her. Nothing mattered but Raylen and the next moment.

Chapter 26

"Blaze, what are you doing here?" Liz squealed when she answered the doorbell.

"Standing out here in the rain freezing my butt off," he said. "What are you doing dressed like Mrs. Santa Claus?"

She slung open the door and stood back. "Come in and warm your hands. There's a fire going in the fireplace, and I brought home leftovers from the café. They're on the stove if you are hungry. And I'm dressed up because this is the first night of my light show. Raylen and I will be giving out candy canes for the next couple of hours."

"Hot coffee?" He stepped inside, gave her a hug, and removed his heavy work coat before heading to the warmth of the fire.

"In the pot. I'll pour us each a cup," she said as she headed for the kitchen. "Why didn't you let me know you were coming?"

He warmed his backside and then turned around and rubbed his hands. "For a fireplace like this, I might…"

She carried two mugs of coffee to the living

room and handed one to him. "No, you wouldn't, so don't say that or even think the words."

"I wasn't going to say I'd leave the carnival business. I was going to say that I'd consider building a house on the property for the winter months. Fireplace wouldn't do me a bit of good in the summertime anyway," he said.

She curled up in her favorite recliner and pulled a fluffy throw over her bare feet. Hooter had raised his head when Blaze came into the house, but he'd settled back down. Blister had barely opened one eye from her new bed on a pillow at the end of the sofa beside the bookcases.

"Talk to me," Liz said.

"Colleen invited me for the weekend, and she took next week off. I'm scared out of my mind, Liz. I don't know whether to take her to Claude or what. She says she wants to get to know the carnival business, but I want her to get to know me first," Blaze said.

Liz gestured toward the other recliner. "Sit."

He settled into the chair and sipped his coffee. "What do I do? And where is Raylen?"

"I helped exercise the mares all afternoon. I'd just come in, got a shower, and was waiting on Raylen to heat up leftovers. You hungry? There's plenty in there for all of us. Jasmine sent them home with me."

"I haven't eaten. Don't know if I could swallow, I'm so nervous. I'm a carnie, Liz. I can't change that. You can, but I can't," Blaze said with a long sigh.

"Hello!" Raylen yelled at the door.

"In here. Blaze is here," Liz said.

Raylen came through the back door in his Santa outfit, but he still wore his cowboy boots and hat.

"Hey, Santa Claus." Blaze smiled. "Have I stolen your chair?"

Raylen kissed Liz and slumped down on the end of the sofa. "No, but what are you doing here? Colleen is over there jumping every time she hears a truck door slam. She's got my old room all fixed for you."

"I'm scared," Blaze admitted.

"That's understandable," Raylen said. "I'd be scared of Colleen, too."

Blaze set his coffee on the table. "We were talkin' about what Colleen and I should do this next week. She's taken a week off work, and Haskell told me we would help Poppa, so I should take her somewhere. She said she'd be happy in Claude in my trailer but…"

"Go on," Raylen said.

"There's this place off the coast of the state of Washington that I've been looking at. I've got plane tickets and the room on reserve, but I have to confirm by midnight. I wanted Liz's opinion before I went to see her," Blaze said.

"What's your heart tell you?" Liz asked.

"It says I don't want to share her," Blaze answered. "It says that I want to spend a whole week in a place where neither of us knows another soul. But I don't know if that's what she wants."

"Confirm your reservations and tell her it's a surprise," Liz said. "Is that the place we've looked at and wished we could go for a week, but never had the time?"

He nodded.

"Tell her to pack a warm coat. The ferry ride out to the island might be chilly," Liz said.

"Thank you." Blaze breathed a sigh of relief. He left half a mug of coffee on the end table and put his coat back on. "I knew talkin' to you would help."

"Don't tell her that you talked to me, Blaze. If I was her, I'd rather think it was all your idea and didn't need a second opinion." Liz walked him to the door and hugged him good-bye. "Guess I'll see you tomorrow at Sunday dinner?"

"Oh, yeah. Our flight is tomorrow evening out of Dallas. We'll have to leave Ringgold right after lunch."

Liz went back to the living room and curled up in Raylen's lap. "Think we'll ever get them raised?"

Raylen didn't answer, so she leaned back and looked into his eyes.

"What are you worried about? Something happen at the barn? Are the horses all right?" she asked.

———

"It's not that. It's…"

The idea sounded so silly in Raylen's head that

he wasn't sure he could put his feelings into words, but he felt like he had to say something if he and Liz were ever going to take another step in their relationship. He remembered when Rye fell head over heels in love with Austin; and now Colleen called him daily wanting to talk about nothing but Blaze McIntire.

It hadn't happened like that with him and Liz. He'd felt as if they'd been put on the earth especially for each other. He hadn't needed to call Gemma or Dewar and talk about it every day—or even Becca back in those days. It didn't mean he wasn't in love with her or that he took that love for granted, but were they missing something that they would regret later in life?

"Okay, now you are worrying me," Liz finally said. "Are you about to tell me that this is over and I'm going to be sitting on the porch tonight all by myself for the first night of the light show?"

Raylen took a deep breath and let it out slowly. "Liz, I'm in this for a long relationship. But I work all year for a living, sometimes from daylight to way past dark like today. I've got land and a house, but I don't have the time or money to book a flight to some remote island for a whole week, as bad as I'd like to. It sounds romantic and I—"

Liz cupped his cheeks in her hands and stared right into his eyes. "Look at me, Raylen. I've had the traveling scene my whole life. Sitting here with you after a hard day's work, having Jasmine's leftovers for supper, looking forward to tomorrow with your family, and cuddling down in your arms tonight is living my dream."

He leaned forward and the kiss they shared was more passionate than any that preceded it. "I love you," he said simply.

"And I love you. Did you ever see a baby chicken fresh-hatched?" she asked.

He shook his head. "Can't say that I have. Is that anything like a newborn colt?"

She kissed him again. "Not at all. Poppa raises a few chickens out on the property. He likes fresh eggs. Little chicken comes out of the egg with these little wings that don't look they'd ever be good for anything, but give them six weeks and they're flapping them all over."

"What does that have to do with spending a week on an island with no one but me and you?" Raylen asked.

She pulled him down beside her and flipped part of the throw over his body. "Colleen just came out of the egg. She needs to grow her own wings. Mine won't fit. She has to get used to a different lifestyle, but she has to know that Blaze loves her enough to keep her safe and protected while she's sprouting her wings."

"I'm not sure I understand it all," he said.

"Okay, cowboy, here's the deal. Right now. Right

here. There's no one else around here and this house is our island," she told him.

"That I understand just fine." He drew her close to his side. "Thank you."

"For what? Forcing you to sit with me two hours every night for the light show?" she asked.

"For making this our island," he said.

"No fortune-teller is an island unto herself. She must have a sexy cowboy with her before it's a real island."

"I see car lights coming this way, so we'd better get out on the porch, Mrs. Claus."

"They're really coming?" she whispered.

"Didn't you think they would?" Raylen said as he took his place in one of the two rocking chairs he had bought for the porch.

"I didn't know, Raylen, but I'm happy they are," Liz said with a smile.

"Honey, in these parts folks have to drive a long way to get a little Christmas light show. You got a write-up on the front page of both the Bowie and Ryan newspapers. People want to see what they read about, and besides, it's free and you are giving out candy canes," Raylen said.

"And I'm entered in the Montague County Christmas contest for the best property decorations," she said. "Aren't they ever going to get here?"

"No, they're takin' it slow and easy, probably

talking about each one of those exhibits. You got the candy canes ready?" he asked.

Liz pointed to a galvanized milk bucket full of red and white candy canes sitting on the table between them. "Right here. All ready."

The first car arrived and the window on the passenger's side slowly lowered. "This is so pretty. The kids had a wonderful time," a lady said.

"It'll be open nightly until Christmas Eve. Come back, and here's candy canes for everyone." Liz handed a fistful through the window.

The next car was there before she could sit down. The third truck pulled off to one side and three elderly cowboys crawled out.

"We want the whole tour, not just the drive-thru," one said.

"Yes, sir." Liz grinned and looked over at Raylen. "You are on candy cane duty," she said and led the men on the walking tour to the barn. "This way, guys. The whole tour is the light show and the barn, which is still decorated because I didn't want to give it up after a big party we had at Thanksgiving."

"Read about this in the paper. Them fool reporters didn't give it the right credit, though. I know you. You are the waitress up at the café who always keeps my coffee cup full. Man alive, Roy, would you look at that tree. Place looks prettier than that mall over at Wichita Falls, don't it?" the oldest cowboy said.

"Mama would've liked the angel on the tree," Roy said and his tone said that his mama wasn't around anymore.

"You and Raylen keepin' company?" the third fellow asked.

Liz nodded.

"We heard that, didn't we, Buddy? Raylen needs a good woman. You be good to him," Roy said.

Buddy, a tall, lanky cowboy in bib overalls, nodded. "This is a fine put-on for a town like Ringgold. Must've took you a spell to put it all together. I got a feeling that you are happy here in Ringgold."

"Yes, it did take a lot of work, but I had a lot of good friends that helped me. And I enjoyed it all. And I am very happy here. I plan to stay forever. Y'all know Haskell? He's my uncle," she said.

"Yes, ma'am, we surely do. Our wives and Miz Sara was good friends in the day. He made all them pretty things, didn't he?" Buddy asked.

Liz nodded.

"Well, guess we'll be on our way. We might come back another day," Roy said.

"It'll be open all month," she said.

Raylen smiled when she sat back down on the porch with him. "I was busy. Was that Roy and Buddy?"

"I guess so. But I'm going to remember them as the three wise men. Look up there." She pointed.

A star was shining brighter than all the others and it hung right above her barn.

———————

Sunday dinner was at the O'Donnells' place and Liz could tell that Blaze still wasn't completely comfortable. He kept touching Colleen's hand, her hair, and her cheek for assurance.

Liz had loved that first-rush phase of excitement with Raylen, but she loved the place they were in now even more. She liked knowing that he would be at her house as soon as he finished work, that if she had a nightmare she could back up into his embrace and it would disappear. Most of all, she loved the confidence in knowing not one ounce of the sizzle was going to fade each time they closed the bedroom door.

Everyone was talking all around her and Raylen, but suddenly she felt as if they really were an island unto themselves. His fingertips gently massaging her neck muscles sent her thoughts to an imaginary clear river where they were skinny-dipping and making love in the water. The vision disappeared when everyone gathered around in the kitchen so Grandpa could say grace.

"What are you thinking about? I think Blaze is doing pretty good, don't you?" Raylen whispered.

"I was thinking how wonderful family and

friends are, and yes, Blaze is doing fine," she whispered.

He kissed her softly on the lips.

Grandpa's voice brought the last few whispers to a halt. "Our Father in heaven."

Liz bowed her head, but she didn't hear the prayer. She was too busy thinking about the surprise that was in store for Colleen, and hoping that she and Blaze had a wonderful vacation.

"Liz?" Raylen said.

She opened her eyes and raised her head. Prayer was over and everyone was lining up around the food tables.

"Where were you?" Raylen asked.

She pulled his head down and whispered, "Thinking about Colleen and Blaze."

"Raylen is blushing," Colleen teased. "What did Liz just say to you?"

The high color that had reached his cheeks deepened. "She said that she's starving. So will you hurry up and get your plate filled? You are holding up the line, Sister."

"I don't believe you," Colleen said.

Liz leaned forward and whispered into Colleen's ear. "Believe it. Food isn't the only thing a woman can hunger after, is it?"

Colleen nodded and grinned. "You got it, sister! You know anything about this big surprise Blaze has in store for me?"

"Now I wonder what I said that made you think of Blaze?" Liz asked.

Colleen's face turned almost the same color as her hair. "Hush! Surprise?"

"Yes, I do know, but I'm not telling you. It's his surprise," Liz answered.

"What can you tell me?" Colleen asked.

"Take a warm coat."

Colleen gave her a stern look.

Liz giggled. "It won't work. You don't scare me anymore."

Blaze grinned. "But you did at first, darlin'. She called me every night and whined about how you wouldn't ever accept her."

"I still might not if she doesn't tell me what you two cooked up," Colleen said.

"Don't care if you do or not, I'm not sayin' another word other than pack a warm coat and have a good time," Liz said.

"You've met your match," Raylen told Colleen.

Liz looked over her shoulder at Colleen. "She scared me worse than Maddie did when I first met her."

"I did not," Colleen argued.

"Yeah, you did," Liz said.

Maddie touched Liz on the shoulder. "As soon as they are gone, you can tell me the big secret. I won't tell her a thing."

Liz smiled and nodded in agreement.

Raylen waited until they were seated and kissed Liz on the ear and whispered, "I love you."

They barely made it home from dinner Sunday night when the parade of cars began to drive down the lane. The very first carload brought two elderly people who parked and headed for the barn. They were dressed in plaid men's robes, belted at the waist and hanging to their ankles. Dark blue towels were held down on their heads with stretchy black headbands, but kinky gray curls had escaped around their ears. "We didn't have time to go home and change. We just came from a Christmas play at the church. Didn't have enough men to be the shepherds so we stepped in. No one knew if they were lookin' at men or women by the time we got our towels on our heads and our Goodwill store bathrobes on," one of them explained.

"Welcome to the Ringgold light show." Liz followed them into the barn.

"Would you look at that, Agnes? That's the prettiest tree I've ever seen. Folks don't use real ones much no more. And look at that angel up there. Can't buy them like that no more. It's an antique for sure," the lady with the white turban said.

"It belonged to my Aunt Sara and Uncle Haskell," Liz said. "Aunt Sara liked Christmas and she must've had a lot of her decorations passed down by her parents because some of the stuff I found isn't available in the stores today. But I love Christmas and I wanted to share it with everyone."

"I knew I recognized that angel. It was Sara Hanson's grandmother's topper. I saw it once when I was a kid," Agnes said.

"Mavis, you can't remember that far back." Agnes slapped her playfully on the shoulder.

"Don't be hittin' on me, woman. Just because you're two years younger than me and was Mama's favorite don't mean you can hit on me now," Mavis said.

"You are sisters?" Liz asked.

"Yep, we are," Agnes said. "Oh, we forgot to tell you, we're the judges for the Montague County contest. We are supposed to tell the folks when we first get there but sometimes we forget."

"Don't be usin' that *we* word. *You* forget. I got my tally sheet right here under my robe." Mavis pulled out a small clipboard from inside her robe and fumbled in her pocket for a pencil.

Agnes fished one from her pocket and handed it to Mavis. "Here's one. See, she does forget."

"Good thing we ain't real shepherds, ain't it? We'd be the kind that lose their sheep for sure." Mavis giggled.

Agnes frowned. "You would. I would know where every one of my little lambs were."

"Don't argue with me," Mavis said.

Liz wondered if someday in the far distant future she and Gemma would be arguing like they were doing. She hoped so—family and friends to share life with were so important.

"I won't if you'll admit that baby they had layin' in the manger just about drowned out the whole show with his little fit," Mavis said.

"If you'd had to lay in a bed of straw with a bunch of weird-looking people all around you, I bet you'd be crying too," Agnes retorted.

The two of them reminded Liz so much of her mother and Aunt Tressa that she got all misty-eyed and emotional. This would be the first Christmas that she'd ever been away from them.

"I'm tired of arguing with you, girl. Next year somebody else can wear our Goodwill robes and our towels. We're going to be on the refreshment committee," Mavis said.

"I'm going back outside. You ladies call me if you need me," Liz said.

"We'll just take our notes and be gone. But honey, as far as I'm concerned, this is the biggest splash in the county," Mavis said.

"Thank you. Don't forget to get a candy cane before you leave." Liz waved over her shoulder as she left.

"We won't. Agnes here loves candy canes. I swear she's been sittin' on Santa's lap for ninety-two years just to get a candy cane. She says the ones at Christmas taste better than the ones you can buy any other time of year," Mavis said.

"Ninety-one years. You can't remember a thing," Agnes said.

Liz giggled. "See you outside. If you need anything holler at me."

"Where's your shepherds?" Raylen asked when she sat back down in her rocking chair.

"The world is a new place this year. They are women"—she lowered her voice to a whisper—"and they're also the judges for the county decoration prize too, so be very nice to them."

Chapter 27

MONDAY MORNING STARTED OFF WITH A BANG. The electricity had blinked off during the night, and Liz woke up fifteen minutes late. Raylen had already gone, so she didn't even get a good morning kiss, and when she got to work that morning, a dozen coffee drinkers followed her inside when she opened the door at exactly six o'clock. That meant she hit the floor in a dead run without even a second to get a cup of coffee.

By midmorning she was wishing she had an energy drink. She finally had time to pour a cup of coffee but barely got a sip before the door opened again.

"That's Lucy," Jasmine called out. "She'll come right back here."

The woman was tiny, just over five feet tall, and slim built. Her brown hair was pulled up in a ponytail. Her eyes were enormous and reminded Liz of the pictures of those little kids that were popular thirty years before. They were even lighter blue than a summer sky.

"Hi, Jasmine." Lucy went straight for the coffee

pot and poured a cup. "You must be Liz. I've heard good things about you."

"With what I've heard about you, I expected you to be six feet tall and able to wrestle an Angus bull to the ground with your bare hands," Liz said.

Lucy shook her head. "Not me."

"What brings you out today? I haven't seen you in a couple of months. I missed you, girl," Jasmine said.

"Been busy with the new therapy group, and the motel is going really good. I started to call this morning, but we only had five rooms to clean and Tasha said she'd take care of them if I wanted to get out. Thought I'd run down to the used bookstore in Bowie and stock up for a month or so. I've got two strays I need to find jobs for." Lucy sipped her coffee.

"I'm not in the market..." Jasmine started.

"You could be," Liz said.

"Oh?"

"Remember back when I started to work, I said it was only going to be for a little while. Maddie has offered me a job at the ranch, so..." Liz shrugged and then went on, "I figured out that I want to work with the horses. It's like fate that Lucy came today. I'll move over and let one of Lucy's girls have my waitress job."

"Thank you," Lucy said. "Bridget is twenty-one. She's got waitress experience. She's living with her folks in Petrolia. I'm afraid if she doesn't get a job, she'll fall right back into her abusive husband's web. If she's got a routine and her own money, she'll be fine with our weekly meetings."

"What meetings?" Jasmine asked.

"Started them a month ago. That's another reason I don't get out much. Sunday afternoons, we all meet in the Baptist church fellowship hall. It's like AA, only for abused women. It's our support group," Lucy said.

"When does she want to start work?" Liz asked.

"She's sittin' out there in my truck. Thought we'd check here before I took her on to her folks' farm," Lucy said.

Jasmine looked at Liz. "You sure about this?"

"I'll miss you, but I figured out what I want to do, and Maddie said I could work with the horses. I'll give Bridget my apron and start work on the ranch tomorrow morning if you say it's all right," Liz said.

She remembered someone in the last few weeks saying that change was a good thing. Though she couldn't recall exactly who said it, she sure hoped they were right.

"I've loved working here," Liz said around the lump in her throat.

Jasmine crossed the kitchen and gave her a hug. "Girlfriend, just because you don't come in to work every day doesn't mean we won't see each other often. We are family now. Lucy, go bring Bridget on in here. She can work with Liz all afternoon and start full-time tomorrow morning," Jasmine said.

Lucy nodded and headed for the door.

"Lucy takes her mission to help abused women very seriously," Jasmine explained in a low tone. "I'm going to miss you like crazy."

"It's the right thing and the right time," Liz said.

Bridget was a short woman, carrying about twenty extra pounds and a few faint yellow bruises around her eyes. After introductions, she held out her hand to Jasmine and said, "Thank you for givin' me a chance. I did some work over at the Dairy Queen when I was in high school, but that was a while ago. I'll learn fast though."

"Minimum wage to start," Jasmine said.

"The tips are really good, though," Liz said.

"I would work for minimum and give the tips to you," Bridget said.

"That isn't the way it works. You keep the tips. Some days they'll be better than your wages. I pay on Saturday at quittin' time. At the end of work today, I'll give you a fifty-dollar advance on your first paycheck for gas to get you to work the rest of the week."

Bridget smiled for the first time. "Daddy said I can use his old work truck until I can get something better. He'd probably fill it up with gas, but if I can do it on my own, I'd like that."

"Then get an apron and follow Liz everywhere

she goes today. Lucy, you want to pick her up on your way back home?" Jasmine asked.

"I'll be here at two," Lucy said.

"Lucy, you said you had two women needing work. What's the other lady looking for?" Liz asked.

"She's fifty years old and never worked outside the home. We got her set up in a little garage apartment in Henrietta, but rent is due at the end of the month. We could only help her get situated and pay one month. She's not qualified for anything," Lucy answered.

"I'm looking for someone to cook and clean and do a little work around my place," Liz said.

"She could sure do that." Lucy's voice was full of excitement. "She takes care of cleaning the fellowship hall when we leave."

"Does she have transportation?" Liz asked.

Lucy nodded.

"Send her down to my house this afternoon. We'll talk. I hate to clean, and I sure hate to cook. We might work up a deal," Liz said.

"What time?" Lucy asked.

"Three. I'm supposed to be at the horse barn at four," she said.

"She'll be there," Lucy said.

Bridget fell right into the work, and Liz had five minutes of free time just before the lunch rush. She called Maddie and told her what she'd done that morning.

"That's a good thing you did, Liz. Then you were serious about working more here at the ranch?" Maddie asked.

"Were you serious about me working as much as I want?" Liz asked.

"I was. Dewar, Cash, and I are leaving tomorrow morning and we'll be gone a week. The hired help will be helping Raylen, and he'll be your boss. Think you can handle that?"

"I'll do my best not to aggravate him so bad that he fires me before you get back," Liz said.

"If you can do that, I'll start you at two dollars above minimum."

"Better make it minimum wage, then." Liz laughed. "I can't promise anything, but I'll give it a try."

"Did Maddie talk to you?" Liz asked Raylen when she arrived at the ranch that afternoon.

"Not since breakfast," Raylen answered. "I meant to run up to the café for dinner, but Grandma made fried chicken and it would have hurt her feelings if I didn't take an hour and eat with her and Grandpa. How'd your day go?"

"I quit my job," Liz said.

Raylen just stared at her with a puzzled look on his face.

"Aren't you going to say anything?" Liz asked.

"I'm afraid of what I'll hear, but go on," he said without a smile or a kiss.

"Lucy needed places for a couple of her abused women. One is working for Jasmine. I quit and gave her my job. Kind of like fate tossed them women in my path. Aunt Tressa says when opportunity knocks, invite it in for a cup of coffee before you send it on its way. So I did. Bridget is working for Jasmine, and she's a hard worker. She'll do all right. The other one is my new housekeeper and cook. She'll be at my house at eight in the morning and she's going to clean, wash, and iron and all those things I hate. And she likes to cook. She'll have our dinner ready at noon and she'll leave at two. She's working five days a week. As of this minute, I'm working for your ranch, and you are my boss."

The grin that split Raylen's face lit up the whole north part of Texas. "What's her name?"

"Who?" Liz asked.

"The new lady at your house." Raylen could breathe a little easier now that he knew Liz wasn't leaving Ringgold.

"Wilma. She has put up with years of mental abuse, but she's a sweet lady and says that's behind her now and she wants to go on with her life. She's so grateful for this job, and I think we're going to get along just fine."

Raylen took off his hat and slapped the dust out of it on his leg. "How can you afford that?"

"I'm going to pay her with what I make working for you." She should tell him about her financial situation, but she wasn't quite ready. "The only time we'll even see her is when we go home at noon. For now, we'd better get busy if we want to be finished before dark. I'm a horse woman now, not a carnie. I can't sleep until noon. So, what are my orders?"

"Kiss me and then exercise horses until dark." He continued to grin.

Chapter 28

CHRISTMAS EVE WASN'T EXCEPTIONALLY COLD, but it was nippy. The O'Donnell family had decided to have their dinner and gift exchange that day, and then on Christmas day, Austin and Rye could take Rachel to Tulsa to spend the day with the other side of the family. Liz and Raylen and Blaze and Colleen could all go to Claude.

"Got to be accommodatin' to the other folks," Cash had said.

Liz awoke in a state of excitement. She'd already wrapped ten presents for Raylen and hid them in a spare bedroom. She had at least one present for everyone in the O'Donnell family and one for Blaze, and now all she had to do was wait for Raylen to come pick her up and help take the gifts out to his truck.

Raylen was running a little late that morning. A mare was down in the horse barn trying to deliver a foal too early and he'd called the vet in for an opinion.

"Merry Christmas Eve," he said with a sweet kiss. "You ready?"

"Once we get all these presents out to the truck."

"That's a lot of gifts," he said.

"Buying them was so much fun. I love shopping and I got to buy so many this year. Usually, it's one for Mama, one for Aunt Tressa, for Poppa and Uncle Haskell, and for Blaze. I love Ringgold," she said.

"Did you buy something for everyone in town?" he asked as she stacked presents in his arms.

"I would have if they were coming to Christmas at your folks," she answered.

Colleen met them at the door and helped Liz unload the presents from Raylen's arms and arrange them under the tree.

"So how are things between you and Raylen?" she whispered.

"First, tell me about you and Blaze," Liz said.

"I'm in love."

"Me too," Liz said.

Dinner was loud and noisy just like all affairs at the ranch. Afterwards when everyone opened gifts, the room was covered in paper and ribbons and more noise and laughter.

Liz opened her presents slowly, savoring every single moment and enjoying watching others open what she'd chosen carefully for each one. To have friends so close that she knew what they would like was the biggest gift of all.

Raylen looked strange when he opened her

gift—a silver belt buckle engraved with the ranch brand—as if he didn't like it or she'd intruded on some kind of private ground by commissioning a silversmith in Amarillo to make the buckle. He kissed her on the cheek and thanked her, but something wasn't right, and suddenly the whole atmosphere between them turned awkward. Before she could ask what was wrong, Maddie dug her phone from her hip pocket and answered it. "Oh, no!" she said.

"What?" Raylen asked.

"It's that mare we've been watching. She's delivering early. I knew she was too old to breed, but I wanted one more colt out of her," she fussed.

"You stay here. Liz and I will take care of her," Raylen said. "Everyone doesn't need to go."

"Get rid of those shoes and use my boots, Liz, and you'd better shuck out of that fancy dress and put on my coveralls too. They're hangin' on a hook by the clothes dryer," Maddie said.

Liz was a little disappointed that she couldn't finish the day in the glow of the family in full Christmas spirit, but she nodded in agreement. She hurried into the utility room and changed into the coveralls, kicked her high heels off and donned a pair of worn cowboy boots that were half a size too big.

Raylen drove so fast that the mesquite trees and fence posts were a blur as they whizzed past Liz's window. They both rushed into the barn to find the mare down in one of the stalls with a hired hand standing over her when they reached the stables.

"I'm on duty every two hours. When I left last time, she was fine," he said.

"The vet checked her early, Carl. We both thought we had it under control. It's not your fault. Go on home to your family. We're here and we'll take care of her." Raylen knelt beside the black horse. "And Merry Christmas, Carl."

"Same to you and Miz Liz." Carl headed out of the barn.

"Come on, girl," he said softly.

Liz dropped to her knees and wrapped her arms around the mare's neck. "Please have this foal and live. Maddie does not need this on Christmas Eve. I promise this will be the last time you have to do this."

=====

"How do you plan to keep that promise?" Raylen could hear a chill in his own voice, but he'd felt terrible when he didn't have a gift under the tree for Liz. Even Blaze had thought to bring something for Colleen, which made matters even worse. But he'd been so wrapped up in getting his gift for her ready for the next day that he had totally forgotten about the gift exchange among the family that day. He gave gift cards every year to everyone. To fancy restaurants for Rye and Austin, to a toy store for Rachel, to a spa for each of his sisters, and a cruise for his parents. Dewar got tickets to a George Strait concert and…

He frowned when he remembered that he hadn't given Blaze anything, either. Now Colleen would be mad at him too.

"What is the matter with you? Didn't you like my present?" Liz snapped.

"I love it. It's beautiful, and I love it. But I didn't have a thing for you or Blaze." Raylen hung his head.

Liz walked across the stall on her knees and wrapped her arms around Raylen. "Tell me you love me."

"You know I do," he said.

She cupped his face in her hands. "Tell me."

"I love you, Liz Hanson," he said.

"That's the best Christmas present in the world. Now let's take care of this horse. She's just about ready. Look at those little hooves coming out." She turned back to the mare.

"It's premature, so it's probably not going to make it," Raylen warned.

"Oh, yes it will. Little or not, it's not going to die. That Mama horse has worked too hard not to be able to keep her baby, and it will live," Liz declared as the next contraction pushed more of the foal out into the world.

It was black except for one white ear and a white splotch on the forehead that faintly resembled a star. Raylen was everywhere at once, wiping its nose, shaking it gently to make it suck in air, and cussing under his breath the whole time.

Liz stayed out of his way until the newborn finally heaved and started breathing, then she helped wipe it down with warm towels. "What now?"

"We baby-sit for a while. See if it can stand on its own, and hope his mama survives," he said.

"Do we call the vet?" Liz asked.

"No, nothing he can do that we can't now," Raylen said.

"Where'd that blaze come from?" Liz asked. "His mama and daddy are both solid black."

"He's only thrown one other one with a blaze. He's won two major races and is almost as famous as Danny Boy," Raylen said.

At midnight, the mare was standing on her own and everything looked fine. The tiny little horse had fed even though it had to stretch its neck to the full extent to reach his mother's teats.

"I'm going to get a shower and grab a few hours sleep," Raylen said.

"Me too. Santa Claus is coming at five in the morning, right?"

Raylen grinned. "Leave milk and cookies."

———

Liz woke up Christmas morning to the aroma of coffee wafting down the hallway. Without opening her eyes, she patted Raylen's side of the bed, only to find a pillow and cold sheets. Then she remembered that he was going to his house after the foal had been born. He'd promised to be at her house at five o'clock because Santa was coming that morning. She jumped out of bed, pulled the curtains back, and gave a sigh of relief. The weatherman had said there was a slim possibility of freezing rain, but the sun was peeking up over the eastern horizon. After presents, she and Raylen should have dry roads all the way to Claude where they were having Christmas with her family.

Raylen slipped his arms around her from behind and pulled her back to his chest. "Merry Christmas, darlin.'"

"Merry Christmas to you." She wiggled in closer and sniffed the air. "Do I smell cinnamon rolls? Does that mean the jig is up? Did you find the milk and cookies on the bar, Santa?"

"I found my milk and cookies. Blister talked me out of the milk and Hooter begged for the cookie so that was their Christmas present. The cinnamon rolls are *not* canned. Wilma had them in the refrigerator with a note on top that said to heat for ten minutes on Christmas morning." He led her to the kitchen. Coffee, juice, and two forks were already on the table. He brought the cinnamon rolls from the oven and put them on a hot pad in the middle of the table.

Excitement reigned in her heart. She'd gotten what she wanted for Christmas. A house that wasn't on wheels and not just any old cowboy picked up under a tumbleweed or behind a mesquite tree, but Raylen O'Donnell. Miracles did happen. She had living proof.

She nibbled at the cinnamon rolls but was too nervous to eat more than a few bites. She'd put out all ten of his presents before she went to bed the night before, had awakened at two o'clock and checked to make sure they were arranged just right and to see if he'd snuck one in for her. At four she woke up again and padded up to the Christmas tree to rearrange them one more time. Still nothing from Raylen.

"All finished?" she asked.

He pushed back the coffee cup. "Wait right here." He disappeared down the hallway and into the spare bedroom where she'd kept all her presents until the night before. When he returned, he was carrying something wrapped in an old quilt.

"What is it?" she asked.

"Your Christmas present," he said.

He laid it in her lap, and a little white head and two black hooves shot out from under the quilt. The foal made a noise that reminded her of a baby and looked up at her with big round black eyes.

"Oh!" Other than one word, she was totally speechless.

"He's all yours, but we have to take him back to his mama. You'll have to go out to the barn to spoil him," Raylen said.

Tears filled her eyes and spilled down her cheeks. "The first of my own herd. And I'm going out to the barn every day to spoil him."

Raylen grinned. "I know you will."

More tears flowed from her eyes. "Oh, Raylen, I love him. Do I get to name him?"

"He's your baby," Raylen said.

"His name is Glorious Christmas Star because of the star on his forehead, and because all winners have to have three names. I will call him Star."

Raylen cocked his head to one side and wiped her tears away with a white handkerchief that he pulled out of his pocket. "Sounds fine to me, but are you sure that's a star? It looks more like a lightning streak to me."

"It's a star that got smeared a little, but it's still a star." She bent forward and kissed the foal on his forehead. "You are going to be a fine racer, aren't you, Star, and we're going to win the same prize that Danny Boy did. Your mama did real good, darlin'." She crooned to the foal. Raylen kissed her on the top of her head and smiled. She looked up and meant to kiss him on the lips but missed and got the side of his mouth. "Now it's your turn. I'm going to sit right here and hold Star while you open your presents, and then we'll take him back to his mama. The big round one first with the red paper and gold bow."

Raylen's eyes widened. "All of these for me?"

He didn't have a single present under the tree for her. He should have bought a hundred presents for her to unwrap in addition to the unwrapped ones out in the yard.

He ripped into a box with a brand-new Stetson hat.

She hugged Star and said, "I promise not to stomp it or throw it on the ground."

The next present was a bottle of Stetson aftershave.

"That scent turns me on," she said with a smile.

He could hardly wait to give her the rest of his Christmas present. Anxiety, hoping that she would like it, made him open faster so he could take her to the backyard and show her how much he loved her.

Liz was suddenly worried that she'd overdone it and he'd think she was smothering him.

The last present was a long black silk scarf.

"It's actually for me when I dance for you," she said.

"Very nice," he mumbled.

Raylen wondered how Liz could have afforded all those expensive gifts. She used what she made working at the ranch for Wilma's salary; she had said so herself. So where did the money come from for a new hat, Stetson aftershave, a hundred-dollar scarf, and all the rest?

But the idea of her finances quickly took a back-seat when he thought about what he'd planned for the rest of her Christmas. He was almost giddy with excitement at that point. "Thank you, darlin'. You did way too much, but I love every one of my gifts."

"So did you. This horse is a son of Glorious Danny Boy. I can't wait to tell Blaze what I got. Someday Star is going to take his place on the ranch." She smiled.

"Well, darlin', can Star get back in his baby bed for now? The rest of your presents are outside." Raylen laid his gifts to the side and stood up.

They carried Star out to the barn and settled him into the middle of a pile of clean hay in the stall with his mother. "Look, Raylen, he's happy. Our new baby is happy in his bed."

Raylen slipped his arm around Liz, and they stood there several minutes gazing down at the new baby horse lying in a bed of hay.

Star shut his eyes and sighed.

"Yes, he is. While he's sleeping, I have a surprise for you, darlin'. Close your eyes," Raylen said.

She didn't have to be told twice. She loved surprises. She was so excited she had trouble standing still. "What is it?"

"Santa Claus came last night and left you a present," he said.

"Is it a new puppy?"

"No, darlin'. I thought about us getting one, but I thought you'd want to help me pick him or her out."

He took her hands in his and pulled her up to a standing position.

She heard a snapping noise and felt a whoosh of air. "What was that?"

He tucked her hand into his and walked her to the porch, then scooped her up in his arms and carried her. "Close your eyes."

"Did you get me a puppy?" she asked.

They didn't go far before he sat down with her in his lap and suddenly, they were swinging. "Now open your eyes."

She gasped. "You bought it!"

They were cuddled up together in the swing that she'd coveted on their first real date. And there was the picnic table and two Adirondack chairs to match.

"I can't believe it. It's a wonderful, wonderful present. I love it, darlin'. It's perfect. It means you want me to stay in Ringgold as long as this wood holds up, doesn't it?" she gushed.

"Longer than that," Raylen said. "I hope this is something that a rancher or a horse whisper woman would have that has roots.

"When I went back to get my keys, that old feller

told me that you could swing the new babies in it and your grandbabies would eat off that table. And speaking of the future..." He dropped down on one knee in front of her and took her hands in his. "When I look into your eyes, I see our future laid out before us. We will love each other, have arguments, enjoy makeup sex, and I see horses, kids, and grandkids. I see us having a full life together. Liz Hanson, I've loved you since we were kids. I want to be the father of those babies that you swing in this swing. I want to sit on those two chairs when we are old and watch our grandbabies eat off that table. Will you marry me?"

"Yes!" she answered without a second's hesitation, locked her arms around his neck, and pulled his lips up to hers in a sizzling kiss.

———————

February is a petulant child in Texas. It can be happy, sunny, bright, and beautiful, or it can spend the day pouting in the corner not knowing what it wants. It was a happy-go-lucky kid on the last Saturday of the month. The sun was out and only a few white clouds floated across the sky above Claude, Texas.

The big barn had been cleaned from top to bottom under Poppa and Haskell's supervision and transformed into a thing of beauty for the wedding. The building was full with the carnival family, the

O'Donnells, and all the friends from the Ringgold area that could make the trip. They were seated in folding chairs when the fiddle music began.

Blaze took his place beside the minister. He was the luckiest man in the whole world. He was even luckier than Dewar and Cash and Poppa, his best men, all supporting him on the most important and most nervous day of his life.

The fiddle music blended beautifully and Gemma, Jasmine, and Pearl, all dressed in bright red satin, made their way to the front of the barn. Then the fiddles struck the first note of the traditional wedding march, and the bride appeared on her father's arm at the back of the barn. Everyone stood up, and Blaze's heart absolutely left his chest in one enormous beat when he saw Colleen in that long white satin dress. White roses were scattered in her red hair, and she wore the silver heart necklace he'd bought her on Orcas Island.

When Cash and Colleen reached the front of the barn, Cash put his daughter's hands in Blaze's and said, "Be good to her. I'm trustin' you with my precious daughter, son."

"You have my promise, sir," Blaze said.

Colleen took the microphone from the preacher. Liz and Raylen's bows hit the fiddle strings at the same time, and she looked deep into Blaze's eyes and sang "Bless the Broken Road," a song made popular by Rascal Flatts.

Liz locked eyes with Raylen's as they made the fiddles whine to lyrics saying that God had blessed the broken road that led her straight to him.

When Colleen finished singing, she handed the microphone back to the preacher. Liz and Raylen laid their fiddles down. Raylen joined the grooms-men, and Liz the bridesmaids. When the ceremony ended, the preacher announced that the wedding party would have a few pictures taken. "But feel free to partake of the food tables and when the pictures are done, the bride and groom will cut the cake so you can have dessert."

While the photographer did his job, Liz sat down in Raylen's lap on a front row chair and waited for their turn to have pictures with the bride and groom.

"I'm glad we did it different," she whispered.

"I was sure nervous about giving you an enve-lope rather than a ring," he said.

"I loved it. A proposal with a marriage license! Bet no one else has ever got that." She held up her left hand and admired the wide gold band. A ring for a rancher's wife who mucked out stalls, saddled up horses, drove a tractor, and hauled hay. "And I will always love my ring," she said, "because it matches yours."

Jasmine sat down beside Liz. "It's a beautiful wedding. This place hardly even looks like a barn. Colleen is beautiful and Blaze can't take his eyes off her. But if I ever get married, I'm doing it the way y'all did, Liz. Propose. Get married in an hour. Put on a nice wide gold band and be married. I suppose my mother would throw a hissy if I did. She's been plannin' my wedding for years."

Ace sat down next to Raylen and patted him on the shoulder. "Blaze has been branded. No doubt about it. His prowlin' days are done. But I got to admit, Raylen, you're the smart one. You'll never forget your anniversary. Been meanin' to ask you, how did you get a judge to marry you on Christmas Day? And how did you work up the nerve to give Liz a marriage license instead of an engagement ring?"

"The judge agreed to open the courthouse and marry us if I would move his name to the top of the list to buy one of Glorious Major's foals. I wanted to be a husband, not a fiancé, and I had a pretty good idea that Liz felt the same way, but I got plenty nervous right there at the end." Raylen smiled.

It was time for Jasmine and Ace to have pictures taken with the bride and groom, so they left and Marva Jo and Tressa sat down beside Raylen and Liz.

"Did you tell him?" Marva Jo whispered.

"I did after we were married. That way it could never be said he married me for my money. I told him all about my inheritance from my father, and I even let him glance at my portfolio and my checkbook." She laughed.

"I married her for twenty acres, not her bank account," Raylen teased.

Tressa patted him on the shoulder. "And you got a sassy piece of baggage with it. We leave in a week for the new carnival year. I'll miss her, but Colleen is a quick study. I swear with that red hair she's a born carnie. She can lay out the cards and tell a fortune better than I ever could. Too bad she can't belly dance."

"I offered her my costumes, but she turned me down," Liz said.

"Parents of the groom, please," the photographer said.

"That's me. Come on, Marva Jo. You're going to stand on one side and me the other." Tressa motioned to Marva Jo.

Lucy sat down beside Liz.

"Wilma is so excited about the move. You are a good woman, Liz," she said.

"I'm a selfish woman. I don't want to lose her, so I settled her in more permanently. And besides, we had two houses. We decided to live in Raylen's house and Gemma moved in with Dewar. So, one house was empty. We opened the fence and put a cattle guard between the two places so on nice days she can walk from one place to the other, and sometimes she even helps clean for Maddie, so everything is working out beautifully."

"Well, she's a happy woman. She's been telling your Uncle Haskell all about how much she loves

Hooter and Blister and how they stayed with her, and I heard her tellin' him that she'd already bought five used Louis L'Amour books for the bookcases," Lucy said.

Lucy meandered away and Pearl and Wil settled in beside Liz and Raylen.

"I heard you bought a couple of Rocky Mountain mares," Wil said.

Liz nodded. "I sure did. Star needed some company since he's gotten big enough to go live in the barn."

Raylen chuckled. "And Dewar spends more time with them than she does."

Liz smiled. "He's got more time than I do. When he finds a good woman, the Vanners will take a backseat. Isn't this pretty close to your first anniversary, Pearl?"

"Wil and I were married a year a couple of weeks ago. Colleen doesn't know how lucky she has it. Maddie is so laid back and calm about everything. My mother about drove me bonkers on my wedding day. You two did it the right way. Get married and then tell Mama. Only if I'd done that, we'd have had a funeral instead of a wedding."

"Yours or hers?" Liz asked.

Wil patted Pearl on the thigh. "Red's, to be sure. Her mama was determined to have a wedding."

Liz pointed at Pearl's pregnant belly and asked, "How are those twins coming along?"

Pearl patted her stomach. "Doc says they're doin' fine. Identical boys. We just found out yesterday. Daddy is ecstatic and so is Wil. I don't know one thing about raising boys but I guess I'll learn."

"And now the whole wedding party," the photographer said.

"That's our cue," Liz said.

Later, after pictures and after the bride and groom had danced to "I Cross My Heart" by George Strait, Raylen and Liz laid down their fiddles, and he led her to the dance floor.

He wrapped his arms around her, letting them rest on the small of her back. "You really aren't disappointed that you didn't have all this?"

"Our wedding was perfect, and I got exactly what I wanted. A house with no wheels and a sexy cowboy, and I got it all just in time for Christmas, including my wedding. Now kiss me, please. Weddings, a sexy cowboy, and good fiddlin' always turn a girl on," she whispered.

had been read and that she had inherited one-third of both the Catfish Fisherman's Hut and Granny Lizzie's house, which was located right beside it. She dried her eyes, forced herself to stop crying, and called Becky. She told her she'd be there before supper, and then she took a quick shower, got dressed in jeans and a T-shirt, and picked up the garment bag holding her wedding dress and took it out to her car first. The thing filled the whole back seat, and she didn't ever plan on wearing it again, but she just couldn't leave it behind. She went back inside her dingy little room and hauled out her two hot-pink suitcases, which contained everything she needed for a honeymoon in the Colorado mountains. The third trip back into the room was just to make sure she hadn't left anything behind. Before she left, she checked her reflection in the mirror on the back of the bathroom door. Her black hair still had droplets of water hanging on her ponytail, and her green eyes had dark circles around them. She should stop by Dallas and try to explain how she felt to Eli, but her hands trembled at the thought of facing him.

"Oh, well, it doesn't matter if I look like crap. I'm going to Catfish, Texas, to work in a bait shop. I'm not having dinner tonight with the queen, not even if Becky acts like she is royalty." She left the room key on the nightstand and locked the door behind her, got into her little red sports car, and headed north toward the Red River.

"I love you, Granny Lizzie," Lainie sobbed as she drove. "Why did you have to die right before my wedding. I needed you to be there to tell me that marriage was tough enough when a woman loves a man, and impossible if she doesn't."

I was there in spirit, and I think you got the message. The voice in her head was as clear as if her grandmother had been sitting right beside her.

She didn't like the idea of working in the Catfish Fisherman's Hut or living with her two older, bossy cousins, but that was better than going back to Dallas. She hadn't even gotten out of Houston when the phone rang. She sucked in a lungful of air and hit the accept button.

"Hello, Daddy," she said. "I'm on my way to Granny Lizzie's place. She's left it to us three girls."

"That's probably for the best," he said. "Your mother has been crying one minute and then yelling the next since you ran away. She can't even hold her head up at the country club. You've made a mess of things, Lainie. You could have had such a good life with Eli, so it seems fitting that you have to live on the river in little more than a slum. It would be best if you call before you come back to see us. Give us time to forgive you for embarrassing the hell out of us."

"Yes, sir," she said and ended the call.

She was almost to Conroe when her phone rang again. This time it was Eli, and she let it ring four times before she finally answered.

"I'm very disappointed and upset." Eli's big booming voice startled her. "Why did you run away? I deserve an answer."

"I figured out that I don't love you," she answered.

"Couldn't you have figured it out a hell of a lot earlier?" His tone was so icy that it sent a shiver down Lainie's spine.

"I did, but you are so controlling that you wouldn't…" She pulled off at the next exit to get a cup of coffee.

"I wouldn't what?" Eli demanded.

"Have let me break up with you," she finished. "It's over. I'm sorry I embarrassed everyone, but I'm not sorry I left. Goodbye." She ended the call before he could say anything else.

"Granny understands why I ran away," Lainie told herself as she parked and ran into the Love's store for a cup of coffee. "I'll try to suck it up and not gag at the smell of fish bait, but I'm not making any promises about getting along with Becky and Jodi. It would have been so much better if Granny Lizzie had left me money instead of a beer, bait, and bologna shop. Then I could have opened my own little restaurant anywhere other than Dallas and could have been happy working sixteen hours a day."

Her phone rang just as she hit the Dallas noon traffic. When Becky's name came up on the screen, she sighed loudly, pushed the accept button, and said, "Hello, how are things in Catfish?"

"Jodi and I have been here since last night. I opened up the shop this morning, and everything is in a mess. Jodi is still in the house trying to get awake. Where in the hell are you?" Becky's tone was covered with a thick layer of ice.

"Coming through Dallas," Lainie answered. "According to the GPS I should be there by two o'clock."

"Well, don't fart around," Becky said. "I've decided that we'll each take two days a week to open up the store at six in the morning, and whoever opens up can leave at three in the afternoon."

"What gives you the right to make the rules?" Lainie asked.

"I'm the oldest, and I got here first, and I've been here at the shop since six this morning, and Jodi still isn't here and it's noon, and Granny Lizzie made me executor over everything," Becky answered. "Do you need any more than that?"

"Who's going to kick Jodi out of bed at five-thirty so she can get to the store by six on her two days?" Lainie asked.

"That's your job," Becky answered.

"You better think again on that issue. She's always been a bear in the mornings, but we can talk about it when I get there," Lainie said.

"Fair enough," Becky said. "Be safe."

"I'll do my best," Lainie said.

About the Author

Carolyn Brown is a *New York Times, USA Today, Wall Street Journal, Publishers Weekly* and #1 Amazon and #1 *Washington Post* bestselling author. She is the author of more than one hundred novels and several novellas. She's a recipient of the Bookseller's Best Award, Montlake Romance's prestigious Montlake Diamond Award, and also a three-time recipient of the National Reader's Choice Award. Brown has been published for more than twenty years, and her books have been translated into twenty-one foreign languages.

When she's not writing, she likes to plot new stories in her backyard with her tomcat, Boots Randolph Terminator Outlaw, who protects the yard from all kinds of wicked varmints like crickets, locusts, and spiders. Visit her at carolynbrownbooks.com.